For Lara

DAUGHTERS
of
SHADOW
&
BLOOD

BOOK I: YASAMIN

J. MATTHEW SAUNDERS

SAINT GEORGE'S PRESS

DAUGHTERS OF SHADOW & BLOOD
BOOK I: YASAMIN

Copyright © 2015 by J. Matthew Saunders

This is a work of fiction. Names, characters, businesses,
places, events and incidents are either the products of the
author's imagination or used in a fictitious manner.

Cover photography copyright © Lefteris Papaulakis
(mosque) and Alex Buts (woman),
courtesy of Shutterstock

Printed in the United States of America

First Printing, 2015

e-book ISBN 978-0-9863331-0-1
paperback ISBN 978-0-9863331-1-8

Saint George's Press
York, S.C.
www.saintgeorgespress.com

DAUGHTERS
of
SHADOW
&
BLOOD

—⚮—

Book I: Yasamin

PROLOGUE

A Letter from Mihai Iliescu

Cluj, Romania
3 March 1999

I WILL MISS THE BOOKS.

I have never had enough space for my entire collection, but I have always insisted on dedicating one room in my house to the library. This house, in particular, is ill suited to handle so many things, least of all the books. They cascade off the shelves onto the floor and collect in the corners, but I know exactly where each and every one of them is.

There are those who expected more from the last scion of Arnold Pavle than an overweight, balding, middle-aged man who likes to hole himself up inside and read dusty tomes others have forgotten even exist. They see monster slayers in films, and they expect a dashing, square-jawed hero, fearless in the face of danger and willing at any moment to rush in and save the day.

I am simply Mihai Iliescu, son of Andras Iliescu, war criminal. My country tells me I should forget our shameful past. I was raised by an aunt who barely tolerated me because I reminded her of what my father was. But how could I pretend none of it ever happened? To deny my father and the events that shaped him as a person would be to deny a part of myself.

I've chased his ghost for almost fifty years. I thought I could understand him by surrounding myself with the artifacts of his universe, but it hasn't worked. I'm no closer to understanding what kind of man my father was than the day I started, and now I'm tired.

Maybe I could have become the true heir of Arnold Pavle, had circumstances allowed, but now I will never have the chance. So perhaps in death my life will finally serve a purpose, and these books, seen by the eyes of others, will continue my family's noble legacy.

I cannot explain everything. The only advice I can give you is to read. "The monsters are real," my father told me, "but we are not helpless against the darkness."

ONE

Berlin, Germany
12 August 1999

THERE WAS NO TICKING CLOCK, no traffic din, no wind in the trees, not even the sound of his own breathing. Nothing broke the silence that followed until her lips parted, and she asked a single, simple question.

"Why are you here?"

Drawn like an adder ready to strike, the woman sat across the room on a divan. He stood near the door by one of the room's tall, narrow windows, a shaft of sunlight cutting across his face. Though the shadows obscured her features, he could feel her dark eyes studying him. He knew the question was coming. He just didn't want to answer it.

Not yet.

"So it's true?" he asked.

She shook her head. "I didn't say that."

He let the beads of the rosary in his pocket slide one by one through his fingers and allowed himself a cautious smile. "Are you familiar with a man named Mihai Iliescu?"

"I've heard of him."

"It's remarkable how many have."

"It's not so remarkable if you have an appreciation for antiques." She glanced around the room. He followed her eyes.

Indeed, the room spoke to her appreciation. It boasted several fine examples of Rococo Chinoiserie, including the divan on which she sat. The value of the two Empire-style tables on either side would have allowed him to retire in luxury then and there. A portrait set in a gilt frame hung on the wall to his right, notable both for its subject and its creator—Rembrandt van Rijn.

The most extraordinary object in the room, however, hung on the wall behind her. Unmistakably Turkish, the giant tapestry could not be any less than three hundred years old. Filaments of dark crimson, blue, cream, and black flowed through the green fabric, invoking lush hills and pomegranate trees heavy with blossoms. In the center the thread formed a tiny mosque with a splendid domed roof and four gleaming minarets. The tapestry's graceful arcs and arabesques danced around the woman's poised figure, the green color in the fabric setting off her olive skin.

"No, perhaps not so remarkable," he said, "but I'm sure it came as a shock to many that a quiet mid-level Romanian bureaucrat had such a passion. He managed to amass quite the collection before he died—furniture, books, artwork, jewelry … relics."

He drew out the last word so that it lingered, haunting the space between them for a moment before fading away.

If she reacted, he couldn't tell. "Remind me again, Mr. Mire. What do you do?"

Give me neither bread nor water,
Give me no rest, nor any sleep.
For the thirst to possess your love,
Is worth my blood a hundred times.

—*Rumi*

"It's Dr. Mire, actually. I teach history at a university back in the States. I've also written a few books about medieval and Renaissance Eastern Europe."

"And what interest does an American university professor have in the antique collection of a Romanian civil servant?"

He held his hand out to the sunlight beaming in through the open window. Adam Mire had learned to appreciate simple things like the warm late summer sun on his skin and the light playing on the leaves of the linden trees outside the woman's townhouse. A part of him felt sorry for her, and he more than understood her reticence to answer what most would see as outlandish accusations.

He returned his attention to the woman still sitting across from him, her face still hidden in the shadows. "I'm not interested in the collection *per se*—but then neither are you. You've been making inquiries into the whereabouts of a certain item rumored to be part of the Iliescu estate."

"And what is this item?"

"A medallion in the likeness of a dragon, formed into a circle with its tail wrapped around its neck. On the dragon's back is a cross, and around the outside an inscription, '*O Quam Misericors est Deus, Pius et Justus.*'"

"'O How Merciful is God,'" she spat, "'Faithful and Just.'"

A cloud passed in front of the sun. The room grew darker and colder and. if possible, even stiller. Shadows reached across the floor toward him like grasping hands threatening to ensnare his feet. Instinctively, he backed away until the sun reemerged. The shadows retreated, though not exactly to where they had been. Around the woman they remained darker.

"And if I did seek such an item, what about this medallion leads you to make the allegations you do, Dr. Mire?"

He swallowed, struggling to suppress the sense of unease that had appeared unbidden in the pit of his stomach, and tried to keep his voice steady. "This medallion is not the type of thing an antique collector would bother with generally, and its value as a museum piece is only marginal. But its worth can't be counted in currency, or what a museum curator might be able to see under a microscope. The stories and legends surrounding it and its owner go back centuries. Some are written. Some are not. Some have even inspired poets and novelists. But what most people don't realize is that there is a tiny scrap of truth in each of these stories. I want to know the entire truth."

"Stories and legends of some ancient, legendary artifact. You have nothing more?"

Adam took a deep breath. "Only that according to his doctors, Mr. Iliescu died of an 'unidentified blood disorder,' just as your husband did."

Her eyes flashed with an emotion hard for him to classify. Pain? Anger? Loss? "You know nothing about my husband or how he died."

The outburst surprised him. He noticed that even though more than a year had passed since her husband's death, the woman still wore her wedding ring on her right hand. He found it curious she would do something so sentimental. "My apologies," he said. "You're right. I don't know. In fact, I don't have proof of anything I've claimed today."

She raised an eyebrow. "But you make claims nonetheless."

"There's no need to worry, Mrs. Ashrafi. I'm not interested in telling anyone anything I know."

Her expression changed again, this time to one he could read a little easier. He had seen it before in others—something feral, something predatory. "There is only one way to ensure you will not tell anyone."

He clutched the rosary still concealed in his pocket. "With all due respect, Mrs. Ashrafi, whom would I tell? My professional reputation demands I verify every claim I make. I could never produce enough evidence to make anyone believe those such as you exist. My career would be over in an instant."

"Then I'll ask you again, Dr. Mire. Why are you here? What is it you want?"

"I want to know why you're seeking this medallion." Adam took a breath. "The very thing that gave Dracula his name."

The minutes passed, measured only by the beating of his heart. Her dark eyes bore into him. Adam wondered if he had miscalculated, if he would be able to reach the door before she pulled him screaming into the shadows. She glanced at the photograph in her hand. He had used it as a calling card of sorts, to gain an invitation inside her home. The woman in the photograph bore an uncanny resemblance to her, though the picture would have been taken long before she was ever born—if the age she was in fact matched the age she appeared.

"You intrigue me, Dr. Mire," she said, brushing her fingers across the picture. "I'll tell you what you want to know, on the condition that you tell me how you found me."

Adam slowly let out the breath he had been holding. "That's a long story, I'm afraid."

The corners of her mouth turned up in a twisted smile.

"I don't mind, Dr. Mire. Unlike you, I have all the time in the world."

TWO

—⟋∽⟍—

A BELL JINGLED AS ADAM opened the door and entered the antique shop. The smell of old books and dusty furniture mingled with the perfume of the flowers from the shop next door and the scent of fresh rain. He hesitated in the entryway, not certain how to proceed. A maze of tables, chairs, books, silver, china, and other random objects collected from hundreds of lifetimes filled the tiny store.

Amidst the chaos, a small, balding man stood at an old drafting table he had conscripted into a desk. Peering over the edge of his glasses, he leafed through a stack of papers. Every so often he made marks with a pencil. When Adam entered, the man glanced up. Adam nodded. The shopkeeper scrutinized him with pale blue eyes and smiled faintly before returning to his task. Adam chuckled quietly. Janos Kovács's reputation preceded him. He catered only to serious collectors, not tourists. He had apparently taken Adam for the latter, exactly what Adam wanted.

Adam pushed into the store, cautiously stepping over a small wooden bench and squeezing himself around a giant Biedermeier armoire. On the other side, he found a stack of books balanced on a shelf much too small for the job. Adam could not detect any pattern in their order. He scanned the titles until he came across one that caught his attention—*Description of the Székely Lands* by Balázs Orbán. He picked it up and opened the worn cover. A name and a date were scrawled in faded pen in the upper-right corner of the title page: Mihai Iliescu, 3 May 1987. He tucked the book underneath his arm and continued reading the titles of the other books. When he finished, Adam turned to discover the shopkeeper standing next to him.

"May I help you?" the man asked in German, his gaze resting on the book underneath Adam's arm.

"I don't know. It's possible," Adam replied in Hungarian. He took the book and opened it to the title page, pointing to the signature written there. "I'm interested in seeing more items from the Mihai Iliescu estate. Do you have anything else?"

"I ... I have many things from the Iliescu estate," the shopkeeper stammered, his face flushed. "You need to be more specific. Are you looking for other books? Mr. Iliescu's library was quite astounding."

"I know. I became rather familiar with his collection on the occasions I visited him in his home. I'd love to see what other books you have, but the truth is I'm looking for something else."

"What might that be?"

"I suppose you could best describe it as a piece of jewelry."

"Jewelry, you say? But Mr. Iliescu was never married."

Adam shook his head. "Not that kind of jewelry. More of a medallion, made into a pin, or even a clasp for a cloak. The design is ... unusual. It depicts an animal that looks like a lizard, or a dragon."

Mr. Kovács's expression darkened. His gaze shifted away, toward the door. "I have never seen anything like what you describe."

"Are you certain? I've been to several other dealers, and they've all told me the same, but you acquired the bulk of the Iliescu estate. I had hoped for better luck here."

"I'm sorry. I'm certain I have nothing like that."

He refused to look Adam in the eye, and as he spoke he twisted the garnet ring on his right pinky finger around and around.

"I'm not the first to ask that question, am I?" Adam asked. "There have been others."

"Please, Mr.—"

"Doctor," Adam said. "Doctor Adam Mire."

"My apologies, Dr. Mire, but I don't intend to continue this pointless conversation with you. I have work to do. Are you interested in purchasing the book you're holding?"

"I think so, but I'd like to look around a little and see what other treasures I might be able to dig up."

"Dr. Mire, I don't mean to be rude—"

The bell on the door jingled again. An older woman wearing a tailored suit and an abundance of jewelry stepped into the shop. The open contempt on Mr. Kovács's face vanished. After one last stern glance at Adam, he beamed at the newcomer, greeting her with arms held out as if the woman were his long-lost sister, and left Adam to his own devices once more.

Adam poked around the shop, picking up another book or two, always trying to keep an eye on Mr. Kovács and the woman, who was apparently looking for a pair of chairs for her living room. As he pretended to browse, Adam made his way closer and closer to the drafting table where Mr. Kovács had left his papers.

They appeared to be nothing more than accounting ledgers—lists of sales with columns for names, inventory, prices. After a glance at Mr. Kovács and the woman, Adam lifted the top sheet. The one underneath was labeled "Iliescu" and followed much the same pattern, except for the note scrawled in one corner.

The bell on the door jingled again. Adam looked up to see the woman leaving. He replaced the papers on the desk and made his way back to the stack of books by the time Mr. Kovács turned his withering glare on him again.

"Did you find anything else of interest?" the dealer asked.

"No, not really," Adam replied, smiling, "but I do believe I'll purchase the book."

OUTSIDE THE SHOP, THE RAIN had stopped, though the sky remained overcast. In Budapest, the August heat had subsided, and with it the flood of tourists. Adam made his way back to his hotel, his new purchase tucked securely under his arm. The doorman, standing ramrod straight, gave Adam a slight nod as he opened the door, the respect evident despite his threadbare uniform. Nearly empty, the Hotel Athena suited Adam perfectly. It provided him the solitude he preferred, yet retained a well-trained and loyal staff who pretended nothing had changed in a hundred years. The front desk and the maids abided his eccentricities without question, even if those eccentricities included stringing heads of garlic across the windows of his room and placing a holy wafer above the door.

As Adam entered his room, his gaze fell on the desk next to his bed. His books and papers lay strewn across the surface. A few extra forints slipped into the hands of the hotel manager ensured the housekeeping staff didn't touch any of his work.

But someone had.

Though the desk hadn't been the picture of order before, Adam knew what his chaos looked like. Nothing was where he had left it. Without hesitating, he stuffed everything from the desk into his leather satchel and walked out the door, planning to find another hotel and send for the rest of his clothes when he did.

Outside dusk rapidly approached, and Adam kept up a brisk pace. Neither the first hotel he tried nor the second had any vacancies. His third choice still lay a few blocks away. He never made it. A cold steel edge against his neck stopped him.

"One move and you die," a harsh voice whispered his ear. "Do you understand?"

"Yes," Adam replied.

A muscled arm pulled Adam into the shadow of an awning hanging over an abandoned storefront. In the window, Adam saw his own murky reflection and that of a well-built, olive-skinned man with a military-style haircut and a closely shaved beard. The man followed Adam's gaze. The corners of his mouth turned up in a sneering grin.

"I don't have much money," Adam said. "My wallet's in my pocket. Take it."

"I don't want your money."

Adam never thought he did. "What do you want, then?"

13

"Where is it?" The man pressed the knife harder against Adam's throat.

"Where is what?" Adam fought the urge to swallow. "I'm just looking for a hotel to spend the night."

"You are not in a position to play games, *effendi*. Where is the *Kazıklı Bey*'s medallion?"

Effendi. Kazıklı Bey. The man was Turkish.

"I don't know what you're talking about."

The knife slipped a fraction of an inch, and Adam felt a trickle of blood run down his neck. The angry red line reflected in the window.

"You lie. I know about your visit this afternoon. You were trying to sell it, weren't you, *effendi*? Do not try to fool me, Dr. Mire. I know exactly who you are. You are not a stupid man, yet you act like one. You know what the medallion is, where it came from. You're damning yourself to hell by hiding it. If you tell me the truth, though, you can die a hero's death and receive your reward in heaven."

"I swear I don't know anything about a medallion, *effendi*."

The man spat on the side of Adam's face and uttered a word Adam didn't understand but was sure he wouldn't want translated. The pressure on Adam's neck eased a little. Dropping his chin, Adam forced the man to turn his wrist and angle the knife away from Adam's throat. Then he grasped the man's arm and slipped underneath to escape the Turk's embrace. He took off running down the street, but he heard the Turk's footfalls behind him.

As he rounded a corner, Adam risked a glance over his shoulder to see the Turk only a few strides behind. Though he was by no means out of shape, Adam knew he couldn't keep his current pace up for much longer. He scanned the area, looking for another way to escape, and failed to see that the sidewalk buckled in front of him. He tripped. His books and papers went sprawling into the street, and when Adam hit the pavement, something in his left shoulder popped. He cried out as searing pain shot through his arm and across his chest. His every instinct screamed at him to get up and keep running, but he could do nothing except lie on the ground and clutch his shoulder in agony.

The Turk stood over him, smiling. He raised the knife over his head, the blade flashing in the light of the streetlamps. "Impressive, *effendi*, but this ends exactly the same."

At the last moment, however, an arm blocked the knife's deadly arc. The newcomer, a slender woman roughly Adam's age, stood between him and the Turk. Adam didn't see where she had come from. The Turk's eyes widened, and then his lips curled back in a snarl. He took a step back and lunged at her, but she dodged every one of his attacks with the grace of a dancer. His frustration evident, he swung the knife in a wide circle. The blade came within a hair's breadth of her chin.

The Turk laughed. "Such a beautiful face. It would be a shame if anything were to mar it."

She rolled her eyes. "Men. The same stupid line every time."

He charged. She sidestepped the knife and brought her arm down on his wrist, making him drop the weapon. She spun around and backhanded him across the face, then kicked him in the chest and sent him flying into the wall. His body ricocheted off the brick surface, and his nose met with the heel of her hand. Bone and cartilage snapped. The Turk crumpled to the ground and didn't move again.

Adam stared up at the woman. Her red hair hung in a

loose ponytail, and her eyes were the deep cerulean blue of the ocean on a cloudless day. She knelt beside him.

"Are you hurt?" she asked, her voice carrying a hint of an Eastern European accent.

"My shoulder. I think it's dislocated."

She gently placed a hand on his upper arm. "May I?"

No sooner had Adam nodded, than she seized his arm and popped his shoulder back into place with a stomach-churning jerk. Adam screamed in agony.

"What did you just do?" he asked.

"I fixed your shoulder. Is something wrong? It does feel better, yes?" She raised an eyebrow. "And I did ask you first. Now come with me, please. We have to get you someplace safe."

Adam made a few tentative motions with his left arm. "Who are you?"

Standing, the woman grabbed him by his other arm. "Later. Now come."

Adam pulled free. "Wait, my things."

"Leave them."

"I can't. My books and papers. I need them."

The woman eyed the unconscious man on the ground. "Fine then, but gather them as fast as you can."

Adam struggled to keep up with her as they ran through the streets. After dozen or so blocks, as Adam felt his legs about to give out, she stopped. Townhouses lined the quiet street. A row of parked cars sat at the curb. The woman climbed into the driver's side of a white Fiat and opened the passenger door for Adam. Before he could even climb completely in, she turned the ignition and punched the gas pedal. The car screeched away from the curb and sped down the street.

"My name is Anya," she said, "to answer your question."

"Adam." He fumbled to buckle his seat belt as fast as he could. "Dr. Adam Mire."

The tires screamed as she rounded a corner. "Oh, I already know your name."

Adam still struggled to catch his breath. "Does everybody in this city know who I am?"

She shot him a sardonic glance. "Not quite, but more than you'd think."

"And why is that?"

She made another gut-wrenching right turn onto a street already teeming with traffic. Horns blared as she cut off a Mercedes and a BMW, but miraculously, the white Fiat remained unscathed. "The truth? You're not the only one looking for Dracula's medallion, Dr. Mire. You're just the only one who isn't armed."

"I don't understand. How do you know about the medallion? And who was that man in they alley?"

"All in good time, Dr. Mire, all in good time."

"Will you at least tell me where we're going?"

She jerked the wheel and veered across three lanes of traffic. More horns bellowed. The car flew up an onramp and onto an expressway.

"Novi Sad," Anya replied.

"Novi Sad?" Adam shook his head. "But I don't have a visa to travel in Yugoslavia."

Anya continued to weave among the cars on the expressway. "Details. Don't worry."

"Why should I trust you?"

"You're still breathing, aren't you? Isn't that enough?" At Adam's silence, she sighed. "Very well. Open the glove box."

Adam pressed the button. The door fell open, revealing

a Glock pistol.

Anya smiled. "Now you're armed. You don't think you can trust me, then shoot me. It's entirely up to you."

The Budapest suburbs sped by. Even the textured grip of the pistol in Adam's hand did nothing to hold his panic at bay. In his mind, pieces of a puzzle began falling into place. He didn't like the picture they revealed. He thought back to the look on Janos Kovács's face at the antique shop when he brought up the medallion. It was a look of abject fear. After the assault on the street, Adam thought perhaps the man's fears were warranted.

And there was something else.

The note in Mr. Kovács's ledger contained a name he had come across before, one almost always accompanied by death.

Yasamin.

THREE

Berlin, Germany
12 August 1999

Y ASAMIN ASHRAFI DRUMMED HER FINGERS on the
arm of the divan, a slow, relentless rhythm that
beat in time with Adam's heart. "Your first experience with a knife to your throat?"

"And hopefully my last," he replied.

"Hopefully. It never does get easier."

Adam watched the rise and fall of her exquisite fingers
as they danced over the dark, polished wood of the divan's
arm. "No, no, I wouldn't imagine it does."

"How fortunate for you, though, that someone came to
your aid, and what a coincidence for this woman to arrive
at the very moment you needed her."

"Not so much of a coincidence, as I discovered."

"Oh really?"

"She was following me."

The drumming stopped. Her expression darkened, if
such a thing was possible.

"Did she follow you here?"

Adam found relief in the sudden silence that before had been so oppressive. "Over the past ten days I've had the opportunity to learn lessons I never wanted to learn. I made certain neither she nor anyone else could follow me here."

"If you're lying—"

"I'm not stupid, Mrs. Ashrafi. Believe me."

Her mouth curled up into the same twisted smile. "Only time will tell if that is true."

"You promised to answer my question if I answered yours."

"And I intend to keep that promise. But I am curious about one more thing. The name you found in the ledger of Janos Kovács. You said you had come across it elsewhere. Where, exactly?"

Adam made every attempt to remain nonchalant. "Odd documents, none of them related to one another, sometimes separated by centuries. A very tantalizing puzzle, but also frustrating. I only recently came upon some information that let me follow the trail down the rabbit hole."

"Quite another coincidence."

"Maybe there are no coincidences," Adam countered. "I've noticed that if God wants to send you a message, he'll often leave clues to follow. They may seem random and unrelated, but they are impossible to miss or ignore."

She began tapping her fingers again. "Be careful Dr. Mire, or you may learn, as I did, that God isn't always the one leaving the clues."

FOUR

—∿—

Buda, Ottoman Hungary
8 Safar 1008
(20 August 1599 Old Style)

YASAMIN WATCHED THE PILLAR OF wax dwindle until it could no longer nourish the tiny flame dancing atop. Sunrise would not come for several more hours, but she couldn't sleep. She cracked the door and slipped out of the room. The light from the waning moon dusted the silent passageways in pallid light, enough for her to make her way, though twice she became lost in the unfamiliar corridors and had to retrace her steps.

Cool air brushed her face as she stepped onto one of the many narrow dirt paths threading through the *haremlık* garden. She breathed deeply and smiled. Though the palace's stone façades would not allow her to forget she was still confined to the *haremlık*, the open air relieved the immediate feeling that she might at any moment suffocate.

The other women had tried to make her room as welcoming and comfortable as they could. Stuffed with silk and satin pillows, her chambers were larger than her old room in her uncle's house in Salonica. She even brought with her the tapestry her mother had made of the little mosque in the woods, but no matter what anyone did, she would never call Buda home.

The path led to the same place as all the others, a central clearing dominated by an ancient oak tree. It was so wide it took four people touching fingertip to fingertip to reach all the way around. Yasamin sat with her back to its immense trunk and stared into the still blackness of the small pond next to the tree.

The tears surprised her when they came. She should have been happy. Her fondest wish had come true, the one she had made so many times, to leave Salonica and be the wife of an important man, not just the only niece of an unimportant public official. As she sat under the old oak she wanted more than anything to take that wish back.

She cried until her tears dried up. She rose to return to her room, but froze when a pebble went skittering down the opposite bank of the pond toward the glassy smooth water that mirrored the clear night sky. With a small splash, the tiny stone sent silver ripples across the surface of the pond, shattering the moon's reflection.

Yasamin stared across the water to find someone standing on the path. Her heart leapt into her throat, but it took Yasamin a mere second to recognize Ayla, another resident of the *haremlık*. Yasamin was certain the relief on Ayla's face reflected her own. She motioned for Ayla to join her, though truth be told, she wanted nothing more than to be left alone.

"You scared me nearly to death," Yasamin whispered once the two of them were seated under the oak tree together.

"My apologies," Ayla replied. "I didn't mean to frighten you. I didn't expect anyone else to be out here in the middle of the night."

"I couldn't sleep. I thought it would be a good place to come and think."

Yasamin paused, struggling for something more to say. She had met Ayla only once before in passing and was unsure what etiquette demanded in the current situation. She knew Ayla was around seventeen, a year younger than she was, and that she was the daughter or niece of one of the chief advisors to Ahmed Pasha, Buda's governor. Beyond those paltry facts, she knew nothing.

Such matters of decorum, however, didn't seem to worry Ayla. "So, what is it you've come here to think about?"

Yasamin could have chosen not to answer. She could have demurred or told Ayla it was none of her business, but instead she told the truth.

"I'm not happy here."

"But you're about to marry Murad Pashazade," Ayla protested. "How could you not be happy to marry the son of a Pasha?"

"It's not him." Yasamin motioned around. "It's this place. I'm not happy here. It's nothing like where I came from. I wanted for so long to leave, to be away from my aunt and her rules. Now I find myself actually missing Salonica. I miss the smell of the sea and the blue of the water on a clear day, the most beautiful blue you could imagine. There, at least I had my pick of satins and silks, or if I wanted I could sit in the afternoon sun and eat citrons until they made me sick."

The relief at saying it all out loud passed over Yasamin like a fresh breeze. She wanted to tell Ayla everything.

"Tonight is not the first time I've slipped out of my room," she continued. "On the first night I was here I came to the garden. These pomegranate trees are from Greece. We had ones like them in our garden at home. I thought if I closed my eyes and touched the bark, or held a bunch of flowers in my hand, I could forget where I was." Yasamin sighed. "I was wrong."

"How?"

"I couldn't plug my ears to the night noises. The wind that blows through the trees is coarse, not like the gentle breezes off the sea. The insects drone at a pitch that seems off to my ears. The wolves howl closer. I should be in Izmir, or even Istanbul, but instead, I'm here, marrying a man I know nothing about."

"I hear Murad Pashazade is a good man."

"Then you've heard more than I have."

Yasamin's soon-to-be husband remained an enigma to her. She gleaned from the gossip within the *haremlık* that he tended to shut himself up in his room for days on end, that he usually refused to speak but a few words whenever he did present himself, and that often those words were poorly chosen. In one story he embarrassed a guest of his father, a celebrated general, by pointing out mistakes the general had made in a particular battle. Even Murad's own mother spoke of him as an idea or a notion, rather than a man.

On the other hand, the stories of Murad's younger half-brother Selim were universal in their praise. He was an accomplished horseman and swordsman, and as young as he was, he had already led soldiers to victory in battle against the Christian armies threatening Buda. By all accounts, Selim was also a swaggering boor, but everyone knew he was a swaggering boor, and he didn't pretend to be otherwise. If she had to be trapped in Buda, Yasamin thought she would prefer Selim to Murad.

She almost told Ayla so, but before she could, she heard a noise. As one, she and Ayla turned toward the sound. Someone else approached on the path. The two of them rounded the oak tree and crouched as deeply into the darkness as they could. Still, as the figure drew nearer, Yasamin couldn't resist peeking around the trunk of the tree.

A tall, lanky man taking long, swift strides passed by on the path. He had tucked his robes into his belt, revealing his baggy trousers. He wore only a mustache, not the beard Yasamin was accustomed to seeing on most men. A fabric-draped, cylindrical hat adorned with a feather rested on his head. He didn't notice Yasamin or Ayla as he passed by.

"A janissary," Yasamin said after he was a safe distance away.

"How do you know?" Ayla asked.

"I've watched them walking down the street outside my home in Salonica countless times," Yasamin replied.

"What is he doing in the *haremlık*? He should know he's not allowed."

Yasamin shrugged. She knew members of the janissary corps were supposed to remain celibate, thinking only of fighting for the Sultan, but underneath the uniform, they were still men. She herself had been tempted more than once to try to catch the eye of one passing by. If some young girl had caught this janissary's attention, he could very well have considered the risk of being found within the *haremlık* to be worth the reward.

"Let it be his problem," she said. "We should go back. It will be light soon."

As they stepped back onto the path, Yasamin's eyes briefly came to rest on a spot across he pond's glassy water. She thought she saw a flicker of a shadow, but when she looked again, the pale moonlight illuminated only the trees and the flowers and the grassy banks of the black pond, nothing more.

FIVE

—◈—

Buda, Ottoman Hungary
10 Safar 1008
(22 August 1599 Old Style)

THE OTTOMAN EMPIRE PRESENTED SOMETHING *of a paradox for those on the outside looking in. The Ottomans gave the land beyond the empire's boundaries where the infidels had their petty kingdoms the name* Dar ul-Harb, *the Abode of War. By contrast, the area within the empire's borders received the name* Dar ul-Islam, *the Abode of Peace.*

In the Abode of Peace, every man knew his place, and from the color of his clothes, every other man could tell as well. If he was Muslim, he prayed five times a day when the muezzins called from the minarets, and he visited the mosque at least every Friday. He plied his trade, whatever that trade happened to be, and prospered.

In every Ottoman town of any importance, baths existed to cleanse the body as well as mosques to cleanse the soul. Over it all ruled the Sultan—the Sublime Porte—from his palace in Istan-

bul, in whose inner chambers no one was allowed to speak, lest his serenity be disturbed

Yet, the Abode of Peace maintained itself through constant warfare.

Conquest kept the machinery of the empire running smoothly. During every campaign season merchants put away their wares, farmers put away their ploughs, fisherman put away their nets, and they all picked up the tools of war. The empire moved to the cadence of the janissary band. Inexorably, the soldiers marched forward, and one by one, the kingdoms of the Abode of War fell under the sway of the Ottomans until the empire spanned from the Arabian deserts to the gates of Vienna, just as it should.

ON THE DAY BEFORE HER wedding ceremony, Yasamin awoke to the sound of cannons booming in the hills across the river. Skirmishes with the soldiers of the German emperor occurred every day. The Hungarian Plain was a battlefield and Buda more of a garrison than a city.

The women of Ahmed Pasha's court, however, were not thinking of battles. That morning the *gelin hamami*, the bride's bath was set to take place, and a visit to the baths meant freedom for a time. They exchanged gossip as they undressed in the outer vestibule of the magnificent bathhouse, a structure completed by Ahmed Pasha's predecessor in order to help integrate the city into the Abode of Peace. Once out of their garments, the women entered into the hot room. The steam was so thick Yasamin could barely see. A girl led her to a large chair in the center of the room, the place of honor. The other women took seats on benches around the perimeter. The idle chatter faded away as they all succumbed to the soothing heat. Attendants came around giving massages.

As they worked Yasamin's tense muscles to the point of pain and scrubbed her skin with coarse straw mitts until it was almost raw, her mind wandered to thoughts of the janissary she and Ayla had seen in the garden the night before. A man entering the *haremlık* placed himself in extreme danger. If he had been caught, he would have been put to death. Only one reason to take the risk made sense to Yasamin.

Love for a woman.

Had a woman seen the janissary one day out of a window and waved a scarf at him—both as a promise of her beauty and a challenge to his ingenuity? Had it been as simple as that? Had he found a sympathetic old grandmother to deliver her a note sealed in a jar? Had that same sympathetic old woman opened the door for him to enter? What had he said on the first night when he scaled the walls and whispered to her through the lattice? Yasamin's mother had told her that love between a man and a woman should embrace all of life and all of death. Yasamin never understood what she meant until then. A janissary risked death every day in battle, but the Sultan wasn't the only cause worth dying for, and wasn't it just as noble a death to be discovered clinging to the window ledge outside a woman's sleeping chambers?

"Yasamin!"

Lost in her own thoughts and lulled into a stupor by the steam, Yasamin had barely noticed when the attendants left her and moved on. The new voice, hard and raspy, tore her from her dreaming questions. Nesrin, Murad's grandmother and Ahmed Pasha's mother, emerged from the swirling steam, wielding her walking stick like a weapon. In the eerie dimness of the room, illuminated only by the orange fire that heated the stones used to produce the steam, the old woman looked like a ghoul.

"Yes, Nesrin?" Yasamin said, trying her hardest not to act startled and struggling to keep her voice even.

Nesrin's eyes resembled those of a prowling leopard prepared to pounce at the first sign of weakness. "I want to have a word with you."

An odd time for a discussion, thought Yasamin, but she kept her opinion to herself. "Certainly, Nesrin."

Nesrin leaned in close, so close Yasamin could feel her breath, cold compared with the steamy air. "I need you to know that if I had my way, you would not be betrothed to my grandson."

Yasamin winced. In the few days since her arrival, she had been forced to endure the insufferable crone's constant scowl. It seemed nothing she did made the old woman happy. Still, the reprimand stung.

"If I have done anything to offend you, Nesrin, I sincerely apologize," she said. "Please tell me what I can do to make amends, and I will gladly do it."

Nesrin shook her head and chuckled, a dry and altogether unpleasant sound.

"Unfortunately, there is nothing you can do, Yasamin. Nonetheless, some things are beyond even my power. Watch yourself. Do not step out of line, or you may find that there are places more unpleasant than Buda."

She turned and hobbled away, vanishing into the steam, the sharp tap of her cane echoing through the chamber as it struck the stone floor with the old woman's every step.

The heat, so calming before, became oppressive, and relief filled Yasamin as she emerged from the hot room into the cavernous hall housing the baths. Steam rose from the large octagonal pool in the center. The caustic smell of the minerals in the water tickled her nose. Eight pairs of great marble columns spaced around the pool held the domed ceiling aloft. Soft light, tinted blue and green by stained-glass panes, filtered into the hall from tiny windows in the dome high above.

Yasamin followed closely behind a girl playing the tambourine while the other women trailed in a procession. Having donned silk robes, they carried bundles containing all the accoutrements they needed for a day at the baths. The unmarried women also carried candles. When the procession reached the central pool, the women circled it as they sang. When the music ended, the unmarried women tossed coins into the pool and made wishes for the husbands they desired. The coins flashed in the light before making tiny splashes in the water.

A smaller pool flanked the main pool. Yasamin set her bundle down at its edge and stepped out of her wooden clogs. She let the embroidered silk robe she wore slide from her body. It glided downward, following the curve of her breasts and hips like caressing hands, and she relished the feeling of the fabric passing over her skin. After the robe fell away and fluttered to the floor, she stood for a moment with her eyes closed, breathing in the damp air. She stepped into the pool's cool water and rapidly dunked her entire body several times, washing away the steam-induced stupor of the hot room.

Invigorated by the plunge in the pool, Yasamin crossed with her *hamam* bundle to the central pool. Fed by an underground spring, its waters were considerably warmer. Out of her bundle, she pulled her soap case, her mirror, and her henna bowl. As she lowered herself into the pool, she willed the healing waters to enter her pores.

Hadice, Murad's mother, walked over to her and began

31

to wash her back. All the women around them paired up in similar fashion, lathering each other with soap and applying henna to their hair. Even as the warm water trickled down her spine, though, Yasamin's knotted muscles refused to relax.

"You know for a bride you're awfully quiet," Hadice said.

Yasamin tried to smile. "My aunt always told me I should make an effort to talk more, but I can never think of anything interesting to say."

Hadice laughed. "Before my wedding, I was so excited they had to tell me to stop talking, and trust me when I tell you none of what I said was interesting. Is something the matter?"

"Not at all," Yasamin replied.

"Then the least you could do is smile. Tomorrow is supposed to be the most joyous day of your life."

The two women switched positions, and Yasamin took her turn washing Hadice's back. "But weren't you nervous the day before your wedding, even if you were excited?"

Hadice laughed. "Of course I was. Who wouldn't be nervous at the prospect of having Nesrin as a mother-in-law?"

Yasamin flinched at the mention of Nesrin's name.

"Really, Yasamin," Hadice continued, "you have nothing at all to worry about. You are very fortunate. Yours is the kind of marriage every woman wants. Murad is a good son. He'll be a good husband. You'll be proud to be his wife as I am proud to be his mother."

Yasamin managed a faint smile. "You're right, of course."

An attendant poured henna into the bowl set out near the edge of the pool. Hadice dipped her fingertips into the reddish-brown liquid and ran them through Yasamin's long, dark hair. "You're a very clever girl. If you remember who your friends are, you'll have no trouble here at all."

A few drops of henna fell onto the stones at the edge of the pool. They reminded Yasamin of drops of blood. Despite the warmth of the water, she felt a chill and looked away. As she applied the henna to Hadice's hair, she glanced around at the other women in the pool, all bathing one another, conversing in groups of two or three. How was she supposed to know who would make a good friend and who would not? All she saw were suspicious faces and unfriendly gazes, except for Ayla, who caught her eye and smiled. They shared a bond at the very least, their middle-of-the-night adventure.

Celibe, Selim's mother, made her way over to them and tapped Yasamin on the back. "May fortune treat you well tomorrow, my dear."

Yasamin forced a smile. "Thank you, Celibe."

Celibe smiled as well, though hers was an odd, twisted smile. "That Hadice has chosen you to be her son's wife speaks a great deal to your patience, and that certainly is a fine virtue to have."

She walked away before either Yasamin or Hadice could respond.

"Don't mind her," Hadice said. "She would do anything to promote Selim over Murad. She's simply jealous that the attention isn't on her own son."

Yasamin understood the sentiment.

The two women finished bathing in silence. Around them the other women gradually took their leave of the pool in favor of the cool room where they could dry off and re-dress. Hadice joined them as well, but Yasamin chose to remain behind a few minutes longer, soaking in the warmth of the mineral water.

The women's chatter faded away until only the sound of the water lapping the sides of the pool remained. Steam swirled around her in fanciful shapes calling to her mind dervishes spinning in their devotional trances. The soft blue and green light from the windows above caused the pool to shimmer in patterns that threatened to entrance her as well.

She felt only a light tug at her hair at first before a violent yank pulled her entire head under the water. She fought her way back toward the surface, succeeding for a moment, only for another hard wrench drag her under again. She didn't have time to scream as the water assaulted her mouth and nose.

As she thrashed, struggling to reach the air, her flailing arms hit something—another person. In an attempt to break free, she pushed off the bottom of the pool and forced her attacker backward into the pool's stone side. The force holding her under the water vanished, and her face broke the surface.

Gasping and choking, she heard the patter of bare feet running across the hard floor. She heaved herself onto the warm stones, where she lay panting. Her mirror, cracked from side to side, rested next to her.

SIX

—◊◊◊◊—

Berlin, Germany
12 August 1999

THERE WERE NO MIRRORS IN the sitting room of the prim townhouse, nor did Adam expect there to be. As Yasamin related the story to him, Adam could still see in her face traces of the innocent, young girl thrown unprepared into the vipers' pit of the Pasha's household.

Only now, her own voice dripped with a viper's poison. "Politics, Dr. Mire, were an ever-present part of life in the *haremlık*. Those who didn't learn how to navigate the intricacies could find themselves on the wrong end of a knife's blade very quickly."

"So we've both been the target of a Turkish assassin," Adam said. "Who would've guessed we have something in common?"

"Does it disturb you to have something in common with me?"

"Let's just say I'd be happy if the similarities ended

there."

"You could go home, you know, back to America, to your comfortable office, your books, your students. You could blot all of this from your memory. Of course, as I'm sure you know, you'll find the politics waiting for you there, too."

"I've seen my fair share of backstabbing, Mrs. Ashrafi, but at least none of my colleagues have tried to kill me."

She cocked an eyebrow. "Yet."

Adam chuckled. "I'm certain that would never—"

"When your last book was so well received, Dr. Mire, how did everyone react?"

Adam fought back the sudden surge of panic. "How do you know about my book?"

"I've read it, of course. Personally I thought it was brilliant. You have a truly unique voice, but I'm willing to bet not everyone agreed. I'm sure there were a few who were not happy with your newfound fame."

Adam thought of the disingenuous grin pasted on the face of the history department's chair as he offered his congratulations. "A few."

She smiled. "I thought as much. You saw the sideways glances, heard the whispered remarks. But being the professional you are, you ignored them and pretended absolutely nothing was wrong. Ill feelings, however, fester if they're not confronted, Dr. Mire. Have you ever really given thought to what it would take to make someone cross the line, do the unthinkable? Not much, in my experience. An imagined slight perhaps, or simple jealousy? It may start as a stray thought, a mere abstract idea, but once the djinni is unleashed ..."

"Mrs. Ashrafi—"

"Please, Dr. Mire, we can dispense with the pretense.

You know my real name."

"If you're trying to scare me away, it won't work."

"I suppose I'll have to try harder."

"Mrs. Ashrafi—"

"Please, Dr. Mire, my name."

The word escaped his lips before he even realized it. "Yasamin."

A chill passed over him, as if he had uttered some dark incantation and opened a door to a black realm. The shadows shifted again as she stood and walked across the room to an antique globe. She brushed her hand across its surface. "When you think about it, it's not so different with nations, really. Imagined slights. Jealousy. Wars have been fought over less. These are indeed interesting times, are they not? As this millennium draws to a close, so much of the world teeters on the edge, waiting for something to push. What do the French call it? *Fin de siècle*. A winding down, the triumph of entropy. So many possibilities."

"Yet, I don't get the sense you want a war."

"Wars are exciting, Dr. Mire, but they're also messy." She glanced around the room again. "I'm comfortable here. I don't really feel like leaving. The state of current affairs concerns me. Tell me, where are the stable democracies your countrymen promised to replace my empire with all those years ago? Iran, Iraq, Syria. Powder kegs, all of them. Europe is no better. Yugoslavia is a shambles. Your bombers have seen to that. And Russia is just as much of a threat as it was when the Sultan resided in Topkapı Palace. If there is one rule I have learned in my years spent in this part of the world, it is this: Do not trust the Russians."

"But do you really trust anyone?"

"I trust Sandhya."

Adam thought the name must belong to the frightened-looking Pakistani girl who had let him in. He slipped her a silver coin as he stepped inside the townhouse. Her small hand closed over it, and she disappeared as soon as she led Adam to Yasamin's sitting room. He thought she must have an interesting story to tell. He hoped to live long enough to hear it.

"What about Janos Kovács?" he asked. "Did you trust him? I'm going to guess many of the pieces in this room came to you courtesy of his little shop. Was he trying to locate the medallion for you? Or were you trying to find it for him?"

Her expression was impossible to decipher. "I could trust Janos Kovács as much as any man like him. I learned quickly that the only thing more precious to him than antiques was the coin passing into his pockets from selling them. What you speak of would be beyond anything he ever knew or cared about."

"Maybe, but he seemed distinctly disturbed when I mentioned the medallion to him. I'm positive he'd at least heard some of the legends, and he obviously believed enough to be afraid."

"I'm impressed you were able to find me that way, from a mere reference in the margins of a Budapest antique dealer's ledger."

"It wasn't that easy," Adam confessed. "I encountered more than a few difficulties."

"What sort of difficulties?"

"Politics, for one."

SEVEN

—⚉—

Near Subotica, Yugoslavia
2 August 1999

ANYA SWORE, BRINGING ADAM BACK from the brink of nodding off. The dark countryside flew by as the white Fiat raced along the expressway. He guessed they were somewhere in hour three of the four-hour drive from Budapest to Novi Sad.

He sat up, doing his best to suppress a yawn. "What is it?"

"Someone's following us," Anya replied. "The black Citroën, two cars back."

Adam twisted around to look. "You have got to be kidding me."

Anya punched him in the arm. "Don't! Are you insane? You'll let them know we've seen them. Use the mirror."

As he rubbed his arm, Adam glanced in the side mirror, and indeed, a black car followed behind at some distance. The darkened windows didn't allow him to see the driver.

"How is that even possible? The way you jerk this tin can around, I can't imagine anyone being able to keep up."

She threw him a sideways glance. "I'm going to assume you meant that as a compliment."

"How long have they been back there?"

"Not long. They appeared right after we crossed the border."

"Any chance it's a coincidence they were able to pick us up there?"

She smirked. "A chance."

At the border crossing Adam had tried to catch a glimpse of Anya's passport, but the only fact he could glean was that it had a red cover. The Yugoslav guard merely glanced at it before handing it back to her. When he took Adam's passport along with his counterfeit visa, however, he frowned. He walked back to the guardhouse, remaining there for several minutes, but then returned and gave both documents back to Adam. Smiling, he waved them on their way.

"Any idea who they are?"

Anya shook her head. "I can't say for certain."

"What are we going to do about it?"

"At the moment, nothing. When it becomes a real problem, we'll figure something out. Until then, it would be best to continue on."

Adam studied the black car's reflection in the mirror. It looked like some jungle cat stalking its prey, waiting for the opportunity to pounce. "Look, if we're about to get into trouble, I think the very least I deserve is for you to tell me what's going on."

Anya sighed. "And what exactly do you want to know?"

"Well, let's start with who tried to kill me. I know this is probably just a typical Monday for you, but fighting off assassins and being stalked by ominous black automobiles with tinted windows isn't my usual fare."

"I'm sorry. I know much of this must be difficult to take in."

"*Difficult* is not the word I would choose."

Anya glanced once more at the black car in the rear-view mirror. "Dr. Mire, what do you know about vampires?"

"You don't have to give me the whole 'there are forces in this world beyond the ken of mortal man' speech, if that's what you're asking."

"I suspected as much. You won't be shocked then, by the things I'm about to say. The man who tried to kill you this afternoon was a member of an organization known as Süleyman's Blade."

"As in Süleyman the Magnificent, the Ottoman Sultan?"

Anya nodded. "Süleyman's Blade is a militant Islamic sect based in Istanbul. They want to bring back the glory days of the janissaries. They combine their military training with a form of religious mysticism similar to what the Bektaşi Order of dervishes practiced in the time of the Ottoman Empire, just as the original janissaries did."

"So why did one of them try to kill me?"

"They believe it part of their God-given duty to rid the world of Turkey's enemies, especially the supernatural kind. Dracula—Vlad the Impaler—was a thorn in the Turks' side for his entire natural life. They see his medallion as the means by which he continues his legacy. They want it so that they can destroy it. They must have made the connection between you and Mihai Iliescu and thought you might become a liability."

"Me? A liability? How?"

"Knowledge is power, and you, Professor, know a great deal. Obviously they see you as a potential threat to whatever plans they have."

"But the one thing I don't know is where the medallion is."

Anya shot him a sideways glance. "How did you even learn of its existence? Did Mr. Iliescu show it to you?"

Adam shook his head. "I didn't know about it at all until after he was dead, and even now I'm not sure I can trust all of what I've been told."

"What do you mean?"

"After Mihai died, I was contacted by the lawyer winding up his estate. He said he had found my contact information among Mihai's things. The lawyer explained that since Mihai had no family, he requested I be the one to catalog his library in the event of his passing. In fact, he said I was probably the only one qualified to do it."

"You must have been flattered."

"I was. I won't lie. It took some time to make the arrangements, though, and by the time I arrived, almost everything was already gone. There was no medallion. The lawyer, a little ferret of a man, explained he had been forced to sell everything in bulk to cover Mihai's debts."

For a few minutes, neither of them spoke. The black car continued to pursue them, always maintaining the same distance. Adam wondered what Mihai would think if he knew the danger Adam had put himself in simply trying to track down some of his old friend's belongings. Mihai probably would have told him he was an idiot for making the trip. He knew his best course of action would be to find a way back to the States and to the safety of his own little book-filled office once they reached Novi Sad.

But he couldn't, because then he'd never uncover the

truth.

"Süleyman's Blade. Are they right about the medallion?" he asked.

"Not entirely," Anya replied.

"What does it do then? Why are you looking for it?"

"It's the key to preventing a war."

"How will the medallion do that?"

"By stopping him before he starts one."

The hairs on the back of Adam's neck stood on end. "Him? You don't mean—"

"Dracula walks, Dr. Mire."

EIGHT

Budapest, Hungary
2 August 1999

WITH THE CHILL OF COLD steel against his throat, Turhan Avci's senses began to return. He smelled the blood in his nostrils and tasted it in his mouth. His head throbbed, and something pushed down on his chest, making it hard for him to breathe. His eyes fluttered open. Dazzling light flooded into his previously dark world, and he grimaced. When the glare subsided, a man's face filled his blurred vision.

The man grunted. "Welcome back."

Turhan lay on the ground while the man knelt over him, one knee pressing on his chest. His memory returned in pieces. He had come there to kill the American professor, and he had almost succeeded, but then that woman appeared out of the ether and stopped him—with little effort. And because of her, Turhan now found himself with his own knife pressed to his neck.

He struggled to make his voice work. "Who ... who are

you?" he asked in little more than a raspy whisper.

The man chuckled. "You know who I am."

Turhan struggled to focus. The throbbing built until he thought his head might burst open, but gradually the image in front of his eyes resolved. The man's hair was black except for a single grey streak that started at the point of his widow's peak and ended somewhere behind his left ear. At least a day's worth of stubble covered his face. His pale eyes studied Turhan as a butcher might study a cut of meat.

He was right. Turhan knew who he was.

"How many more of you are here?" the man asked.

Turhan remained silent.

The man pressed the knife down harder, threatening to cut off Turhan's breathing. "I am not feeling very patient today," he spat. "How many are here in Budapest?"

Turhan smiled and began to pray, whispering the sweet words of the Prophet. "I seek refuge in the Lord of mankind, the King of mankind, the God of mankind …"

He did not operate under any delusions. He was dead, whether he told the man what he wanted to know or not. He would not give up his place in paradise and condemn his soul to eternal torture by betraying his brothers.

The man sneered. "I see you have some sense after all." He thrust an index finger in Turhan's face. His hand was clad in a black glove. "But know this. I will find all of you, and I will make you regret trying to take what is mine."

He silenced Turhan's whispers by slashing open his throat with the knife, yet even as Turhan's warm blood spilled out onto the floor, his lips continued to move, reciting the words that would carry his spirit to its ultimate reward.

NINE

Berlin, Germany
12 August 1999

YASAMIN'S BLACK EYES SHONE WITH something akin to amusement. "I am aware of Süleyman's Blade. It is an organization full of idiots thinking they can recall the glory days of the Ottoman Empire. Süleyman the Magnificent, indeed. A more accurate name for him would have been Süleyman the Imbecile. I'm not surprised they couldn't even kill a naïve, unarmed academic."

Adam let the sidelong insult pass. "Why do you say Süleyman was an imbecile?"

"He was a love-struck fool who could not refuse the silly whims of his own wife. He had his best friend murdered simply because she asked him to do it."

The story of how Süleyman the Magnificent betrayed his best friend Ibrahim Pasha for the love of a woman was one taught to every schoolchild in Turkey. A cautionary tale about the importance of trust and loyalty as well as the limits of those virtues, the story contained no heroes, only villains.

Adam raised a finger, unable to resist the bait. "What you're saying is only speculation. While it's true Roxelana and Ibrahim Pasha were not on the best of terms, there is no evidence she was directly involved in Süleyman's fatwa against him, or his execution."

"Dr. Mire, which of us is in a better position to know the truth?"

He let his hand drop back to his side. "You have a point."

"It's such a romantic notion you have in the West, that Süleyman fell in love and raised a slave to be his queen. You try to make it into some grand story, as if Roxelana—as you call her—were a real-life Scheherazade. He may have loved her, but she didn't love him."

"Now that's something you can't possibly know," Adam protested.

She drew herself up even more, her eyes blazing. The shadows swirled around her. "But how could she? Taken from her home against her will, sent to a foreign place, forced to change her religion, made to offer her body to a man she'd never even met. She merely made the best of her situation. I was still only a girl when I left my home, Dr. Mire, though by the standards of the time I was old to be marrying." A pang of bitterness entered her voice. "I wish I had possessed Roxelana's guile."

"You sound as if you have regrets," Adam said.

"A few, Dr. Mire, but there is no use dwelling on what is past."

A dry laugh escaped his lips. "Dwelling on the past is all I do."

"Perhaps if you focused more on your present, you wouldn't find yourself in the position you are in now."

"What position is that?"

"A precarious one."

The rosary beads still hidden in Adam's pocket slid through his fingers one at a time. "I've already weighed the risks."

"I'm certain you have." Her eyes narrowed. "It won't do you any good."

Adam endeavored to redirect the conversation before it went to an even darker place. "Tell me, Mrs. Ashrafi, is what Anya said true? Does Dracula walk?"

Another emotion entered into her enchanting eyes, hard to define again, but if pressed, Adam would have called it sadness. "He does, Dr. Mire, but he is not yet a part of the story."

TEN

—ᘺ—

Buda, Ottoman Hungary
10 Safar 1008
(22 August 1599 Old Style)

AS THE SUN SET, THE women gathered behind the veils and drapes concealing the *haremlık* from the rest of the palace. Hundreds of candles stood sentry against the darkness while the women lounged on pillows around tables laden with food.

It was Henna Night, an opportunity for the women of the household to come together to charge the bride with a happy marriage. Except the bride had failed to appear. Ayla found Yasamin sitting in the dark in her room.

"What are you still doing here?" Ayla asked. "Everyone is expecting you. We can't have a celebration without the guest of honor."

Yasamin didn't move. "I don't feel very well. Perhaps I shouldn't go."

Ayla laughed. "Nonsense. Whoever heard of a bride not going to her own Henna Night?"

Yasamin told Ayla what had happened at the baths that morning.

Ayla's smile melted away. "Are you hurt?"

Yasamin shook her head. "Except for a few bruises here on my arms, I'm fine."

"Do you have any idea who could have done such a thing?"

"None at all."

In reality, Yasamin thought immediately of Nesrin and Celibe, the two people who for different reasons didn't want her to marry Murad, but she couldn't see either of them going as far as trying to kill her to stop the wedding.

"Have you told anyone else?"

"No. Do you think I should? Maybe I should tell Hadice. She would know what to do."

Ayla shook her head. "I'm not certain I'd tell anyone."

"Why not?"

"Because you don't know who it was. You can't even prove it actually happened. There are a hundred ways you could have gotten those bruises. You could be accused of making everything up."

Yasamin again thought of Nesrin and Celibe. She could see either of them doing such a thing in order to discredit her or Murad. "What should I do then?"

Ayla thought for a moment. "Nothing. Act like nothing at all has happened."

"But how will that help?"

"I can be your ears. No one knows that you've told me. If you act as if nothing happened, it will give me a chance to listen and see what I can discover. Women let all kinds of things slip out they shouldn't when they're gossiping. If I find out something, then we can tell Hadice. Are we agreed?"

Yasamin nodded. "Agreed."

"Now let's go. We have a celebration to attend."

Yasamin entered to cheering and singing. A girl followed her with a bowl of henna. The women gathered around and set to work. They placed silver coins in Yasamin's palms and began to paint intricate patterns in henna on her hands.

Yasamin smiled at Hadice as she took her turn at the brush. She made a point to smile at all of them—even Celibe and Nesrin. Over the next hour, graceful curves spiraled around her hands, forming leaves and flowers and swirling abstract motifs.

To her, though, it seemed the red-brown lines snaked and coiled around her fingers and up her arms like thorny vines, rooting her to Buda and her fate. She wanted to pull her hands away. She wanted to run, but everyone was looking at her, and she forced the smile to remain on her face while the brush danced over her skin. Once the women finished, they passed the henna bowl around and began to decorate their own hands.

Yasamin studied their work, only to notice a small waver in one of the lines making up the stem of a rose on her left hand. When she brought her hand near her face, she gasped. The waver was not a mistake, but rather minuscule writing. "Seek refuge in the Lord of mankind," it said. "The djinn are here."

She tried but couldn't remember who had painted the rose on her hand. She surveyed the happy, smiling faces of the other women, all busy decorating their hands with the henna. None of them paid her attention at that moment. She glanced back down at her hand.

The djinn are here.

When Yasamin stared at the spaces between the other

women and the bobbing shadows which the candles cast, she could almost see the spirits referenced by the words on her hand. She shut her eyes tight to banish the vision.

One of the eunuchs led in a *kemençe* player who was blindfolded so that the women could dance and enjoy themselves without having to wear their veils. He drew his bow across the strings and began to play a lively tune. Most of the women rose to dance, though Yasamin was not among them. The message on her hand left her so unnerved she couldn't bring herself to even pretend to enjoy the evening. As she sat, she felt the eyes of the other women on her, but she couldn't do anything but gaze at her hands.

At length, Ayla came over to her. "Come dance with me. If you don't, people will think something is wrong. There's nothing wrong, is there?"

With a sigh, Yasamin stood and joined the other women. She only halfheartedly moved with the music at first, but gradually, she gave herself over to the *kemençe* player's song.

As the evening progressed, the music grew wilder and darker. The *kemençe* player's rhythms became more complex and his harmonics more dissonant. Yasamin no longer recognized the song, but she continued to dance. In her head, she saw images of high black mountains looming over an impenetrable forest.

She had seen such places on the journey from Salonica to Buda, but these images possessed a familiarity beyond mere glimpses from a carriage. She knew the contour of the land underneath the canopy, where it fell for a creek bed or rose for a ridge. She knew where the oak and beech trees gave way to conifers as the forest reached up the mountains. She knew secret ways across those mountains.

The moon rose, and the candles dwindled down. Yasamin paid no attention to the time. She merely concentrated on the song, moving her body to the wild rhythm. She didn't remember going to bed, but found herself there all the same the next morning. The grey, predawn light filtered in through her window. Someone was screaming.

ELEVEN

—〰—

Buda, Ottoman Hungary
11 Safar 1008
(23 August 1599 Old Style)

I N THE DARKNESS, YASAMIN MIGHT have mistaken the lump for a pile of old clothes, an odd sight in the *haremlık* garden for certain, though nothing sinister. The approaching dawn, however, revealed more than a mere pile of rags. A man lay in the path, and as the new day grew even brighter, it became apparent he was no ordinary man. His feathered hat lying askew, the colored sash around his waist, and his lack of a beard marked him as a janissary. The sightless gaze on his ashen face also made evident he was quite dead. Blood stained his tunic and pooled on the ground around him.

Nesrin's young servant girl Ine found him while she was fetching water for the old woman. Normally a quiet girl who took Nesrin's reprimands in silence, Yasamin would never have guessed her capable of such a cacophony. As dawn broke, the cries of the muezzins calling the faithful to the first prayer of the day joined Ine's screams in chilling counterpoint.

As Yasamin wrapped a caftan around herself, she glanced at her henna-covered hands. The last thing she clearly remembered from the night before was dancing to the music of the *kemençe* player. She had almost forgotten about the vine-like lines of henna camouflaging masterful calligraphy in a rose's stem—a cryptic message for her. *Seek refuge in the Lord of mankind. The djinn are here.*

By the time Yasamin arrived in the garden, several other women had already gathered, and as the echoes of the call to prayer faded away, Ine's shrieks subsided into whimpers. Yasamin followed Ine's gaze past the broken water jar at the girl's feet to the blood-soaked body and found herself staring into the lifeless eyes of the janissary she and Ayla had seen in the garden.

Images flashed in Yasamin's mind. A pool of blood. A broken sword. A man lying on a cold marble floor, mouth agape, eyes glazed.

Images of a scene Yasamin never witnessed.

A young girl, a late arrival to the grisly party, pushed her way through the semicircle of women. When she saw the dead janissary, her face contorted in the purest expression of agony Yasamin had ever seen. A wail escaped her mouth, and she rushed toward the body—only to be stopped by one of the ebony-skinned eunuchs who had charged into the garden. She kicked him, pounded him with her fists, even bit him, but he didn't waver. After a while she stopped resisting and collapsed into a sobbing heap on the ground.

The eunuch knelt by the body and barked orders to two others. The pair ran off, only to return a few minutes later with a rug rolled up over their shoulders. They laid the rug flat on the ground, lifted the body of the janissary onto it, then rolled him up and carried him away.

An auspicious beginning to Yasamin's wedding day.

Mere hours after the eunuchs carted away the janissary's body and the shards of the broken jar were gathered up, Yasamin found herself dressing to meet her husband. Ayla assisted her as she donned a lush caftan of green silk that set off her olive skin. The elaborate vine pattern embroidered in gold echoed the meandering henna covering her hands. She wrapped a belt made of gold coins around her waist and fastened a matching necklace around her neck. Carefully, she folded a cream-colored silk scarf over her head, and Ayla helped her fasten a red fez trimmed in more gold coins on top. Finally, she pulled the red veil over her face.

After the days of celebrations, feasts, dancing, prayers, and rituals, the ceremony itself was a simple affair. Legally, Yasamin had married Murad without being anywhere near him when she assented to be his wife in front of witnesses from her own family. The appearance of the married couple before the imam was simply meant to bring the blessings of Allah down onto the already completed union.

The guests gathered in the open air of the palace's central garden in the late afternoon. Yasamin emerged to gasps and murmurs from those assembled. Hadice came forward to receive her. With one hesitant step toward her mother-in-law, Yasamin left the world she knew. She thought about her family as she had last seen them on her departure from Salonica—her uncle Hamid; her aunt Fatima, wearing yards of gold brocaded satin meant to impress the representatives of the Pasha; her young cousins Azmiye and Emine, giggling at something only they would understand; her cousin Hasan, looking proud and almost defiant; and his wife Piraye, looking bored. For almost as long as she could remember, they had been her only family. At the time, she felt like she was escaping. Now her departure felt more like a boat leaving a safe harbor in the midst of a storm.

When she reached Hadice, the older woman smiled and took Yasamin's hand in her own. She slipped Yasamin a silver coin for good luck and pulled her into a tight embrace. "Don't worry, my dear," she whispered into Yasamin's ear. "Everything always works out for the best. You'll see."

From behind Hadice, Murad Pashazade emerged, flanked by his brother Selim Pashazade and their father Ahmed Pasha. High turbans adorned with ostrich feathers rested on each of their heads. The imam called for Yasamin and Murad to both step forward. For the first time, Yasamin stood face-to-face with her husband.

His build was slender, and he stood with his shoulders slightly hunched. His face reflected more of his mother than his father. Even under his black beard, Yasamin could see Hadice's long, narrow features. His eyes, though, were nothing like his mother's. They lacked her passive complaisance. In them, Yasamin saw a restless, nervous alertness. His eyes met hers only briefly before his gaze darted to his mother, then to his father, the imam, and finally her again. His demeanor reminded Yasamin of a trapped hare.

At the imam's instruction Murad held out his right hand. It trembled. The imam placed Yasamin's hand atop Murad's and held a string of prayer beads over their hands clasped together. He sang out exhortations from the Qur'an and prayers in Arabic, asking Allah for happiness and long lives for them both, as well as many children of course. Yasamin didn't know how long she stood holding Murad's hand. The longer the imam spoke, the more Murad's hand shook. She watched a bead of sweat make its way down his forehead.

When the imam finally finished, he raised his arms in the air, and the guests cheered. Musicians and servants with trays of food materialized. Guests gorged themselves on piles of *sis kebab, dolmas*, and slices of fresh melon while others danced to the rhythms of the zither and the drums. Among the men, potent, anise-flavored *raki* flowed, and even as twilight gave way to night, the revelry continued unabated by torchlight.

Eventually, Murad appeared at Yasamin's side, holding a candle. Without a word, he gently took her hand and led her away from the crowd, up the staircase, and through the corridors of the palace. The sounds of the celebration faded away. He paused for a moment outside the door to his private chambers, his face flushed and hands shaking. When he opened the door, Yasamin stepped over the threshold and caught her breath. Holding a candle, Nesrin awaited them in the single, small room. Nothing covered the white walls. Only a pallet and a single blanket lay on the floor. A small window opposite the door allowed in a little air and a sliver of moonlight.

Yasamin nearly panicked when Nesrin reached out a bony hand, but with her rough fingers on Yasamin's forehead, she began to mutter in Arabic—verses from the Qur'an regarding good fortune and a prosperous future. Yasamin felt foolish when she realized Nesrin was merely playing her part in the ritual, praying and conferring further blessings on the newly married couple. When Nesrin turned to Murad and touched his forehead to repeat the prayers for him, Yasamin thought she saw something resembling affection.

As soon as Nesrin finished, servants brought in trays full of more food and set them down on the bare wooden floor. They exited quickly, as did Nesrin. When the door shut, Yasamin found herself alone with a man for the first time in her life. Neither of them said a word. They merely looked at one another in the flickering light of the candle.

His eyes commanded her attention again as they scanned every part of her body. No man had ever paid such attention to her. Self-conscious, she averted her gaze, studying instead the cracks in the white plaster walls. When she looked back at him, he too was looking away, his no-longer-eager eyes fixed on the floor.

"My apologies," he said. "I'm forgetting my manners. Please, let's have a seat."

He tentatively grasped her elbow and with no small amount of awkwardness sat her down before the trays of food. Once he seated himself, he turned and extracted a small bundle from beneath the single blanket on his simple bed. "I should give this to you."

Yasamin took the bundle from his outstretched hand, a piece of crimson silk wrapped around something heavy. When she unwrapped it, she found a silver necklace made to look like a chain of pomegranate blossoms, each segment embedded with rubies representing the delicate petals. She traced her fingers over and around the small gems and the fine lines wrought in the metal. She removed the gold necklace she wore and fastened the pomegranate necklace in its place. The silver sparkled in the candlelight.

After a moment, she removed her veil and revealed her face to her husband.

He smiled. "You are more beautiful than I was told."

As Yasamin's heartbeat thundered in her own ears, an uncomfortable silence filled the room. Murad seemed content merely to stare at her. She glanced down at the trays of rapidly cooling food.

Murad picked up a tray and offered it to her. "Please, I know your stomach must be tied in knots right now. Mine is. But we should eat. It would be a shame to let this wedding dinner go to waste."

Yasamin smiled faintly. The thought of eating turned her stomach even more, but she picked up a *dolmas* and bit into it. Murad did the same. While they ate, his eyes never left her.

As she bit into a piece of baklava, a dribble of sticky, sweet honey ran down her chin. She met Murad's gaze, hoping he didn't notice. He laughed.

"Allah is truly good to me for giving me a beautiful wife such as you." He took the baklava from her hand, then placed his hands on either side of her head and pulled her toward him until their lips met. She pushed him away.

"Is something the matter?" he asked.

"No," Yasamin replied. "I didn't mean it. You startled me. That's all."

"My apologies again then."

He leaned in and kissed her once more. She struggled not to resist, but he sensed her reluctance. He stopped and sat back on the pallet. "Are you sure nothing's the matter? Aren't you happy?"

"Of course I'm happy." With the lie, Yasamin's stomach tightened even more. "Allah is truly good to me for giving me a husband as handsome as you."

He smiled again and reached out a hand to stroke her hair. "My heart soars to hear you say that."

He kissed her a third time. While he did, he slid her

caftan off her shoulders and ran his fingers over her bare skin. Yasamin played her part as best she could, despite the awkward moments when neither of them knew how exactly to turn their heads or what to do with their hands. When Murad brought her into a tight embrace, she wrapped her own arms around him, hoping maybe she could become caught up in his enthusiasm, but as she moved her hand across his right side, he flinched.

"What's wrong?" she asked.

Wordlessly, Murad sat back and fumbled to remove his caftan and shirt. A freshly healed cut ran along his right side, from just underneath his ribcage to his pelvis.

Yasamin gaped at the pink line. "What happened?"

"Nothing," Murad said. "A careless mistake."

He moved closer again and, placing a hand on the small of her back, lowered her onto the pallet. Yasamin hoped she could fool Murad into believing she thought only of him, but when she closed her eyes, she saw his brother Selim with the broad shoulders and square jaw of their father and eyes that burned with a focused intensity Yasamin found impossible to banish from her mind.

TWELVE

Buda, Ottoman Hungary
12 Safar 1008
(24 August 1599 Old Style)

YASAMIN WOKE AGAIN IN THE hours before dawn, but on this morning only silence greeted her. The moonlight filtering into the room allowed her to make out the form of Murad sleeping next to her, his bare chest rising and falling in a slow rhythm. She winced as she tried to sit up. It had hurt, just as her aunt said it would. She wished more than anything to have a basin full of water so that she could wash herself and then go back to her own room with its real bed and soft blankets. She bit her lip as the tears fell down her cheeks, and she continued to cry until the first rays of the sun pierced the gloom and the muezzins cried out. Next to her, Murad stirred. She hastily dried her eyes.

"Good morning to you," he said when he found her awake already.

"Good morning." She turned away from him, her voice

still shaky.

He reached up and ran a finger down her bare arm. "Was it really that awful?"

"No," she whispered. "No, it wasn't. I'm sorry."

"Don't be sorry. It would be better if you weren't."

They sat, neither of them speaking. Though Murad continued to caress Yasamin's arm, she couldn't bring herself to look at him.

"Do you want some time to yourself?" he asked.

Yasamin nodded.

He stood up, revealing for a moment the scar on his side. He pulled on a robe and went outside to rouse the servant boy who slept in the alcove opposite his room. A few minutes later, he came back with a basin full of water. Murad waited outside while Yasamin washed herself. When he returned, the frantic excitement she had seen in his eyes earlier was gone, but the sudden coolness she now found there unnerved her even more.

YASAMIN FELL ASLEEP THINKING OF the stories her aunt used to tell to scare her into behaving—stories of the demonic *ifriti*; the *al basti*, said to take horses at night so that they were exhausted the next day and couldn't perform a day's work; the *karakoncolos*, that led lost travelers to their deaths during winter storms; the *karakura*, that tormented sleepers in their dreams.

Above all, she remembered the stories of the djinn. Allah created them from fire, just as he created men from the earth. Immensely powerful and long-lived, they inhabited the empty places of the world. Though they normally concealed themselves from men, they could make themselves known if they wanted, but encountering a djinni was not always a fortunate thing. They were often treacherous, her aunt had warned her, and even when one seemed helpful, it often had its own carefully concealed agenda. The very last chapter of the Qur'an itself referred to the djinn. The warning written in henna on her hand echoed it. "I seek refuge in the Lord of mankind, The King of mankind, The God of mankind," the chapter began, and it appealed to all who heard it to avoid the false whispers of djinn as well as men.

A whisper awakened her. With a start she sat up to find herself in her own bed. Murad had not sent for her that night.

"The djinn are here," the whisper said, echoing the words written on her hand.

Yasamin wondered why such words would come to her in her sleep, but then she heard the whisper again.

"The djinn are here."

The voice, deep and hoarse, came from close by. She jumped up and pulled back the sheer curtains hanging around her bed. Once she convinced herself no one was there, she ran to the door and threw it open. Outside the corridor was empty.

"The djinn are here."

The words snuck up from behind her. Yasamin spun around to see the eyes of a man staring at her through the latticework covering her window. She had seen those eyes before, fixed in silent terror. The eyes of the dead janissary. She opened her mouth to scream, but before any sound could escape, he vanished and left her to gaze into the empty darkness.

THIRTEEN

—◊◊◊—

Berlin, Germany
12 August 1999

"THE DJINN ARE HERE," ADAM said.

Yasamin stood near the antique globe, staring down at a small patch of dull green. The color marked the Ottoman Empire's European territories in the vanished world depicted on the spherical surface. "As good an explanation as any, Dr. Mire."

"At the time," he added.

She turned to look at him. "It still is. After all, what are the djinn but creatures of the night, the empty places, the negative space?"

"But the djinn were always part of God's plan," Adam pointed out.

"Who can say Shaitan himself was never part of God's plan?"

"I didn't come here to have a theological debate with you."

She let out a chuckle. As she spoke, she walked back

toward the divan, pulling the shadows behind her. "Of course you did, Dr. Mire. You came here with a crucifix around your neck and rosary beads in your pocket. I'm sure you have a vial or two of holy water hidden somewhere as well. Your beliefs couldn't be more evident. How do you even know your little charms will work?"

"Faith," Adam replied, even as he chided himself for thinking he had been clever enough to hide the rosary from her.

She passed her hand over the surface of the tapestry behind the divan, tracing out the shape of the tiny mosque in the woods with fingers that hovered over the delicate fabric, but never quite touched it. "I had faith. My charms didn't protect me."

"Did you want them to?"

"An absurd question, Dr. Mire."

"Is it? I've read that djinn can be quite beguiling, and that when dealing with one, you can't let your guard down, even for a second."

Yasamin's eyes narrowed. "You have read too many books."

Adam raised an eyebrow. "You can't deny what I'm saying."

"I don't have to affirm it."

"Fair enough." Adam's gaze went to the wall behind the globe, where floor-to-ceiling bookshelves housed hundreds of antique volumes. "Speaking of books, I've always been curious about something."

"What?"

"'Two were dark, and had high aquiline noses, like the Count, and great dark, piercing eyes, that seemed to be almost red when contrasted with the pale yellow moon. The other was fair, as fair as can be, with great masses of golden hair and eyes like pale sapphires. I seemed somehow to know her face, and to know it in connection with some dreamy fear, but I could not recollect at the moment how or where. All three had brilliant white teeth that shone like pearls against the ruby of their voluptuous lips. There was something about them that made me uneasy, some longing and at the same time some deadly fear. I felt in my heart a wicked, burning desire that they would kiss me with those red lips.'"

The shadows in the room became agitated again, though Yasamin hadn't moved. Adam almost expected the Impaler Prince himself to appear.

"*Dracula*," she said. "You have a very impressive memory, Dr. Mire."

"Chapter Three, Jonathan Harker's diary, dated May 16," said Adam barely above a whisper. "The passage still gives me chills."

"A brilliant work of atmosphere."

"That it is, but it gives me chills for a different reason. I know the truth. Did Bram Stoker?"

"The truth, Dr. Mire? Mr. Stoker wrote a novel. The events he portrayed all came from his very active imagination." Her mouth twisted into a condescending sneer. "Surely you know the difference between fiction and reality."

"I thought I did, but what happens when your reality turns out to be fiction, and the fiction becomes your reality?"

FOURTEEN

Near Novi Sad, Yugoslavia
2 August 1999

THE OVERCAST, LEADEN SKY HAD long vanished into blackness by the time the rolling countryside gave way to the suburbs of Novi Sad. Few other cars shared the road with the white Fiat and the black Citroën, which had been following several car lengths behind. Mere feet separated the two speeding automobiles by the time Adam realized the larger black car had closed the gap.

"Get ready," Anya said, glancing in the rearview mirror.

Adam closed the book he had bought from Janos Kovács and replaced his penlight in his pocket. "And how exactly am I supposed to do that?"

"Just brace yourself."

She barely finished her sentence before the Citroën rammed their car from behind. Almost too late, Adam grabbed the dash with both hands. The Fiat lurched and swerved. Anya jerked the wheel, somehow managing to keep the car on the road while propelling it across three lanes amid shrieking tires. The Citroën receded, but only for a moment.

Anya glanced over her shoulder and scowled. She shifted gears and floored the gas. The car's engine roared in protest, but their lead widened as the Citroën struggled to match the Fiat's speed.

For a second, Adam thought they might get away, but the Citroën surged forward, slamming into the Fiat again. The little white car came within inches of the concrete barrier separating them from oncoming traffic. Anya grappled with the steering wheel.

"I don't think they're going to give up," Adam said.

"Neither do I." Anya scanned the road ahead. "And I don't think this car is going to take another hit like that. I believe it's time for a backup plan."

Adam raised an eyebrow. "I'm almost afraid to ask."

"Trust me."

"Do I have a choice?"

Anya didn't reply. She spun the steering wheel, and the car careened back across the road. Ahead, an off-ramp rushed at them. Anya took it at full speed, and the Fiat became airborne for a moment. Once off the expressway, the Fiat barely slowed down.

She glanced at the glove box. "You should retrieve the Glock. You're comfortable using a gun, are you not?"

"I hate guns. Won't have one in the house." He pulled the Glock from the glove box, dropped the magazine and checked the ammo, then popped the cartridge back in place before pulling the slide to lock and load the pistol. "Doesn't mean I don't know how to use one."

Anya smiled. "Just what I was hoping."

"So what's the plan?" Adam asked.

Anya glanced over her shoulder. The Citroën bore down on them. "We're going to wreck, but on our own terms."

Adam stared at her. "We're going to what? Are you crazy?"

"Just be ready."

The Citroën was almost on top of them again. Adam's heart pounded. Whatever Anya planned, she didn't have much time. He squeezed the handle of the pistol so hard his knuckles turned white.

The road, which abutted the green fairways of a golf course, was lined with beech trees. Ahead of them it took a sharp turn to the right, but when they reached the bend, Anya rammed the Fiat into the wide trunk of a tree instead.

The airbags deployed, blinding Adam. He could hear only the crunch of metal and the jangle of shattering glass. When the airbags deflated and the dust began to dissipate, Adam found himself conscious and uninjured, much to his surprise. Then he saw Anya slumped over the steering wheel, her eyes closed.

He nudged her shoulder. "Anya?"

Her eyes opened. She shot him a withering look and placed an index finger over her lips. Then she closed her eyes again. Following her lead, Adam slouched down, trying to imitate Anya's limp pose.

The Citroën stopped behind the wrecked Fiat. Adam watched in the mirror through half-closed eyes as two men exited the vehicle, both tall and pale with short blond hair, close-set eyes, and high Slavic cheekbones. They split up, one of them approaching the car on Adam's side, the other crossing to approach on Anya's.

The man on Anya's side yanked her door open, only to be met with a swift jab to his midsection. He doubled over, and Anya drove an elbow between his shoulder blades, sending him to the ground. Before his partner on Adam's side could react, Adam sat up and pointed the Glock at him through the shattered window.

"Stay where you are," Adam barked in German, guessing at a language the man might understand.

Adam pushed the car door open and stood up. His hand shook as he held the gun. The man smirked, but didn't try to move. As close as he was, Adam didn't need perfect aim, a fact the man no doubt knew. Behind him, Adam could hear Anya and the other man scuffling, but he couldn't see them.

"Your woman, she's a feisty one," the man in front of Adam said. "Clever, catching Drago by surprise."

"She's not my woman," Adam replied.

The man chuckled. "Whatever you say."

Adam glared. "Let's remember who has the gun here, okay?"

The man continued. "Drago, though, he was a boxer. He represented Yugoslavia in the Olympics. Always bet on Drago in a fight, I say."

Anya cried out. The man, still grinning, cocked an eyebrow. Adam's confidence in Anya's plan began to waver.

"Anya?" he called. "Everything all right?"

No answer.

The man's smirk grew even wider. "It looks to me Drago is gaining to upper hand."

"Here's a thought," Adam said through clenched teeth. "Why don't you stop talking now?"

At that moment, Drago went sprawling across the smashed hood of the Fiat. Adam glanced to his left before realizing his mistake. When he looked back, he saw only the other man's boot as it collided with his hand and sent the gun flying. The man grabbed Adam by the arm and twisted it behind his back. Then he slammed Adam against the car and held him there. He grasped a shock of Adam's hair and propelled his head into the car's roof. Fireworks exploded in front of Adam's eyes as the pain radiated outward from his forehead.

"Drago's not the only boxer," the man growled.

Still clutching Adam's arm, the man pushed him along toward the Citroën. Dazed from the blow to his head, Adam didn't put up a fight, but about halfway there the man's grip vanished. Adam turned in time to see him crumple to the ground. Anya stood over him, cradling her fist. Behind Anya, Drago lay sprawled on his back.

Adam reached up and dabbed at the blood from the cut above his right eye. As he caught his breath, he looked from one unconscious blond-haired man to the other. "These two don't look like members of Süleyman's Blade."

Anya shook her head. "They're not."

"Who are they then?"

"Chetniks, I'd say."

"I know that word," Adam said. "Nationalist paramilitary groups in Serbia before World War II. I'm guessing these Chetniks aren't the same."

"Actually, they are," Anya replied.

Adam held up a hand. "That can't be."

"You should know better by now than to say things 'can't be,' Dr. Mire. The Chetniks still operate throughout the Balkans."

"Operate doing what?"

Anya shrugged. "They are a much looser organization than Süleyman's Blade, based around individual cells. If you ask each cell what the Chetniks' goals are, you'll get widely varying responses."

"Such as?"

"Some are simply anarchists, wanting to create chaos for the sake of chaos," Anya replied. "Some want to recreate Yugoslavia. Others merely quest after Greater Serbia. But they are above all Slavic chauvinists who worship an idealized and inaccurate view of history. They actively oppose other ethnic groups in the Balkans and routinely harass them to try to force them out."

"Ethnic cleansing," Adam said. "I hate to say I'm not surprised. I'm assuming they want the medallion as well?"

"They believe it is the map to some treasure trove of medieval Slavic relics, one that will help the Slavs secure ultimate supremacy in the game of 'We were here first.'"

"Let me guess. The medallion isn't a map either."

Anya smiled. "Not the kind the Chetniks believe it is."

"What is it then? You keep dancing around the truth."

"It shouldn't be in the hands of anyone who wants to use it. It's a thing of evil."

"Well, if it's the focus of so much evil, why not let Süleyman's Blade destroy it?"

"It can't be destroyed, at least not by ordinary means."

"But extraordinary ones?"

"They exist, but they aren't for the faint of heart."

"No, I'm sure quite healthy human hearts are required."

Anya frowned. "This mission is not something to be taken lightly. Many have already died because of the medallion. Many more will, unless we find it."

"And if you find it, what are you going to do with it?"

"Hold it, for safekeeping."

"That's it? You think that will work?"

"God willing."

Adam shook his head. He wasn't sure God had anything to do with it. "If what you say is true, I don't think we need to be going to Novi Sad. What's there anyway?"

"A safe house."

Adam began walking toward the Fiat. "We've already been followed. I'm no expert on the subject, but based on my close observation of more than a few James Bond films, that means the bad guys are probably there waiting for us."

"Where would you suggest we go then?" Anya called after him.

"Banja Luka."

In only a few quick strides, Anya caught up with him. "Bosnia? It won't be easy to get there. Most of the roads were destroyed during the war. Not very many have been repaired."

"Still, I think it's the place we need to be."

"Why is that?"

Adam snatched his satchel from the wrecked Fiat. "Mihai told me."

FIFTEEN

Budapest, Hungary
2 August 1999

JANOS KOVÁCS WATCHED AS THE man picked up another vase. He turned it around in his hands and held it
up so the light shown through the delicate porcelain.
Hand-painted pink and red roses adorned the surface. A
gilded line traced the scalloped opening.

"Tell me about this one," the man said.

"That's ... that's a Limoges porcelain vase from the
eighteenth century," Janos stammered. "Several just like it
were made for the household of the comte d'Artois,
brother to King Louis XVI."

"How much?"

Janos gasped.

"How much?" the man repeated.

"3,450,000 forints, about fifteen thousand U.S. dol-
lars," Janos said quietly.

The man's peculiar appearance had immediately
roused Janos' suspicions when he entered the store. He

wore a suit more appropriate for the end of the nineteenth century than the end of the twentieth, and his hands were clad in black leather gloves. His hair was black except for a prominent streak of grey. A tasteful amount of stubble covered his face. Over his shoulder, he carried a worn leather satchel. Janos had not taken him for an admirer of French china.

As it turned out, he wasn't.

The man let the vase fall from his hand. It shattered on the floor, the shards joining the remains of the other two vases the man had dropped. Janos, his hands and feet bound to a chair with rope, could do nothing to stop him.

"Please," he said through teary sobs, "please, no more. I've told you I don't know anything."

"You said that before I dropped the first vase," the man replied coolly, "but then you were able to remember the name of the woman who contacted you about the Iliescu estate. After I dropped the second one, you remembered the conversation you had with her in fairly vivid detail. What do you remember now?"

"I may remember another detail I forgot earlier. The woman, Yasamin, she said something curious toward the end of our conversation. I asked her why she was so intent on finding this one piece, this medallion. She said it held a djinni's magic. She told me she promised once to keep it safe, but broke her promise. I told her I didn't understand. She laughed, as if what she said were all some joke, but I don't think it was. That's all. I swear. I don't know any-more."

The man grinned. "I believe you."

"You do?" Janos asked.

"Absolutely."

Relief washed over Janos when he thought he might be

freed, but the man didn't untie him. Instead he produced a small can from his satchel. He lifted the lid, revealing bright green paint. He then pulled a paintbrush from the satchel and walked behind Janos.

"What are you doing?" Janos asked as he heard the man kneel behind him.

The man didn't respond. He grabbed Janos's right hand, and Janos soon felt the brush coat his palm with wet paint. When the man finished, he stood and walked back around. Any hope Janos had that the man might let him go vanished when Janos saw the metal gleam of the knife's blade. He didn't even have time to scream. In one clean swipe, the man slit open his throat. As the life drained from him Janos watched the man tip the entire shelf of vases forward. He closed his eyes for the final time as it came crashing down on top of him.

SIXTEEN

—⚉—

Berlin, Germany
12 August 1999

"CHETNIKS," YASAMIN SAID, "I HAVEN'T heard that word in quite some time."

Adam shifted his feet in the shaft of sunlight. "Neither have I."

"The Ottomans ruled over the Serbs for five hundred years. And what did the Serbs do when they gained their freedom? They forgot at once what it is like to be a people without a country. Now their leaders incite violence against their own neighbors. Human nature will never change." The corners of her mouth turned up. "I suppose I should be grateful for that."

Adam sensed a hesitance in her voice. "But?"

"I think about what has been lost—the art, the books, the knowledge. When Matthias Corvinus was king of Hungary, Buda Castle housed the largest library in the world, but by the time I arrived, the library was gone, the volumes scattered to the four winds. I would have liked to see it at the very least. I was forced to make do with stories."

Adam's eyes widened. "Matthias Corvinus held Vlad the Impaler prisoner in Buda Castle. He would have seen the library himself."

"In the stories I heard, bronze doors depicting the Labors of Hercules led into a great hall where light poured in through tall stained-glass windows illustrating scenes from the life of the king. The domed ceiling portrayed the twelve signs of the zodiac surrounding the king's seal, a black raven holding a gold ring in its beak. Everywhere, books rested on tables, bound in leather covers encrusted with sparkling jewels and inlaid with gleaming gold." Yasamin's mouth twisted into a sneer, erasing her wistful expression. "The palace was nothing like that during Ahmed Pasha's time. Only half of it was inhabited. He allowed the other half to fall into ruin."

"What I wouldn't do for the chance to see that library myself, or at least talk to someone who has," Adam said, "but Ahmed Pasha had other priorities, I would imagine."

Yasamin nodded. "The enemies of the Sultan preoccupied him."

"I imagine it wasn't pleasant knowing that at any moment, the Holy Roman Emperor could send his armies over the frontier and lay siege to the city."

"Far from pleasant, Dr. Mire, but there was something more. A darkness arrived the day of my wedding in the form of a dead janissary in the garden. In the months that followed, it spread down every corridor, into every forgotten room, underneath every door. Everyone felt it, to one extent or another, even if no one could name it."

"Could you?" Adam asked.

"Not at first. Not until much later."

SEVENTEEN

Buda, Ottoman Hungary
19 Rabi' al-awwal 1008
(29 September 1599 Old Style)

YASAMIN STOOD IN THE HAREMLIK garden, gazing up at the window to her room. She could find no foothold, no means of climbing up. No one could reach the window. Yet the janissary had done it.

No, not the janissary.

She had seen him lying dead in the garden. The face at the window did not belong to him, but she couldn't force the stories from her childhood out of her head.

As she made her way back to her room, she passed by the washroom where she overheard two of the servant girls arguing. She huffed. Typical. They were always fighting or gossiping when they should have been concentrating on their chores. She went to reprimand them but stopped first at the doorway to listen, hazarding a peek around the corner.

Ine, Nesrin's servant girl, took a soggy pair of trousers and spread them out to dry. "You're lying. No one dies of mere fright." She paused. "I should know."

"I'm not lying. Hafza swears it is true," said the other girl as she wrung out a shirt into a pail of cloudy water. She had brilliant green eyes. Yasamin had seen her around the *haremlık* before but didn't know the girl's name.

"What are the two of you clucking about?" Yasamin demanded as she entered the room.

Her entry gave both girls a start, and the wet clothes fell to the floor with a splat. They scrambled to pick them up. Neither of them looked Yasamin in the eye or answered her.

"I'm waiting," Yasamin said.

After another long pause, Ine spoke. "Sitti was telling me a story of how one of the janissary cadets was scared to death."

"Ine, be quiet!" the green-eyed girl snapped.

Yasamin turned to her. "Really, Sitti? Scared to death? Why don't you tell this story to me?"

Sitti still didn't look at Yasamin, glaring at Ine instead. "It's nothing."

"It's something, or you wouldn't be discussing it at the expense of the laundry."

Sitti was silent for a moment. Then she sighed and, without removing her hateful gaze from Ine, began to tell the story. "A few days ago, the captain of the janissaries was very sick and close to dying. Ahmed Pasha brought a doctor all the way from Izmir, but he could do nothing, so Ahmed Pasha called for the imam. When the imam came to pray over the man, he would not wake up. His breath was shallow and raspy, and his skin was the color of unbaked dough."

Yasamin remembered the sight of the janissary lying dead in the morning dew. His skin was the same color. "You saw this?"

Sitti shook her head. "No, Saruca told me."

"Then she saw it?"

"Hafza told her," Sitti said in a quiet voice.

"Really? So Hafza witnessed the tragic event?"

"No," Sitti admitted. "One of the eunuchs told her. But the eunuch saw it. I swear."

Yasamin stifled a laugh. "A fourth-hand account. Very trustworthy. Please, continue."

Sitti did not seem to catch Yasamin's sarcasm. "The imam prayed over the captain, but when he touched the old janissary's forehead, he cried out as if in pain. The imam ordered the janissary cadet who had been attending the old man to fetch some water. He did, but when he came back, the imam said it was too late. The janissary captain was dead."

Yasamin placed her hands on her hips. "What does any of this have to do with scaring janissary cadets to death?"

"That comes next," Sitti replied. "The imam went out of the room to speak with Ahmed Pasha, leaving the cadet alone with the body. A few minutes later, when the imam returned, the dead janissary was lying on the floor far from his bed. A trickle of blood ran from his mouth. The cadet lay next to him, dead, a look of terror frozen on his face. No one knows what really happened, but the old janissary must have climbed out of his bed and staggered toward the cadet when he went to set down the pitcher of water he brought."

"See, you're making it up," Ine said. "He couldn't have walked across the room if he was dead."

"He could if he was possessed by a djinni," Sitti replied.

"They do such things, you know. My grandmother knew of a spell to bind a djinni. She taught it to me. You take a rock that's perfectly round and you wind a string around it—"

"Sitti, that's enough." Yasamin did not want to hear any more about the djinn. "You're not to repeat such stories or say such things. Do you understand?"

"Yes, *hanım effendi*," Sitti said.

"Good," Yasamin replied. "Now both of you concentrate on the wash and leave the gossip for another time."

"Yes, *hanım effendi*," the two girls said in unison.

Back in her room, Yasamin struggled to banish the incident from her thoughts, but images of the dead janissary captain lurching toward the doomed boy refused to be put away. She couldn't stop herself from glancing toward her window, expecting each time she did to see a face staring back at her. She made so many mistakes in her embroidery she had to tear all the thread out. She was about to start over when another visitor interrupted her, one almost as terrifying.

"Yasamin!"

She cringed at the raspy voice. Nesrin stood in the doorway to her room, cane in hand. Behind her, a eunuch stood with two large bags.

Yasamin stood and bowed. "Yes, Nesrin."

"It has come to my attention that you have been engaging in gossip with the servants."

Yasamin's jaw dropped. "What? I never—"

"Remember your place, Yasamin. More is expected of the wife of a Pashazade. A good wife constantly seeks ways to bring honor to her husband and shuns things that do not."

She sounded exactly like Yasamin's aunt Fatima. *A good*

wife is her husband's best weapon. A good wife does not vex her husband. A good wife is worth ten thousand horses. Whenever Fatima began one of her lectures, Yasamin always found her mind wandering, especially on sunny days when sailing ships crowded the harbor. Yasamin appreciated the advice even less coming from Nesrin.

"Who told you I was gossiping?"

"Ine and Sitti."

The heat rose in Yasamin's cheeks. "Those silly girls? They were the ones gossiping and neglecting the wash. I merely stopped long enough to correct them."

"Did you, now? From what I hear, you were extremely interested in what they had to say."

"Nesrin, if I have offended in any way, I apologize."

Nesrin's scowl deepened. "Apologies are mere words. They may be silly servant girls, but you are not. People pay attention to what you say and do, Yasamin, and not all of them have your best interests at heart. Do not pry into topics that are none of your business."

She made a small gesture with her hand, and the eunuch entered the room and emptied the bags onto the floor at Yasamin's feet. They were full of clothes.

"You like using a needle and thread so much, I didn't think you would mind mending these clothes."

With that, the crone turned and hobbled out of the room, followed by the eunuch, leaving Yasamin feeling as if she might throw up. She thought about Nesrin's words as she stared down at the clothes all around her. They smelled of sweat. She kicked them away. She never would have had to mend clothes in Salonica. Mending clothes was for the servants. In fact, that was exactly who would mend them. She would have Ine and Sitti do it since they were the ones who had thrown her to the wolves.

Yasamin searched for them first in the washroom. They were not there, though the laundry was far from finished. Pile after pile of dirty clothes still dominated the room, and cloudy water still filled the tub in the center.

As she stormed back to her room, Yasamin swore to herself that when she found them, they would receive the tongue-lashing of their lives for betraying her to Nesrin and for being so lazy. She had almost reached her room when she heard familiar bickering coming from up ahead. Beyond her room the corridor turned a corner. She crept up and peered around to find Ine and Sitti arguing in front of one of the countless doors of the palace.

"We have to tell someone," Sitti said.

"Why?" Ine asked. "Why can't we just pretend we never saw it?"

"That wouldn't be right."

"But, Sitti, what if we get into trouble?"

"Why would we, Ine? We didn't do anything wrong."

"And what is it exactly that you didn't do?" Yasamin asked, revealing herself.

Again the two girls jumped. They both looked at Yasamin with terror in their eyes.

"If you have time to exchange gossip and report on my comings and goings to Nesrin, the two of you apparently don't have enough to do," Yasamin said. "I have some mending that ought to keep you busy for a while."

"But *hanım effendi*—" Sitti began.

"No, Sitti," Yasamin said. "I will not change my mind on this matter."

"*Hanım effendi*, we apologize for leaving the wash," Sitti persisted. "We were only going to take a short trip to the kitchen, but ... we found something."

Ine looked daggers at Sitti, but Sitti remained resolute.

"See, right here," she continued.

Sitti pointed to the floor. A small spot of dark red peeked from underneath the door. Yasamin knelt in order to have a better look. She reached down and dabbed her finger in the glossy liquid.

An image filled her mind. Blood. The caustic smell of rust. Sticky on her fingers. She wasn't in Buda or Salonica. She was ... somewhere else. She couldn't remember anything more.

"It's blood, isn't it, *hanım effendi*?" Ine asked.

"I'm afraid so," Yasamin replied.

"This is Rabiye's room," Sitti said. "We haven't seen her since yesterday afternoon."

"Rabiye!" Yasamin called out. "Rabiye, are you in there? Are you hurt?"

No one answered. She looked back at Ine and Sitti. Both stared wide-eyed at her, frozen in place. She turned again toward the door, and with a deep breath, she opened it, only a few inches at first. When nothing happened, she nudged the door again. The gap widened. Still nothing happened. She opened the door all the way. The room was empty.

She and the two girls entered. Inside they found another spot on the floor by the window and a red smear on the sill, right up to the lattice.

More images overwhelmed Yasamin. Men running through the hallways. Her hands smeared in blood. The horrible smell. They seemed like memories, but they couldn't be. They never happened.

"*Hanım effendi*, are you all right?" Ine asked.

"Yes, I'm fine." Yasamin turned to the other girl. "Sitti, can you tell me more about your grandmother's spell to bind a djinni?"

EIGHTEEN

—ᗯ—

Buda, Ottoman Hungary
22 Rabi' al-awwal 1008
(2 October 1599 Old Style)

"RABIYE TOLD ME ABOUT HER janissary once."
Yasamin glanced at Ayla. The two of them
sat huddled under the great oak tree in the
center of the *haremlık* garden. Even as summer gave way to
fall, they still met under the tree whenever they could. As
the days grew shorter, Yasamin felt more grateful for Ayla's
company. The longer nights brought little comfort.

"What was he like?" Yasamin asked.

"Handsome, with silky black hair and chestnut-brown
eyes. He was from somewhere in Anatolia, he told her,
though she didn't remember exactly where. Rabiye's focus
was probably on his strong arms, broad chest, and muscu-
lar thighs."

Yasamin felt her cheeks go flush. "Ayla!"

Ayla grinned. "It is where *my* focus would be. Come
now, you can't tell me you've never had similar thoughts."

"Of course I have. I think I would want more, though. Did he sing to her? Or read her poetry?"

"Both," Ayla replied. "He told her she was his heart and that without her he would cease to live, that in his darkest hours all he had to do was close his eyes, and the vision of her face compelled him to go on. The morning Ine found him dead in the garden, Rabiye said her entire world unraveled, like a rug with one loose thread."

"Love can be powerful."

Ayla nodded solemnly. "Sometimes it can be too powerful. Such a pity. I suppose a vanished girl would be more cause for alarm, if circumstances were different."

Yasamin looked at Ayla in astonishment. "What do you mean, 'if circumstances were different'? Surely her family must be going mad with worry."

"Ahmed Pasha is her only family," Ayla replied, "and if the rumors about her and the janissary are true, she may have run away out of shame."

"But the blood—"

"You yourself said there was only a small amount, and any number of things could have happened. In any event, I believe Ahmed Pasha has more pressing matters on his mind these days."

"Like what?"

"Yasamin, seriously, you need to stop spending so much time with your needle and thread. Half the janissaries have been afflicted with some disease. Ten of them have already died."

"Ten? I had only heard about the janissary captain."

Ayla smiled. "Then you do know something."

"Gossip by some of the servant girls. Just ridiculous rumormongering I thought."

"How do you think I found out? Rumormongering has

its place."

"But how do you know it's true?"

"I trust my source."

"Who would that be?"

"Nesrin."

"Nesrin!" Yasamin said a little louder than she intended.

"Is something the matter?"

Yasamin shook her head. "No, it's only that Nesrin does not strike me as—"

"A rumormonger?"

"No."

"I was helping Ine bring Nesrin's supper to her. The poor girl, it's not her fault she's a little dull. In any event, Nesrin had trouble seating herself to eat. Ine and I had to help her. She said it could be worse for her and that at least she was in better health than any of the janissaries seemed to be."

"Do they know what is causing their illness?"

Ayla shook her head. "No. And no one can find a cure. The afflicted just gradually get weaker until they die."

"How horrible."

"Nesrin said it is almost as if a djinni is stealing their lives."

"A djinni? Where would she get an idea like that?"

"Oh, there are stories. My grandmother used to tell me about the place where she grew up, not far from here, just over the mountains. She said there is a special kind of djinn that takes the body of a deceased person and visits in the night to steal life from the living."

"I've never heard of such a thing."

"My grandmother was full of such stories," Ayla said.

"What were these djinn like, in the stories she told?"

"Like all the djinn, really. Strong as a bull, fast as a hare, agile as a cat. Able to see in the dark better than you or I can see in broad daylight. Capable of hearing a whisper from miles away. Able to move without a sound and pass through locked doors."

The phrase echoed through Yasamin's head. *The djinn are here.*

"Could they be stopped?" Yasamin asked.

Ayla wrinkled her nose, apparently pondering the question. "I think I remember silver repelling them, or a string of prayer beads. They also could not move about freely during the day."

"They had weaknesses, then," Yasamin said.

Ayla shrugged. "I suppose, but you know how djinn are. They can attract people to them, lure them close, enchant them so that they ignore the danger until it's too late."

Yasamin remembered the leering face through the lattice. "These djinn are repulsed by prayer beads you say? What would happen to one if someone recited verses of the Qur'an in the presence of one of them?"

Ayla raised an eyebrow. "I have no idea. They are fairy-tales, after all, aren't they?"

"Of course."

The two of them sat in silence for a few minutes. Yasamin pulled her shawl around her as the wind whipped up, though it was not the wind that chilled her. "You haven't happened to learn anything about who attacked me in the baths, have you?"

Ayla shook her head. "Not even a hint, but I'll keep listening. I promise. As long as we're speaking of gossip, though, do you know what else I learned today?"

Yasamin smiled. "Do tell."

"A group of traveling merchants has come to the city."

"So? That happens every day."

"Not a group that will be passing through Salonica."

Yasamin had not heard from anyone in her family since she had come to Buda. Her heart skipped a beat at the though of being able to contact them. "Would they deliver a letter for me?"

"Why do you think I brought it up? They won't be leaving for a few days. You have time to give them a letter."

"It would mean a lot to me to be able to write to my family."

Ayla placed her arm around Yasamin. "I thought it might."

Silence reigned in the garden again, disturbed only by the call of a crow circling in the sky above.

NINETEEN

Berlin, Germany
12 August 1999

OUT OF THE CORNER OF his eye, Adam spotted a bird, a single magpie, as it lit in the linden tree just outside the window. He remembered a line from a nursery rhyme his grandmother used to recite to him.

One for sorrow,
Two for mirth,
Three for a funeral,
Four for a birth,
Five for heaven,
Six for hell,
Seven's the devil his own self.

The black-and-white bird turned its head to one side and scrutinized him with one eye.

"This sickness, it afflicted only the janissaries?" Adam

asked.

Yasamin nodded. "So it seemed."

The magpie croaked once and took flight again. Adam returned his full attention to the dark, still room and took a deep breath as he realized the momentary distraction could have cost him his life. "Rather inconvenient, with the war between the Ottoman Sultan and the Holy Roman Emperor simmering."

"I lived daily with the sound of cannon fire, Dr. Mire. I was well aware of the state of affairs between my people and the Christian infidels."

"But with the enemies of the Sultan on the move—not only along the frontier with the Holy Roman Empire but in places like Transylvania—I'm betting Ahmed Pasha couldn't spare even one man," Adam continued.

The twisted grin returned to her face. "You have a point, I assume?"

"This illness—it was part of a deliberate plan, wasn't it?"

She laughed. "How could such a sickness be planned, Dr. Mire?"

"You know as well as I do. It wasn't a sickness."

Her eyes narrowed. "Then what do you suppose the janissaries were dying from?"

"Blood loss. This is where Dracula enters the story."

"Such conviction. How would you know?"

"I read it in a book."

TWENTY

—⚬—

Banja Luka, Bosnia and Herzegovina
3 August 1999

JUST BEFORE DAWN THE BLACK Citroën stopped in front of a townhouse on a deserted street. Anya exited the vehicle the two Chetniks had graciously provided, and Adam followed her up the steps and inside.

She flipped on the lights, revealing an interior out of place in the run-down neighborhood. A white, modern, expensive-looking sofa and two equally white, modern, and expensive-looking chairs surrounded a marble-topped coffee table. A white carpet covered the floor while black-and-white abstract art decorated the walls. Adam looked about for any hint of personality—photographs, books, knickknacks. He found none.

"What is this place?" he asked.

"Another safe house," Anya replied.

Adam continued to gawk. "How many of these things do you have?"

Anya pointed at the set of stairs off the entryway. "I'm

sure you'd like a shower. The bathroom is upstairs, first door on the right. Tonight you can use the bedroom across the hall. While you're cleaning up, I'll get you a change of clothes."

Until then, Adam didn't realize how exhausted he was. He muttered a simple thank-you to Anya and climbed the stairs. His legs felt like lead weights were strapped to them, and his satchel might as well have been a cinder block. He dropped the satchel inside the door of the bedroom Anya had indicated and crossed the hall to the bathroom.

He pulled his shirt off and winced as the searing pain surged through his shoulder. His back and legs aching, he examined himself in the mirror. After a few minutes he stopped trying to count the bruises. He had definitely looked better. Hell, he'd seen bodies in the morgue that looked better. At the sight of the small cut on his neck, a thin garnet line against his pale skin, he shivered.

He turned on the shower and stood beneath the scalding water, breathing in the moist air. The heat soothed away some of the pain, but none of the fear. Thankfully, when he had explained to Anya why they needed to come to Banja Luka, she believed him, but now that they were there, he wasn't really sure what to do next.

After staying in the shower far longer than he should have, he wrapped a towel around himself and crossed the hall again to the bedroom, shutting the door behind him. True to her word, Anya had left a set of clean clothes on the bed, all in his size.

Glancing around the bedroom, he saw the theme from below continued on the second floor. A plain, white bedspread lay across the bed. More abstract, monochromatic artwork adorned the walls. Adam heard the door to the bathroom close, soon followed by the sound of the shower. He dressed as quickly as he could and slipped out of the bedroom.

The bathroom door was still firmly shut. The only other door on the hallway stood ajar. Adam crept past the bathroom and paused for a moment trying to slow the pounding of his heart before he prodded the door with a finger. It moved barely an inch before the hinges creaked. Wincing, Adam stopped and glanced over his shoulder toward the bathroom. He could still hear the water running. Reminding himself he didn't have much time, he pushed the door all the way open to reveal another bedroom. The ubiquitous black-and-white art hung on the walls. Another white bedspread covered the bed. On top of it rested Anya's travel bag.

Adam crossed the room. He pulled the bag open, hoping to find some indication of who the woman was who had commandeered his life. What he found instead was an assortment of passports and visas declaring half a dozen nationalities and just as many names. They all contained the same woman's portrait, though—masses of red curls framing an aristocratic face with the most intense blue eyes he had ever seen. Digging deeper, he discovered more passports and visas, except his own face stared back at him from the counterfeit documents. His hands shaking, Adam set them all aside and kept rummaging.

At the bottom of the bag, he hit something hard and bulky. He removed a book—not an ordinary book, an antique. Its worn, leather-bound cover still bore tiny traces of gold leaf, but the image embossed in the leather caused him to catch his breath: a dragon resting on a crag, its wings partially extended and its tail curved around in a wide circle, almost touching its forked tongue.

"So I see you've made yourself at home."

Adam spun around. Anya stood in the doorway wrapped in a white terrycloth robe. Her loose, damp hair framed her face in red waves.

Realizing there was no way to salvage the situation, he put on his best shamefaced grin. "Just looking for the secret passage to the conservatory."

Anya smiled. "That's in the kitchen."

Adam exhaled, letting his shoulders slump. "Look, I'm sorry—"

Anya held up a hand. "Don't be. If I were you, I would have done the same thing. Only I wouldn't have gotten caught." Her gaze went to the book in Adam's hand. "I was waiting to show that to you later, but since I see you found it, now is as good a time as any I suppose."

"What is it?" Adam asked.

"A book."

"Thank you. I never would have gotten that from the binding and the pages. Where did you get it?"

"From the Kunsthistorisches Museum in Vienna. I borrowed it."

Adam cocked an eyebrow. "You stole it."

"Borrowed," she repeated. "When we're done with it, I'm going to put it back."

"An ordinary person doesn't 'borrow' books from museums. Who are you really? Who are you working for? And no games."

She sighed. "If you must. My full name is Anna Fyodorovna Yakovleva, and I don't work *for* anyone."

"Russian, then. So if you don't work *for* anyone, who do you work *with*? Some KGB version of *The X-Files*?"

Anya shook her head. "Certainly not amateurs like the KGB, and as for *The X-Files*, let's just say they got a lot of things wrong. My allegiance lies with an institution far older than my country's current political arrangement."

"The only institution in Russia that old is the Orthodox Church."

"Did you think the Vatican alone stands against the darkness in the world? Let me assure you, Dr. Mire, there are rooms in St. Basil's Cathedral that would reduce you to tears if you could see what they contain. The Russians have saved mankind from the world on the other side of the veil more times than can be counted."

"Back to my first question. Why do you have this book?"

"It's another piece in this puzzle, Dr. Mire, one I'm hoping you can fit into place for us."

"So we didn't just meet by chance. You were looking for me."

"You have a ... unique perspective on matters, a dedicated scholar who believes in vampires." She glanced at the book. "Most people tend to dismiss anything they find inconvenient. You are one of the few who will read with an open mind."

"Read what, exactly?"

"A biography. You're familiar with Prince Michael the Brave of Wallachia?"

"I wrote my doctoral dissertation on the man. I'm more familiar with him than I want to be sometimes." Adam opened the book and leafed through it. "Judging by the paper, the binding, and the type, I'd say mid nineteenth century?"

"Good eye. It was written by a Romanian nationalist named Ioan Nicolescu."

"That fits. Michael the Brave was the darling of the Romanian nationalists, the first person in history to unite all the parts of Romania, never mind his kingdom only lasted one summer. Still, there's one thing that tells me this book can't be genuine."

"What's that?"

"I would already know about it."

Anya shook her head. "Nicolescu had some rather ... unorthodox views, and his sources are more than suspect. Most of your colleagues would consider him a crackpot. This book has spent the last hundred years in a vault in the Kunsthistorisches Museum—until it was stolen a few weeks ago."

"So you admit you stole it."

"I said I borrowed it. We recovered it from the people who did steal it. The question is, why did they want it?"

"You can't ask them?"

Anya pursed her lips. "It's currently not an option."

Adam nodded solemnly. His fingers brushed the soft leather cover. "Options are running out for all of us," he muttered, opening the book.

TWENTY-ONE

From The Life and Death of Michael the Brave
by Ioan Nicolescu

Târgoviște, Wallachia
6 October 1599 Old Style

I HAVE ENDEAVORED WITH THIS *volume to create a complete account of the last years of the life of the great Romanian hero Michael the Brave, which has, to date, been lacking. My sources include letters from the prince himself as well as those who were close to him during that tumultuous time. If I have taken liberties, I ask the reader's forgiveness now. I mean only to provide a more cohesive narrative. The events I present are factual.*

THE BOY, PROBABLY NO MORE than ten years old, gasped for breath after having run all the way to the top of the tower. No doubt he was eager to deliver his message, but the prince did not acknowledge the boy right away, even

though it was a message he was surely just as eager to receive. Instead, he watched the sun rise over the battle-
ments in silence. Michael rarely slept anymore because of
the nightmares, dreams he described as being full of violence, blood, and death.

The lack of sleep and the dreams were clearly taking
their toll on the prince. Many remarked—privately of
course—that he no longer even seemed like the same person.

He was not Prince Michael *Viteazul,* Michael "the
Brave," who stood at the banks of the Danube in defiance
against the arrayed armies of the Ottoman Empire; who
took the citadels of Giurgiu, Silistra, and Hârşova against
incredible odds; who routed the celebrated Ottoman general Sinan Pasha and liberated Bucharest, Brăila, and
Târgovişte. And no one knew if he ever would be that man
again, least of all himself. Medieval Wallachia was a dangerous place, most of all for its ruler.

Watching the eastern sky grow lighter by increments,
Michael had much on his mind that morning and knew
once the boy delivered his message he would have very
little peace, either by day or by night. With the sunrise
came his last fleeting moment of calm.

Only when the sun's disc finally cleared the ancient
stones did the prince turn to the messenger boy. "You have
news?"

"Yes, Your Grace," the boy said.

"And what does our fat Albanian friend have to say?"

"General Basta says that the German emperor has
agreed to your plan. He will support your claim to the
throne of Transylvania."

From the top of the tower Michael could view the entire plain. Just over the mountains to the north lay the

principality of Transylvania. Four years earlier, with the Turks clamoring at Michael's back, he was forced to humiliate himself by pledging fealty to Prince Sigismund Báthory in return for help. Since then the Turks had become less of a concern, and Michael decided the time had come for that fealty to end.

"Good news, then," Michael said. "Where is Alexandru? Does he know yet?"

The boy's eyes grew wide with fear.

"What's the matter?" the prince asked.

"No one can find Alexandru this morning," the boy replied.

Michael sighed. "Then send someone to look for him."

The boy ran down the stairs, nearly falling as he did, as if he couldn't make his legs move fast enough. It was not the first time the prince had given such an order.

Absolutely nothing is known about the earlier life of the *boyar* who called himself Alexandru Dragan. Sporadic mentions of him began appearing around the same time as Michael the Brave rose to power. There is no doubt that in matters of war, he was a tactical genius. The prince himself credited him with many of his victories. But according to others in the Princely Court, he was also erratic, temperamental, and prone to disappearing at inopportune times.

Michael, however, always forgave his odd behavior. He had watched Alexandru in battle and described the way Alexandru killed as "divinely inspired." When the prince pursued the retreating forces of Sinan Pasha to Târgoviște, Alexandru seemed to know what the Turks would do before even they did. The Ottoman forces regrouped and reformed outside the city walls, putting together a hasty counterattack certain to fail, but Alexandru told Michael it was a trick. He devised a plan to trap the Turks instead. Everyone else considered his idea insane, but Alexandru's passion convinced the prince, and his plan worked. The Turkish lines broke down, leaving the city for the taking.

Michael remained at the top of the tower after the messenger boy left, watching in solitude as the morning sun illuminated the fields around the palace, his thoughts on the battle for the city.

"Standing there, I could see in my mind's eye the impaled Turkish soldiers high atop blood-slicked pikes outside the city gates," he wrote in a letter to his cousin Livia Cantacuzinos a few years later, mere months before his death.

"They wailed in agony, the weight of their own bodies pushing them farther down onto the wooden stakes. There were thousands, if not tens of thousands of them—an entire forest of writhing, screaming men. It would take some of them days to die. Yet I knew, as I still know, that no such forest ever existed. The Turks either were killed in battle, or they fled. I knew, but I could still see it. I could see each and every face, contorted in pain, those not already dead begging for the relief death would bring."

TWENTY-TWO

Berlin, Germany
12 August 1999

"I MPALED OTTOMAN SOLDIERS," YASAMIN SAID. "Such a curious vision. What a tortured soul."

Adam cocked an eyebrow. "A tortured soul maybe, but what Michael the Brave claimed he saw wasn't just a vision. You know full well it really happened, only a hundred years earlier. Vlad the Impaler erected a macabre forest of tormented men to intimidate the Ottoman army advancing toward the city. It worked. The Turks were so terrified they retreated without so much as firing a single arrow. It and a thousand other stories like it gave Vlad the Impaler his brutal reputation."

"A reputation he does not deserve."

"You don't think so?"

"I know so. His people loved him. Before he rose to power, war and death loomed like constant specters over Wallachia. When not worrying about starvation and illness, everyone lived in fear of the Turks or the Germans or the Poles. Prince Vlad kept them safe."

"But at what cost?"

"One they were willing to pay."

"One you were willing to pay as well?"

"I had no choice in the matter."

"Didn't you? Trapped in an arranged marriage to a man you didn't love? I'm sure the minute you saw the opportunity to get out, you took it."

Moving faster than Adam's eyes could even track, she rose from the chair and rushed toward him, stopping mere inches from the small patch of sunlight in which he stood. Fiery rage burned in her eyes. "How dare you question my motivations. You have no right—"

"I have every right." He pulled the rosary from his pants pocket and thrust it in her face. "You don't know what I've lost, the hell I've gone through to get here."

She shrank back, gathering the shadows around her once more. The fire in her eyes cooled, from blazing hatred to smoldering malice. "Be careful with your words, Dr. Mire. *Hell* is an easy one to throw around. I doubt you've had even a taste of true hell. And don't think for a minute your trinkets or your little square of daylight will protect you from me, should I—for any reason—grow bored with your company."

Adam trembled as he clutched the rosary. The cross dangling from it swung back and forth, glinting in the light from the narrow window. Slowly, he lowered his arm, but did not put the rosary back in his pocket. "I know how it works," he whispered. "You had to give your consent."

"What does your Bible say, Dr. Mire? 'Judge not lest ye be judged'? You don't know my full story, not yet."

"You don't know mine either."

"Then by all means, continue." She returned once more

to her divan and shot him a look that would cause the pope himself to waver in his faith. "And pray, dear doctor, that I don't grow bored."

TWENTY-THREE

Banja Luka, Bosnia and Herzegovina
4 August 1999

THE NIGHT BEFORE HAD BEEN different. Sleep had come easily to Adam, possibly easier than it ever had, but then, in the previous twenty-four hours he had been beaten up twice, involved in an automobile accident, and chased across three countries. No one could really blame him for collapsing into the bed and immediately falling unconscious.

That night, however, he found himself lying awake, staring up at the ceiling. *Description of the Székely Lands*, from Janos Kovács's antique shop, lay open on the nightstand, as did the book Anya "borrowed" from the Kunsthistorisches Museum. He had spent the entire day studying both. A mistake, perhaps. Every small sound sent his heart racing as he imagined furtive assassins scaling the wall outside and bursting through the bedroom window to end his life.

"I assure you the townhouse is well protected from the

likes of Süleyman's Blade and the Chetniks," Anya told him.

But Adam remained unconvinced. "You've covered everyone breathing. What about everyone not breathing?"

"Now you know as well as I do vampires aren't able to enter a person's dwelling without first being invited," she replied with a reproving smile.

Her words did little to put Adam at ease. Anya had evaded the question when he asked exactly who dwelled in the townhouse. Regardless, he knew vampires had ways around that particular limitation.

The hoot of an owl outside directed Adam's attention back to the window. He had left the garlic in Budapest. The window was unprotected, but the holy wafer above the door gave him some degree of comfort, as did the feel of the cold metal crucifix around his neck.

It also helped to think of his last happy memory with Nadiye, walking hand in hand in Istanbul along the banks of the Bosporus, watching the sun rise across the strait to bathe the Asian part of the city in pink and orange. They had paused near the Ortaköy Mosque.

He brushed her long dark hair away from her ear and leaned in to whisper words he never thought he'd say to another person. "I love you."

She smiled and rested her head on his shoulder. "Took you a while."

He clutched his chest, feigning a wounded expression.

She laughed. "But I'm so happy you finally said it. I love you, too."

He leaned in to kiss her. Neither of them knew she would never see another sunrise.

A small click jarred him back to the present. In the weak light filtering in through the gaps in the blinds,

Adam watched as the window slid open and a black figure slipped silently into the room. The furtive assassins, right on time. As slowly as he could Adam moved his hand to the vial of holy water lying next to him.

The figure drew closer. Adam waited until the last possible moment before sitting up and throwing the holy water in the intruder's face. A gunshot deafened him. The bullet parted the air as it flew past his head and lodged in the wall. The man yelled—a Russian curse. Adam turned on the lamp.

The man stood, pointing a pistol at Adam's head. Dressed in dark military fatigues, he was perhaps a few years older than Adam, with grey creeping into his closely cropped black hair and beard. Water dripped from his nose and chin.

"Who are you?" the man barked. "What are you doing here?"

Before Adam could answer, Anya's voice came from the other side of the bedroom door. "Dr. Mire? What happened? Are you all right?"

She tried to open the door, but Adam had locked it. Without altering his aim, the man went to the door and opened it. Anya, in a T-shirt and sweatpants, stood in the doorway leveling a pistol at the intruder. Adam, who expected a repeat of the earlier scene on the street in Budapest, soon realized he was going to be disappointed.

Anya lowered the pistol and crossed her arms in front of her. "Kostya, put the gun down."

The man smiled at her. "Anya, it's been a while. I was beginning to think you didn't love me anymore."

Anya rolled her eyes. "You're free to use the front door. There was no need to come in through the window."

Kostya pointed at Adam. "But there is a stranger here."

"He's not a stranger," Anya said. "This is the American I was telling you about."

Adam nodded, wishing he were wearing more than his boxer shorts. "Adam Mire. Pleased to meet you."

Kostya ignored him. "You're not even supposed to be here. You should be in Novi Sad."

"We ran into some trouble on the way," Anya said.

"Chetniks?" he asked.

"Yes."

Kostya grimaced. "But why here? The next closest safe house would have been in Belgrade. Why go so far out of your way?"

Anya nodded in Adam's direction. "Ask him. It was his idea."

"His? Really?" Kostya eyed Adam. "This is who you went all the way to Budapest to retrieve?"

"I can explain everything to you," Adam said, "but first, I'd like the gun pointed somewhere other than my head, if you don't plan on using it."

Kostya didn't move. "How do you know you can trust him, Anya?"

Anya placed her hands on her hips. "Kostya, please, he's standing there in his underwear. Let the man have some dignity."

Kostya glared at Adam again, then sighed and lowered the gun. "We'll wait downstairs for you," he said to Adam. "You have five minutes. Do you understand?"

"Perfectly," Adam replied.

After dressing, Adam found them both seated downstairs in the sterile living room, Anya on the sofa, Kostya in one of the chairs.

Kostya stood and offered his hand as Adam entered. "Mr. Mire, glad to see you again. Anya here has been telling me about you. You'll pardon my unorthodox entry from earlier. Please, have a seat."

Scowling, Adam ignored Kostya's outstretched arm, dropped his satchel on the coffee table, and fell into the other chair. "It's *Dr.* Mire, and pardon my lack of manners, but I'm not up on my Emily Post. I don't really know the etiquette for when someone breaks into your room at four o'clock in the morning and puts a gun to your head. Who the hell are you?"

Kostya's smile faded as he sat back down. "Konstantin Danilovich Markov."

"Look, Konstantin Danilovich—"

"*Father* Konstantin Danilovich Markov."

Adam eyed him. "Father? You mean you're a priest?"

Kostya nodded. "Special forces."

"The Russian Orthodox Church has special forces?" Adam asked.

Kostya shrugged. "The Vatican has the Swiss Guard."

Adam shook his head. "They're the pope's personal bodyguard. They don't go around sneaking into people's bedrooms and pulling guns on them."

Kostya raised an eyebrow. "As far as you know."

In light of the previous day's adventure, Adam thought better of continuing the argument. "You have a point," he muttered.

Kostya turned to Anya. "See? He doesn't know his ass from a hole in the ground. I don't understand why we're wasting our time here."

"I explained it to you earlier, Kostya. He's a valuable asset," Anya said. "He's already made more progress in a day than we have in months."

Kostya shook his head. "He's too much of a risk. He's not prepared."

"He has already survived two attempts on his life."

"That's not what I meant."

"I know what's in the shadows," Adam said, "and I'm still here."

"For how long?" Kostya snapped. "Luck will only get you so far, Dr. Mire, but if you're so versed in the darkness, then tell us, why are we all in Banja Luka?"

Adam choked down a pointed response and reached for his satchel. "I wasn't a hundred percent truthful before when I said Mihai didn't leave anything for me. He left me a book." He drew a tome with a worn leather cover out of his satchel and opened it to show Anya and Kostya. "It's a first-edition copy of *Dracula*. It would be worth a small fortune if there weren't scribbles and notes in the margins of almost every page. Mihai made them. A lot of it looks like obsessive-compulsive doodling, but it's not. He wrote a virtual treatise on vampires, all in the blank spaces of the book. Among the topics he covers is Dracula's medallion. There's more, though. This book is the key to a road map that might lead to the medallion."

"He couldn't think of something less ... dramatic?" Kostya asked.

"He was being pragmatic," Adam replied. "I'm not among those who believe Mihai died a natural death. He uncovered something he knew could get him killed. He was making sure his knowledge outlived him."

"So what does the book tell you?" Anya asked.

Adam flipped to a part near the beginning, to an entry in Jonathan Harker's journal in which he comes to realize he is a prisoner in Dracula's castle. A business card for the antique shop of Janos Kovács rested between the pages. Several lines of text were also starred and heavily underlined, part of a soliloquy by the Count, boasting of his ancestors:

We Szekelys have a right to be proud, for in our veins flows the blood of many brave races who fought as the lion fights, for lordship. Here, in the whirlpool of European races, the Ugric tribe bore down from Iceland the fighting spirit which Thor and Wodin gave them, which their Berserkers displayed to such fell intent on the seaboards of Europe, aye, and of Asia and Africa too, till the peoples thought that the werewolves themselves had come.

"An odd detail," Anya said, "Dracula calling himself a Székely when everyone knows the real Dracula was a Wallachian."

"That wasn't the only liberty Bram Stoker took, but in this case, it's easy to see why he did." Adam drew another book from his satchel, *Description of the Székely Lands.* "This is the book I bought from Janos Kovács' antique shop. Stoker used an English translation of it as a reference when he was doing his research. Based on the underlined reference to the Székelys in *Dracula*, I guessed it might contain another clue." Adam opened it to reveal an old postcard tucked in the pages. On it was a painting of a tiny mosque surrounded by woods. "Turns out I was right."

Kostya smirked and snatched the postcard out of Adam's hand. "A postcard? Unless it's from Dracula himself, I don't see how that helps us."

"It isn't the only thing I found," Adam replied, glaring at Kostya anew. He opened the book to a different place and removed a folded piece of paper covered front and back with typewriting. "As near as I can tell, this is part of a transcript from an interview with a Serbian woman who was a small girl living in Banja Luka during the early part of Word War II. She tells the story of how the old caretaker of a mosque hid her and her father from Croatian soldiers one night."

Kostya waved the postcard in the air. "So you think this mosque holds the answers we're looking for?"

"Some of them."

"How do you intend to find it? After all, Banja Luka was home to quite a few Muslims before the civil war, and the Serbs haven't succeeded in tearing down all the mosques, yet."

"Turn the postcard over," Adam said.

Kostya did so. "There's a name. Ibrahim Zorić. Do you know who that is?"

Adam shook his head. "No, but I'm certain if we ask around, we can find him. My plan was to pay him a social call later this morning, at a decent hour. Care to join me?"

Kostya sat, absently stroking his goatee. "Fine. I'll play along, for now, but I'll still wager you end up just like your friend Mihai Iliescu."

Adam smiled, looking from Anya to Kostya. "How could I, with the Russian Orthodox Church as backup?"

TWENTY-FOUR

Near Novi Sad, Yugoslavia
4 August 1999

THE MAN IN THE BLACK gloves dragged the body toward the middle of the golf green by the light of the waning moon. This one wasn't as heavy as the first, but transporting two dead bodies several hundred feet proved strenuous, even for him. He stopped to rest for a moment.

As he stood and surveyed the manicured fairway spread out in front of him, a breeze rustled the trees and set the moonlit grass shimmering in waves. Up above, the stars shone in the clear sky. The form lying on the ground stared at them with lifeless eyes. The wet, glossy edges of the wound slicing across the dead man's neck reflected the silvery light. The gloved man inhaled the earthy scent of the golf course, and for the first time in his recent memory, he felt at peace.

He reflected on his earlier encounter with the pair of men, when they were both still breathing. Neither told him anything useful. The one called Drago never said anything at all, only glaring from his place on the ground, his hands and feet bound. The other was more talkative, but still knew enough to keep his mouth shut when the questioning began. It didn't matter. Gathering information was secondary to his real job, the one he used his knife to accomplish.

Having rested, he continued with his task. When he arrived on the green, he arranged the second man's body next to Drago's. Bright green paint covered each man's right palm. The killer made certain to place the palms open and facing upward. He wanted them to remain that way when rigor set in.

He drove away in the direction of Novi Sad, leaving the two dead Chetniks to be found by a groundskeeper or perhaps an overzealous golfer the following morning. By then the media in Budapest would also be reporting on a Hungarian shopkeeper found murdered in his ransacked shop and a dead Turkish immigrant left in a dark alley, each with their right palms painted green. If he was lucky, there might even be mention of a missing American university professor. By the following evening every police agency in Europe would be on alert, all trying to uncover the conspiracy behind the bizarre string of events.

The corners of his mouth turned upward in a devious grin. None of them, including the American professor, would realize the truth until much too late.

There was no conspiracy.

TWENTY-FIVE

Berlin, Germany
12 August 1999

A S THE SUN PROGRESSED ACROSS the sky, the light shining through the window shifted, and Adam shifted with it—closer to her and away from the view of the warm summer day outside. The shadows around her continued to obfuscate her features.

"What did I tell you about trusting the Russians?" Yasamin asked.

"I didn't have the benefit of your wisdom at the time."

She laughed. "If you had, you wouldn't be here at all. I would have told you that you were making a mistake trying to find me."

"Maybe I was."

"I'm curious about what you discovered in Banja Luka. I was born in the palace there."

"I know."

She had taken to strolling around the perimeter of the room, pausing for a second or two to consider some small artifact on a table or picture on the wall. Adam watched her. There was nothing casual about the way she moved. She was a tigress pacing her den. "Murad asked me once what Banja Luka was like. I lied to him."

"Why?"

"Because he was not interested in the truth."

"What was he interested in?"

"His own thoughts and schemes, dwelling in his own jealousies and bitterness and regret."

"What did he have to regret?"

"Nothing, other than the fact he was not the person everyone else wanted him to be. He was thoughtful, quiet, shy. He would have been happy locking himself away and devoting his entire life to study." A faraway look came over her face. "He had many great ideas about the world, about men and their relationship to God. He should have been allowed to pursue them."

"You sound almost affectionate."

Her gaze hardened once again. "You mistake my feelings at your own peril, Dr. Mire."

"Why was he not allowed to pursue his own interests?"

"He was a pashazade, and the son of a pasha does two things—govern and fight. There is no room for anything else."

"Not even love?"

She shook her head. "Never. All marriages are marriages of convenience. My first was no different."

"What advantage did you gain?"

"I was the wife of a pashazade. I had social standing I never could have dreamed of growing up in my uncle's household in Salonica."

"And for him?"

She hesitated, as if taking time to choose the precise

words. "He gained a wife."

Adam struggled to mask his bemusement. "A wife? No other reason?"

"For him, that was everything. He never could have achieved anything without me."

"There's something you're not telling me."

She grinned. "Astute."

"So, how did you help him?"

The faraway look returned. "I saved him from all of those things he hated about himself. Because of me, he finally learned to look past the jealousy and the anger that had eaten away at him. I set his soul free."

"Would he see it that way?"

"For what I did, in the end, he would thank me a thousandfold."

TWENTY-SIX

—◦◦◦—

Buda, Ottoman Hungary
26 Rabi' al-awwal 1008
(7 October 1599 Old Style)

O N THAT CHILLY MORNING, YASAMIN decided to cover the shawl in tiny crimson and pink pomegranate blossoms. She set about embroidering the delicate flowers, letting herself go in the rhythm of the needle passing back and forth through the fabric. At the knock on her door, she jumped and pricked her finger.

"Yes, what is it?" she called, allowing the irritation to come through in her voice as she sucked the blood from her fingertip.

"*Hanım effendi,*" the voice of a eunuch replied, "your husband wishes to see you."

Yasamin's mind raced as the eunuch escorted her to Murad's room. They did not part on the best of terms, and Murad had made no effort to contact her for several months, since the day after their wedding. Her reaction to him had no doubt hurt his pride. She could apologize, but she feared the damage was already done.

In the daylight the room looked even sparer. Whereas the candlelight of their wedding night had softened its severe edges, the harsh sunlight now reflecting off the bare white walls revealed every flaw in the plaster, every tiny crack, every chip. The pallet passing for Murad's bed appeared as an afterthought, crammed into a far corner, as if doing so could make it disappear altogether. A stack of scrolls and parchments rested on the floor at the foot of the pallet.

Murad stood, waiting to greet her. She smiled when she saw him. He did not smile back.

"I apologize for not having sent for you before now," he said once the eunuch had left. "Circumstances have prevented it."

"What circumstances?" Yasamin asked.

Murad shook his head. "It's complicated. I'm not sure you would understand."

"Why not? I'm your wife. Is it that you don't trust me?"

"How could I when even you would prefer my brother, the great hero, over me?" Yasamin opened her mouth to protest. He didn't let her. "It's no use denying it. I can see it in your eyes." He looked away. "It has been difficult for me."

"Difficult for you?" Any intention Yasamin had of offering her own apology evaporated as her cheeks flushed with anger. "Did it ever occur to you that it has been difficult for me, too? I've been taken away from my home. I don't know anyone here. I don't understand the way people act. Most of the time they may as well be speaking a foreign language. And before the day of our wedding all I knew about you was what I could piece together from the gossip of others—except everywhere I turn, everyone is talking about your brother instead."

Murad laughed, though there was no humor in his tone. "Whatever you have heard about Selim is wrong. He is no hero."

"What are you saying?"

Murad touched his side. "Do you remember this scar, the one you asked about? I received this memento of war saving my brother's life. I'm sure you've heard the story of the great battle—hundreds of infidel soldiers defeated by a handful of men led by Selim. It is far from the truth."

"What is the truth, then?"

Murad shook his head. "There was no battle. German soldiers constantly test for weaknesses along our borders. We were involved in a small skirmish—nothing more. They retreated as soon as they met resistance, but in the chase that followed, some of us were cut off. We struggled to catch up, but Selim managed to lead us into woods so thick, we had to dismount and guide the horses on foot. That's when we found a group of about twenty lost infidel soldiers, all emaciated and hollow-eyed, like they had been wandering in the wilderness for years. When we attacked them, they were so confused and frightened they started to cut each other down. What followed should never have happened."

"What followed?" Yasamin asked.

"One of them found the strength to defend himself. He leapt upon Ilker first and dragged him to the ground. Ilker broke free by unsheathing the dagger at his waist and burying it deep in the infidel's leg, but he could not stop the infidel from wounding him in return. Then, as if Ilker's dagger had left him with nothing more than a scratch, the infidel went after Selim, who was too busy gloating over the bodies of two slain soldiers to see him. I didn't think. I ran and threw myself in the knife's path as the wounded man was about to run Selim through. The infidel impaled himself on my sword. As the sword went through him, his eyes held no surprise, only hatred, for me—for all of us. He sputtered and coughed up blood, but to my horror, he retained his grip on his own weapon and pushed himself farther onto my sword to reach me. I twisted my blade and ended his infidel life, but not before he gave me this scar." Murad closed his eyes.

"He collapsed to the ground, and his blood stained the underbrush red as his hate-filled eyes glazed over. The whole thing made me sick. I never wish to see a man die like that again."

"Why have you not corrected anyone?" Yasamin asked. "If what you say is true, why let your brother steal the glory that should belong to you?"

"No one would believe me. Besides, there are other ways for me to distinguish myself."

"Do you really think being a religious ascetic will impress anyone?"

Murad frowned. "What makes you think I am a religious ascetic?"

Yasamin glanced around the bare room. "I should imagine this is hardly the style in which a pashazade lives. Why do you go without, if not for religious reasons?"

"I have what I need."

Yasamin moved toward the scrolls stacked against the wall. "What are these documents you've collected? They weren't here before."

Murad blocked her way. "I didn't bring you here to talk about them."

"Then why did you?" Yasamin asked. "You don't speak to me for months and then greet me like you would greet a servant."

"I want to offer my apologies, Yasamin. You are my wife. I shouldn't have kept you away. Let us spend some time together, and perhaps I can convince you I am a better man than my brother." Murad drew close. "And you are not the only one who knows so little. I would like to learn more about you, if you would care to share."

"But you already know everything. I grew up in Salonica in the household of my uncle, who is the official keeper of the weights at the market. There is nothing more."

Murad shook his head. "I don't believe you. There must be more. What about your parents?"

"They died when I was very young."

"Do you remember them at all?"

"Only vaguely. I remember my mother was very beautiful. At least everyone has always told me she was."

"Then you must get your features from her."

Yasamin blushed. "Actually, I've been told I look like my father."

"What about him? What do you remember of him?"

"I don't remember anything about him really. My aunt said he was a very important person. He was a personal friend of your grandfather, Ferhat Pasha."

"That is all you remember?"

"Should there be more?"

Yasamin observed Murad's hands out of the corner of her eye. They still trembled. She imagined Selim would not be so nervous around a woman.

"I have never been to Banja Luka," he said. "My mother tells me it's a beautiful place. What do you remember of it?"

Yasamin shrugged. "I rarely left the palace. I only remember going to the mosque a few times. The first and last time I really saw the city was the day I left to live with my aunt. It was winter. The sky was grey, and all the trees were bare. There wasn't much to see."

Murad let his shoulders slump, and a pang of guilt knotted Yasamin's stomach. He thought she was being short intentionally, though she truly didn't remember much from the time before her parents died. She could recall bits and pieces, but that part of her life never seemed real to her, as if it all happened in a dream.

Then a hopeful smile spread across Murad's face. "I see you're wearing the necklace I gave you."

"I always wear it. It reminds me of Salonica."

"I thought it might. I had it specially made for you. I wanted you to have a piece of your home here."

"Thank you."

Murad offered his hand. She took it, and he led her to the pallet on the floor. He leaned in and kissed her. She didn't flinch.

BY THE TIME YASAMIN RETURNED to her room in the company of another eunuch the predawn sky had lightened to a deep cerulean. She waited until she was sure the eunuch had left, then reached into her caftan and pulled out the documents she had taken from Murad's room.

Most of them, she discovered as she read, were accounts of plagues spanning back hundreds of years. She spent hours scouring the descriptions made by doctors, holy men, and travelers of various sicknesses they encountered in their wanderings. She came to realize Murad was looking for accounts similar to what was happening to the janissaries, perhaps to find a cure. She wondered if that was how he intended to distinguish himself.

At length, she came across a series of letters written more than a hundred years earlier by a captain in the Sultan's army named Kemal. He wrote them while he took part in a campaign in some rebellious part of the Sultan's domain.

Yasamin imagined him a dashing figure with dark features. In her mind's eye, she saw a rugged face with a well-maintained beard and an ample mustache. He was the son of a physician or an accountant perhaps, and no doubt, he plied the same trade when he was not fighting in the Sultan's army. The letters were all addressed to his wife in Izmir. Yasamin wondered if she ever received any of them.

TWENTY-SEVEN

Letters from Kemal, a soldier, to his Beloved

Războieni, Moldavia
6 Rabi' al-thani 881
(29 July 1476 Old Style)

Y HEART ACHES FROM THE distance between us, my Beloved. You are my last thought before I sleep at night, and my first when I awaken each day. Our time apart tortures my soul, but Allah willing, my love, we will not be apart much longer. The Sultan's army has achieved a great victory against the infidels.

His Excellency, the Lord of Kings himself, led the charge against the infidels and their prince, and when the infidels saw his power, they immediately fell into chaos. Many we simply cut down. The rest fled the field in terror. We pursued them to a fortress not far away, where they have decided to take their stand. We have begun preparations to lay siege. Our cannons will bombard them day and night. We expect them to surrender quickly ...

Cetatea Neamţului, Moldavia
27 Rabi' al-thani 881
(19 August 1476 Old Style)

I CLOSE MY EYES, MY Beloved, and I can see you. I imagine you brushing your hair as you ready yourself for bed, the silver-handled brush I gave you on our wedding day gliding through your raven hair. Your emerald-green eyes are focused somewhere in the distance. Perhaps as you twirl your hair with your fingers you're thinking of me. I could spend all day like this, my love, with my eyes closed, looking at you. I hope our time apart will be over soon.

The infidels impress us with their tenacity. The citadel has not yet fallen, despite the fact that our barrage has caused severe damage to the structure, and we know they are nearing starvation. For days now, we have expected their surrender. Instead, this morning our positions on the hill overlooking the fortress came under heavy fire. We thought we had destroyed their cannons. Still, the cannonballs rain down at an impossible rate. We may have to break the siege before we lose all of our artillery ...

Neamţ, Moldavia
3 Rajab 881
(22 October 1476 Old Style)

I KNOW MY PLACE IS in the service of His Excellency the Sultan, but I grow weary of the life of a soldier. All I want is to smell your perfume, to hear your voice, to feel your hand in mine. Alas, I cannot do so yet. While His Excellency the Sultan has returned to Istanbul, we who are left must subdue these lands for his and for Allah's glory.

As we feared, we were forced to break the siege. The infidel prince has escaped, and we have word he is amassing a new army. Meanwhile, small raiding parties are a constant source of annoyance. We are preparing to leave here and march against a fortress some distance away to the north. I hope we meet with greater success there ...

Suceava, Bukovina
12 Ramadan 881
(29 December 1476 Old Style)

IT IS UNFORTUNATE WINTER HAS set in. It is never a merciful time for soldiers. I should not be here. I should be with you. I should be looking into your eyes. I should be holding you in my arms. The thought of seeing you again has become all I live for. I beg Allah for it to come to pass, and I have received news today that makes me think Allah has heard my pleas. The *Kazıklı Bey* is dead.

So hated was he that he was shot through the heart by one of his own archers at the outset of a battle a few days ago. He has cheated death so many times, though, that his head has been cut off and sent to Istanbul, where the Sultan ordered it set on a pike outside the gates to the palace, to prove he is indeed dead.

The crimes of the *Kazıklı Bey* were so vile I cannot write them in this letter, but they were sufficient to earn him the name "Impaler Prince." With his atrocities at an end, however, I expect these rebellious principalities to be subdued quickly. Allah willing, I will be able to return home to you, my Beloved ...

Hotin, Bukovina
7 Shawwal 881
(23 January 1477 Old Style)

I AM NOT TOO PROUD to admit I am afraid, my Beloved. I hold onto the image of your face more tightly than ever. An invisible, silent assassin, more deadly than any enemy arrow, creeps through the camp.

It is an illness. Its victims are robbed of their strength seemingly overnight, and no matter their original complexion, their skin becomes a sickly, pale color. Their breathing becomes labored and rasping. Some, after a few days, begin to drool blood.

I have not been afflicted yet, thank Allah. I don't know what the future holds. We haven't met with any success against the infidels for some time. It appears now to be a lost cause. If we don't withdraw soon, I fear we will be lost. Pray for me, my love ...

Hotin, Bukovina
29 Shawwal 881
(14 February 1477 Old Style)

I EXPECT YOU ARE SAD for me that I've contracted this dreadful sickness. You shouldn't be. My understanding has begun to extend beyond notions of life and death. They are, in truth, meaningless labels humans use in a futile attempt to understand the world in which they find them-selves. I see that now. Do not mourn for me.

I am not dead ...

TWENTY-EIGHT

Berlin, Germany
12 August 1999

"CURIOUS TIMING ONCE AGAIN," ADAM said. "The *Kazıklı Bey*—the Impaler Prince—dies, and a plague overtakes the Sultan's army, forcing them to retreat from the Romanian principalities."

"Very curious," Yasamin replied.

"And this Kemal's last words to his beloved, 'I am not dead'—"

She held up a hand. "I would prefer not to dwell on it."

Adam raised an eyebrow. "Curious indeed."

"Think whatever you will, Dr. Mire. Even I can understand the tragedy of lost love, especially in situations where it is unavoidable."

"Unavoidable? What made it unavoidable?"

"Come now, Dr. Mire, I'm not going to spell out everything for you."

"Just like you didn't spell out everything for Murad."

"Why should I have?"

132

"He was your husband."

"I had my reasons for not being completely truthful."

"You mean about stealing the scrolls?"

"I mean about a great many things, including Banja Luka," she said. "I saw more of the city than I said, and it used to truly be a beautiful place. On the occasions we left the palace to go to the baths, I remember seeing the green gardens with flowers that bloomed in the springtime; passing by the marketplace and smelling the fresh bread, the spices, and the salty meat cooking; looking up at the pointed minarets touching the sky. It was a lively city. It made me happy to be there, and I would have been happy to stay."

"Have you been to Banja Luka recently?"

She shook her head. "Not since the war ended. I don't have any particular interest in going back now. It's not the same place. I've heard the Serbs have destroyed all the mosques."

"There are plans to rebuild several of them."

She glowered. "For whom? All the Muslims are dead or have left. It is an academic exercise, Dr. Mire, meant to appease the collective conscience of the West, which let it happen to begin with. They can rebuild all they want. It will never replace what has been lost."

"There is one mosque I found there that they didn't destroy, at least not all of it."

"Which one?" she asked.

Adam pointed to the mosque in the tapestry behind her. "That one."

TWENTY-NINE

From the transcript of an interview with Katerina Lukić

Banja Luka, Independent State of Croatia
7 February 1942

O N 7 FEBRUARY 1942, FASCIST *Ustaše paramilitaries murdered 2,300 Serbs near the city of Banja Luka, then part of the Independent State of Croatia, a Nazi puppet. In the early 1990s, when ethnic violence broke out again in and around Banja Luka, a reporter for the BBC named Edwin Reynolds tracked down several witnesses to the 1942 massacre, most of whom had been children at the time. Weymouth resident Katerina Lukić immigrated to England with her father shortly after the war. When Reynolds interviewed her, he heard a story he did not expect.*

Katerina Lukić: I'm ... I'm not sure where to begin.

Edwin Reynolds: Why don't you talk about what you were doing when you found out the soldiers were coming?

Lukić: My father and I were sitting down to dinner. It was already dark because it was winter. Petar, our neighbor, pounded on the door until Father answered. Petar told him Croatian soldiers were coming down the street rounding up Serbs and that we needed to leave right away. I started to cry. I remember saying I didn't want to go. Father knelt in front of me and told me to be brave. We barely made it out of our house.

Reynolds: Where did you go?

Lukić: There was an old mosque not far from our house. It had always been there, as long as I could remember, but I never paid much attention to it. Sometimes I saw the old man who was the caretaker tending the garden. He always wore a fez and a tired but pleasant smile on his face. I don't remember my feet even touching the ground as Father clutched my hand and dragged me along. I could hear the soldiers behind us, their heavy footsteps growing louder and louder.

Reynolds: Your father thought you would be safe there.

Lukić: It was what he hoped at least. When we reached the mosque, we ran around to the back where there was a door and next to it a tiny square window. The curtains were drawn, but I could see the glow of lamplight from inside. Father banged on the door until the old caretaker answered in his fez and slippers. He frowned at the two of us, but when he saw the fear in Father's eyes, his expression softened. Father begged him to let us inside, before the soldiers found us. I still remember what my father said. "I know we do not share the same faith, but we serve the same God. I have heard from others that you are a good man. Please help us."

Reynolds: Did he?

Lukić: The man motioned for us to come inside and hurriedly shut the door behind us. We stood in a cozy living room. My stomach rumbled at the smells drifting from the kitchen. We had to leave our own dinner uneaten. A plump woman wearing a scarf over her head walked in. A boy close to my age peeked from behind her. The woman looked at her husband. He explained to her what was happening, and I remember her eyes growing wide, her jaw set in horror. Then her expression softened. She smiled at me, but the sadness did not leave her face. "I suppose I'll have to set two more places at dinner then," she said.

Reynolds: It must have been a very tense meal.

Lukić: It was, but the man, the woman, and their son were extremely gracious. I have often wished I could have found them later and thanked them. The war made it impossible. We ate mostly in silence. I do remember the food was very good. Every few minutes, we heard bursts of gunfire from outside, and every time, both the caretaker and my father paused and muttered a quiet prayer.

Reynolds: So the Croatian soldiers passed you by, then?

Lukić: If only. Toward the end of the meal, another knock at the door came. It was insistent and accompanied by angry yelling. I clung to Father.

Reynolds: What did you do?

Lukić: The caretaker's wife shoved us into the tiny bedroom where we hid underneath some blankets, holding tight to one another.

Reynolds: Did it work?

Lukić: No. I heard the caretaker open the door and speak with the soldiers, their voices muffled through the bedroom door and the blankets. I could tell the soldiers were becoming angrier and angrier. They yelled at the caretaker. Then I heard a sharp smack. The caretaker's wife screamed, and the boy cried. Heavy boots thudded across the floor. The bedroom door flew open, and rough hands yanked the blankets off us. Light flooded back into the world, and I stared into the leering face of a Croatian soldier. I could smell the alcohol wafting off him. He took me by the arm and yanked me up, away from Father. Another soldier pulled him to his feet. The soldiers dragged us both back into the main room where two more waited for us, guns drawn.

The caretaker huddled in a corner with his wife and son. The soldiers threw Father and me in the corner with them. The caretaker had a bleeding cut over his left eye. The soldiers took aim. I buried my face in my father's chest, but for a third time that evening, a knock at the door came.

Reynolds: Who was it?

Lukić: To this day, I don't know the answer to that question. The soldier who had found us motioned for one of the others to answer, but when he opened the door, no one was there. The soldier walked outside and looked around, then turned to face the others. He shrugged. "Nobody is out—" he started to say. He didn't get the chance to finish.

Reynolds: What happened to him?

Lukić: Something tackled him to the ground and dragged him out of sight. It moved so fast, I couldn't see what it was. I would have guessed a wild animal mauled him judging by his screams.

Reynolds: What did the other soldiers do?

Lukić: Two of them ran to the door while the last kept his gun trained on us. As soon as the two soldiers crossed the threshold they were attacked. First one soldier and then the other fell to the ground, bright red blood spurting between their fingers as they clutched their throats, gagging, gurgling, thrashing around, struggling to breathe. I was terrified, but I couldn't make a sound. I watched in horror as a hand grabbed each soldier by an ankle, then pulled them both into the shadows.

Reynolds: A human hand?

Lukić: Yes.

Reynolds: What did the last of the soldiers do?

Lukić: His gaze alternated between our group in the corner and the door, and for the first time fear crept into his eyes. His hand shook as he held the gun. Father glanced at the caretaker. Their eyes met, and the caretaker nodded. Before the soldier could react, they sprung up. Each took one of the soldier's arms, and together they shoved him outside. He stood for a moment in shock before being knocked down. He clawed at the dirt in vain while he too was dragged away.

Reynolds: And you never discovered what killed them all?

Lukić: Not her name.

Reynolds: Her?

Lukić: After the last soldier's final cries faded, a woman appeared at the door. She was Turkish by her complexion, with long, raven hair and olive skin. She would have been beautiful, save for the blood covering her hands and dripping from the corners of her mouth. "Do not mistake what I have done tonight for mercy," she said. "I was protecting this place, not you." Then she vanished into the mist.

THIRTY

——ɷ——

Banja Luka, Bosnia and Herzegovina
4 August 1999

KOSTYA HESITATED BEFORE HE KNOCKED on the
door. "Are you sure about this?"

"No," Adam replied. "But it's all we have. If
this Ibrahim Zorić can't shed some light on the location of
the mosque in the postcard, then I doubt anyone will be
able to."

"Maybe he can tell us too why he hasn't had the sense
to leave this pit yet."

The side of the street where they found themselves was
lined with residences, but many of the houses were abandoned. The same held true for the shops on the opposite
side. Plywood filled in broken windows, and graffiti—
mostly hate-filled slogans in Serbian Cyrillic—covered the
storefronts.

A wizened Muslim wearing a fez opened the door a
crack, enough to scrutinize the two strangers standing
there. His suspicious gaze passed from Kostya to Adam.

"Ibrahim Zorić?" Adam asked.

The man grunted and tried to shut the door. Kostya's hand shot up. His palm smacked the door and held it open. As the old man struggled against the far stronger Kostya, his dour expression changed. Fear crept into his eyes.

"Wait," Adam said in Serbian. "We're not here to hurt you. We just want to ask you a few questions."

"I have no answers for you," the man replied as he continued to push against Kostya. "I cannot help you. I don't want any more trouble. Please, go away, now."

Adam frowned. "More trouble?"

The man looked past Adam's shoulder. Adam turned to see two men standing across the street, sheltering themselves from the bright sun under an awning over the entryway of a coffeehouse, one of the few businesses still open. One had a shaved head. The other was dark-haired, with tattoos visible on his arms and his neck. Though they looked nothing like the two who had chased him and Anya on the way to Novi Sad, Adam knew who they were. *Chetniks*. He and Kostya traded glances.

"Please, not now," the man said. "Come back later."

"When?" Adam asked.

"Never," Kostya said before the man could reply. "If we come back later, someone else will answer the door and claim no one by the name Zorić has ever lived here. Isn't that so?" The man began to stammer in protest, but Kostya brought his fist down on the doorframe, silencing him. "Please don't lie anymore. We've already said we're not here to hurt you. We're not with *them*. We just want to talk to you. Surely you have a few minutes to spare."

The man lowered his eyes and nodded, opening the door wide enough to let them in. He shut the door behind them, and beckoned for them to follow him into the next room.

"You didn't have to do that," Adam whispered to Kostya in Russian.

"Yes I did," Kostya replied.

A low table surrounded by pillows took up the center of the room. A cheap-looking oriental rug covered the floor. Other mismatched rugs hung on the walls.

"Please, sit," the man said.

Adam and Kostya each perched on top of a pillow while Zorić left the room for several minutes. When he returned, he held two saucers, each with a cup balanced on top. The china rattled as he placed the cups of thick, black Turkish coffee in front of Adam and Kostya. With his guests served, he retrieved a cup for himself.

When everyone was seated around the table, Adam saluted with his cup and took a sip of the strong brew. "My name is Adam Mire. My colleague is Konstantin Markov. We're ... journalists. You are, in fact, Ibrahim Zorić, yes?"

The man nodded. "You must accept my apologies for failing to offer you hospitality before. Since the war, there are so few Muslims left. We live every day in fear of harassment. We cannot afford to be too trustful."

"Can't you go to the police?" Adam asked.

Zorić threw his hands up. "The police are all Serbs. They simply look the other way."

Kostya snorted. "The 'peace' your country has brought to Bosnia, Dr. Mire."

Adam shot him a sideways glance. "I'm very sorry, Mr. Zorić. I promise we won't take up too much of your time. We are looking for information about a mosque. We don't know the name of it, or even its exact location, only that it was somewhere in Banja Luka, at least as recently as

1942. We have a picture of it."

Adam took the old postcard out of his satchel and showed the picture of the mosque to Zorić.

The old man's eyes grew wide. "Where did you get this?"

"From a friend," Adam answered.

"Your 'friend' visited me almost a year ago and showed me this exact picture. He told me I was well respected for my knowledge of this area's history. I do know much about the history of Banja Luka, but really it is because I am old and my family has lived here for a very long time. I don't deserve anyone's respect for it."

"Mihai came here?" Adam asked.

Zorić nodded. "Yes, that was his name. A Romanian. Mihai Iliescu."

"What did you talk about?"

"Our conversation concerned private matters," Zorić replied.

"Please," Adam said, "it's important."

Zorić refused to look either of them in the eye. "Why come all this way to talk to me? Why don't you discuss it with him?"

"Because we can't," Kostya said. "Mihai Iliescu is dead."

Zorić's face went chalk white. His hands shook so much his coffee spilled over the side of his cup. "All the more reason for me not to say any more."

"All the more reason for you to talk to us," Adam said. "Mihai was killed by someone or something far more sinister than those thugs outside. We need to understand what happened to him—so we can put a stop to it."

Without a word, Zorić struggled to his feet once more and left the room. A few minutes later, he came back with a rolled-up piece of paper and handed it to Adam, who unrolled it to discover a watercolor print of a small mosque nestled in the center of a grove of blooming pink pomegranate trees. Its white walls and four minarets gleamed in the midday sun. It was the same mosque pictured in the postcard. The print, signed by an English painter Adam had never heard of, bore the date 1852, a time when anything "oriental" was all the rage in Britain.

"It was called the Foreigner's Mosque." Zorić said.

"Odd name," Kostya remarked. "Why did they call it that?"

Zorić shrugged. "That was simply its name."

"What did Mihai say when you told him you recognized it?"

"He asked me where it was and if he could visit it."

"Did you take him there?"

Zorić clenched his jaw. His mouth flattened into a grim line. "You have not been listening. I would have been more than happy to take him there, but such a visit is not possible. The mosque was destroyed during the Second World War and never rebuilt. The city has, of course, grown since then. An apartment block stands on the site now."

"Why was it never rebuilt?" Adam asked.

"The mosque had no imam, no devoted worshipers, no one to speak for it," Zorić explained. "There was only an old caretaker, and no one ever listens to the caretaker."

"What did Mihai say when you told him all of this?"

"He seemed disappointed, but of course, you can't change the past. The mosque was very old. Its odds of surviving were not the best."

Adam paused before he asked the next question. He had not cleared it with Kostya first. "Have you been contacted by a woman named Yasamin?"

Whatever color was left in Zorić's face fled. "Mr. Iliescu asked me the same question."

"What did you say to him?"

"I told him I had not."

Kostya grunted. "Would you say if you had?"

Zorić fixed him with his stare. "I am a man of integrity. I do not lie."

"Very well," Adam said. "Did he explain his reason for asking?"

Zorić turned his gaze to Adam. "He said only that artifacts of Banja Luka's Ottoman past might be of particular interest to her, but he told me that if she did contact me, I should not under any circumstances agree to meet her in person."

Kostya raised an eyebrow. "Why might that be?"

"He did not elaborate." Zorić gazed down at his coffee cup, which was by then empty. "If you will, please excuse me for a moment. There is something I have forgotten."

Adam waited until Zorić left. "There's more going on here than Mr. Zorić is letting on."

Kostya crossed his arms. "I get that feeling as well, but something tells me you and I are not referring to the same thing."

Adam pointed to a basin resting in one corner of the room. "That's a washbasin Muslims use before saying prayers. See the calligraphy around the edge? A work of art. It shouldn't be here. And the tiles that border the ceiling—they're out of place too. The pattern is too elaborate for a simple home."

"What are you trying to say?"

"These things were taken from a mosque."

Looking at the floor, Adam realized that it, too, was

made of tile. He lifted up one corner of the rug. Underneath he could see the very edge of a mosaic. He stood and began clearing away pillows.

"Help me move this table," he said to Kostya.

"Why?" Kostya asked.

"There's an image in the tile on the floor. I need to see it."

They set aside the table, then Adam turned back the rug. He held his breath. Though badly damaged, enough of the mosaic remained for Adam and Kostya to discern the large lizard-like animal, its body curved into the shape of a circle and its tail wrapped around its neck. A ring of Arabic calligraphy similar to the rim of the washbasin encircled the creature.

Kostya knelt over the mosaic. "This certainly changes things."

At that moment Zorić walked back into the room carrying several books. When he saw what Adam and Kostya had done, he yelped. Dropping the books, he shoved Adam out of the way and picked up the edge of the rug. "What are you fools doing? Hurry, we must cover it up again." Kostya stopped him. "Wait, where did this come from?"

"From the Foreigner's Mosque," Zorić grunted.

"But how?" Adam asked.

Zorić glared at Adam. "The last caretaker was my father."

Adam ran his finger along the edge of the washbasin. "He took these things from the ruins?"

"He saved what he could. The men in my family were caretakers for the mosque for as long as anyone could remember—forever, maybe. My father hid and protected these things, and now I do, but I am the last. I have no children." He covered his face with his hands. "I am afraid of what will happen to all of this when I am gone."

Adam held up a hand, trying to calm the agitated old man. "If I promise you I'll do what I can to help save all of it, will you tell us what you know?"

Zorić eyed him. "And you can actually help me?"

Adam nodded. "Absolutely."

"Very well," Zorić said.

"What does the writing around the edge say?" asked Adam.

Kostya looked at him in surprise. "You mean you don't know?"

Adam shook his head. "I never learned Arabic."

"It is the last chapter from the Qur'an," Zorić explained, "admonishing the faithful to seek refuge in the Lord of Mankind and to beware the whispered lies of men and djinn."

"And the creature in the middle? Do you know what it means?"

"No. I'm sorry. I do not. Given the chapter, my father assumed it was a representation of Shaitan."

Adam scratched his chin and said almost to himself, "Or perhaps some other evil." He shot a look at Zorić. "Katerina Lukić. If your father was the caretaker, you were there the night of the Banja Luka massacre in 1942. Your parents sheltered a man and his daughter from the Ustaše. You saw what happened to the Croatian soldiers."

Zorić stiffened. "What I saw were members of the Serbian resistance kill the Croatians to rescue the girl and her father. I had nightmares for months."

"But that's not—"

"It is what happened."

Adam glanced at the books Zorić had dropped on the floor. "What are those?"

Zorić picked up the books and handed them to Adam. "They are books I wanted to show you. Your friend Mihai sent them to me several months ago. I am not certain why, except perhaps to thank me for my help. They seem very old and valuable. The letter he wrote implored me to keep them safe, though truthfully, I would have sold them if there were someplace I could."

As Adam glanced over the three volumes, one title stood out to him, *The Land Beyond the Forest* by Emily Gerard. Bram Stoker had consulted it in addition to *Description of the Székely Lands* when writing *Dracula*. Adam pulled the copy of *Dracula* Mihai had sent him and opened it to a page with another underlined section in which Abraham van Helsing explains to Jonathan Harker and the others exactly what Dracula is:

He must, indeed, have been that Voivode Dracula who won his name against the Turk, over the great river on the very frontier of Turkey-land. If it be so, then was he no common man, for in that time, and for centuries after, he was spoken of as the cleverest and the most cunning, as well as the bravest of the sons of the 'land beyond the forest.' That mighty brain and that iron resolution went with him to his grave, and are even now arrayed against us.

"I'll buy these books from you right now," Adam said. He retrieved his wallet. "Will German marks do?"

Zorić smiled at last. "They will do nicely."

With the transaction complete, Adam and Kostya helped put the room back in order. Adam thanked Zorić for his time and headed toward the front door. Kostya's hand on his shoulder stopped him.

"How can you make a promise to protect these things,

knowing you won't be able to keep it?" he asked, reverting to Russian and motioning for Adam to stay back while he crept toward the door. His hand went to the gun concealed in his jacket.

"I had to say something," Adam replied. "Besides, how do you know it's a promise I can't keep? I have contacts at the University of Sarajevo. As soon as I can, I'll get in touch with them."

"I would not be so optimistic about speaking with them any time soon," Kostya said as he peered through the curtains. "Our friends are not there anymore."

"Do you think they've moved on?"

"Not a chance. As soon as we open the door, we're dead. Now you see why I insisted we come in for a chat."

"You were buying us time."

Kostya nodded. "Exactly."

"Then what do we do?" Adam asked.

"Use the back way out."

"Are you sure there is one?"

Kostya grinned. "There is always a back way out."

He was right. Zorić led them through his house to a window that opened up on a ten-foot drop to an alleyway behind Zorić's house. Kostya climbed out first, followed by Adam. No sooner than his shoes hit the pavement did the two Chetniks appear from around a corner.

"So much for that plan," Adam said. "Now I wish Anya had come with us."

Kostya surveyed the two men advancing toward them, guns already drawn. His hand inched toward his own gun but stopped when two other men appeared in the opposite direction. Their assailants could fill them both with bullets before Kostya ever had the chance to draw. The four Chetniks rapidly closed in.

He glanced from side to side. "I'm not sure Anya would have been able to help us in this situation."

"Against the wall!" the bald Chetnik barked, aiming his gun at Adam as they drew closer.

He never made it a step farther. Gunshots echoed through the alleyway. In less time than it took to blink, all four Chetniks lay on the ground, dead. Adam glanced at Kostya who seemed just as surprised as he was. His gun still holstered, he hadn't fired a single shot. Adam wondered at their luck until their saviors materialized from around the same corner where the first two Chetniks had appeared, three men with Mediterranean features, guns also drawn. They were not smiling.

"Süleyman's Blade?" Adam asked Kostya.

Above their heads the window from which they had just exited slammed shut.

Kostya frowned. "Zorić has connections, apparently."

The one in the middle of the group, a tall, lanky man with a goatee, stepped forward. "Dr. Adam Mire, Father Konstantin Danilovich, please come with us."

THIRTY-ONE

Berlin, Germany
12 August 1999

A GAIN YASAMIN SWEPT HER FINGERS over the tapestry. "This mosque was one of my father's favorite
places. I'm happy to know at least part of it survived."

"So you do remember your father," Adam said.

She shook her head. "I only remember that much because I visited the mosque once. I was perhaps five or six. I
was told it was a special occasion and that I should be on
my very best behavior for the day. The sky was grey and all
the trees were bare. I shivered outside in the cold, yet
even as I think about it now, I recall feeling a sense of
peace."

"They call it the Foreigner's Mosque. Do you know
why?"

"Dr. Mire, the answer to that question is right in front
of your face. Where is the 'Land of the Foreigners'?"

"Wallachia," Adam replied, even as the significance

dawned on him. "That's the literal translation of the name."

"And he was prince of Wallachia."

"But that doesn't make any sense," Adam protested. "Vlad the Impaler was one of the Ottomans' bitterest enemies. Why would they name a mosque for him? And why would they put a depiction of his dragon emblem on the floor? Not to mention the fact that it violates Islamic law to depict animals in religious art. Doing so would defile a holy place."

"The depiction of animals may violate Islamic law, but it does not violate the rules of Islamic magic. In fact, it is often necessary. Think about the writing around the circumference of the mosaic, Dr. Mire: 'I seek refuge in the Lord of Mankind.'"

"I've thought about that phrase quite a bit."

She nodded. "The last chapter of the Qur'an is an important one. It is often recited as a spoken amulet against evil. After the death of the *Kazıklı Bey*, they stripped his medallion from his corpse. The Foreigner's Mosque was built to house it, as a symbol of his defeat, or so the Sultan said."

"But if they wanted it to serve as a symbol of his defeat, they would have sent it to Istanbul, not a small mosque in the middle of the woods in a backwater province," Adam said. "They built the mosque because they were trying to contain it, to keep the evil in."

"Or perhaps to keep it out."

"The day you visited the mosque as a child, did you see the medallion?"

Her attention went to a small dagger with a jeweled hilt displayed on a table next to her divan. "No, not then. Later."

THIRTY-TWO

Buda, Ottoman Hungary
26 Rabi' al-awwal 1008
(7 October 1599 Old Style)

A TINY DROP OF BLOOD stained the paper next to the very last word of Kemal's last letter. Yasamin stared at it for a long time. *I am not dead.* As she focused on those four words, she thought she saw a shadow move at the edge of her vision. She jerked around but only her own belongings occupied the room—her blankets and pillows resting where she had placed them that morning, her tapestry hanging on the wall. She turned her attention back to Kemal's last letter. Without knowing it, she began to mouth the very last sentence, as far as she knew, the last thought this captain in the Sultan's army ever expressed.

I am not dead.

I am not dead.

"I am not dead."

Yasamin froze. The creaky whisper came from so close

she could feel the speaker's breath caressing her ear, but no one was there. She sat by herself on that cold, clear autumn day, reading letters she had no business reading.

YASAMIN COULDN'T FALL SLEEP THAT night. Long after the last candle went out, Kemal's words echoed in her head. When she closed her eyes, she saw only the sinister face of the janissary at her window. She nearly jumped out of her skin at the knock on her door.

"Yasamin!" a girl's voice called from the other side of the door

Yasamin tiptoed across the room. "Who is it?"

"Let me in quickly," came the breathless voice. "It's Ayla."

Yasamin opened the door. Ayla stood on the other side in her nightshirt, out of breath.

"Yasamin, come with me," she said. "I have to show you something."

"Why are you up this late? It's the middle of the night. You're going to get into trouble."

Yasamin peered into the black, empty corridor behind Ayla. In truth, Yasamin feared a ghoulish janissary looming over Ayla's shoulder more than any trouble she and Ayla might find themselves in.

"I promise you, Yasamin, I wouldn't be here if it weren't important."

"Then tell me what it is now, and we can discuss it in the morning."

"It won't wait."

"Why not?"

"Because it won't. It has to do with who tried to drown you at the baths and what happened to Rabiye."

Yasamin drew in a sharp breath. Her fear did not go away, but her curiosity pushed it aside, at least for the moment. "What have you found?"

"Please," Ayla said, "just come with me."

The *haremlık* garden glowed in the light of the stars and the waning moon. The bare trees cast shadows everywhere, like bony hands reaching out, trying to grab them. Ayla led Yasamin down a corridor on the other side of the garden. They were in the oldest section of the palace, a part rarely used. The still, empty rooms reminded Yasamin of a mausoleum.

Ayla stopped in front of a door at the end of the corridor. "It's in there. Go ahead. I'll be right behind you."

Yasamin opened the door and walked into a tiny washroom that hadn't seen use in years, judging from the dust and the cobwebs and the hole in the ceiling. She glanced around. "I don't see any—"

Had the moonlight shining through the hole above not glinted on the metal, Yasamin never would have seen the dagger. She moved out of the way as the knife slashed the air where she had been standing. Ayla lunged at Yasamin again, but she was clumsy with the small knife, and Yasamin was able to dodge her attacks. She knew, however, that with one lucky jab, the pool of blood on the palace floor would belong to her.

"Ayla, what are you doing?"

Ayla didn't reply. She advanced toward Yasamin again, the menacing point of her dagger reflecting the pale light.

Yasamin retreated until her back pressed against the wall of the tiny room. "Please, I'm begging you. Stop before he comes for us."

"Before who comes for us, Yasamin?" Ayla spat. "The eunuchs? They're all asleep. No one knows where we are."

"I ... I don't know who I mean," Yasamin replied, "but I can feel him watching. Can't you?"

"If you're trying to scare me, it's not working. There's no one here but you and me."

"It's him. He's here."

"Who? Who is here?"

"Rabiye's janissary. Please, I'm begging you to believe me. I know he's supposed to be dead, but I saw him at my window. He spoke to me."

Ayla narrowed her eyes. "Don't think you can play games with me, Yasamin."

"I'm not playing games." Yasamin ducked another swipe from Ayla's blade. "Why are you doing this?"

"You know very well."

Yasamin shook her head. "If I did, do you think I would have agreed to come here with you in the middle of the night?"

Ayla heaved an exasperated sigh. "You think you're so much better than everyone else. You think you can come here and take what you want, like you took Murad from me."

"How could I have taken Murad from you? It was not even my choice to marry him."

Ayla didn't move. "*I* was promised to Murad a long time ago. My father made an agreement with Ahmed Pasha. He helped Ahmed Pasha to acquire the office he now holds, and in return, I was to be wed to his older son, but since my father is dead, Ahmed Pasha has chosen not to honor his promise. Eliminating you won't give him a choice."

She charged at Yasamin again, the dagger raised above her head. Yasamin managed to grab her wrist, but the blade danced perilously close to Yasamin's throat as they struggled. Yasamin pushed back as hard as she could, but Ayla's crazed anger only made her stronger.

"Please," Yasamin said, "we're both in danger here."

Ayla broke free from Yasamin's grip. "You're the only one in danger."

Yasamin tried to jump out of the way as Ayla slashed toward her, but the dagger ripped through her shirt and grazed her side. Despite herself, Yasamin cried out and stumbled to the ground clutching her side. Before she could recover, Ayla fell on top of her and held her down.

"I never expected you to be delivered to me like this. Since I failed in the baths, you've been so careful. It seems Nesrin is never more than a shout away. You even stopped leaving your room after dark. I feared I would never get another opportunity, but Rabiye offered me the perfect way to coax you out. The djinn have granted me good fortune."

The djinn.

"Wait, you're the one who wrote about the djinn on my hand," Yasamin said.

Ayla sneered. "This is just more trickery."

"No, someone wrote, 'Seek refuge in the Lord of mankind. The djinn are here,' on my hand. You just attributed your good fortune to the djinn. Are you telling me you didn't write it?"

"I didn't, not that it matters. Farewell, Yasamin. May Allah have mercy on you."

She raised the dagger high above her head. Yasamin closed her eyes and braced herself for the fatal blow, but it never came. The weight of Ayla's body lifted. Yasamin sat up to see her lying on the ground in the corridor outside the abandoned washroom. A man stood over her. He wore a janissary's uniform.

"Ayla, no!"

From her pocket Yasamin took a small round rock she had picked up from the pond in the haremlık garden and a piece of her embroidery string. She began to wrap the string slowly around the rock. As she did, she recited verses from the Qur'an, as Sitti had shown her when teaching her the spell for binding a djinni.

As soon as she began reciting the verses from the Qur'an, the janissary fixed his gaze on her. Wincing, as if in pain, he tried to walk toward her, but he stumbled.

Ayla leapt to her feet and rushed at him, her eyes burning with rage, nostrils flared, and lips drawn back in a snarl. Startled, Yasamin stopped her recitations. Immediately, the janissary pivoted and caught Ayla by the arm. She kicked at him, but his grip seemed to be made of iron. Her struggling made no difference.

The janissary squeezed her arm until she dropped the knife. Then he spun her around and, holding her pressed against him, placed his free hand over her mouth. Yasamin heard a sickening crunch when he snapped her neck. The janissary let her limp form fall to the ground in a heap at his feet. He turned toward Yasamin again. Yasamin scrambled backwards, but she had nowhere to go in the little washroom.

"Are you all right, *hanım effendi*?" he asked, holding out his hand.

As he spoke, he gazed at the ground. Yasamin realized he was taking care not to look at her unveiled face. Seeing him clearly for the first time, Yasamin was also shocked to discover he was not Rabiye's janissary, the one she had seen dead in the garden and afterward at her window. She didn't say anything. She couldn't speak. She couldn't move.

"I'm not going to hurt you," the janissary said. "Are you all right?"

"Yes," she answered softly.

She took his hand, and he helped her to her feet.

"Please, then, *hanım effendi*, run quickly. I'll see that everything is taken care of."

But Yasamin didn't run. She stood, looking at the janissary's profile as he gazed toward the ground. His aquiline nose gave him a hawk-like appearance. It protruded a bit too much for Yasamin to consider him handsome, but something oddly familiar about his face compelled her to speak nonetheless.

"Who are you?"

"Who I am is not important," the man replied in a firm but not harsh tone. "Now run! I mean it. Go!"

Yasamin obeyed. She ran faster than she had ever run before. Not once did she look back to see what became of the janissary. She staggered through the door of her room and collapsed on top of her bed. For hours, her mind raced, replaying the events of the evening over and over, but as the dawn neared, exhaustion eventually overtook her, and she fell into a sleep so deep even her nightmares couldn't find her.

THIRTY-THREE

Buda, Ottoman Hungary
2 Rabi' al-thani 1008
(13 October 1599 Old Style)

SNOW.

Yasamin practiced saying the word a dozen times. The servant girl who brought breakfast told her what the curious precipitation was. Her food sat uneaten as she stood at her window watching the snow drift silently downward and cover everything in a thin layer of white. She reached through the lattice to catch the snowflakes, only to have the delicate crystals melt away as soon as they touched her hand. She wanted a closer look.

In the courtyard, she pulled her cloak tightly around her to ward off the wind. She walked around the old oak tree magnificently draped in white, studying it from every angle. Every so often a gust of wind came up and caused the snow to whirl around in tiny cyclones.

The day's stark white tone made the sudden flash of color she saw out of the corner of her eye even more strik-

160

ing. It appeared and then vanished so quickly Yasamin couldn't even be sure she saw it. She called out, but no one answered. The snow continued to fall all around her without a sound, and for the first time, she became aware of the silence. She slowly made her way around the tree again. Ahead of her and to the left a staircase led to the second level and back to her room. Beyond stood the archway leading to the old part of the palace, still in shadow at that time of day. She shivered, and not because of the cold. She decided she should go back to her room and to the embroidery she planned to do that day.

She made it up only a few steps before she saw another flash of color. This time, she was certain she had seen it. She turned around. A man stood in the archway, staring at her with smoldering eyes. It was the janissary who had saved her from Ayla. Even with the shadow falling across his face, his eyes held a fire that captivated her. In fact, they seemed to glow.

His uniform was standard for a janissary—trousers tucked into high boots, a modest but precisely tied turban, and no beard, only a mustache. He smiled when their gazes met. They stood facing each other for a second or two longer, until she remembered she was unveiled. She averted her eyes for only a moment, but when she looked back, he was gone.

YASAMIN FELL ASLEEP THAT NIGHT with the needle in her hand. She awoke to someone singing. As she neared her window, the long, doleful melody stopped, but seconds later, a man call her name from outside her window. She jumped back. She was certain the dead janissary had returned, at least until he spoke again.

"Don't be afraid, *hanım effendi*."

The voice belonged to the janissary who saved her life. Yasamin approached the window again. The moonlight allowed her to see glimpses of him through the lattice.

"What are you doing?" she asked. "You shouldn't be here."

"My apologies, *hanım effendi*." He grinned. "You're right. I shouldn't."

"Why are you, then?"

"To see you, Yasamin."

Her heart skipped. "How do you know my name?"

"I went to a great deal of effort to discover it."

"I'm afraid I'm at a disadvantage, then. You know my name, but I don't know yours."

"I am called Iskander."

He began singing again, the same low, mournful song. From somewhere in the distance, a wolf joined in. He shifted, and Yasamin saw a flash of moonlight on metal, the clasp of his cloak. It looked like some sort of serpent, its body bent into a circle with its tail wrapped around its head. As he continued to sing, she recognized the tune, the same song the *kemençe* player played on her Henna Night.

"Iskander," she said, "don't think me ungrateful for what you have done, but you're making me nervous. How is it you're able to perch outside my window?"

"You're very beautiful," he said.

She looked away. "I'm married."

"I know."

"My husband is a pashazade." She turned to face the window once more. "I could scream right now, and twenty eunuchs would come and cut you down."

"Then why don't you scream?" he asked.

Yasamin hesitated. "You saved my life."

"Tell me, *hanım effendi*. How did you come to be in that unfortunate position?"

"Ayla, the girl you ... saved me from, she disagreed with my being chosen as Murad Pashazade's wife."

He cocked his head to one side. "No, that's not what I meant."

"I don't understand."

"Every story has a beginning," Iskander explained, "and what we think is the beginning. You're telling me what you think is the beginning. Go back. Tell me everything from the very start."

"I don't want to do that."

"Why not?"

Yasamin closed her eyes. "You're a perfect stranger."

Iskander laughed. "I think I ceased being a stranger when I stopped that girl's knife from harming your exquisite neck. Come, now. I want to know all about you. Would it be easier if I asked you more specific questions? We can start with a simple one. Where were you born?"

"Banja Luka."

"I've been there," said Iskander. "Of course, that was many years ago. It is a beautiful place. The jewel of Bosnia. The most beautiful moon I have ever seen was over Banja Luka—a splendid white disk hanging in the cold, dark blue sky over the pines."

"I don't really remember much about living there. I was very young when I left."

"Why did you leave?"

"My parents both died."

"I'm terribly sorry. It was an accident then?"

Yasamin was about to answer that it had in fact been

an accident. Someone left a candle burning, but before she could say anything, the images flashed in her mind again— a man lying on the floor in a pool of blood, her own hands covered in sticky red.

"I don't know."

"When you left, where did the whims of life take you?"

"To live with my aunt and uncle in Salonica."

"Also a very beautiful city."

Yasamin bowed her head. "Yes, it is, more than I ever realized."

"You're not happy."

She peered at the janissary through the lattice and tried vainly to read the expression on his face. "I'm happy enough. Who are you to presume how I feel or what I'm thinking?"

"It is easy to see. All anyone has to do is look. You haven't been happy since you left Banja Luka. You had a comfortable life with your aunt and uncle in Salonica, but you didn't get along with them. If I had to guess, you couldn't understand their limited ambitions, and you chafed under your aunt's instruction."

Yasamin felt her cheeks flush. It was as if he knew her already. "My uncle is happy to be the keeper of the weights at the market. They wanted nothing more for me than to marry someone exactly like him. My aunt punished me every time I questioned her about my lessons. She insisted on teaching me things useful for a bureaucrat's wife."

"Not the wife of a pashazade."

"No."

"And yet, here you are."

"Yes, here I am."

"It is what you always wanted, but not what you expected," Iskander said. "You dreamed every day about living in a palace again, married to a man of prominence, but you always thought the palace would be in Istanbul, and the man of prominence would be broad-shouldered and square-jawed. Instead, you're in a backwater province, married to a man you don't find attractive."

"Murad is not a bad man. I could learn to love him."

"Could you?"

"I don't have much of a choice."

"There is always a choice."

"Not in this case. I have to find a way to be content with my life."

"But for someone like you, why should that be the case?"

"Why? Because I have responsibilities to my family, to my husband, to his family. I can't simply turn my back on them. I can't believe you would ask such a question. A janissary would know more about responsibilities than anyone."

"I am a janissary in the *haremlık* speaking to a woman who is not my wife," Iskander retorted. "Even a janissary can dream of a life free of the artificial ties that keep us away from what we want. What do you want, *hanım effendi*?"

"I don't know."

"I think you do. Snow this early in the season is quite unusual. A warm room full of pillows and blankets would be much more pleasant than the chilly air out here. If I came to your door, would you let me in?"

"What?" Yasamin was unsure she had understood the question.

"If I came to your door, would you let me in?"

"You can't," she said.

"I can, but that's not what I asked."

"You'd never be able to make it. There are guards—"

"Who are usually asleep."

"Still, the risk would be too great."

"Perhaps," he said, "but great rewards await those who take great risks."

And he was gone. Hardly a minute later, Yasamin heard a faint knock at her door.

"*Hanım effendi*." The janissary's whisper carried through the door like a shout. "It is Iskander."

Yasamin went to the door and opened it.

"Will you let me in now?" he asked.

A thousand voices whispered in Yasamin's head. They all told her not to let him cross the threshold, all but one. Acidic and unrelenting, it whispered the loudest, hissing and spitting about all of the wrongs people had committed against her. Out of hatred for all of them, it told her to let him in.

"Please, come in."

He stepped into the room. Before she shut the door, she glanced out into the corridor.

"No one saw me."

"Are you certain?"

"As certain as the sun will rise in the morning."

"I shouldn't be doing this."

"You are even more beautiful without the lattice between us," Iskander said.

"It's dark. How can you say that?"

"Would it be trite of me to say your beauty is enough to illuminate even the darkest place?"

Yasamin smiled, despite herself. "Perhaps."

"I would still say it."

She could barely see him, but she could feel him in the

darkness. His presence disturbed the very air. He drew closer to her. She didn't retreat. She closed her eyes. When she opened them again, he stood mere inches from her.

"Your necklace," he said.

She glanced down. The silver glinted in the wan moonlight filtering in through the window.

"A gift from my husband." She said the word *husband* a bit harsher than she intended.

"Pomegranate blossoms," Iskander said. He reached up as if he were going to touch the tiny garnets set among the silver leaves, but instead his hand merely hovered over the necklace. "Do you know what pomegranates represent?"

"My aunt always told me they represented fertility and good luck. They're my favorite flower. They remind me of home."

"Did your aunt ever tell you they also represent bloody death?"

Yasamin backed away from him. "That's horrible. Why would you say something like that?"

"It's true."

She fingered the necklace. "I don't believe you."

"Take it off."

"Why?"

"Just do it, please."

She did. He leaned into her and kissed her lips. She didn't try to stop him, nor did she try to stop him when he brought his hand up to caress her cheek and her neck. She heard the music again, but the energy was gone from it. The melody had become a long wail, like the cry of a wolf. She closed her eyes and let it take her over.

THE ROOM WAS STILL DARK when Yasamin awoke. She called out Iskander's name, but received no response. She was alone. Part of her, the part that listened to her aunt, felt the full weight of the shame at what she had done. But the same voice that told her to let Iskander cross the threshold had grown stronger.

For a long time, all that disturbed the silence was her own breathing and the pounding of her heart, until she heard footsteps outside in the corridor. They grew louder until they stopped outside her door. Yasamin held her breath. After a few moments, the footsteps resumed, this time retreating until the silence prevailed again.

Yasamin crept to the door and cautiously opened it. A peculiar object rested at her feet, one that had no business being there. Try as she might, Yasamin could not think up one rational explanation for its appearance. She bent down and picked it up.

A single head of garlic.

THIRTY-FOUR

Berlin, Germany
12 August 1999

Y ASAMIN RAN HER FINGER OVER the dagger's jeweled hilt. "When I met him, he did not tell me how he came to possess the medallion, nor did I understand its significance. I assumed it was a simple trinket, one that held only some sentimental value for him."

Adam did not take his eyes off her fingers as they traced around the jewels encrusting the small knife's hilt. "You never asked him about it?"

"Once. It was a mistake. He replied evasively, telling me it was 'a gift.' I knew he was lying. I persisted, though I shouldn't have."

"Why not?"

"He grew angry. He shouted. He told me it didn't concern me and that I ought to rein in my curiosity before it brought me harm. I knew the way he reacted was wrong, but at the time I was more concerned with making sure I didn't lose his affection. After that I was careful never to mention the medallion again."

"You risked death to be with him. Why was it worth it to you, if you thought his feelings for you were so fragile?"

"Because I loved him, and because he loved me."

"Did he?"

"Say what you will about him, Dr. Mire, but he loved me." Her eyes narrowed, and in the shadows, Adam could have sworn he saw a red glint reflecting off them. "Now believe me when I tell you that you wish to take this conversation in a different direction."

Adam struggled to steady the tremor in his voice. "Okay, getting back to the medallion. You know now it's not a simple trinket, right?"

She nodded. "I do."

"Why do you want it?"

"Do I want it? Now who's making the assumptions, Dr. Mire?"

"I saw your name in the margins of Kovács's ledger. And Mihai warned Ibrahim Zorić about you. In both cases, there must be a reason."

"There is, but I am not looking for the medallion."

"What are you looking for, then?"

"Not *what*, Dr. Mire. *Who*. I'm looking for him. Let Süleyman's Blade and the Chetniks and the rest fight over the medallion. I want him."

"Then I think you've made a slight miscalculation."

She hissed, a sound that froze Adam's blood. "What miscalculation would that be?"

He swallowed. "Süleyman's Blade doesn't want the medallion, either."

"What do they want?"

"Not *what*. *Who*. They want you."

THIRTY-FIVE

Banja Luka, Bosnia and Herzegovina
5 August 1999

SWEAT FROM THE SATURATED BLINDFOLD stung Adam's eyes. His clothes were drenched. The air in the hot room was so stifling he had trouble even breathing, but with his hands and feet tied to a chair, he could do nothing but sit and wait.

To keep himself from going insane, he thought again of his last day with Nadiye.

After watching the sunrise, they walked a little farther along the bank of the Bosporus to a café where they could have coffee and look at the boats drifting by.

"I wish you didn't have to go back to the States in a week," Nadiye said.

"I can probably arrange another trip in a few months," Adam replied. "I'll come up with some excuse."

"Still, a few months is a long time."

"We'll just have to make the most of the time we have, then. What are you doing tonight?"

She shook her head. "I can't. I promised Serhan and a few of his friends I would make them dinner."

Adam frowned at the mention of her brother's name.

"Don't be that way," Nadiye said. "My brother is all talk. He's not a bad person. He's just young and impulsive. He'll come around. You'll see."

Adam smirked. "Yeah, he'll come around when I convert to Islam and suddenly become Turkish."

"I choose who I have a relationship with, not my brother." There was steel in her voice. She placed her hand on top of Adam's. "And if I choose to have a relationship with a smart, handsome American doctoral student, then Serhan will have to accept it."

Adam smiled. "Tell me about this American doctoral student. How smart and handsome is he?"

Nadiye laughed and squeezed his hand, causing Adam's heart to skip a beat. Puffy white clouds floated in the blue sky above, the pink of early morning almost gone. The sunlight glinted off the water, which by then teemed with boats of every shape and size—from cargo ships to water taxis to small caïques. They finished their coffee the same way they always did on mornings like that one, talking about anything and everything, as if they had all the time in the world.

Adam's ears perked up when the door opened. Multiple footsteps told him several people entered the room. Someone stopped directly in front of him, and a pair of rough hands removed the blindfold. When Adam could focus his eyes again, he found himself looking at a familiar face, one he was not surprised to see.

"Hello, Adam," the man said.

"Hello, Serhan," Adam replied, his voice a little more than a rasp.

"How long has it been?"

"Eight years."

"Can you believe it?"

Adam glared at Serhan and the three men who flanked him. "Seems like yesterday."

"Would you like some water?" Serhan asked.

Adam wanted to refuse, to spit in his face, but he didn't have enough saliva left to do it. He nodded and hated himself for it. One of the other men held a bottle of water up to his lips. He drank all of it without taking a breath.

"I'm terribly sorry for the heat," Serhan said. "The air conditioning is unfortunately broken, and as you can probably guess, finding someone who can repair it is difficult given the current state of affairs."

"I know what you're doing, you know."

Serhan smiled. "You do? Please then, enlighten me."

"Psychological Torture 101. Random cruelty followed by random kindness. Create enough cognitive dissonance, and eventually the victim breaks down."

"Really, you think that's what I'm doing? As you well know, Adam, a true follower of Allah does not abide torture. The air conditioning really is broken. Look at Tarik. He's dripping. Do you think he would be this uncomfortable if he could help it? Believe me when I say if we could have put you anywhere else, we would have."

Tarik and the other two men stood stone-faced. Adam couldn't help but notice the guns holstered at their sides.

"And what exactly am I doing here?" Adam asked.

"I simply want to ask you a few questions."

"And then I'm free to go?"

"If you give me the correct answers."

Adam smirked. "Of course. Well, in that case, I have a

dinner date later, and it would be ungentlemanly to keep her waiting. Your questions, please."

Serhan bowed. "As you wish. Where is the medallion?"

"What medallion?"

Tarik slapped him.

"You will excuse Tarik," Serhan said. "He is not as far along on his spiritual journey as I am. And you just lied." He held out a hand. One of the other men gave him Mihai's copy of *Dracula*. "This book you showed to Ibrahim Zorić. It's a road map of some sort written in code. It tells where the medallion is. As I recall, you were always very fond of letting everyone know how smart you are, and I'm quite certain you've figured it out."

"I haven't. Sorry to disappoint."

Tarik slapped him again. The salty, coppery taste of blood filled his mouth, and he could feel it trail down his chin.

"Another lie," Serhan said.

"Why do you want it?"

Serhan tilted his head to the left and pulled down the collar of his shirt to reveal two small, round scars on his neck. "I was more fortunate than my sister, though it depends on how one defines 'fortunate.' I nearly went insane in those first few weeks. I have nightmares every night still. Süleyman's Blade saved me. They gave me a purpose, and I will stop at nothing until the world is rid of its evil."

"You led Nadiye there that night."

"She followed me. I told her not to."

"She was trying to save you."

"I didn't need her to save me. I can take care of myself."

Adam snorted. "Clearly."

Serhan slapped him.

Adam coughed and spit out a bit of blood-tinged

phlegm. "I thought a true follower of Allah didn't condone torture."

"I was justified," Serhan replied. "I'm tired of this. I have the book. I don't need you."

"You don't need me? You said yourself the book is written in code. If you don't know what you're looking for, it's just a collection of random notes scrawled in the margins. To make sense of it, you'd have to know how to read Romanian, Medieval Latin, and Old Serbian."

Serhan smiled weakly. "You're not the only professor."

"What if I told you finding the medallion isn't the only use for the book? What if you could use it to find who killed Nadiye and get your revenge?"

"You're lying again."

Adam leaned forward as far as he could. "And if I'm not? You're not the only one who loved Nadiye, as much as you wish it weren't so."

Serhan wrinkled his nose in disgust as he wrapped the blindfold around Adam's head again, pulling it painfully tight before tying the knot. "We'll talk again soon, Professor."

"Where is Kostya?" Adam asked. "What have you done with him?"

Serhan let out a dry chuckle. "The Russian? Rest assured he is being well cared for. But if I were you, I wouldn't be worried about him."

Footsteps retreated from the room, and the door slammed shut. Adam didn't know how much time passed after that. At some point the exhaustion overtook him. He dozed fitfully, moving in and out of consciousness until his half dreams blended with reality. At one point, he thought he heard Nadiye calling to him, but her voice strange—harsh, guttural, like it was the night she died.

Then a hand slapped his face.

The blindfold vanished, and Adam opened his eyes to see Kostya staring back at him. A purple bruise encircled his right eye.

"Kostya? How did you get here?"

Kostya smirked. "It's my job to keep you from getting killed, remember? I'm your lucky charm, like a four-leaf clover or a silver bullet." He unsheathed a knife hanging from his belt and cut the ropes binding Adam's arms and legs to the chair. "Can you walk? We need to move quickly."

Adam rubbed his wrists where the rope had made his skin raw. "I think so."

He stood and tried to take a step but his knees promptly gave out, and he would have collapsed to the floor had Kostya not caught him. After a few moments spent leaning on the Russian priest, he took another tentative step and found himself a little more surefooted. Kostya raised a questioning eyebrow.

Adam nodded. "I'm good. Let's go."

Kostya lifted a bag by the door and handed it to Adam. "I brought your satchel."

"Thanks." Adam shouldered it. "How did you get it?"

Kostya beckoned Adam to follow him. Just outside the door, a man lay on the floor. The unnatural angle of his neck told Adam all he needed to know about the man's status as living or dead.

"If the Blades have one weakness, it's that they're predictable," Kostya said, stepping over the body. "It's a top-down organization, and what the lower levels have in devotion, they tend to lack in brains. Obvious strategies. Obvious counterattacks. Obvious hiding places. Your bag was in the only coat closet with a posted guard."

They continued down a stark industrial corridor with concrete floors and cinder-block walls broken only at intervals by grey metal doors.

"Serhan is not obvious," Adam said, glancing over his shoulder at the dead guard. "Serhan is dangerous."

Kostya turned and pointed to his black eye. "I am well aware how dangerous Serhan is. He is also not here. I watched him leave before I came to retrieve you."

"Where were you? How did you get out?"

"I was in a room much like the one we just left. As for how I escaped, that's a trade secret, mostly involving the knife hidden in the sole of my shoe."

They came to a place where the hallway branched in two directions. To the right, it continued past another set of identical doors. To the left, a set of stairs led upward.

"Which way?" Adam asked.

Kostya pointed to the stairs. "Up. At the top there should be a door leading outside."

"Should be?"

"I didn't see it, but I heard people entering and leaving, and I saw the sunlight coming in from outside."

Adam wrinkled his nose. He didn't like the idea of basing their salvation on a guess, even an educated one. "What is this place?" he asked.

"An old warehouse, I think," Kostya said. "Abandoned now, overtaken by vermin."

The sound of a door opening caused them both to turn their heads. A man—Mediterranean complexion, average height, and slightly portly—stepped into the corridor from one of the rooms to the right. Kostya's eyes narrowed. Adam saw the glint of metal as Kostya drew his knife. The portly man grappled with the firearm at his side, but wasn't able to draw it before Kostya slammed him against the wall.

The Blade died without making a sound. Kostya let him slide down the wall, then cleaned his knife on the man's pant leg and dragged the body back into the room he had come from.

Adam stared at Kostya when he reemerged.

"What?" Kostya asked.

"Anya didn't—"

"Anya didn't have to." Kostya looked over his shoulder at the door. "I say a prayer for every one of them. Come, let's get out of this place."

They turned, only to find their way blocked by another Blade, one who had been with Serhan when he paid his visit to Adam. He already had his gun drawn. Kostya pushed Adam to the floor and threw himself against the wall. Adam's ears rang as gunshots reverberated off the concrete. Kostya hurled his knife at the Blade, and it sank into the man's thigh. With an anguished cry, he dropped his gun and fell to his knees.

Kostya pulled Adam up from the floor. "Now we really have to move."

They climbed the stairs, Adam first and Kostya a few steps behind. Two flights up, Adam could see a door. Kostya had guessed right. Behind them, men shouted and footsteps echoed. By the time Adam and Kostya reached the second flight, the Blades had almost caught up. Adam glanced backward to see Tarik on the landing below, gun drawn. A single shot echoed through the stairwell. Adam ducked and kept running, but he didn't hear Kostya behind him. He paused for just a second and turned to see Kostya standing, grasping the railing.

A bright red bloom spread across the front of his shirt.

"Run, you lucky bastard," Kostya whispered before falling backward down the stairs.

Adam took the remaining steps two at a time and leapt at the door, throwing his entire weight against it. The door flew open, flooding the stairwell with dazzling sunlight. Adam tumbled through the doorway with his satchel and onto the dusty ground. He scrambled to his feet and continued to run. Even when he could no longer hear the footfalls behind him, he kept running until he couldn't anymore. When he stopped, he collapsed to the street curb and buried his face in his hands, gasping for air and sobbing. It took him a few minutes to pull himself together. Wiping the hot tears from his eyes, he glanced up and down the street. Not far on the opposite side was a tavern.

When Adam entered, the few patrons regarded him with narrowed eyes and furrowed brows—not surprising, given what he must have looked like. He staggered toward the bar.

"I was just mugged," he announced in Serbian, loud enough for everyone to hear. "They took all my money and papers. Please. I just need to use your telephone to call my uncle Vanya."

The barkeep raised an eyebrow. "You don't look like a person who has an Uncle Vanya."

Adam sat down at a stool. "I didn't know I had one until just recently. My mother's brother. A little bit of a black sheep. Please, your telephone. I'm begging."

The barkeep glared and slammed the old rotary phone on the bar in front of Adam. Next to the phone, he placed a full glass of water. "For your trouble," he said.

Adam threw his head back and gulped down the drink, realizing as the liquid stung his throat that it wasn't water. He didn't care. He set the empty glass down, picked up the phone, and dialed the number Anya made him memorize. The phone rang three times before an answering machine picked up and a robotic voice told him to leave a message.

Adam recited the lines Anya had taught him, "Uncle Vanya, it's your favorite nephew Alyoshka. I've run into a little trouble …"

After he delivered his message, Adam waited. An hour passed, maybe more. The sun began to set, but eventually, a black Citroën pulled up to the curb. Adam gathered up his things, and with a nod to the barkeep, left. Once he was outside, the Citroën's window rolled down to reveal Anya.

"Get in," she said.

Without replying Adam opened the door and climbed into the passenger seat.

Anya's gaze moved from his bloodied face to his dirty, sweat-stained clothes. "You look wretched. What happened? Where's Kostya?"

Adam didn't answer.

"Adam, where is Kostya?"

Adam sighed. "Anya, I'm sorry."

Adam told her the entire story, from the visit to Ibrahim Zorić to being chased through the streets of Banja Luka. Anya remained silent for several minutes. All Adam could hear was the low hum of the Citroën's engine.

"Bastards," she said finally. "They'll pay one day. But right now we obviously can't stay in this city. Any suggestions on where to go?"

Adam stared straight ahead. "Dubrovnik."

"You've been doing some reading, then?"

"I figured I would make use of my time."

"What's in Dubrovnik?"

"I don't know."

The Land Beyond the Forest, one of the books he had bought from Ibrahim Zorić, contained the clues pointing to Dubrovnik, but he had just lied. He knew exactly what they would find there. He wished he didn't. He rummaged through his satchel until he found the biography of Michael the Brave. As Banja Luka vanished behind them in the falling darkness, he began to read.

THIRTY-SIX

From The Life and Death of Michael the Brave
by Ioan Nicolescu

Near Şelimbăr, Transylvania
16 October 1599 Old Style

D ESPITE THE SEASON, WINTER'S BITE swirled in
the air around Michael the Brave and his men.
His breath came out in thick, white puffs, as did
the breath of his horse. The ancient road upon which they
traveled followed the River Olt northward to the mountains. At the narrowest part of the pass, rocky walls closed
in on either side, and mountain pines crowded the way,
their branches undulating in the wind, needles creating
ever-shifting patterns in shades of green.

The rustling of the trees in the wind sounded like the
ghostly whispers of the armies that used the very same
pass to traverse those mountains over the centuries. Romans, Goths, Huns, Slavs, Byzantines, Turks—they all left
their footprints there. From the road, Michael glimpsed

the abandoned and crumbling structure that gave the pass its name—the Pass of the Red Tower. It served as a reminder that the specters of the past could never be completely exorcised, only appeased. An act of appeasement had brought him there.

After the pass opened up again, the road turned away from the river spilling down the mountain. Close to forty thousand men followed Michael, stretched out in a line along the narrow roadway. In addition to the soldiers, the families of many of the nobles had joined the march, fearful of being attacked by Tatar raiders if they stayed behind. It was not the prince's first choice to bring them along, but others convinced him it would be a compassionate gesture, after reminding him that even with all he'd accomplished, his hold on power was too fragile to defy the *boyari* completely.

Several yards ahead, a dark figure on a dappled horse emerged from the forest and stepped into the path. Michael's hand went up in a silent signal for the line to stop. His other hand went to the sword at his side. The wind died down, and the rustling of the trees ceased. The figure in the path remained motionless.

Michael's horse quietly neighed, his breath rising up in small clouds. The stranger's horse snorted as if in reply. The prince could tell he wore armor only by the glint of his metal gauntlets and greaves. A drab brown cloak shrouded the rest of him, including his face. Silhouetted against the steel-grey sky, he looked like a shade from the underworld.

But after a brief moment, the stranger nodded, and Michael relaxed his grip on his sword. He signaled for the line to begin moving again. When they met, Alexandru's horse fell into step alongside his.

"It's good to see you again, Alexandru," Michael said.

"It is good to see you, Your Grace," Alexandru replied.

"Did you deliver the message?" Michael asked.

"I did, Your Grace."

"And how was it received?"

"Very well. The Szeklers are no friends of Cardinal Báthory. When the time arrives, they will throw their lot in with you."

Michael nodded. "I'm glad to hear it. What of the rest of your travels through the Cardinal's lands? Uneventful, I hope."

"Uneventful," Alexandru said, "but unsettling."

"How do you mean?"

"They say Sigismund Báthory is unstable," Alexandru replied, "but Sigismund at least had the good sense to recognize the Turks for the menace they are, Your Grace. Andrei obviously lacks such judgment. Already, Turkish merchants are returning to the marketplaces of the cities. It will only be a matter of time before those whom Sigismund drove away return in full force."

"And what of Sigismund's abdication? Does anyone know the reason behind it?"

Sigismund's sudden abdication in favor of his cousin Andrei Cardinal Báthory had provided Michael with the perfect opportunity to renounce his oath of fealty to Transylvania's Hungarian prince.

Alexandru shook his head. "Unfortunately, no, Your Grace. There are only rumors. Some say he intends to pursue his estranged wife. Others say he means to live out his life as a hermit in a monastery somewhere in Silesia."

Michael chuckled. "For the sake of his wife, I hope he's chosen the latter."

For a time, they rode in silence while up in the sky, a

lone eagle swooped and circled over the moving line of men. Its cry threatened to shatter the cold, brittle air.

"In two days, it's going to rain," Alexandru said suddenly. "We should make every effort to reach Sibiu tomorrow."

Alexandru's cloak kept his face in shadow and his expression hidden. He wore a medallion as the clasp, a dragon with its tail wrapped around its head and a cross on the back. The cross was partially obliterated. Michael had asked once about the medallion. Alexandru said only that he had inherited it from his father.

"Reaching Sibiu in a day will be nearly impossible. It would be difficult even if we didn't have the women and the children to consider."

"Yet it must be done," Alexandru replied. "The women and the children chose to come. They should be subjected to the same rigors as the rest of your soldiers."

"A heavy rain would be disastrous," Michael said.

"That it would."

"And you do have an uncanny ability to predict the weather."

"As you say, Your Grace."

Michael nodded. "Very well then. We shall be in Sibiu by sunset tomorrow."

Soon they crested the final ridge before the road turned and began its long winding descent. The valley beyond opened up before them, an explosion of red, orange, and yellow foliage.

In the Latin language, the word *Transylvania* means "The Land Beyond the Forest." Yet even today, the primeval wood full of ancient oaks and beech trees speaks of a place where the forest is a present, sentient force.

As the line of men moved forward, the road turned

back on itself again. Negotiating the uneven topography of that wild country proved to be slow work. Michael worried reaching Sibiu in a day would indeed be impossible. He was growing fatigued, and he knew those who followed were as well. Only Alexandru appeared unfazed by the long journey. When they stopped to make camp for the night as the light began to fail, he displayed the same amount of vigor as he had earlier in the day.

WOLVES PROWLED AT THE EDGE of the camp, darting from shadow to shadow, their eyes reflecting red in the light of the fires. The fires kept them at bay, but they made for a fitful night's sleep. More than once, their curt barks and yelps and their petrifying howls set a child crying.

Michael stood outside his tent, gazing into the blackness beyond the reach of the fires. A dream had awakened him again, full of violence and death like the others, but this time there was something different. Amidst the blood and the gore, someone quietly recited the liturgy. Only it was not the litany for the dead, as he might have expected, but the rite spoken to repel the Devil. As he played the dream over in his mind, a shadow of something stirred in the darkness—another wolf he thought—but then he felt a presence beside him and turned to find Alexandru standing by his shoulder.

"The wolves certainly are restless tonight," the *boyar* said.

"How very strange it is," Michael replied. "The wolves seem to prowl about as if they have a purpose."

Alexandru laughed, a low rumble, almost a growl. "Your Grace, they're just animals responding to instinct.

You should be sleeping. Tomorrow will require all of your strength."

Michael shook his head. "I can't sleep."

"Something troubles you?"

"Dreams, Alexandru. Dreams trouble me."

"I'm sorry to hear it."

"I don't suppose they ever trouble you."

"I don't sleep," Alexandru admitted, "at least not for more than a few hours at a time. My dreams never have the opportunity to become troublesome."

"Then you are fortunate."

"I wouldn't consider myself so, Your Grace."

The prince recounted the conversation in another letter to his cousin Livia shortly before his death. "In the dim light of the fires, I could barely see the outline of Alexandru's aquiline nose and abundant mustache," the prince wrote. "I have never asked Alexandru about his disappearances. Alexandru has never volunteered an explanation. He always returns a few days later as if nothing has happened. As long as Alexandru's tactical genius lasts, I am willing to tolerate his eccentricities, but if I admit the truth, it is fear that keeps me from asking. I am afraid of learning too much about Alexandru's private demons, lest they become public."

THIRTY-SEVEN

From The Life and Death of Michael the Brave
by Ioan Nicolescu

Near Șelimbăr, Transylvania
17 October 1599 Old Style

A T DAWN THE NEXT DAY, they appeared. Several thousand of them strode into the camp to join the prince's cause. Michael greeted them with the appropriate amount of esteem.

Though the Szeklers speak a language almost identical to that of their Hungarian neighbors, they claim to be the descendants of Attila the Hun. By their reckoning, they were in Transylvania centuries before the Hungarians themselves, and they resented the interference of an upstart like Andrei Cardinal Báthory in their affairs.

Unfortunately, they also brought with them unwelcome news—that the army of Cardinal Báthory had gathered near the town of Șelimbăr, less than a day's march away. Michael and his men were cut off from Sibiu. He would meet Andrei Báthory on the battlefield before the sun set. Michael sent soldiers racing from tent to tent, raising the call to battle. What had been a quiet camp clamored with the sounds of preparation.

In the midst of the chaos, a lone *boyar* approached the prince.

"We will not join this battle," he said quietly.

Michael stopped and turned, his eyes wide with incredulity. "What did you say?"

"We will not join this battle," the *boyar* repeated. "You would have us leave our wives and our children here unprotected. We cannot do that."

Michael moved closer until his face was only an inch from the *boyar*'s. The nobleman's breaths came long and measured. "Have you forgotten who I am?"

"No, Your Grace."

"Then you will follow me into battle today," the prince said. "You chose to bring women and children here, knowing full well the dangers involved. Don't tell me you came all this way never intending to fight."

"We will not join *this* battle," the *boyar* repeated again. "The mayor of Sibiu promised us shelter in his city. Sibiu has fortifications, and our wives and our children would be safe there. I don't see any fortifications here."

The color rose in Michael's face. "How dare you turn your back on what is your duty! I saved you from the Turks. You are bound to me as your prince. Does that mean nothing to you?"

"Your Grace," a voice said behind Michael. He turned to see Alexandru. The drab brown cloak had been replaced by a bright gold one, but it still hid his face. "We're wasting time with this argument. Let the cowards stay here. It won't matter. The day will belong to you."

The nobleman pointed at Alexandru. "Why do you listen to this dog, Your Grace? He's been your bloody spy here for weeks and he didn't know about this? He culled not one scrap of information about a massive army gathering against us, something every shepherd in this valley probably knows? I'd say that's mighty suspicious. Almost as if we were being led into a trap."

With remarkable speed, Alexandru knocked the *boyar* to the ground and pinned him there, pressing his gloved forearm down on the other man's windpipe.

"Do not *ever* question my loyalty to the throne of Wallachia," Alexandru spat as the man underneath him struggled to breathe. "The next time you do, you'll find the sharp edge of my knife across your throat instead of simply my arm."

He released the *boyar*, leaving him on the ground to gasp and choke, and without another word, he strode into his own tent. Silence reigned over those who had witnessed what happened. Michael glared at each of the assembled *boyari* in turn.

"All of you who choose to follow me," he cried, "prepare to leave now!"

MICHAEL'S ARMY CAME UPON THE town of Şelimbăr a little after noontime. The town sat huddled against a tributary of the River Olt in the middle of a broad valley. It consisted then of a few dozen squat grey stone buildings with red-tiled roofs, the only structure of note being the church with its red-roofed steeple reaching heavenward. The persistent grey skies cast an unhealthy pallor over everything. The prince and Alexandru sat upon their mounts at the crest of a ridge. Behind them, twenty-five thousand soldiers arrayed themselves into formations. In the valley below, the Hungarian army of Andrei Cardinal Báthory faced them. Transylvania's black falcon standard flew in the wind.

"By my estimate, Your Grace, the Cardinal commands about thirty thousand men," Alexandru said.

"I fail to understand why you thought that knowledge would somehow comfort me," Michael replied.

Alexandru didn't respond. Subtly, almost imperceptibly, he motioned toward the left side of the Hungarian's lines. "Do you see how that small hillock creates a gap in the ranks of the infantry there on the left?"

Michael strained to see what Alexandru saw. It required some effort, but he finally spotted the small irregularity in the Hungarian lines. "I do."

"The weak point is there. If you concentrate on that point, you can isolate the cavalry on the left flank, removing it from the battle. With the Szeklers aiding us, the Cardinal's numbers won't matter."

"It's done then," Michael said. "Marshal the men accordingly."

"As you wish, Your Grace." Alexandru pulled on the reins of his horse so that he could go convey the prince's orders to the other *boyari* and the rest of the men.

"Alexandru, wait," Michael said.

"Yes, Your Grace?"

"Promise me something."

"Anything," Alexandru replied.

"Promise me you didn't know Andrei's forces were planning on cutting us off from Sibiu."

Michael had no way to gauge Alexandru's reaction through the closed visor of his helmet.

"Your Grace, I would never betray you," he said.

"That's not what I asked."

"I promise you that Andrei Báthory has managed to surprise even me."

Michael said nothing further. It was as close to a reassurance as he would get from Alexandru.

"I would request one thing, Your Grace," Alexandru added after a moment.

"What's that?"

"That I be allowed to lead the cavalry charge."

Michael hadn't expected such a request. He shook his head. "Out of the question. You know I need you to remain with the rear guard. If, in the course of the fighting, things start to go badly for us—"

"My failure led to this battle. Allow me to make it right."

"Redemption isn't necessary, Alexandru."

Alexandru gazed out toward the opposing army. "I'm not speaking of redemption, Your Grace."

His voice held a steely edge Michael never heard before.

"I've told you what you need to do to defeat the Cardinal," Alexandru continued. "Do it, and you'll be the victor today. Just allow me this one indulgence."

Michael sighed. "Very well, but do not abuse my trust, and if you are foolish enough to get yourself killed, there will be repercussions."

"Understood," Alexandru replied.

Alexandru left to relay the orders to the other generals. The men lined up rank and file according to Alexandru's plan, and once Michael received the ready signal from each of his generals, including Alexandru, he drew his saber and raised it in the air. Across the expanse, his rival, Andrei Cardinal Báthory, did the same. Michael imagined a twisted smile on the face of the Transylvanian prince. His saber sang as it slashed through the air, and it began. The army's vanguard rushed past and charged toward the enemy lines, cavalry on the left and the right, infantry in the middle with the pikemen in front to protect the musketeers.

Michael remained with the rear guard. He watched as Alexandru stormed down the hill toward the Hungarian army. With his gold-colored cloak flying behind him, he looked like Wallachia's own gold eagle standard brought to life. The horses of the men who followed him shook the ground as they barreled toward the weak point in the Hungarian lines Alexandru had identified.

The cannons, ones the Wallachians took from the Turks and brought over the mountains, thundered in turn. The savage rhythm grew more and more frantic until it became the foundation of a violent and deadly dance. Pops of musket fire joined in counterpoint as the armies collided on the battlefield.

With a flash and a puff of smoke, man after man fell. With the slice of a blade or the jab of a pike, rider after rider fell. Back and forth, life for life, the two armies fought for what Michael thought might be an interminable length, were it not for Alexandru.

He and the other riders thrust deep into the enemy ranks while avoiding the sharp end of any pikeman's weapon. The Hussars—the puffed-up Hungarian riders who made up Andrei's cavalry—pushed back, but they could not break through the cordon the Wallachian riders established. Alexandru's bright gold cloak allowed Michael to spot him without much effort in the midst of the battle. He was unstoppable. Every time Alexandru's saber met an enemy soldier, it found a gap in the armor, and with every felled enemy, Alexandru's frenzy grew. It was exquisite.

The Hungarian lines, unable to receive any relief from the Hussars, strained under the cannon and musket fire. Michael expected them to waver and break at any moment, proving Alexandru's tactical genius once again. He caught sight of the golden-clad *boyar* in the thick of the battle, his saber slick with blood held triumphantly aloft.

But then his heart leapt into his throat when he saw the Hungarian musketeer raise his weapon. An orange spark and a puff of white smoke erupted from the bell-shaped muzzle. Alexandru lurched forward as the shot struck his back. Armor provides ample protection from musket fire at a distance, but at close range, Michael knew the shot would rip straight through. Alexandru fell from his mount, and his gold cloak disappeared into the muddy, bloody brown of the battlefield.

When the other riders saw Alexandru fall, they fell into confusion, and the tide turned at once. The Hussars stormed into the fray, and the Wallachian lines began to break.

Michael took in several deep breaths of the cold, damp air before doing the only thing he could. He raised his saber high above his head and with it slashed the air. With a roar, the rear guard stormed down the hill with the prince in the lead.

While the pikemen and musketeers took up positions among their fallen comrades, Michael and the other riders rushed to engage the Hussars. The cavalries clashed together, the resulting cacophony like the explosion from a match hitting a flash pan. A shot from Michael's pistol dispatched one Hussar, a swipe of his saber another. Michael maneuvered around men and horses alike as he strove to reach the spot where he had seen Alexandru fall.

The prince didn't hear the cannonball until it ploughed into the ground next to him, spraying him and his mount with dirt and rocks. His horse reared up and threw him to the ground. His last thought before his world went black was that his dream had become reality.

"I SLOWLY OPENED MY EYES," Michael recalled later in one of his letters. "At first I could see nothing but hazy white light. I shut my eyes again as I struggled to clear my head. I could hear sounds—men talking—but I could not tell where the voices came from or make out any words. When I opened my eyes once more, a dark shadow obscured the light in the center of my vision, but as I concentrated, the world gradually came into focus. The dark shadow resolved itself into Alexandru, standing against the pale grey sky. He reached out his hand to me. 'It's finished, Your Grace,' he said. 'Transylvania is yours.'"

THIRTY-EIGHT

From The Life and Death of Michael the Brave
by Ioan Nicolescu

Alba Iulia, Transylvania
1 November 1599 Old Style

THE SUN SHINING THROUGH THE narrow windows failed to reach the cathedral's darkest corners, but the shadows did not keep one very dim side chapel from drawing Michael's attention as he entered. The chapel's ornate, flamboyant style gave it away as a later addition when compared with the sturdier, more austere architecture of the rest of the church. The chapel housed the tomb of one of Hungary's greatest heroes, Jan Hunyadi, whose military genius had pushed the borders of the Kingdom of Hungary to their greatest extent.

The friezes on the sides of his sarcophagus depicted his victories over the Turks at the Battle of Smendria and the Battle of the Iron Gates, in which he drove the forces of the Sultan out of Europe north of the Danube. His Hungary was gone forever, though, split into three parts, a third ruled by the German emperor, and another third by the Turks. Only Transylvania managed to retain some of its independence, and three weeks after defeating Andrei Cardinal Báthory's army, Prince Michael the Brave came to Alba Iulia to claim it as his own.

At the Battle of Şelimbăr, the charge of the rear guard made all the difference. Cardinal Báthory inexplicably refused to send in his own rear guard, and the Hungarian lines could not hold up against the full force of the Wallachian assault. As for Alexandru, what looked like a fatal shot from a musket was only a glancing blow. Alexandru was knocked from his steed and stunned, but otherwise survived unscathed. Cardinal Báthory fled after the battle. He was found dead a week later in the woods outside Sibiu. It appeared a wild animal had ripped out his throat.

The Roman Catholic Bishop Napragy greeted Michael in front of those assembled in the sanctuary. He knelt before the clergyman and kissed his hand. After he rose, Bishop Napragy presented him with the keys to Alba Iulia's citadel.

The prince then turned to face those assembled. Everyone—his own *boyari*, the Hungarian nobles who now owed him fealty, the Saxon burghers, General Basta—they all awaited his proclamation, but it did not come.

"I felt something wet and warm hit my forehead," Michael wrote to Livia. "I reached up and touched my face, and when I pulled my hand back, red blood coated my fingers. I looked up to see Bishop Napragy suspended over my head on a sharp wooden pole, the end of which protruded from his chest. A trickle of blood ran from his mouth, contorted in a silent scream. Another drop of blood fell and hit my face. A peal of laughter echoed through the church, a low rumble, almost like a growl. And then the light shifted. Bishop Napragy was alive, standing next to me, waiting for me to speak."

Michael compelled his voice to work. "In the name of His Imperial and Royal Majesty Rudolf II, King of the Romans and Emperor of the German Nation, I Michael, Lord of Muntenia and Oltenia and Prince of Wallachia, claim authority over the lands of Transylvania."

Those assembled cheered, but the prince felt only cold dread in the pit of his stomach.

THE REVOLTS BEGAN ALMOST IMMEDIATELY. Mere hours after his installation as Prince of Transylvania, Michael received word a Hungarian noble had lost his head to the peasants who worked his estate near Sighişoara. Both Alexandru and Father Dumitru Leandros, the prince's personal priest, were with him in what once had been Cardinal Báthory's chambers.

"General Basta's men can take care of it," Michael said. "Those responsible should be captured alive, if possible, so they can be publicly executed."

Father Dumitru protested. "But Your Grace, the people have suffered so much at the hands of the Hungarians. You speak the same language they do. You pray in the same way. Surely you can understand that they might expect their lot to improve with you as their prince, and you can understand that there may be those who will be impatient for change. Perhaps you should show mercy."

"To show mercy is to show weakness," said Alexandru.

"To show mercy is God's commandment," Father Dumitru admonished.

Michael had expected Father Dumitru to disagree

with his decision. "I'm sorry, Father. Alexandru is right. Things are not settled yet. Unfortunately, my place as prince is secure only because of the presence of Basta's army. I cannot afford to show the peasants mercy at the expense of the Hungarians right now."

"Your Grace—"

"There will be time enough for mercy later, Father." Michael turned toward Alexandru. "Now. I need to speak with the father about a matter in private."

"As you wish," Alexandru replied, and with a curt bow to both His Grace and to Father Dumitru, he left.

"You see," Michael said once Alexandru was gone, "I don't confide in Alexandru about everything."

"What is on your mind, Your Grace?"

"Today in the church, I had a vision. The dreams are bad enough, but to be unable to trust my own eyes when I'm awake—it is unsettling."

"What did you see?"

Michael told him. The priest remained silent, gazing at the shadows thrown onto the wall by the dim lamp.

"Father, I need your guidance," Michael said. "I think I am being warned away from some terrible future. Please tell me, what must I do to avoid more of these visions?"

Father Dumitru shook his head. "Your Grace, I cannot offer you a straightforward answer to that question. I can only advise you to continue to seek God's will, and I can give you absolution for your sins, if you have a penitent heart."

The prince clenched his fists. His anger at Father Dumitru's platitudes surprised even him. "That is all you can offer me?"

"That is everything."

"Useless nonsense," the prince hissed.

"Your Grace—"

"Go away, Father. I want to be alone."

"But—"

"Now."

Father Dumitru turned to leave, but paused near the door. "I will tell you this, Your Grace. If you put your crown in heaven at risk for the sake of your crown on earth, then you are in danger of losing both."

THIRTY-NINE

Berlin, Germany
12 August 1999

"ARROGANCE," YASAMIN SAID. "IT IS probably the most destructive form of the sin of pride. I have seen the ruination arrogance can render on a person, a family, a nation. It was no different for Michael the Brave."

Adam let out a rueful chuckle. "Except for one thing. I find it odd that out of the hundreds of books I've read, the thousands of documents, the countless hours I've spent in research, I have never come across the name Alexandru before. Why is that?"

"A mistake, perhaps?"

"Not a mistake I would ever make."

"Arrogance, Dr. Mire. Remember?"

Adam ignored the remark. "Either this Alexandru never existed except in the head of Ioan Nicolescu, or he's been purged from the historical record. Normally I would go for the former, but now ... *He* was Alexandru, wasn't he?"

"And if he was? Michael the Brave still made his own choices. They undid him, just as Serhan's choices will undo Süleyman's Blade."

"I wouldn't underestimate Serhan," said Adam.

"I have nothing to fear."

"He knows your weaknesses, and how to exploit them."

"And I just told you his. He is only a man, and he will make the same mistakes men always do. He will assume God is with him. It will make him careless. In fact, it already has. You're here, warning me about them, a loose end I would have wrapped up tightly."

Adam shifted where he stood, uncomfortable with her implications.

"All of you," she continued, "Süleyman's Blade, Chetniks, Michael the Brave, you hide behind your righteousness. You create your petty kingdoms—and for what? In the end they all fall. You'll never learn your lesson."

"What lesson?"

"That your sins are what define you."

"My faith tells me otherwise." Adam knew as soon as the words left his lips he had made a mistake.

She laughed. "Your faith? Weak evidence, Dr. Mire. Let's look at history, something you of all people should understand. How many major historical events can you directly attribute to pride? What about lust? Greed? Wrath? Envy?" She fixed him with her gaze. "Now, can you think of any sprung from humility, chastity, charity, temperance, or kindness?"

"Gandhi," Adam whispered. "Oskar Schindler. Nelson Mandela."

Yasamin raised an eyebrow. "What Gandhi did wouldn't have been necessary were it not for the British

Raj. The same holds true for Schindler and the Holocaust, as well as for Mandela and Apartheid. The evil came first. It still defined them, if only by contrast."

Adam stood silent.

Her mouth curled up in a triumphant grin. "Now look at your own life. How many of the turns your life has taken have occurred because you made the *right* choice first?"

Adam felt his face flush. She had reached into his heart and plucked out his darkest fear, and now she forced him to stare at the black, twisted mass. "The fact that my sins may have put me on my present path is something that haunts me."

FORTY

—⚋⚋—

Near Dubrovnik, Croatia
6 August 1999

ONLY THE LOW HUM OF the Citroën's engine broke the silence. Neither Adam nor Anya had said much of anything since leaving Banja Luka. The biography of Michael the Brave lay closed in Adam's lap. He rested his head against the window, watching in the rearview mirror as the sky behind them lightened from deep indigo to cobalt blue.

"Are you willing to answer a question for me?" Adam asked.

Anya gave him a sidelong glance. "Are you willing to live with the answer?"

Adam smiled, despite the black mood that hung over the car. "Fair enough."

"What do you want to know?"

"How did you stumble upon this line of work? You know being a secret agent for the Russian Orthodox Church? I can't imagine they post job openings in the want ads."

"I didn't 'stumble upon' it. I became involved because of my father."

"So it's a family business then?"

Anya shook her head. "Not exactly. My father disappeared when I was a child under circumstances that were ... unusual to say the least. My search for answers led me to where I am now."

"Did you ever find him?"

"No."

"I'm sorry to hear that."

She scowled. "Why?"

"Because I know what it's like to lose a parent. It's hard, never knowing what happened, never being able to fill that void."

Her fingernails dug into the steering wheel. "That's something I will never understand about Americans."

Adam frowned. "What do you mean?"

"The need for a happy ending, a resolution. 'Closure' I think is the term you use? Life is what it is. Sometimes there are no answers."

Adam brushed his hand over the leather cover of the book in his lap. "So why look? Why are we on this chase now, if you don't expect to find any answers? What's the point?"

"The point, Dr. Mire, is in the trying, the doing, the effort. Maybe we'll fail. Maybe we'll all end up like Kostya, but if we don't put forth the effort, then we're just as complicit in the evil as those who commit it."

Adam smirked. "How very Russian of you."

"Something my father taught me," Anya said.

"How old were you when he disappeared?" Adam asked.

"It was the day after my eleventh birthday."

"And these unusual circumstances, they were …?"

"Unusual, Dr. Mire."

Adam took the hint. "Another question I've been meaning to ask you. Back at the safe house in Banja Luka, when I was—"

"Going through my bags?"

"I was going to be more diplomatic, but yes, when I was going through your bags, I found counterfeit visas and passport with my picture."

"What of them?"

"How long had you been following me?"

"Since you started making inquiries about Dracula's medallion."

"So several months then. Any chance you'd tell me how you found out I was asking around about the medallion?"

"No."

"Didn't think so. But theoretically, if you found out, then so could Serhan."

"Anything is possible, Dr. Mire."

Adam gazed out at the twilight world speeding by. "I never imagined I'd be this far in over my head."

"What did you imagine? Did you expect anything other than blood and violence and death to accompany your search for the medallion? This is no game. Kostya is dead."

"I know. I'm sorry. Were you … close?"

Anya pursed her lips. "We were colleagues. That doesn't mean I didn't care for him."

"We should make sure he didn't die in vain then."

"Everyone dies in vain, Dr. Mire."

FORTY-ONE

Banja Luka, Bosnia and Herzegovina
7 August 1999

IBRAHIM ZORIĆ HEARD A NOISE. He struggled out of bed and pulled on his old robe, then clambered through the house in the darkness. In the front room, he turned on a lamp to find a man wearing black gloves crouched over the dragon mosaic on the floor. The table and the rug had been shoved aside.

When he saw Zorić, the gloved man stood and smiled. It was not a warm smile. "Hello, Mr. Zorić."

"What are you doing here?" Zorić asked.

"You called me, remember? I'm here to settle up with you."

A flutter of hope filled Zorić's chest. "You've come with my payment?"

The man shook his head. "Not exactly."

Zorić pushed down a wave of panic. "But I did what I was supposed to do. I contacted you as soon as I could. I want my payment. I need that money so I can leave here."

"But you didn't contact only me, did you? You called in your friends. That was never part of the plan. First, they tried to take Mire in Budapest, and now the incident here. Do you have any idea the harm you've caused?"

"Harm? Süleyman's Blade does the work of God."

The man's eyes narrowed. "Not everyone shares your opinion."

Zorić pulled himself as upright as he could and thrust his chin out. "It is not an opinion. It is the truth."

"Even so, it is not what we bargained. I'm sorry. I cannot pay you."

Zorić deflated. He tried to seize the man by the arm. "But you have to. You can't leave me here."

The man grabbed Zorić and twisted him around, then drew a knife and held it to Zorić's neck. Zorić had no chance to break free of his grip. "I never said anything about leaving you here."

"You're a madman," Zorić croaked.

"I'm no less sane than anyone else."

"You are taking joy in this."

"I am doing no such thing. Death is a necessary part of life. I am merely facilitating it."

"But what will my death serve?"

"Merely one less person who knows the truth," the man said as he drew the knife across Zorić's throat.

FORTY-TWO

—ᴡ—

Dubrovnik, Croatia
7 August 1999

I N THE SMALL HOURS OF the morning, Adam sat in a
chair by the hotel room window. Outside, the lights of
Dubrovnik's Old Town shimmered, illuminating the
red tile roofs of the buildings and the narrow streets gently
sloping down to the indigo-blue shore of the Adriatic Sea.
The Italians still called the city Ragusa. At one time it
rivaled Venice in its wealth and splendor, but like Venice
its fortunes had ebbed and flowed over the centuries. The
city suffered heavy damage when the Yugoslav army
shelled it during the early part of the civil war. The physi-
cal scars had since been covered over, but Adam knew the
emotional ones might never go away.

Adam felt a presence beside him and glanced over to
see Anya seated in the chair next to him. The two of them
had signed into the hotel as Annika and Adam Meyer, a
married German couple. The desk clerk hadn't even asked
to see their passports, though Anya had the counterfeit

documents at the ready. She wore only a nightshirt. A hair clip, a gold rose, held her loose ponytail in place. Adam had bought the trinket for her earlier in the day, partly to keep up their ruse, but mostly because he thought she'd like it.

She motioned to the book resting in his lap. "Must be riveting reading."

"I can't sleep," Adam said, "so I though I might as well make productive use of the time." He held up the book. "Mihai's copy of *Dracula*. Looking through it I found more than just his scribbled notes. He inserted pictures of a woman, some he drew himself. Others are copies of portraits showing her in period dress."

"Which period?" Anya asked.

"Several. There are even some newspaper clippings with photographs. A few look like they're from the fifties or sixties while others seem more recent. It's the same woman, the same olive skin, dark hair, and dark eyes."

"You think she's Yasamin?"

"It makes sense."

Anya smiled a sad, wistful smile. "You don't have to do this anymore. You can go back home and forget about all of this. We can arrange for you to return to the States. It was perhaps unfair to involve you in any of this. You aren't prepared for what is coming."

"What's coming?"

"More death."

Adam studied her form illuminated in the weak light. "Death and I have a long relationship. Besides, I don't really have anything to go back to. I'm not even sure I have a job anymore. I was supposed to return from my sabbatical in June, and yet here I am in August."

"Why didn't you go back?"

"This book. Mihai's gift to me. He was a friend. I owe it to his memory to find out what happened to him."

"But you have family, friends. You must miss them."

Adam shook his head. "My parents died in a car accident when I was very young. My grandmother raised me."

"Is she …?"

"Gone."

"Were you close?" Anya asked.

"Not at all. She was hyper-religious. To her, the only book that wasn't evil was the Bible. Truth be told, my childhood was a living hell. It didn't help being in Bayou Redneck, Louisiana, either. Most people there consider camouflage a color. Try being the quiet, bookish, skinny kid in a place like that."

Anya reached over and placed her hand on top of his. Her skin was as soft and smooth as fine silk. "I'm sorry. I know a little about less-than-ideal childhoods. Obviously, you were clever enough to find an escape."

Adam laughed. "Funny thing, being smart isn't what got me out of there."

Anya cocked her head to one side. "No?"

"In high school I started to practice boxing just to survive," Adam explained. "I bloodied a nose or two and after that the bullies left me alone for a little while. Turns out I was pretty good. After about the fourth time I got called to the principal's office, he started paying for me to take real lessons. He told me he used to box, too, and was impressed by my 'irrational tenacity.' He even brought down a coach from the University of North Carolina to meet me. To this day, I don't know where the money came from, but I had all four years of college paid for. All I had to do was compete. And I've used what I know to get out of a few scrapes since then."

"Have you ever gone back to your home?"

"The day I left, my grandmother told me God would punish me for abandoning her. When she died two years ago, I went to her funeral, but no one knew me. I left without even talking to anyone."

"Even if you have no family, you must have friends? Loves?"

"There was … someone, but not anymore. She decided she'd had enough and ended the relationship about three months ago."

"Why?"

He shrugged. "Because I'm not there."

"You still aren't," Anya said.

"I know."

"Will you be prepared for tomorrow?"

"I think so," Adam replied.

"I can still come with you, if you'd like."

"No. I think it might scare him away. I'm afraid I'm going to have enough trouble getting any information out of him as it is."

"I won't be very far away."

Adam smiled. "I appreciate that."

Anya stood. "You should really come to bed."

He picked up the book again. "In a little while."

She took the book from his hands and closed it gently. Then she leaned over and kissed him on the mouth. Her lips tasted sweet, like honey and ripe raspberries. He wanted more, but she pulled back, drawing him up out of his chair, toward the bed.

She smiled and removed the clip from her flame-red hair. It cascaded down around her shoulders. Then she slipped off her nightshirt. Her flawless ivory skin shone in the moonlight. Adam's gaze followed the curves of her body and the tantalizing shadows they created, from her teardrop-shaped breasts down toward her hips.

Adam wrestled out of his shirt and struggled to unbuckle his belt, but Anya's nimble hands stilled his fumbling fingers. His belt cracked like a whip when she took it off, and her touch threatened to drive him mad as she helped him slide off his pants. Once they were both unencumbered, she pulled him in for another kiss. Together they toppled onto the bed.

Adam felt clumsy as he lay pressed against her, but the more they explored one another's bodies—with their hands, their lips, their tongues—the less he thought of himself. Images he couldn't explain filled his mind—misty woods at twilight, ancient moonlit ruins, bluffs high above stormy grey seas. Anya was in each of these places—*was* these places somehow. They beckoned to Adam, and he heeded their call.

Their motions took on the rhythm of ocean waves until finally the pleasure crested and broke over him, sending his mind rolling and tumbling, unable to surface. When his senses returned, he found himself staring at the ceiling of the hotel room, panting for air. He whispered her name. Anya laid a hand on his chest. He drifted off to sleep with her curled next to him, dreaming of the places he had seen. When he woke up the next morning with sunlight streaming into the room, he was alone.

FORTY-THREE

Berlin, Germany
12 August 1999

Y ASAMIN SNEERED. "WHEN WILL YOU understand you will never rise above your own self? You are a professor at one of the most prestigious universities in the world, an amazing accomplishment at your age. But what do you really have to show for your life? You spend all your time alone, amid stacks of books and old papers."

"I'm proud of what I've accomplished," Adam said through clenched teeth.

"Indeed. But are you really any different than you were growing up alone, with only books to keep you company? When you think about it, you've really done nothing at all. Why else would a night's dalliance take on so much significance for you?"

"You don't know what you're talking about."

"Did you think everything would be perfect if you proved yourself to everyone who tormented you? Do they even care? Have you managed to exorcize your personal demons, Dr. Mire? Or are you still the hurt little boy who doesn't understand why no one likes him?"

"You don't have any right—" Adam took a step out of the sunlight without even realizing. He caught himself, though, before he ventured any farther into the room and retreated into the relative safety of the small illuminated rectangle on the floor.

"Impressive," she said, an amused look on her face. "Someone weaker would have allowed emotions to overcome rational thought ... regardless of the obvious consequences."

Adam struggled to keep his voice even. "Clever trick. Is that what he did, trick you?"

"He always told me the truth."

"Except for his real name, of course. He lied to you about that. Interesting choice of an alias, by the way."

"How so?"

"*Alexandru* and *Iskander* are both derived from the Greek name *Alexandros*. It means 'defender of mankind.' Ironic, isn't it?"

She shook her head. "It's not ironic at all, Dr. Mire."

FORTY-FOUR

—∿—

Buda, Ottoman Hungary
7 Dhu al-Qi'dah 1008
(10 May 1600 Old Style)

THE GIRL WAITED FOR YASAMIN in the middle of the *haremlık* garden, underneath the leafy branches of the oak tree. On more than a few occasions over the previous week, Yasamin had spied her lurking in the corridors near her room or staring at her through lattice-covered windows. Every time their eyes met, the girl looked away. A meeting was inevitable, Yasamin supposed.

She reminded herself not to turn her back.

When Yasamin was a few paces away, the girl turned and smiled. She had long, dark hair but pale blue eyes and light, cream-colored skin that almost sparkled in the shafts of sunlight piercing the oak tree's broad canopy.

"*Hanım effendi*," the girl said, bowing, "after all these years, it is nice to see you again."

Yasamin smiled politely and bowed in return, though she didn't recognize the girl at all. "And you as well."

The girl's face fell. "You don't remember me, do you? Yasamin, it's Sanem, from Banja Luka. We used to play together."

Hazy memories stirred in Yasamin's mind. A girl with a broad smile and blue eyes so light they were almost grey. Laughing. Running. Stealing pastries from the kitchen and eating them in the cool shade of a tree. Happy memories.

Yasamin's smile broadened into a genuine grin. Impulsively she reached out and grasped the girl's hand. "Sanem. Of course. I'm so sorry. Please forgive me. It was such a long time ago. Very much has changed since then."

Sanem nodded. "Indeed it has."

"But how do you find yourself here?"

Sanem's smile faded. "My aunt passed away a few months ago. I have no more ties in Banja Luka. My aunt was not the best matchmaker, and her efforts to find me a husband failed. She arranged for me to come here. She thought perhaps Hadice would have better success."

Yasamin let out a chuckle. "Hadice does have a particular talent in that area. It does my heart good to see you again, Sanem."

"Mine as well. You left Banja Luka so suddenly, without even saying good-bye. No one would tell me what happened. I didn't find out until much later."

Yasamin shifted her gaze toward the ground. "No one told me at first, either. They only said something horrible had happened and that I had to go. I didn't want to."

Sanem squeezed her hand. "My aunt spoke very highly of your parents, always. She was very close to your mother. She said they did not deserve to die the way they did."

Yasamin raised an eyebrow. "I can't imagine anyone deserving to die in a fire."

Sanem frowned. "A fire? That is not what my aunt

said."

"What did your aunt say?"

"She said they were murdered."

Yasamin let Sanem's hand drop.

YASAMIN CLASPED ISKANDER'S OFFERED HAND, and their fingers intertwined. Even in the dim, flickering light of the candle, the contrast between the dark olive of her skin and the pale tone of his was apparent.

"I have a theory," she whispered.

He laughed. "You sound so serious. What theory do you have, my dearest?"

She pulled away. "No. I'm not going to tell you if you're going to make fun."

He reached for her and brought her close again. "I'm not making fun. I promise."

She made no serious attempt to fight his embrace. "You think I care only about my clothes and my needlework and how I should plait my hair. You think I don't know or care about the wider world."

"I would never make such a mistake. Please tell me your theory."

"Only if you swear you won't laugh anymore."

"I swear it."

"You are not Ottoman."

The corners of his mouth twitched, but he remained true to his word. "Well then, what am I?"

She shook her head. "I don't know, but I think you come from some part of Europe the Sultan's armies have subdued, and I think you were taken when you were nine or ten in the *devşirme*."

Every Christian household in the Abode of Peace was

required to give one son to the Sultan's service in the *devşirme* or boy tribute. The boys were taken to Istanbul, where they converted to Islam and received new names. For the rest of their lives, they remained proud slaves of the Sultan.

"I think your name was perhaps Miloš or Stefan," she continued, "though you don't look quite like the blond-haired, blue-eyed soldiers I sometimes spied walking down the street in front of my uncle's house."

"What you say is close to the truth."

"Only close?"

He kissed her wrist before lowering her onto the pillows. "What my name was doesn't matter. Now it is Iskander, and the path my life has taken has led me here, to you."

For months, he had come to her during the night, and they had made love like this. She never saw him enter or leave. She simply turned around to find him there, and later he vanished from the room as if made of smoke. Though how he arrived or departed mattered very little to her.

His hot breath danced over her skin as his lips traced their way down her neck, over her small, round breasts, and across her taut stomach. She ran her fingertips over the compact muscles of his arms and his back. Pleasure rippled through her as their bodies moved together, finding the perfect rhythm.

In her head, she heard the song of the *kemençe* player from her Henna Night, and the same images flashed across her mind's eye—the tall trees in the dark forest, the cold mountain streams, and the high passes. The melody rose and fell while the strange yet familiar images flooded her mind, and Iskander's body, slick with sweat, pressed against her. Faster and faster the music went, louder and louder until she lost herself.

Iskander released her from the grasp of life itself. All the pain, longing, base toil and petty competition involved in living ceased to matter when she looked into his gleaming green eyes.

Afterward though, even as she lay amidst the pile of pillows with Iskander's powerful arms curled around her, the troubles of life began to creep back in. Iskander kissed her on the neck. She smiled weakly.

"Something is the matter," he said. "Are you still upset with me?"

"No, of course not."

"Then what is it?"

"Nothing."

"It must be something or it wouldn't worry you so."

"How do you know I'm worried?"

"I know you."

Yasamin sighed. "There is a girl. Her name is Sanem. She said something to me today. I haven't been able to rid it from my mind."

"What did she say?"

Yasamin told Iskander about her conversation with Sanem under the oak tree.

"Do you believe her?" he asked when she finished.

Yasamin thought back to her vision of the dark crimson pool of blood on the white marble. "No."

"Then you shouldn't be bothered. This Sanem is a petulant brat. She should know better than to be so careless with her words."

She nuzzled his chest. "I'm certain you're right, of course."

Iskander whispered, "There is no need for you to ever

worry. Remember who you are."

She smiled. "Who am I?"

"Your name is Yasamin, and the path your life has taken has led you here, to me."

FORTY-FIVE

Berlin, Germany
12 August 1999

I T'S NOT IRONIC AT ALL, *Dr. Mire.*
Like a black spider crawling its way on eight spin-
dly legs through his brain, the grim sense that he had
made a fatal error played at the edge of Adam's thoughts.
He rushed through everything he had said so far and every
response she had made, looking for his misstep. As he did,
his fear and frustration threatened to bubble over. "What
you're saying doesn't make sense. Dracula is an enemy of
mankind, not a defender."

"If that is what you think, then you have seriously
misunderstood his motivations," Yasamin replied.

"Did you ever understand them?"

"Not always."

"Do you know why he left you?"

"It was not his choice."

"But I suppose the result was the same regardless. You
were alone. You can't tell me you were never resentful for

what he did."

She raised her eyebrows. "Resentful? As intelligent as you are, you really don't understand very much, do you, Dr. Mire?"

"Why don't you enlighten me?"

"I've been trying to. Yet you stand there, still, insisting I tell you something you most assuredly don't want to know. *I* left *him*. He and I parted ways because of *my* mistake and *my* desire to right my wrong. Nothing more, nothing less. It does not diminish the bond between us."

"But the others you found to fill the lonely nights, did they diminish the bond between you?"

She glared. "You mock."

He held up his hands. "It is a legitimate question."

"One you really have no business asking." She paused. Adam held his breath and watched for the shadows to shift, but then she smiled. "Fortunately for you, I do not take offense easily. Over the years, I have, from time to time, sought out other companionship, but it has always been of a transitory nature."

"These others, where are they now?" Adam asked.

"Most are dead. Others are … not. I don't know where they are."

"So you've simply abandoned them."

"There are no obligations among us."

Adam thought of the letter Mihai had slipped in between the pages of the book he sent to Ibrahim Zorić, the one that had led Adam and Anya to Dubrovnik. He held up a chiding finger. "But there are consequences, even for you."

FORTY-SIX

A letter from Dom Marin Pavlović to his sister

Lastovo, Republic of Ragusa
18 June 1738

IN THE YEAR 1738, THE *Archbishop of Ragusa summoned residents of the island of Lastovo to his court to testify about accusations of grave desecration and corpse mutilation. Over the course of several months, hundreds of pages of testimony were transcribed regarding a deadly epidemic of gastric fever the island's residents blamed on vampires. Digging up the bodies was necessary, they argued, to destroy the demonic creatures. The ecclesiastical court disagreed, finding seventeen people guilty and sentencing them to do penance. It was the last recorded outbreak of vampirism in Ragusa. It was not the last unexplained death.*

BEFORE I END THIS ALREADY overly long letter to you, my dear Irenka, I must recount to you an odd conversation I had recently with His Excellency Sebastijan Basiljević upon his unexpected visit to our island. If you have received my other letters, then you know about the recent … unpleasantness we have endured here. I though the matter closed until I heard word His Excellency had arrived and wished to see me.

I soon found myself walking with the nobleman along the stony path above the village. The wind whipped around us. Far below the sea was the color of dull steel. Ahead lay our destination, a small stone church set against the grey sky. I am certain you remember the Church of St. Erasmus. Of course no one calls it that anymore. It is simply the Church on the Hill.

"Your Excellency, these are simple people," I said as we walked. "You should have mercy on them."

His Excellency glared. I am convinced it is the only expression he knows. "We are not talking about a mere harmless superstition, Father, not that any superstition is completely harmless. These men desecrated graves, mutilated and dismembered bodies looking for vampires. Some of your fellow clergymen even aided them. It must stop."

"I assure you I have made every effort," I protested, "but the beliefs on this island, they run deep. Every time there is a plague or illness, vampires are blamed. The stories are legion—bloated, ruddy corpses that bleed fresh blood when stabbed, cadavers that remain undecomposed for months or years, even bodies leaping out of coffins, felled only by silver bullets."

"Abominable," muttered His Excellency.

I held up my hands. "Any time a grave is opened, the men charged with the task say a prayer for the deceased and ask for forgiveness."

"It does not excuse what they have done."

"No, it does not, Your Excellency."

"And it will not happen again. I will see to it myself," His Excellency said as we reached the top of the hill and paused at the gate to the churchyard. "Our Republic's foundation must remain in God. Otherwise all is lost."

His words rang hollow. I know what kind of man Sebastijan Basiljević is. Stories of the intrigues he orchestrated to secure his position as president of the Small Council have reached even this tiny island. He came for some other reason, something that would no doubt further his own ambitions.

"Tell me about the Sicilian," he said.

I frowned, perplexed. "But your Excellency, I gave testimony—"

He held up a hand. "I know what you said in your testimony, but I also know you left out a few details for the sake of propriety. I want the entire truth."

I sighed. "He came to the island several months ago on a fishing boat from Brindisi. One night he fell from the deck of the boat while undoubtedly intoxicated and drowned. There is a strong belief here that the devil claims the souls of those who drown, so when gastric fever began striking down people in the village, everyone naturally thought of him."

"No one thought of fetching a doctor?"

I shook my head. "There are no doctors here, and outsiders are generally not trusted. After a day the story took on a life of its own, as these stories often do. Some began to say they saw the Sicilian entering the houses of people who later fell ill and died. Sometimes they said he was accompanied by a woman."

"A woman?"

"A beautiful woman with long black hair and olive skin, like a Turk."

"Does anyone have any idea who she might be?"

"No one knows, a demon some say." At that I crossed myself.

"What do you believe?" His Excellency asked.

"Flights of fantasy, of course. Although the night they chose to dig the Italian out of his grave almost made me believe otherwise."

"What do you mean?"

"A storm blew in unexpectedly, gusts of wind and torrents of rain. I was told they were coming here, to the churchyard where the Sicilian is buried. I ran all the way from the village, but by the time I caught up with them I was too late. I found the four of them had already dug the coffin out of the ground. They were preparing to drive an iron spike through it to pin the corpse inside. The lightning flashed, and in that moment, I was convinced I saw a fifth figure standing next to the grave. In the next instant, it was gone. Then, as the men drove the spike into the coffin, I thought I heard a voice coming from inside. The others heard it, too. It sounded like a woman's name—Jasmina."

"Is that all?"

"That is everything."

"Where is the grave?"

I pointed across the churchyard. His Excellency started toward the patch of freshly turned earth and modest stone marker. I followed after.

"Thank you, Dom Pavlović," he said as he stood over the grave, "but I won't be needing your services anymore. You may leave."

I raised an eyebrow. "You do not want me to accompany you back to the village?"

"I can find my own way. Thank you," he replied.

I turned to leave, but looked back over my shoulder to see His Excellency kneel next to the grave and pick up a handful of dirt ...

FORTY-SEVEN

Dubrovnik, Croatia
7 August 1999

A LIGHT BREEZE CARRIED THE salty scent of the sea. Though the warm sun shone down from a cloudless, blue sky, Adam pulled his jacket around him as a chill worked its way up his back. The house looked abandoned. While all the other buildings on the street had been repaired, a hole still gaped in its red roof, and jagged broken glass adorned most of the darkened second-floor windows.

Adam knocked on the door again and waited. He was turning his back to leave as the door opened a crack.

"Dr. Mire?" a voice called.

Adam turned around. "Yes? Josip Basiljević?"

A man's face appeared in the opening. He was perhaps in his fifties, gaunt, with pale blue eyes and wisps of grey-blond hair. "I'm sorry to have kept you waiting. Please, come in."

The door opened a little wider. Adam stepped inside

and into a different world. As soon as Basiljević shut the door, the languid, sun-drenched city on the sparkling blue sea disappeared, replaced by damp, dim rooms and the smell of mold and rotting wallpaper. Basiljević led Adam down a corridor so dark Adam worried he might stumble, though the older man didn't seem to have any trouble.

At the end, he pushed open a door leading into a large formal parlor, or at least the room had served that purpose at one point. A few chairs and a sofa were arranged around a low table in the center of the room in an apparent attempt to impose some normalcy. Other pieces of furniture were either scattered about or stacked in the corners. Basiljević invited Adam to take a seat.

"So, I hear we have a mutual friend," he said as he sat in the chair opposite.

Adam nodded. "Mihai Iliescu. Did you know him well?"

A calculated risk. Apart from the story of Dom Pavlović, Mihai had inserted only two other items related to the city of Dubrovnik in *The Land Beyond the Forest*. One was a drawing of a coat of arms, a pattern of red and white stripes. Adam had confirmed it belonged to the Basiljević family, one of Dubrovnik's oldest patrician houses, that morning at the city's Assumption Cathedral. The other item was a newspaper clipping from 1976 relating the brutal murder of a prostitute found with her throat torn open.

Basiljević drew his thin lips up in an apologetic smile. "No, I'm afraid I didn't know him very well. He came to Dubrovnik several times a few years ago. We met because he said he was researching vampire panics throughout history for a book he was writing. He wanted to talk about the trial of the vampire hunters on the island of Lastovo in the 1700s. My great-great-great-great-great-great-grandfather was one of the prosecutors. I still have many of his papers. Since then Mr. Iliescu and I have corresponded by letter from time to time. I was very shocked to hear of his passing."

Out of the corner of his eye, Adam thought he saw a flicker, something darting over his head. He looked up.

"Bats," Basiljević said calmly. "Since the shells opened a hole in the roof, they have made their home in the upper levels of the house. Occasionally, one gets lost and finds its way down here."

"Pardon me if I'm overstepping, but why haven't you repaired the house?" Adam asked. "The shelling was over eight years ago."

He shrugged. "My family is very old, dating back to the time of the Republic, but that does not mean we are wealthy anymore. There is no money to repair the house. It is just as well though. I am the only one who lives here at the moment, and I don't need half the rooms."

"But this is an historic building. There is help—"

Basiljević fixed him with a glare. "My family does not ask for help."

"Fair enough," Adam said. "When did you last speak to Mihai?"

"When he came to visit a few months ago. He arrived unannounced, wanting to meet with me."

"What did he want to talk about?"

The corner of his mouth twitched. "Nothing important."

"Surely it must have been something for him to make the trip."

"I don't think it is appropriate for me to say."

"Why not?"

"I do not wish to speak ill of the dead."

"I don't understand. Why would you be speaking ill of him if you told me what he came here to talk about?"

"I … I cannot say. That is all."

"Mr. Basiljević, I have come here because I believe something happened to Mihai, and I am trying to uncover what that was. I understand your hesitance, but please listen to me when I say I would not ask if it weren't vitally important."

Basiljević studied Adam with his pale blue eyes, then sighed. "You are familiar with the story of the Lastovo vampire panic, yes?"

"I am," Adam replied.

"Some say the Sicilian 'vampire' called out the name of a woman as they drove an iron spike through his coffin. Mr. Iliescu said he had discovered the identity of this woman, this Jasmina."

Again Adam saw a flutter overhead. "Did he tell you?"

Basiljević shrugged. "I did not ask. Besides, what he said next made no sense at all. Jasmina, he told me, was still alive, at least in one sense of the word."

Adam feigned surprise. "But she would be almost three hundred years old. That would be impossible unless—"

"Unless she were a real vampire," Basiljević said. "Now you see why I did not want to tell you anything. Mr. Iliescu seemed nervous, excited, at times almost manic. I was afraid something had happened to cause his mental health to suffer."

"How did he come across this information?"

Basiljević shook his head. "He would not say. He asked me if he could go through the papers I have again, to see if anyone might have mentioned a female visitor to Lastovo. Of course, there have been countless others who have pored through them, looking for the same. I told him so. I did not see what he could find that all the others have missed."

"How did he react?"

"He was disappointed, but gracious. He thanked me for my time, apologized, and left. He even sent me several books from his library, as a token of his gratitude for my help. The note that accompanied them said they were ones he though I might enjoy. Frankly the jumble of titles had me questioning his mental state again. I put them aside. My eyes are too weak to read very much anymore."

At the word *books*, Adam's ears perked up. "The books. Do you still have them?"

"Of course. One does not simply dispose of books, no matter what they are."

"May I see them?"

"I suppose, though I don't understand—"

"Please, Mr. Basiljević. I know none of this may make any sense to you. Honestly I'm shocked and a little disturbed that it makes sense to me, but it does. Trust me."

Basiljević exhaled sharply through his nose. With exaggerated gestures, he pushed himself up from the couch and left the room. Sitting alone in the dimness, Adam couldn't help but glance up at the ceiling. The room reached so high, the shadows concealed the corners. He imagined all sorts of things in those shadows, none of them bats. If he stared long enough, he thought he could see the shadows swirling. His hand closed around the rosary in his pocket. The activity overhead subsided.

After a few minutes, Basiljević came back holding a stack of books. He set them on the coffee table in front of Adam, who scanned the gold leaf on the leather spines until he came across a title that interested him: *Bulfinch's*

Mythology. His copy of *Dracula* came out of his satchel again. Adam flipped through it until he found another underlined section describing how the ship Dracula used to travel to England ran aground near the Yorkshire town of Whitby during a storm. The ships name was *Demeter*, after the Greek goddess of agriculture:

There was of course a considerable concussion as the vessel drove up on the sand heap. Every spar, rope, and stay was strained, and some of the 'top-hammer' came crashing down. But, strangest of all, the very instant the shore was touched, an immense dog sprang up on deck from below, as if shot up by the concussion, and running forward, jumped from the bow on the sand.

Adam picked up *Bulfinch's Mythology* and opened it to the story of Demeter and her daughter Persephone. Immediately a photograph fell out onto the table. In it a man and a woman walked arm in arm down a busy city street. Both had black hair and dark olive skin—possibly Turkish or Persian. Adam had never seen the man before, but the woman staring out of the photograph made the hair on the back of his neck stand on end.

"Yasamin," he whispered.

Basiljević frowned. "Don't tell me you believe such things as well."

"I understand how you could doubt Mihai's grip on reality, Mr. Basiljević, but I'm afraid he was perfectly sane. I know who this woman is."

Before Basiljević could respond, the vampire landed with a thud on the table between them. Adam tumbled backwards over his chair. As quickly as he could, he scrambled to his feet. A man, or rather something that had once been a man, leered at him with pupilless eyes. His chalk-white skin hung loose on his thin frame. His clothes were no more than rags. Adam's attention, however, remained focused on the fangs protruding from his mouth and the claw-like nails at the ends of his fingers.

"Where is she?" he rasped, as if unused to using his voice.

Behind the vampire, Basiljević sat, his face expressionless and detached. For the first time, Adam noticed the two small reddish marks on his neck.

"Where is she?" the vampire repeated.

"I ... I don't know," Adam stammered.

"You lie. You said you had seen her."

"Pictures and drawings of her made over a period of more than a hundred years. That's all. I want to find her as well."

The thing that was once a man stepped off the table. Adam knew the vampire could reduce the chair separating them to splinters in a matter of seconds. "Why?"

"Because someone will kill me if I don't."

An awful gurgling escaped the vampire's throat. Horrified, Adam realized he was laughing. "I don't think you have to worry about that anymore."

He stepped closer.

"Wait," Adam said. "I'll tell you what I know, if you tell me what you know."

"Bargaining for your life. Quaint."

"Do you want to find her or not, Sicilian?" Adam asked.

The vampire scowled. "You have a brain between your ears. Congratulations. Unfortunately, it will gain you nothing."

Adam glanced at Josip Basiljević. "The Basiljević family, they've protected you all these centuries."

"Correct again."

"Why?"

"They had no other choice."

"She did, though. And she left you. What did you do to drive her away?"

He glared. "You obviously know nothing about us, or you would never ask such a question."

"Did she ever tell you about Dracula's medallion?"

"Why do you use his name?" the vampire growled.

"Do you know why she's looking for it now?"

"She would never do such a thing. Why would she want to meddle in his affairs again?"

"You're jealous. You're much more human than you want to admit."

The vampire sneered. "Your mistake. The truth is that she came here fleeing from him. He drove her away because of that blasted medallion. She was the one who lost it to begin with."

"Lost it? How?" Adam asked.

The vampire lunged. Adam drew a gun he had concealed in his jacket. The vampire paused, his clawed hands easily within reach of Adam's jugular vein.

"Idiot," the creature spat. "Do you honestly think a gun will harm me?"

Adam pulled the gun's trigger, and a stream of water shot from the end of the muzzle. It hit the vampire, and his skin sizzled and smoked. Shrieking, he backed away.

"No!" Basiljević screamed.

The vampire fell over the table and continued to flail. The skin burned away from his face, exposing the bloodless musculature underneath. Adam stood over the writhing creature.

"Amazingly realistic, the water guns they sell here," he said. "You can't find anything like this in the States."

"What did you do?" Basiljević asked.

"Holy water," Adam replied, holding the gun up. "Father Milković of the Assumption Cathedral sends his regards."

Basiljević threw himself at Adam, rage and hatred burning in his eyes, and tackled Adam to the floor. Adam struggled to throw him off, but Basiljević was tenacious and maneuvered his hands to Adam's neck. The man's iron grip closed around Adam's windpipe.

"You've ruined everything," Basiljević said through clenched teeth as his fingers closed tighter.

As the edges of Adam's vision began to darken, he raised the water gun and pulled the trigger. The brief stream of water hit Basiljević in the face. The older man reared back, and Adam bucked to throw him off before rolling away and jumping to his feet. Basiljević clambered upright as well, prepared to charge again, but Adam drew a second gun from his jacket.

"I'd stay back," Adam whispered, his vocal cords still burning from the assault. "This one doesn't shoot water."

Basiljević obeyed, standing stone-still, an odd smile on his face. Adam didn't have to wait to find out why. Behind him the vampire rose.

"Okay, Anya, where the hell are you?" Adam muttered under his breath.

The vampire hissed through his deformed mouth. Adam dropped both guns and grabbed a poker from where it hung next to the fireplace. The vampire charged, and Adam swung, but the creature's hand closed around the poker. He wrenched it from Adam's grip and sent it flying across the room where it lodged in the wall.

Adam pulled the rosary from his pocket and held it out in front of him. "*Crux sacra sit mihi lux. Non draco sit mihi dux.*"

The vampire recoiled, giving Adam enough time to retrieve the third weapon from his jacket, a sharpened wooden stake. Enraged at the sight, the vampire growled and swiped a clawed hand at him, but Adam remained out of reach. Out of the corner of his eye, Adam saw Basiljević inching toward the poker embedded in the wall.

Again, he wished Anya were there to even the odds.

"*Vade retro satana. Numquam suade mihi vana.*"

But since she wasn't, he'd just have to even them himself.

"*Sunt mala quae libas. Ipse venena bibas.*"

Rosary held high, Adam launched himself forward with all the force he could muster. The vampire's claws grazed him, tearing his shirt and leaving four red jagged lines across his chest, but he managed to sink the stake in the creature's side. It slipped between the vampire's ribs, into what Adam prayed were the remnants of the thing's heart.

The vampire shrieked and staggered backward, then collapsed to the floor again. His body shuddered before becoming still for good. Like flash paper it burst into flames, leaving a pile of smoldering ashes only seconds later.

Basiljević let out an anguished wail. He fell to his knees, his body convulsing as he sobbed. Adam picked up the copy of *Bulfinch's Mythology* and left him crying over the vampire's ashes.

Outside, threatening grey storm clouds filled the sky, a drastic change from earlier, but not unusual for Dubrovnik in August. The downpour started when he was halfway back to the hotel. He sprinted the rest of the way, thinking what a story he would have to tell Anya. Drenched by the time he arrived, he climbed the stairs to their room, only to find the door ajar. Inside everything was in shambles. Anya wasn't there. On the bed lay a scrawled note:

May Allah protect you and what is with you and deliver you to your destination. —Serhan

FORTY-EIGHT

—⊸〰⊷—

Dubrovnik, Croatia
7 August 1999

JOSIP BASILJEVIĆ SAT IN HIS parlor, sipping tea. He barely looked up when the man entered, only long enough to register the shock of white in the man's black hair and the smirk on his face.

"I have no money to give to the poor," he said, "and I am in no mood for a social visit at present. Please, whoever you are, show yourself out."

"But I have not come here for either reason," the man replied, "and you know me, Josip."

Josip gazed up at him, studying his face for the first time. In the man's cold eyes, he did recognize something, having seen the same calculating, predatory gaze many times in his life. But Josip dismissed the idea that this man was a vampire. No, he lived and breathed. He had no excuse for his actions.

"I'm sorry," Josip said. "You are mistaken. I have never seen you before."

"Ah, but you have, Josip Basiljević. We met eight years ago."

"Before all this trouble started," Josip said absently.

"As you say, before there were holes in your roof, before you lived in the darkness amidst shattered glass, alone with *that thing*." He pointed to the pile of ash.

Josip straightened up and thrust out his chin. "Vittorio was not a thing. He was our charge, our burden. He elevated the Basiljević family to a place of honor. How many of the other old patrician families of Ragusa can say they have any honors left? None. And now it is all gone, because of that vile American."

The man shook his head. "Not because of him, because of you."

"How can you say that?"

"Think, Josip. Think about how we met."

"I ... I don't remember."

The man grunted and rolled his eyes. "Then let me help you. I came here to warn you, to tell you that you needed to leave before the Yugoslav army surrounded the city and began shelling. But you wouldn't leave. You were too proud."

"I couldn't. I couldn't leave him."

"There was nothing keeping either of you here. I offered you both a safe place."

"At a price."

The man smiled. "So you do remember."

"It's coming back to me now." He sneered. "You wanted to use me and Vittorio. You wanted to turn him into a weapon, your personal assassin."

"He was your family's personal assassin for how long?"

"He was more than that."

The man dismissively waved a gloved hand. "If you say

so. If you had let him come with me, he would have had his fill of human blood. No need to scrounge, settling for the occasional tourist or prostitute, worried all the time about arousing the suspicions of the police."

"He would have been your slave. No, I have lived in the darkness among the ruins of my family home for the last eight years, but I do not regret the decision to stay."

"As you wish."

Josip took another sip of his tea. "You have come to kill me, haven't you?"

The man nodded.

With deliberate movements, Josip placed his teacup on its saucer, then set the saucer down on the table. He stood to face the man. "Then by all means, just do it."

FORTY-NINE

A letter from Dr. Johann Flückinger to his brother

Medveđa, Austrian Serbia
27 January 1732

IN THE EARLY 1700S, A *vampire scare raged across parts of the Austrian Empire. In village after village, whenever death or disease struck, bodies were exhumed and examined for telltale signs of vampirism. If any were found, the bodies were burned or beheaded. Several cases became famous when they were documented by government officials. One of the most notorious, the case of Arnold Pavle, caused a sensation when the report of the doctor who investigated the claims was published in the Viennese newspapers. Finally, Empress Maria Theresa sent her personal physician to investigate the claims. After he concluded vampires did not exist, she issued a decree banning the exhumation of bodies, but of course, her decree did not stop the vampire hunters—or the vampires.*

I HAVE DONE EVERYTHING HERE I can possibly do. All the reports have been filed, and I am set to return to Belgrade tomorrow, but I fear I won't be able to tear myself away. I know I must sound insane, to be so taken with a place such as this. It cannot even be called a proper village, merely a collection of ramshackle buildings surrounded by farmland and populated by illiterate, superstitious peasants. I have seen horrible things here that will haunt me forever, but there is beauty here, too.

Take care of my lovely Louisa. Tell her I'm sorry for staying away so long. I know she grows impatient with me. Our engagement is now going on two years, and in her last letter to me, she was quite forthright, imploring me to set a date for the wedding, but I cannot bring myself to do so. Perhaps there is a reason.

Yesterday I called on a woman named Alisa Pavle. She is a widow. I made the call as part of my official duties, but really, I simply wanted to speak to her. When she opened the door and saw me, a steely defiance entered her pale blue eyes, bloodshot and swollen from crying. I found her gaze both captivating and a little terrifying. Despite the cold, she did not invite me any farther than her porch, however, and our subsequent conversation did not progress as I had envisioned.

"What business do you have here, Dr. Flückinger?" she asked.

"I need to speak with you," I replied.

"About what?"

"Your husband—"

"Arnold was not an evil person," she said. "Do you understand that? He did nothing wrong. He had nothing to do with what happened five years ago, and he certainly had nothing to do with the most recent deaths."

"Seventeen people are dead," I said. "I have seen the bodies myself. They were complete and undecomposed, plump even, with a red and vital color to the skin. Their chests were filled with fresh blood. They had even grown new fingernails and hair. I cannot think of a scientific explanation for any of it."

"Isn't that your job, Dr. Flückinger, to use your knowledge to find an explanation? Can you not come up with something to say to your superiors that does not make my poor husband into a monster?"

"It's too late. The report is already written."

"Then change it."

"It was dispatched to Belgrade yesterday."

She slapped me. "Then go. Why did you even come here? Was it so you could throw your 'conclusion' that my husband murdered his friends and family in my face?"

I touched my stinging cheek. "I came to apologize, madam. I tried, for your sake, to draw another conclusion. I failed."

She crossed her arms. "Well, now that you've made your apology, you can go back to your nice, safe office."

I hesitated. She had endured enough pain. The last thing I wanted to do was cause her more. Yet I simply couldn't leave things the way they were. "Madam, my report contains my observations and the testimony of your neighbors, but you refused to give an account. I'm asking you now to tell me what happened five years ago. There will not be an official record."

"If I tell you will you go away?"

The chill in her voice crushed me. I wish she hadn't reacted so.

"I promise," I said.

She set her jaw and lowered her eyes. "Arnold was part

245

of the militia that patrolled the border. He had just come back from serving for several months. He said that while he was gone, not a day passed that he didn't think about me and his life here on the farm. It was wonderful to have him back. Those first few days were some of the happiest of my life. Then everything changed."

"How so?"

"Arnold started to withdraw. Before he left, he was the warmest, most generous man I'd ever met, but he became cool and distant, and not only toward me. Our neighbors, our families, they began making comments to me about the way Arnold was acting."

"Did you try to talk to him?" I asked.

She shot me a withering glance, and I immediately regretted the question. "Of course, Dr. Flückinger. He refused to discuss anything for a very long time."

"But he did, eventually."

She nodded. "Eventually. One night I woke up, and he was not in our bed. I found him in the barn. He held a knife in his hand. He was cutting his own arm and watching the blood drip on the ground. I made him tell me what was wrong then. I told him I would leave him if he didn't. He cried and begged, but I held firm, for his sake and for mine. I couldn't stand to see him suffering so."

"What could possibly make him do such a thing?"

"He said he had done something wrong. While his militia company was encamped on Kosovo Plain, he snuck away one night to a nearby farm he knew was abandoned. He intended to look for things the owners had left behind."

"He was looting."

"Call it what you will, Dr. Flückinger, but don't judge. You have not lived my life."

I stared at the floor and shifted my feet. "I'm sorry.

Please continue."

"He found something there at the farmhouse, a medal. It looked old and possibly valuable, but no sooner did he put it in his coat than he was attacked by … something. He wouldn't say what. He fought it off and escaped the farmhouse, but over the next several days, a dark cloud settled over his mood, as if the color drained from the world. He thought returning here and picking up his life again would help, but it didn't. He said he thought he was cursed."

She began to cry. I wanted to wipe the tears away from her cheeks, but I knew better than to try. After a moment, she dried her own eyes and continued. "He showed me this trinket he had taken from the farmhouse. He hid it in a box in the barn. It was hideous, a snake with its body wrapped around in a circle. I asked him why he kept it. He said he just couldn't seem to part with it."

"How long was this before his accident?"

"He fell from the hay wagon about a month later. You know the rest. The animals started getting sick and dying, then our neighbors. People claim they saw Arnold in their houses at night. It was not him, Dr. Flückinger. Do you understand me?"

"Where is this medallion now?"

She shook her head. "I don't know. It disappeared not long after Arnold died. Good riddance, I say. Let it be someone else's problem."

I did not want to ask the next question, but I knew I had to. "What will you do now?"

A young boy, around five, ran to her side. He had his mother's bright blue eyes.

"I have my son to think about," she said. "Five years ago, I thought everything would be all right once the panic died down, but after this latest bout of madness, we can't stay. I don't want him to grow up in a place where everyone thinks his father is a monster."

"Where will you go?"

"We have some relations in Hermannstadt who have agreed to take us in. It will be hard, but at least we'll be safe."

I nodded. "I wish you Godspeed on your journey then."

A faint smile played across her face, then disappeared. "Thank you, Dr. Flückinger."

With nothing else to say, I turned to leave, and as I walked away, I wondered what might have been, if the two of us weren't who we were ...

FIFTY

Berlin, Germany
12 August 1999

YASAMIN COCKED HER HEAD TO one side. "Consequences? I don't see what consequences you could possibly be referring to."

"You are responsible for the panics in Dubrovnik as well as other places," Adam said, "and the deaths of God knows how many innocents. Get enough people riled up, and you'll have the villagers coming for you with their torches and pitchforks. The things you have done will come back to haunt you."

"Will they?"

"You can't possibly think you can survive forever."

"I have managed for more than four hundred years."

"That creature you created in Dubrovnik lasted for more than three hundred. It took mere minutes to destroy him." Adam knew he walked a fine line—provocative enough to keep her interested and talking, but not enough to get himself killed.

"Perhaps you are right, Dr. Mire," she said, "but today is not the day."

Adam hoped it would not be his day either. "The Sicilian, what was his name?"

She smiled. "Poor Vittorio. He did not deserve to come to such a low end."

Again, Adam chose to ignore the implications of her statement. "Is it true, what he said? Were you responsible for losing Dracula's medallion?"

The smile melted. "Yes."

"How did it happen?"

"That man, that *farmer*." She spat the word. "Playing at war just like all the rest. The Germans had invaded my land again, driving the people from their homes. I saw him one evening sneaking away from their encampment and followed him to an abandoned farmhouse. I knew his type. He was planning to steal what he could find there."

"Arnold Pavle," Adam said, "or Paole as it became in the stories."

The letter from Dr. Johann Flückinger to his brother concerning Arnold's widow Alisa had been tucked into the pages of Mihai's copy of *Dracula* as well.

Yasamin nodded. "That was his name, as I discovered later, but by then all trace of him had vanished. I found him that night in the bedroom of the farmhouse, rooting through an old trunk. I ... overcame his hesitations. He came to me easily. I felt the heat radiating off him and listened to the rhythm of his heart. It beat strong and fast, like yours, Dr. Mire. I kissed his lips and then his neck. He moaned as my mouth passed over his skin. He jerked only once when my teeth pierced his throat. I relished the savory taste of his blood spilling over my tongue. The thought of drinking my fill that night drove me to ecstasy."

Adam squeezed the rosary in his hand, trying to banish the images that came unbidden to his mind.

"I drew my dagger and cut open my wrist," she continued. "My blood oozed out. I held it up to his mouth, and I made him drink, but then the image of a woman came to his mind, a kind smile, blue eyes filled with laughter—his wife. His love for her filled him, and his touch seared. The pain was too much. I pushed him away. When his senses returned, he unsheathed his own knife and sunk the blade into my stomach. I fell backward, clutching at the wound, trying to stanch the flow of blood that nonetheless percolated through my fingers. I stumbled over my cloak and ripped it. The medallion holding it around my shoulders fell to the floor. He snatched the medallion up and stumbled out of the room into the night. I was too weak to give chase. I knew it would be only a matter of time, though. I had tasted his blood, and he had tasted mine. The 'curse,' as you refer to it, would eventually take him."

"Why did you have the medallion?"

"Its allure is ... difficult to resist, once you've held it. I wanted to hold it again. And my family guarded it for so long. I didn't see the harm in wearing it."

"And so after this happened, you ran away from him. You came to Dubrovnik, to do what? To hide?"

"I told you I was not running away."

"Then why leave?"

"I had to fix my mistake."

"The medallion is more than just a sentimental bauble, isn't it? What does it do?"

"Do you really want to know?"

"I wouldn't have asked if I didn't."

"Every moment for the rest of your life you will live in peril."

"To hear you talk, I'll be spending the rest of my life in this room."

She nodded. "As you wish, then. The medallion, Dr. Mire, has the ability to unmake him, if used properly. I couldn't let it fall into the wrong hands, even if it meant my own undoing."

"If the tables were turned, do you honestly think he would have ever sacrificed himself to save you?"

"I know he would have. He would have done anything for me."

FIFTY-ONE

Buda, Ottoman Hungary
8 Dhu al-Qi'dah 1008
(11 May 1600 Old Style)

RUMORS FLEW AROUND THE HAREMLIK like vicious, pecking ravens. Even under the dark cloud cast by the plague and the twin disappearances of Rabiye and Ayla, the lifeblood of the *haremlık*'s denizens remained gossip. Yasamin did not tell Iskander about the other slights and barbs she received every day, the complimentary remarks containing hidden insults. She imagined he wouldn't want to be bothered with such petty details of her life.

Such talk centered mostly on the fact that Yasamin and Murad had little to do with one another. Hadice tried to help, in her own way, though Murad's ambivalence toward Yasamin hung in the air between them as thick as pipe smoke.

"Be patient with my son," she told Yasamin. "Murad has always been content with his own company. Perhaps it is my fault for coddling him when he was a boy. Still, I can sense he is destined for something great. Just give him time."

But for a pashazade to treat his wife in such a lukewarm manner was unseemly, the others said. There must be a reason. After all, as odd as Murad sometimes behaved, he was still a man. If Yasamin didn't stoke his desires, then the fault must be with her.

Celibe, Selim's mother, was much more imaginative.

She approached Yasamin as she sat in the garden, basking in the morning sun and watching the bud-laden branches of the pomegranate trees sway in the breeze.

"It's a beautiful day, isn't it?" Celibe said as she took a seat next to Yasamin in the grass. "I'm so glad winter is finally gone. Spring was quite late in arriving this year, don't you think?"

Yasamin forced a smile and demurely shook her head. "I wouldn't know. The weather in Salonica never varies much."

"Do you miss it? Greece? I lived there when I was a girl. I found it oppressively hot in the summer, but I was much farther south."

Every minute of every day I miss it, Yasamin thought. "I'm fortunate to be here."

Celibe reached out and placed her hand on Yasamin's. "Please, Yasamin, you can be honest with me. I want us to be closer. I truly do. We are a family. We have to watch out for one another, especially here in the *haremlık*."

"Do you think I'm not being truthful?" Yasamin asked.

"I've watched you, Yasamin. There is melancholy in your every move and expression, even when you pretend to be happy. My dear, I know your relationship with Murad is not what you expected it to be. I want to let you know your secret is safe with me."

Yasamin snatched her hand away. "What secret?"

Impossible. She couldn't know.

Celibe chuckled. "Really there is no need to play coy with me."

"I'm not, Celibe. I swear to you," Yasamin said.

Her heart pounded. She wanted to run. Celibe could never know about Iskander. It would ruin everything.

"Your arrangement with Murad," Celibe said. "I know all about it."

She gave Celibe a puzzled look. "Arrangement?"

Celibe laughed, as if Yasamin were trying to play some great joke on her. "Yes, your arrangement. It never occurred to me before, but it all makes sense now. I was with Ahmed Pasha just this past evening. As I was leaving his chambers, I saw someone else leaving Murad's room. I couldn't tell who it was. I didn't see anything more than a shadow, but I didn't need more. The silhouette couldn't have been anything but a janissary. Now, I have heard that life out on campaign for months at a time can get very lonely, and sometimes janissaries will turn to one another for companionship. I have also heard there are those who prefer such companionship, even when not in the field. I must say, Yasamin my dear, you're very brave."

Yasamin's words came out in an angry torrent. "You don't know what you're talking about. You yourself said that you saw little more than a shadow. It could have been anyone. It was probably Murad's servant. If I were you, I would be more careful about what I say."

"Oh, I am always careful about what I say," Celibe replied. "And as I said, your secret is safe with me, though I cannot vouch for those with looser tongues."

Yasamin shook with rage as she watched Celibe walk

away. Murad didn't deserve to have such accusations aimed at him, but she knew many would believe the story Celibe concocted. Such trysts might be overlooked among the janissaries, but one would never be tolerated for a pashazade. Murad would be turned out of his father's household, and her with him. Or worse, they could both be put to death.

If only everyone knew how Murad had saved Selim's life in battle, that he was the hero everyone believed his brother to be. Then everyone would see Celibe's lie for what it was. He had to be persuaded to tell the truth.

Yasamin became so lost in her troubles she failed to notice Nesrin standing next to her until the old woman cleared her throat. Yasamin looked up with a start.

"Daydreaming, Yasamin?" she asked.

"No, Nesrin," Yasamin replied hastily, "nothing of the sort, I assure you."

"It looked like you were daydreaming to me. I do not care for idleness. I have not lived as long as I have by being idle. A lesson you'd do well to learn." Yasamin opened her mouth to protest, but Nesrin waved her hand dismissively. "No matter. We can discuss it later. I've come to ask you if you've seen Sanem today."

Yasamin's heart skipped a beat. "No. I haven't."

Nesrin's brow furrowed. "Curious. She was supposed to help with preparing the coffee this morning, but she didn't. No one has seen her today at all."

"She is not in her room?"

"She is apparently nowhere. Rabiye, Ayla, and now Sanem. Three girls, all vanished. Most disturbing."

"Can't you ask Ahmed Pasha for help? Surely he cannot ignore what is happening."

Nesrin's eyes flashed. A bitter note entered her voice.

"My son is still occupied with matters of his own. Come now, Yasamin. The sun is already high. Enough dawdling. You may help me back to my room. After that there is the matter of the laundry."

Neither of them spoke as they passed through the corridors, Nesrin holding onto Yasamin's arm for support. Only the rhythmic crack of Nesrin's cane disrupted the silence. Yasamin glanced at the stooped woman. Nesrin's stern countenance offered no reassurances, only grim realities.

FIFTY-TWO

Buda, Ottoman Hungary
9 Dhu al-Qi'dah 1008
(12 May 1600 Old Style)

ISKANDER KISSED YASAMIN IN THE pale light. His lips on her skin, his fingers running down her spine to the small of her back, his powerful arms around her—they all threatened to make her forget what had happened that day. But Yasamin could not forget, and Iskander sensed her worry.

"What's wrong?" he asked as he stroked her dark hair. "Did Sanem say something else to you today?"

Yasamin shook her head. "No, not her."

"Then who?"

Yasamin bit her lip and glanced toward the lattice-covered window. Diamonds of moonlight littered the floor underneath. She didn't reply.

Iskander placed a hand under her chin and turned her head back to face him. "Come now, why this reluctance? You can tell me anything."

Staring into his emerald eyes, Yasamin knew he was right, but she thought of Sanem, and some small part of her said she should be afraid of him. "I … I want to believe that."

"But?"

Sanem was the one person who could have possibly helped Yasamin fill in the holes in her memory. She was missing, and the only other person who knew what Sanem had said about her parents was Iskander, in whose arms she had so trustingly fallen asleep the night before.

"But I've come to realize I know almost nothing about you," Yasamin said.

He stepped back and held open his arms. "What would you like to know?"

Yasamin paused for a moment to consider. "Where were you born?"

He chuckled. "An easy one. In a small town in Transylvania. But you can do better than that. Ask me something harder to answer."

"Do you remember anything about your family, from before you were taken in the tribute?"

"I don't remember very much. The one clear memory I do have is the day my father and older brother were murdered—buried alive. I remember the soldier who came with the news, muddied and bloody. He had ridden his horse to exhaustion to reach us. My mother screamed and threw herself to the floor. I'd never heard such a sound before."

Yasamin shivered, despite the warm night. "How horrible. Who would do such a thing?"

"My father had enemies, but it doesn't matter anymore. The killers received their due."

The small dark spot of fear in Yasamin's mind grew

again. "Is that when you were taken to Istanbul?" she asked.

"That happened ... later. I was taken to Istanbul against my will, and for almost the entire year that followed, I was beaten daily for disobedience. In truth, though, I owe a great deal to the Sultan. I could never have received the education or the training I did in my birthplace. I am the man I am today in many ways because of him."

"But?"

"Duty has its place, certainly, but those who do their duty and nothing else are fools who throw their lives away for others. The first time I saw you, I knew I had to find a way to be with you, even though the vows of a janissary forbid it. I love you, Yasamin. I understand you may not feel the same, but if you don't, please don't tell me. I don't think I could bear it."

The fear did not go away, but Yasamin couldn't deny what she felt. "I love you."

"Then please don't keep anything from me. Tell my why you're so upset."

Yasamin told him everything Celibe had said.

As she spoke, his expression darkened. "She can't be allowed to do that."

Yasamin began to cry. "I don't know what to do. I don't want her to wrench us apart. Maybe ... maybe we could run away together. Maybe we could find somewhere to make a new life for ourselves."

"I don't think that's possible."

"But why not?"

"It's just not." He pulled her close, then reached up and wiped away her tears. "But we will find a solution to this. I promise you I will not give you up, not without a fight."

"But what can you do?"

He kissed her neck. "Leave me to worry about it."

As they made love, Yasamin heard the *kemençe* player's music again, but it was different, darker, angrier.

YASAMIN STOOD PARALYZED OVER CELIBE'S contorted form, unable even to scream. The older woman lay in the garden on the path Yasamin always took to the great oak tree, in a position almost identical to that of the dead janissary and with the same unnatural pallor to her skin. The morning dew had washed away the thick makeup she normally wore, and the lines crisscrossing her bloodless face spoke of a life far rougher than she ever let anyone know.

Iskander's words from the night before floated back to Yasamin on the breeze rustling in the pomegranate trees. *I promise I will not give you up. Not without a fight.*

Yasamin could see no marks, but the expression of horror frozen on Celibe's face told Yasamin she did not die quietly. She knelt and gently closed Celibe's sightless eyes. As she did, she spotted something on Celibe's neck and turned the woman's head so she could see better. It looked like a bite mark, a human bite, with two deep, round punctures where a person's eyeteeth would be. But there was no blood, and there were no bruises.

Yasamin heard voices. Without anywhere to run, she quickly found her voice and screamed with all her might. Two of the other girls rounded the bend in the path. When they saw Celibe lying on the ground, their screams joined Yasamin's. Several black eunuchs appeared a few minutes later, and the rest of the women in the *haremlık* as well. The eunuchs took control of the situation, some forcing the women back while the others picked up Celibe's body and carried it away with a tenderness they had not shown the janissary.

Yasamin sat in the wet grass and wailed. Maybe the others thought her outburst was an expression of her shock, or perhaps even a result of some affection she had for Celibe.

It was neither.

FIFTY-THREE

Berlin, Germany
12 August 1999

ADAM COCKED HIS HEAD TO one side. "How do you know he would do anything for you? Or that what he did was even for you? How do you know it wasn't simply part of his plan?"

Yasamin pursed her lips. "I know."

"That's it? You know?"

"Perhaps if you continue with your narrative, I may share more. At this point I'm dying to know where you went after Dubrovnik."

"There was a sign in Greek in the background of the picture I found in *Bulfinch's Mythology*," Adam replied, trying to ignore her sardonic choice of words. "I also found a transcript of an interview with a French World War I veteran named Jean-Pierre Allard, who talked about the great fire that destroyed much of the city of Thessaloniki in 1917. Of course, you knew the city better as *Selanik*, or *Salonica*."

"I have known the city in many guises."

"I imagine it must be difficult for you, watching the changes."

"The only thing constant in this world is change," Yasamin said. "A platitude maybe, but we call them platitudes for a reason. My centuries on this planet leave me in a better position to understand than most, and I have accepted it."

"But just like Banja Luka, so much of Thessaloniki has been destroyed and rebuilt—bombing, fires, ethnic conflicts. It doesn't trouble you now to walk its streets? After sunset, of course."

"Salonica and I are intertwined, Dr. Mire, more so than any other place. It is the only place I was ever happy in life, though I didn't know it at the time. My Banja Luka is gone, but my Salonica is still there, if you know where to look. I feel at times as if the fortunes of the city reflect my own."

"Do you believe in destiny?" Adam asked.

Yasamin gazed past him, as if she were seeing something different in the portrait on the wall behind Adam. "Once, not anymore."

"What changed?"

"I have seen too many 'destinies' unfulfilled, Dr. Mire. Too many people waste their lives chasing futures as substantial as pipe smoke. The truth is that we each make our own destinies. Anyone who believes otherwise is an idiot."

"Prophecies, then?"

"Any particular prophecy you have in mind?"

"One, though I'm sure you're already familiar with the story."

She grinned. "Tell me anyway."

A cat, toying with a mouse before it makes a kill. Adam

forced a smile onto his own face. He knew his time was running short. Still, he played his role as best he could.

FIFTY-FOUR

From The Life and Death of Michael the Brave
by Ioan Nicolescu

Jassy, Moldavia
26 May 1600 Old Style

B Y MAY OF 1600, MICHAEL the Brave had defeated Prince Ieremia Movilă, puppet of the Polish king, and added Moldavia to his realm. In doing so he achieved something no one else has accomplished since. The three Romanian lands—Wallachia, Transylvania, and Moldavia—were finally one. He regarded it as his destiny. Even though the Poles were still a threat, even though the Germans and General Basta had abandoned him, and he had not yet subdued the Turks, he believed God was with him and that only God could reverse his fortunes. He may have been correct.

At this point the rift that had been developing in Michael's relationship with Father Dumitru opened into a chasm. For a while, the prince had been relying almost exclusively on Alexandru's counsel. Michael believed Father Dumitru felt slighted. He justified his actions by reasoning that he did only what was necessary to be a modern ruler. From Father Dumitru's own scant writings, however, it is evident that the priest was concerned about altogether different matters.

Michael was forced to borrow an exorbitant amount of money from several wealthy Turks in order to secure his place as Prince of Wallachia. Naturally, his creditors were not happy when he overthrew Cardinal Báthory and began to expel the Turks from Transylvania. With Moldavia subdued, he felt it might be time to appease them, and so he invited them to dinner in a new dining hall he had added to the palace in Jassy. When they were all assembled, he ordered the doors barred and the hall burned to the ground with them inside. Alexandru proposed the efficient method of freeing himself from his debts.

When Father Dumitru learned of the incident, he stormed into the prince's private study to confront both him and Alexandru. "You are a Christian, Your Grace," he shouted. "This is no way for a Christian to act. To murder an unarmed man, even a nonbeliever such as a Turk is simply wrong."

"But Father, His Grace is merely following precedent," Alexandru explained coolly. "One of his predecessors, Vlad Țepeș, employed the practice on more than one occasion to remove Wallachia of undesirable groups."

Father Dumitru turned his anger on the *boyar*. "Vlad Țepeș was universally hated and was eventually killed by his own men."

With a speed both men had trouble believing possible, Alexandru pinned the priest to the wall. "Vlad Țepeș was felled by a Turkish arrow in battle," he hissed, his face inches from Dumitru's. "To say otherwise is to dishonor the memory of a hero."

"Alexandru, let him go," the prince ordered.

Alexandru glared at Dumitru. "In any event, is it not better for a prince to be feared than to be loved?"

He released Dumitru and stormed out of the room.

"Your Grace," Dumitru began.

Michael held up a hand. "Your concerns are duly noted. Now to other matters. Have you made any progress into the cause of my nightmares?"

"No, Your Grace."

Already nettled by Father Dumitru's confrontation, Michael perhaps let his anger get the better of him. "What good are you then?"

"I came here to offer you guidance, Your Grace. If you do not want to hear what I have to say, then I'll waste no more of my time here."

"You haven't said a thing."

"But I have, Your Grace. You need only to listen. I cannot tell you the meaning of your dreams. You must look inside yourself. Perhaps God is testing you."

Michael struggled to keep his voice even. "How do I pass such a test?"

"Faith."

The prince actually laughed. "Is that all?"

If Father Dumitru was offended, he did not indicate so. "Nothing more is necessary."

Michael took off the ruby ring he always wore on his right hand. "Do you see this ring? I have ten others like it. I am a very wealthy man, but at this point, Father, faith is a luxury I cannot afford."

DISSATISFIED WITH THE ADVICE FROM Father Dumitru, Michael decided to seek it elsewhere, according to the last of his letters to his cousin Livia. That evening he gave the same ruby ring to an old man. The Gypsy palmed it after peering up and down the deserted corridor. The prince himself had foregone his usual garments for plain ones much like the old man wore.

"No tricks," he said. "You know who I am."

"I don't play tricks," the old Gypsy retorted.

"Well, what did you see?"

The Gypsy shook his head. "I don't think I will tell you. You would not like it."

"What do you mean? Whether or not you tell me what you see in my future is not your decision to make."

"Still, I do not believe I should."

For someone to behave with such insolence, especially an old Gypsy, was inexcusable, and for a moment Michael forgot he was supposed to be in disguise. "Remember Gypsy, this is my realm, now. I can have you executed on the spot."

The old man chuckled. "If you must know, then. You are going to die."

"We are all going to die, old man."

"Soon. You are going to die soon."

He only confirmed what Michael already knew, based on the prince's letter.

"How do I stop it?" Michael asked.

"You can't," the Gypsy replied, "unless you kill the man who binds himself with the snake."

"The man who binds himself with the snake? What does that mean? Who is this person?"

The Gypsy held up his hand, a calm smile on his face. "I cannot. It is a riddle only you can solve."

FIFTY-FIVE

—m—

Excerpt from an interview with Jean-Pierre Allard
in the newspaper L'Eclaireur de l'Est

Thessaloniki, Greece
5 August 1917

O N 5 AUGUST 1917, A *fire destroyed two-thirds of the*
city of Thessaloniki, leaving 70,000 people homeless
and almost 10,000 structures, mostly in the city's an-
cient heart, nothing more than smoldering ashes. Officially, the
cause of the fire was ruled accidental. In a small house where a
group of French soldiers were garrisoned, a spark from the
kitchen fire ignited a pile of straw. Water was in short supply,
and Thessaloniki lacked an organized fire brigade, so the fire
quickly spread out of control.

But years later, in 1939, a different story emerged from a
convalescent home for soldiers outside Rheims, France. A man by
the name of Jean-Pierre Allard, who had a history of mental
problems dating back to his service during the First World War,
claimed he started it. When asked why, he said simply, "I was

trying to destroy a vampire."

The hospital administrators and local authorities attempted to downplay the incident as the product of a deranged mind, but a curious reporter from a local paper managed to gain access to M. Allard under false pretenses. The paper printed his account, and soon, papers in Paris and London picked up the story. Within a week people as far away as New York City were talking about the "Salonica Vampire." Several British and German insurance companies, which had been coerced into paying out hundreds of thousands of pounds in claims, even pressured the Greek government to reopen the investigation.

Their policies, after all, did not cover vampire attacks.

However, as fast as the story spread, it was forgotten. On 1 September 1939, German tanks rolled across the Polish border. M. Allard died quietly in his sleep a few months later. Still, among certain circles in the port city of Thessaloniki, one may still hear the word vrykolakas, *the Greek word for vampire, used to describe a dark, alluring, honey-lipped beauty who may yet stalk the streets looking for her next victim.*

I COULD NOT BELIEVE MY good fortune. The girl stood out on the street, staring up at me. Looking down at her from the second-story window, I was able to see her enticing profile in the lamplight. She was obviously a local Turkish girl, somewhat common, but it didn't matter to me. She had dark olive skin, beguiling almond-shaped eyes, and full lips that quivered as she waited.

"Well?" she called up to me in broken French. "Don't you like what you see?"

"Of course," I replied.

"Then invite me in."

But then I heard a voice behind me. "Close the window, Jean-Pierre. You're letting the night air in. Who are you talking to?" It was Charles, the good-looking bastard.

"No one," I shouted. I knew if Charles and the others found out about the girl, they would take her from me, and I would never have a chance. I turned back around and was glad to see the young girl hadn't left. "There is a side door in the alley to your right. Meet me there."

She smiled. Moments later, I opened the door to find her standing on the other side. Her beauty took my breath away.

"Please," I said after I remembered to speak, "come in."

She stepped over the threshold without a word.

"What is your name?" I asked.

"You may call me Jasmine," she replied in the same broken French.

"Jasmine," I repeated. "You are just as lovely as the flower after which you are named. I am afraid the only place where we may have some privacy is the kitchen. You don't mind, do you?"

"Not at all," she told me.

I led her to the small kitchen where the fire still smoldered. The summer heat was oppressive, but the girl didn't seem to care. She sat on the table and pulled up her skirt to give me a view of her exquisite calf and thigh. I took off my coat and my shirt. She leaned back. Her thin blouse outlined the contours of her round breasts and supple waist. I leaned into her and brought my mouth to her neck. As my lips touched her skin, electricity shot through my body. I imagined it would feel the same to be struck by lightning. I pushed her skirt out of the way.

"I am but a soldier," I said. "They do not pay us much, but whatever you ask, I will give it."

"I don't ask for much," she purred. "Only your life."

Her beautiful features melted away. Her face distorted, becoming bestial. Her teeth grew into fangs and her fingers into razor-sharp claws. She launched herself from the table and pinned me to the floor, her legs straddling my midsection, her hands pressing down on my chest. I tried to push her off, but she had the strength of many men. I couldn't even gather up enough breath to scream.

"If you struggle," she said, "it will only hurt more, but feel free to struggle as much as you like, if you want it to hurt ..."

My eyes darted toward the glowing embers in the hearth. As Jasmine opened her mouth wide to reveal the full extent of her fangs, I stretched my arm and reached into the ashes. Despite the searing pain, I grabbed a burning hunk of wood and used it to bash the monster across the temple. She fell off me, crying in pain, and I sprang to my feet. Sparks from the log landed in a pile of straw that ignited as I ran out the door. Though I did my best to raise the alarm, fire engulfed the house in minutes, killing everyone inside. I was the only one who escaped.

At least I pray I was.

FIFTY-SIX

Thessaloniki, Greece
9 August 1999

ADAM SAT ALONE AT A table at a small sidewalk café, watching the bustle of Thessaloniki swirl around him. After a while, a woman approached his table. Seeing his friend Marina Dimitriou in her tailored suit, not a strand of her long brown hair out of place, Adam felt self-conscious about his rumpled appearance. He stood, took her hands in his, and kissed her on each cheek.

"I didn't know you were planning a stop in our Thessaloniki, Adam," she said as they both took a seat. "If I had, I would have made time for more than a cup of coffee." "I didn't know I would be visiting myself. Thank you for sparing a few minutes for me, Marina."

She looked him up and down, and the smile on her face faded. "Is something the matter? Pardon my saying this, but you don't look well."

He shook his head. "Just tired. The last several days

have been ... hectic. A lot of traveling. Not much sleep."

"What's going on?" she asked.

He flagged the waiter. "I'm actually here about our old friend Mihai Iliescu."

"I was shocked when I heard the news. I'll miss him."

"So will I, but I'm curious. Had you heard from him lately?"

"As a matter of fact, yes. He was here last December. I met with him then. He looked haggard, much like—"

"Much like I do?"

"I'm sorry, Adam. I'm only concerned. What's this all about?"

"Marina, I know I'm going to sound a little crazy, but I think he ran into a bit of trouble that may have led to his death. I think someone—" Adam's glance darted to the approaching waiter. He stopped talking and pressed his lips together in a forced smile. After Marina ordered her coffee he continued. "What did Mihai talk about when you met with him?"

"Not very much. He said he was in town looking for a few books for his collection." She smiled again. "You know how much he loved his book collection."

"Did he tell you what kind of books?"

"Not exactly. If you can believe it, he wanted to talk more about celebrity gossip than anything else."

"That doesn't sound like him at all."

"No, but he seemed very keen on the comings and goings of Bahram Ashrafi."

"Who?"

"The son of a German businessman," Marina replied after the waiter brought her coffee. "He was on the German bobsled team in the last Olympics and apparently appeared in a number of racy underwear ads in Germany and Austria."

"Bahram Ashrafi doesn't sound like a German name."

"His family is Persian," Marina explained. "He was on vacation here at the time of Mihai's visit. The paparazzi were thick around him, as well as the woman who hung on his arm."

"A woman? Who was she?"

"No one seems to know, really."

"Why was Mihai interested?"

Marina sipped her coffee. "I'm not sure, but after Ashrafi returned to Berlin, he announced his engagement to this girl. Within weeks, they were married, and a few weeks after that, he was dead. I wouldn't have paid attention to any of it at all, were it not for Mihai."

"Dead? How did he die?"

"No one knows. The doctors said it was some peculiar type of anemia, but they never found a cause."

Adam produced the photo he had found and showed it to Marina. "Is this Bahram Ashrafi and his mystery woman?"

Marina glanced at the picture. "Yes, but how did you—"

"It's a long story." Adam sat silent for a moment. The doctors may not have known what killed Bahram Ashrafi, but he did.

"I think I have something that might be of interest to you," Marina said. "Mihai gave me something while he was here."

Adam perked up. "A book?"

"Of sorts. His father's journal."

"Did he say why he gave it to you?"

"He said he thought it would interest me, given my research."

"Have you read it?"

"I don't know Romanian. I've actually been afraid to show it to anyone else. I don't think Mihai was being completely upfront with me. Somehow I get the impression he left it for me to give to you. Would you like to see it?"

"Of course. Where is it?"

"In my office." She glanced down at her watch. "I have a class soon, but I'll be done by two o'clock. Why don't you stop by then?" She reached over the table and touched his arm as she stood. "It's good to see you again, Adam."

Adam watched her walk away, feeling a tinge of sadness. When she was some distance down the street, she paused and looked over her shoulder. Adam smiled and waved. She waved back. If some things had worked out differently Adam thought, maybe ...

Walking back to the hotel, Adam failed to notice two bicycle couriers until they almost hit him. When he bumped into the German tourist, he mumbled an apology and kept walking, ignoring the string of curses thrown in his direction. The doorman greeted him as he opened the door. Adam didn't reply. The desk clerk said something to him as he crossed the lobby. He didn't pay attention. He didn't remember riding the elevator to the fifth floor or entering his room. Something about what Marina said didn't seem right. Of course, it made sense the journal of Mihai's father would be another piece of the puzzle, but it was not the book Adam expected to find.

ADAM ARRIVED AT MARINA'S OFFICE ten minutes after two o'clock. He ran his fingers over the gold letters on the door that spelled out in Greek, "Dr. Marina Dimitriou, Department of History." As he did, the door opened.

Adam peered inside. All he could see at first was her desk, papers and books strewn across the surface. It looked a lot like his own.

But it shouldn't have.

Marina was meticulous in the extreme. She would never have allowed anything on her desk to go askew. Adam attempted to push the door open farther, only to meet resistance.

"Marina?"

He forced himself through the opening to find the rest of the office in similar disarray and Marina on the floor.

"Marina!" He knelt over her, but he knew it was already too late. Her sightless eyes were fixed on the ceiling. A red gash crossed her throat, and a viscous maroon pool of blood spread underneath her crumpled form.

Her right hand was painted green.

FIFTY-SEVEN

Berlin, Germany
12 August 1999

TIME CONTINUED TO PASS AS if in a dream, every second drawn out like honey dripping into a jar. The two of them, the vampire and the professor, were the only ones in the world. Nothing else existed. Nowhere else existed, but it would not last.

"It would seem, Dr. Mire, your destiny would be to bring death wherever you go."

"It would seem."

"I do find the green paint curious, if a little theatric. Any idea what it means, exactly?"

"Green was the color of the Order of the Archangel Michael, better known as the Iron Guard," Adam explained, "a paramilitary fascist organization that took over the Romanian government before World War II. One of their symbols was a green fist. I'm afraid it means they've come back, if they ever went away at all, that they are tied up the search for the medallion as well."

"Another player on the board, then?"

"Another player," Adam repeated.

"One playing a very dangerous hand. This game is becoming increasingly complicated, more complicated than you expected, I would imagine."

"I never thought of this as a game."

Her eyes narrowed, and she wrinkled her nose in annoyance. "Why do you insist on continuing to deceive yourself in every way, Dr. Mire? Of course this is a game for you, one with high stakes and dire penalties, but a game nonetheless. You enjoy the challenge I can see it in your eyes."

"*Enjoy* would not be the word I use."

"Very well, but you do thrive on it. Admit that in the last two weeks, you've felt more alive than you have ever felt."

He shook his head. "I can't do that. I haven't felt alive in … a long time. Besides, what do you know about feeling alive?"

"More than you might think, Dr. Mire."

FIFTY-EIGHT

Buda, Ottoman Hungary
26 Dhu al-Qi'dah 1008
(29 May 1600 Old Style)

Yasamin plaited her hair into a long braid and
secured it to the top of her head, then covered her
face in a thick layer of white powder, bound her
breasts, and put on her bulkiest clothes. As she surveyed
the results of her efforts in the mirror, she hoped she had
done enough to pass as one of the white eunuchs so that
she could leave the *haremlık* unescorted.

Voices swirled in her head—the childhood tales her
aunt had told her, Murad's account of his encounter with
the crazed German soldier in the wild forest, the stories
Ine and Ayla had told about plagues and djinn, the letters
of Kemal the soldier, Iskander's whispered reassurances.
She couldn't quiet the cacophony.

She rushed through the garden, pausing only to fold the
sheet she carried into a small turban on her head before
she came to the gateway to the men's area of the palace. A

black eunuch stood guard. She lowered her eyes and hurried past him. He never said a word.

From there Murad's apartment was only a short distance away. She could not think of anyone else she could talk to about what was happening. As she neared, the door opened, throwing a pool of lamplight into the corridor. Yasamin pressed herself against the wall. A man emerged from Murad's apartment, dressed in the uniform of a janissary. Yasamin recognized the black mustache and the hawkish nose instantly.

Iskander turned. Their eyes met. The corners of his mouth curled up into a slight smile before he turned his back and walked the other way.

Then Murad's door closed, leaving Yasamin in darkness once more. Her heart pounded. She didn't know whether to knock on the door or race back to the safety of her own room, if safety even existed there. She took a step toward Murad's room when a large hand reached from behind her and covered her mouth.

"Such a pretty face," a voice whispered. "What a waste on a eunuch."

The hand let go, but Yasamin dared not scream. Her assailant seized her shoulders and spun her around.

"I knew it must be you," Selim said. "I've only ever seen your eyes, but I could never forget them. Now that I see the rest of your face, its beauty is equally burned into my mind." His forward words and brash smile did little to hide the pain in his eyes. "So tell me, what are you doing lurking outside Murad's apartment?"

Yasamin stood as tall as she could and thrust out her chin. "I could ask you the same."

Selim laughed. "You have fire. That's good. You need fire to survive here. But I have every right to be here. You have none. I could have you put to death."

"I ... I needed to speak with Murad."

Selim raised an eyebrow. "There are other ways, if you want to talk to your own husband."

"It's urgent. I couldn't wait for him to send for me, and I didn't know if I could trust a eunuch with a note."

"Urgent? What could be so urgent for you to risk your life?"

"It's about what happened to Celibe today."

Anger crept into his voice. "What do you have to tell Murad about my mother? She is dead. She can no longer slight you."

"No, it has nothing to do with any difficulties between us, I promise you. And I never wished her harm. I am truly sorry for what has happened."

"Not as sorry as I am, I'm certain."

"There is more. There is something terribly wrong—the crazed German who attacked Ilker, the dead janissary in the garden, the plague afflicting the others, the disappearances in the *haremlık*, Rabiye and Ayla and Sanem, the djinn."

Selim held up a hand. "Wait. Slow down. You're not making sense."

Yasamin opened her mouth to explain, but closed it again and lowered her eyes. "Nothing. It's nothing. I've been foolish. I'm so sorry."

"Yasamin, look at me." When she did, Selim continued. "You are not a fool, and for what it is worth, I disagree with the way my mother treated you, but you should not have come here."

"What are you going to do with me?"

"Nothing, as long as you leave now."

"Of course."

She turned to go.

"And Yasamin?"

She paused. "Yes?"

"Think twice before you try a similar trick in the future. That costume may fool a half-asleep eunuch, but not anyone else. You're fortunate I came across you first."

Yasamin nodded and then ran all the way back to her room, ignoring the startled shouts of the eunuchs at the gateway to the *haremlık*.

ISKANDER WAITED FOR HER IN her room. He crossed to her and kissed her. She shoved him away. The fog from before had lifted. For the first time in a long time, she could think clearly.

"What are you?" she demanded.

He furrowed his brow in confusion. "What do you mean?"

"What are you? Are you responsible for all the terrible things happening? These deaths and disappearances? What sort of darkness have you brought here?"

"Yasamin—"

"Are you even a man? Or are you something else in disguise?"

Iskander held out his arms. "I am only what I am."

He moved to embrace her again, but she stepped back.

"Why were you talking to my husband?" she asked.

"That is none of you business."

"But he's my husband," Yasamin countered, "and you're my—" She stopped.

Iskander's mouth formed into a twisted smile. "Your what?"

Yasamin bit her lower lip. "Why were you talking to

him?"

"Yasamin, please. There are some things you shouldn't stir up."

She glared. "Now who's keeping secrets?"

"I'm trying to protect you."

"I don't need you to protect me."

"Don't you? Could you have stopped Celibe from spreading rumors meant to ruin you?"

"I didn't ask you to do what you did."

"Come now. You are not a stupid person, Yasamin. After Ayla, after Sanem, you knew what might happen if you told me what Celibe said to you. You were hoping for it."

Yasamin shook her head. "No, no I wasn't. I would never—" She paused again. "You made me tell you. I didn't want to, but somehow you made me."

"Nonsense. I've never made you do anything you didn't want to do."

He was right. A small part of her had hoped Iskander would do something to Celibe, but she would never admit it to him.

"Fine. Keep your secrets. Plan your schemes." Yasamin turned from him. "Just go somewhere else to do it."

"Yasamin." Iskander's tone conveyed more warning than pleading.

"My aunt was right. She always said Allah put us in places for a reason, and because he does so, we should be happy where we are. I should never have allowed you in."

"But you did."

"I want you to leave. Now."

"As you wish."

When Yasamin turned around again, Iskander was gone.

FIFTY-NINE

Buda, Ottoman Hungary
11 Dhu al-Hijjah 1008
(13 June 1600 Old Style)

ISKANDER DID NOT APPEAR THE following evening or any evening after. Two weeks passed. Every night Yasamin remained awake as late as she could, hoping to see his familiar shadow. Every morning she woke up alone. She didn't know if she wanted to wrap her arms around him and lose herself in him again, or if she wanted to slap him and spit in his face. It didn't matter, she supposed. She knew she wanted to see him again.

The black eunuch who brought Yasamin her breakfast set the tray down with a flourish. The bracelets on his wrists jangled as he spread out his arms in a grand gesture and bowed. He gazed up at Yasamin, and with a broad, toothy grin and a glint of mischief in his eye, he nodded and winked.

Yasamin had noticed him a few weeks earlier. His easy smile and boisterous laugh had quickly made him a favorite in the *haremlık*. His lithe form was unlike most of the other eunuchs, and Yasamin admired his long, elegant fingers as he lifted a carafe and poured her a cup of thick, black coffee that filled the room with the scent of the forest on a crisp spring morning. Once his task was complete, he turned to leave.

"Wait," Yasamin said.

He glanced at her, one eyebrow raised. "Yes, *hanım effendi?*"

"What is your name?" Yasamin asked.

"Simon."

"Would you ... would you sit with me for a few minutes?"

He furrowed his brow in puzzlement, but only briefly before his smile returned. He nodded. "Of course."

He sat down cross-legged on the floor facing Yasamin. She studied him as she took a sip from her coffee cup. Simon could go places Yasamin could not, and from what Yasamin had heard, he knew all the secrets worth knowing.

"How did you come to be here, Simon?" she asked.

Again, he looked at her, brow furrowed, but then he nodded and embarked on the narrative of his life. His voice a rich tenor, he told Yasamin of being captured as a boy and being ... put into service as he called it. He served in a household in Damascus before being taken to Izmir, and then Sarajevo, and finally Ahmed Pasha's court in Buda. When he finished, he looked at Yasamin, the mischievous glint still in his eye. "But *hanım effendi*," he said, "surely the life of a mere eunuch is of no interest to the wife of Murad Pashazade."

The corners of Yasamin's mouth turned up in a faint smile. "It has become a slight obsession of mine lately, how

Allah arranges all the events of our lives. Today our lives, yours and mine, intersected. I was just curious to know the circumstances leading up to our meeting."

Simon chuckled. "Such serious thoughts for—"

"A woman?" Yasamin felt her cheeks flush. "Should I be thinking instead of my needlework? Or the latest bit of petty gossip? Or perhaps even my husband?"

Simon cleared his throat. "I mean no offense, *hanım effendi*, but someone of your beauty, to have an equally beautiful mind, it is a rare thing indeed. Incidentally, your husband does think of *you*."

"He does? He speaks of me then?"

"Occasionally."

Yasamin gazed into her cup of coffee, wondering for a moment if she should try to divine her future. "Well, it's nice to know I haven't been completely forgotten. What else does he speak of?"

"Many different things," Simon replied, glancing at the door.

"Simon, he is my husband. You are not betraying any confidences by telling me the things you have overheard. I promise not another soul will ever know we spoke."

Simon sighed. "War, *hanım effendi*. He talks of war."

"The war with the Germans has made everyone wary."

Simon shook his head. "That is not the war I mean."

"What other war is there?"

"I shouldn't talk about it."

"Simon, please. My husband does not send for me. I only wish to understand why."

Simon looked at her fearfully, but then his expression softened, and he broke into a resigned smile. "Very well, *hanım effendi*, I will do it for you, but this is dangerous knowledge."

Yasamin nodded. "I understand."

"You have no doubt heard of the illness that continues to afflict many of the janissaries. Ahmed Pasha consulted an old woman, a witch, who told him it was a curse placed upon him by his enemies, and that the only way to lift it was to send soldiers east, over the mountains, to kill an upstart prince."

Yasamin felt a chill in her veins. Ayla had said her grandmother, the one who told stories of the sinister blood-drinking djinn, was from someplace to the east over the mountains. "Has he already done so?" she asked.

"Not yet," replied Simon, "but he intends to soon, though Murad Pashazade is adamantly opposed."

"Why?"

Simon shrugged. "No one knows for sure. He had visitors to his room late into the night to discuss strategies."

"Strategies? What sort of strategies?"

"I do not know any more."

Yasamin gazed through the window to the garden.

"I'm sorry if I've troubled you," Simon said.

Yasamin managed a faint smile. "No, Simon, it's not you. Thank you for telling me. Now I'm sure you have other duties. I don't want to keep you any longer. Perhaps some other morning you can keep me company again."

Simon stood up and bowed. "It would be my pleasure, *hanım effendi.*"

HOURS STILL WERE LEFT UNTIL sunrise. Yasamin sat up in her bed, struggling in vain to stave off sleep, when she heard the music. The singer, a woman, keened the same song the *kemençe* player had played on her Henna Night; the same one Iskander had sung the first night he had come to her; and the same one she heard in her head every time she was with him.

She looked out her window to catch a glimpse of a figure in white meandering through the pomegranate trees in the moonlight. The figure turned and for a moment their eyes met. Yasamin backed away from the window as fast as she could. She had just seen Rabiye, only not as Yasamin remembered her, crying over the body of the dead janissary in the garden. Her skin was paler, her lips redder, and in her eyes, Yasamin saw something she could not describe, something feral, almost predatory. Yasamin peered out the window to see Rabiye disappear among the trees. She rushed out of the room and through the dim corridors down to the garden. Running down the path past the red-blossomed pomegranate trees, she stopped from time to time to listen for the song. She caught up with Rabiye again at the pond by the giant oak tree. Her janissary lover was there, the same one Yasamin had seen three times in the garden—the first time alive, the second time dead, and the third time alive again, peering into her window. He gripped a struggling Ine. Rabiye knelt down in the grass in front of the terrified girl. Yasamin gasped when she saw that Rabiye cast no reflection in the water of the pond.

One look at Rabiye, and Ine's face grew lax. The janissary let her go, but she didn't try to run away. As softly as one would touch a small child, Rabiye took Ine's head in her hands and guided her down until Ine's head rested in her lap. Not once did Ine resist. Rabiye stopped singing once more. She looked down at the girl and smiled, revealing long, inhuman fangs. She sunk them deep into Ine's neck. The servant girl's body twitched several times, and then went still. When Rabiye lifted her head again, blood covered her mouth and ran down her chin. She looked at Yasamin again and smiled.

Yasamin's fear took control of her body, and she ran. The jeering laughter of Rabiye and her janissary echoed off the stone walls. When she reached her room, she barricaded the door with whatever she could find. Until the sun rose, Yasamin stood watch. Even as the muezzins called the faithful to the first prayer of the day and sleep finally overtook her, she could not hold images of the bloody rite at bay when she closed her eyes, a rite she knew was staged especially for her.

SIXTY

—⟋m⟍—

Berlin, Germany
12 August 1999

"LIFE AND DEATH ARE CLOSELY intertwined," Yasamin explained. "To truly experience life, one must, on a certain level, experience death. Rabiye's janissary understood. He risked his life to be with her. Rabiye also understood. She risked her life as well. Without that risk, their love for each other would have meant nothing."

"But the death they received was not the type of death either of them contemplated," Adam replied.

"Does it matter?"

"It does. To their eternal souls."

"What do you care about their souls? Honestly, you are the last person I would expect to hold any beliefs at all. What has God ever done for you?"

"What I experienced growing up was nothing like Christian compassion. I had to believe in something better just to survive. Besides, I've seen too much since not to believe."

"And how many instances of Christian compassion have you seen in your life, Dr. Mire?"

Adam thought about Nadiye, the compassion in her eyes and her touch, her kindness to him when he needed it. He thought about Clara too, the "someone" he had told Anya about, though she had made it clear she wasn't willing to put up with his obsessions. He missed their endless talks, her readiness to laugh at his bad jokes, the way the corners of her mouth crinkled when she smiled. They were the only two people he would have ever died for, and he had failed them both in that regard. He was prepared to remedy his failure.

"Enough."

"Another lie, Dr. Mire. If that were so, you wouldn't be here. No, if the kindnesses you've experienced were enough to sustain you, you would be content to live your little life in your office, surrounded by your dusty books, listening to your students' petty problems."

Adam, again, couldn't answer.

"In fact," she continued, "you've endured so much to get here, I can't imagine simple curiosity over a magical trinket would justify any of it. Why are you here?"

Adam squeezed the cross on his rosary until it cut into his palm. "Revenge."

SIXTY-ONE

—⁕—

Thessaloniki, Greece
9 August 1999

"HELLO, DR. DIMITRIOU."
The man must have been hiding behind
her door. Marina spun around at the sound of
his voice. His pale eyes bore into her. He grinned, baring
his teeth.

"What are you doing in my office?" she asked.

A streak of white ran through his black hair. He wore
an old-fashioned waistcoat and, even more unusual for
Greece in August, black leather gloves. He bowed slightly.
"I'm waiting to speak to you."

"How did you even get in?"

The man shrugged. "The door was unlocked."

He blocked the only way out. Marina's blood ran cold.

"No, it wasn't."

The man's expression darkened. "Fine, then, I picked
the lock."

"If you don't leave now, I'm going to call security." She

couldn't keep her voice from wavering. She picked up the telephone on her desk, but in a fraction of a second, he covered the distance between them. He seized her arm and squeezed until she dropped the telephone. Maintaining his grip, he replaced the receiver.

As hard as she tried, she couldn't break free. "I can cry out."

The man retrieved a knife from his pocket and held it against her throat. The edge of the blade was stained brownish red. "I would recommend against doing that."

"What do you want?"

He drew her close and whispered in her ear. "You."

Marina's heart pounded. She scanned her desk for anything she could use as a weapon, but nothing was in reach. "I have an appointment. Any minute now he's going to be here."

The man chuckled. "Dr. Mire? Don't you worry. I'll be long gone by the time he arrives." He squeezed her arm again, and she winced. "I would like you to answer a question for me now."

"What?"

"Why did you lie to Dr. Mire?"

"I didn't—"

He jerked, and her protest ended in a choked whimper. "You told Dr. Mire you didn't know what Mihai Iliescu's father wrote in his journal. That's not entirely true, though, is it? You showed it to a colleague in the Department of Romance Languages, one who speaks Romanian. He translated it for you."

"Only a small part of it."

"Enough to bring me here."

"Who are you?" Marina asked.

"I am Chaos. I am Discord. I am Strife."

"You're insane."

"You're not the first to say that. Now answer my question. Why were you less than truthful with Dr. Mire?"

"I ... I wanted to help him," Marina said. "He looked so haggard. I knew he was in trouble, but I also knew he'd be too stubborn to let me help. The part of the journal I read, it described a medallion Mihai's father owned. He spoke of it almost as if it were cursed. I was going to see if I could find out more about it."

"Did Dr. Mire talk to you about this medallion?"

"No, but ... but I think I saw it once."

The man pressed down with the knife. "Where?"

"Mihai had it. Adam and I, we sometimes used his library for research. He had a number of books that ... weren't available anywhere else. I found the medallion when I was pulling a book off of a shelf. I thought it had fallen behind by accident. I showed it to Mihai, but he snatched it from me and put it back. He wouldn't talk about it."

"What you say is impossible."

"I swear it's the truth."

"You would stake your life?" the man asked.

"Yes," Marina replied, hot tears sliding down her face. "Please. You don't have to do this."

The man grinned again, showing his teeth. "Don't worry. I'm going to leave you to your appointment with Dr. Mire."

But he didn't put the dagger away.

SIXTY-TWO

Thessaloniki, Greece
9 August 1999

B EFORE HE COULD STOP HIMSELF, Adam reached
down and touched Marina's face. His hand came
back covered in her blood. His mind flashed back
to eight years earlier, when he found himself crouching
over the body of another woman. The same anger he felt
then exploded into searing rage. He snatched up a paper-
weight from Marina's desk and threw it through the window.

When he turned around, he came face-to-face with a
startled student standing in the open door. She looked
from him to Marina's body to his bloody hand, then
dropped her books and ran. Adam's first impulse was to
run after her to try to explain himself, but he knew it
wouldn't do any good. Instead, he ran in the opposite direction, hoping to make it back to his hotel.

His angry gesture, however, was already attracting a
crowd of students outside beneath the shattered window.

When Adam ran by, someone called out. Several members of the crowd gave chase. Adam stepped up his pace, but even as a few of his pursuers dropped off, the others gained. He scanned about, thinking he might have a better chance in the streets of Thessaloniki itself, away from the wide walkways and open, manicured lawns of the university campus. He turned a corner, only to find a pair of university security guards confronting him.

The two students still chasing him caught up and tackled him to the ground. One of the security guards pressed his face down into the concrete walkway while another handcuffed his hands behind his back. Then they jerked him upright and told him to stay seated. They didn't have to. He didn't even want to run anymore.

Over the next hour, while Adam sat bleeding from the scrapes on his face, something of a jurisdictional turf war went on in front of him. The police from the city of Thessaloniki joined the campus security, along with two men in suits Adam assumed to be representatives of the Hellenic Police. Judging from the heated gesturing and sharp-sounding words, he guessed they were arguing over who would get to interrogate him first.

Finally, one of the Hellenic Police officers pulled out a cellular phone and made a call. He talked to the person on the other end of the line for about a minute before handing the phone to one of the Thessaloniki policemen. The policeman listened and then handed back the phone, a stern look on his face. He and the others left, leaving only the two Hellenic Police officers.

The one with the cellular phone walked over to Adam and knelt in front of him. He said, in English, "Hello, Dr. Mire. A lot of people have been looking for you over the past few days."

"I didn't kill her," Adam said, barely above a whisper.

"I know," the officer replied.

He grabbed Adam underneath the arm and pulled him to his feet. He and the other officer led Adam to a white Citroën and shoved him into the backseat.

As they drove off, the officer spoke up again. "Of course, you understand you're still being held for questioning. You've left quite a string of bodies across southern Europe."

"Bodies?"

"Oh yes. Turhan Avci and Janos Kovács in Budapest, Drago Loncar and Slobodan Ilić near Novi Sad, Ibrahim Zorić in Banja Luka, Josip Basiljević in Dubrovnik. Impressive."

And Adam would bet his life that each and every one of them had a hand painted green. "I don't know anything about who murdered any of those people. I can prove I left each and every one of them alive."

"Of course you can. But you did have an accomplice."

"Accomplice? There's no accomplice. What are you talking about?"

"Several people have reported seeing you with a red-haired woman."

"Anya?"

"So that's her name, then?"

"No, I mean, yes, that's her name, but she's not my accomplice. In fact, she's in trouble, and she needs my help."

"Oh? How so?" he asked.

Adam opened his mouth to explain, but realized he couldn't. No matter what he said, the two police officers would never believe him. "I want a representative from the American consulate present when you question me," he said instead.

"Naturally," the officer replied. "But you understand there is protocol to follow. I can't guarantee a representative will be available right away. It may take a few days. In the meantime, we probably won't be able to release you. You'll be held in a cell, but if you cooperate, other accommodations could be made."

"Thank you for the kind offer, but I'll wait, if it's all the same to you."

The officer turned and looked him straight in the eye. "Trust me when I tell you our hospitality is far more preferable to the alternative. Things don't have to be difficult. Surely we can find common ground. The dead travel fast, Dr. Mire. We must travel faster."

For the dead travel fast.

A quote from *Dracula*. Adam shot him a questioning glance. If Adam had learned anything over the last several days, he had come to understand that nothing was a coincidence.

Adam had a hundred questions, but he would never have the chance to ask any of them. A car pulled into the Citroën's path. The officer driving punched the brakes, but the Citroën slammed into the car, throwing Adam against the back of the seat in front of him. When he sat up, the driver was slumped over the steering wheel. The other officer was shouting and fumbling for his cellular phone. Another car pulled into the street behind the Citroën and blocked them in. Four men emerged. Adam knew who they were immediately.

The Chetniks advanced toward the car. The officer stopped fumbling for his phone and reached into his jacket for his gun.

"Get down!" he barked at Adam before leveling the pistol and firing through the Citroën's back window. The

Chetniks scattered, drawing their own firearms. The officer fired again. One of the Chetniks went down, but the
other three continued to advance.

"Damn Chetniks," the officer said. "Where the hell did
they come from?"

"You know who they are?" Adam asked

"Of course. It's part of the job."

Bullets whizzed past the car. The officer fired, and another Chetnik went down. A thought nagged at Adam.
The remaining two Chetniks continued their slow advance
on the police car, firing back whenever they had the opportunity, but it was all wrong. The Chetniks were being
too cautious. The officer couldn't cover both of them at
once. They could have rushed the Citroën if they wanted.

Not until the fifth Chetnik loomed at the window did
Adam realize he had failed to account for the driver of the
car the Citroën hit. The Chetnik fired through the window, spraying the officer's blood and grey matter over the
front seat.

He yanked the back door open and pulled Adam out,
then shoved him toward the second car while the others
helped their wounded compatriots. All of them glared at
Adam with a hatred he couldn't understand. The largest
among them stuffed Adam, still handcuffed, into the backseat between two others. As they drove off, Adam could
hear the wail of sirens. After a few blocks, they changed
cars, one Chetnik remaining behind. They repeated the
maneuver again several minutes later. None of them
talked. The police sirens died away, and with them any
hope Adam had of being found.

"How did you even know I was here?" Adam asked in
Serbian after the third car change.

None of the Chetniks answered.

Adam smirked. "Magic, then."

The comment earned him a few angry glares, but sill none of them said a word. Adam scanned the buildings lining the streets they drove, hoping maybe for some clue he could use later, but after more than an hour of riding around Thessaloniki, he gave up. He was hopelessly, irretrievably lost. The car pulled into an alley behind a generic apartment building. The big Chetnik pulled Adam out of the car and forced him through the door used for deliveries. Several more pushed past him in the opposite direction, toward the two wounded Chetniks waiting in the car.

The barrel of a gun digging into his back, Adam walked down a hallway to an unadorned metal door. The Chetnik jerked the door open and shoved Adam inside, then slammed it shut. The door locked with a click. Adam found himself in a cramped storage closet without much in it, except for a bucket. High overhead, a window let in a small amount of light, but Adam couldn't see a way to reach it. With nothing left inside him, he slumped to the floor, thankful only that he wasn't running anymore.

SIXTY-THREE

Berlin, Germany
12 August 1999

THE SUN CONTINUED TO SINK lower in the sky. Adam shifted with the orange-hued light filtering through the window. With only a little time left until sundown, he hoped he would not have to wait much longer.

"I want revenge for Nadiye's death," he said.

"Revenge will not fill the emptiness you feel inside," Yasamin replied.

"Don't you think I know that?" He shook his head. "I'm not trying to fill the emptiness."

"Then what are you trying to do?"

Adam clenched his jaw. "All I want is for the person who killed her to suffer."

"You should be careful, Dr. Mire, when you wish suffering on others. You often bring down even more on yourself."

"An acceptable risk."

She leaned forward in her chair and extended an elegant hand toward him. "Look at yourself. You had an opportunity for happiness, and you let it go. You should leave now. Go away, back to America, back to this woman you say you left there."

"You just mocked that life."

Her eyes flashed with anger once more, but her voice lost some of its edge. "You have mocked that life by your actions. You have squandered opportunities and ignored every warning. You have failed to understand the value of a complacent, uneventful life. You don't deserve to have one, but if you leave now, there is a chance you can salvage what you've thrown away."

"And how do you propose I do that?"

"I cannot tell you everything, Dr. Mire, only that you don't have to make the same mistake as—"

"The same mistake as what?"

"The same mistake as I did."

SIXTY-FOUR

—〰—

Buda, Ottoman Hungary
18 Dhu al-Hijjah 1008
(20 June 1600 Old Style)

"Y" OUR HUSBAND, HANIM EFFENDI, WISHES to see you."

The eunuch at Yasamin's door refused to meet her gaze. With resignation, she pulled her veil across her face. She couldn't refuse a summons from her husband, no matter how much she wanted to remain hidden in her room, safe from the dark things she knew to lurk in the palace corridors. She expected Murad to make another awkward attempt to seduce her, but when she entered his chamber, he was not smiling.

"You told me your parents died in an accident—a fire as I remember," he said without any word of greeting.

Yasamin frowned, puzzled at the question. "Yes. My aunt told me."

Murad shook his head. "She lied."

Yasamin felt her cheeks start to burn. She balled her

hands into fists. She didn't understand why Murad would say such a thing, but she suddenly felt like striking him. "She would never do that. What possible reason could she have to lie?"

"To protect you from the truth, Yasamin."

"What truth?"

"This," Murad said, holding up a scroll. "There was a fatwa issued against your father, Yasamin, your entire family, actually. Your father and your mother were lawfully executed."

"Now you're the one who's lying, Murad. My father was a respected man. He served Allah faithfully. No one would dare accuse him of doing anything wrong without proof."

She tried to snatch the scroll out of Murad's hand. Each time he pulled it just out of reach. On her third attempt, he let her have it. She unfurled it and read while Murad watched her. When she finished, she let it drop to the floor.

"A fake," she said. "What it accuses my father of doing he couldn't have done. How could anyone do these things? How could anyone say these things about him? That he denounced Allah, that he drank the blood of animals? It isn't real. Can't you see?"

"So you don't believe he did those things?"

"He didn't." She threw the scroll at him. "I know he didn't."

"What if I told you he confessed?"

"I would say you were lying again." She glared at him. "Tell me you're lying."

Murad shook his head. "That I cannot do."

He held up another scroll. This time, she didn't have to grab it from him.

"This is a forgery," she said when she was finished reading. "It's not true. It's not. Where did you find these?"

"In my father's records room," Murad replied coolly.

"How long have you known about this?"

"A while."

"Since before we were married?"

Murad nodded.

"Then why did you marry me?" Yasamin asked.

"A calculated risk," Murad replied, "one that would have been well worth it, had we succeeded. Imagine my shock to discover it was all completely unnecessary."

"I don't understand."

He ignored her. "My father has been such a fool. All he understands is brute force. It's his solution to every problem, and Selim is exactly like him. Neither of them can see there are often better ways to defeat one's enemies, that swords and cannons are not always the best weapons." As he talked, he walked to the room's small window. He took a red sash from around his waist and hung it through the opening. "He doesn't even know what's in his own records room. It's a mistake he's going to pay for very soon."

"How soon?"

A twisted smile snaked across his face. "Now."

As soon as Murad spoke, a clamor arose, as if the gates of hell themselves had opened. Yasamin could hear men running and shouting, and soon screams echoed through the corridors. As quickly as it began, it ended. Silence blanketed the palace.

"Ahmed Pasha and Selim are dead now," Murad said. "It's a shame it had to happen this way. If my father had just listened to me, he would have been able to deal with the Germans, and he wouldn't have lost favor with the Sultan." He clenched his jaw. "If he had just listened."

Yasamin was not paying attention, however. Her strange visions all fell into place, like bloody shards of ceramic forming a grizzly mosaic. She remembered it all at once. Her father and her mother lying in a pool of blood. Kneeling next to her mother's body, her hands covered in sticky, red-purple liquid. A man standing over her as she knelt, holding a sword. Being scooped up into the arms of another man and carried away. Screaming and fighting him until he told her to be quiet, that he was saving her. He made her hide in a room full of blankets. He piled them on top of her and warned her not to move. She nearly suffocated, but she survived. Hadice was the one to find her hours later and arrange for her to be smuggled out of Banja Luka to Salonica to live with her aunt and uncle.

Yasamin remembered, because the sound of the murder of Ahmed Pasha was the same as the sound of the murder of her parents, a roar of frenzied violence followed by perfect stillness, as if the world needed time to adjust to the new reality before continuing.

"I won't make the same mistakes as Pasha as my father did," Murad said.

His words brought Yasamin back to the present. "Pasha? You?"

"Yes," Murad replied, "I am the new Pasha of Buda. The Sultan has already decreed."

"But how could the Sultan have already decreed?"

"I told you. My father should have listened to me. None of this had to happen. None of it would have if he had just listened. As usual, his stubbornness and his lack of imagination prevented him from seeing the bigger picture."

"What is the bigger picture?" Yasamin asked.

"That God is reflected in all things, even the Evil

One," Murad replied as he walked toward her. "It's a shame things didn't work out better between us, but you are my wife."

He grabbed her by the shoulders and kissed her.

She pushed him away. "What are you doing?"

"Taking what is mine."

He grabbed her again and pulled her to him for another kiss. She struggled but couldn't break free. He forced her down onto the pallet, his weight atop her body immobilizing her. She only began to scream, though, when she saw the two small punctures on his neck, in the same place Rabiye had bitten poor Ine.

AFTERWARD SHE LAY UNABLE TO move, even as Murad dressed himself.

"I hate you," she said, staring at the ceiling.

"I wish things had turned out differently between us, Yasamin." He knelt and stroked her hair. "I wish you could have come to love me, but in the end I suppose it doesn't matter."

Yasamin jerked away from him. "My aunt will know the truth. She'll tell me you're lying."

Murad snorted. "Don't be stupid, my dear. She'd inform you that you were considered unmarriable until my mother chose you to be my bride. She'd also tell you that she would have agreed to any marriage, no matter what the circumstances or conditions. She would tell you those things, that is, if she could."

"What do you mean?"

Murad picked up another scroll and threw it at her. She unfurled it and began to read.

"Honorable Murad Pashazade," it began. "I am Imam

Rakim of Salonica. I wish I were writing under better circumstances, but unfortunately, this letter comes to you bearing sad news. Your wife's family, her aunt and uncle and all of her cousins, have died in a terrible accident—a fire."

SIXTY-FIVE

—⟨⟨⟩⟩—

Buda, Ottoman Hungary
19 Dhu al-Hijjah 1008
(21 June 1600 Old Style)

PEALS OF THUNDER SHOOK THE window lattice like the cannon fire that still echoed across the hills. The thunder and the pounding rain woke Yasamin from a fitful sleep. The lightning revealed she wasn't alone in her room. A man sat with his back against the wall opposite her bed, watching her.

"Iskander?" she called out. "Is that you?"

Before the man could respond, another flash of lightning illuminated his face. It wasn't Iskander, but Selim, who was supposed to be dead. Moments later, the lightning revealed him at her bedside. He grabbed her and crushed his hand over her mouth. His hold was firm, but not harsh.

"Don't look at me," he said, "and don't scream when I take my hand away from your mouth. Just listen to what I have to say. Do you understand?"

She nodded. He removed his hand.

"First, who is Iskander?" he asked.

"No one," Yasamin replied. "You misheard me."

Selim grunted. "Whatever you say, though you know I'm in no position to judge you."

"Murad said you were dead."

"He was mistaken."

"How did you escape?"

"I'm Selim Pashazade, hero of a hundred battles against the infidels. Murad should have known better than to send only two soldiers to dispatch me. I sent them to their eternal rewards instead."

"What are you doing here, Selim Pashazade?"

"I want to warn you."

Yasamin laughed. "Warn me of what? Of Murad? I'm afraid you're a bit late. I hope you didn't risk your life for that. Now go away before you get us both killed."

"You could come with me."

"Come with you? Where?"

"Sarajevo. I think we can both find refuge there."

"Why are you doing this?"

"Because you deserve better than Murad."

"You don't know that to be true."

"How is what I said untrue?"

"You don't have time for me to number the reasons."

"I don't care about the reasons."

Yasamin sighed. "You're a fool to say that. You're also a fool to think you'll make it to Sarajevo alive."

"Then I'm a fool. But I have to try. All I have left is the hope that tomorrow, when the sun comes up, things will be better somehow. In that, I think we are a lot alike. Please, come with me."

He offered his hand to her. Yasamin started to place

her hand in his, but she hesitated. "Murad told me he saved your life once. Is that true?"

"It is," Selim said, an edge in his voice.

"What happened?"

Selim exhaled a long breath through his nose. "I made an error. I got lost. I led our division into a thicket where we stumbled upon a group of German soldiers. Most of them were too weak to even fight us, all except for one. He attacked like a crazed animal. He would have killed me, had it not been for Murad. Until yesterday, it was the worst day of my life. "

"Why did you tell everyone that you saved his life?"

"I didn't. You of all people know how gossip makes its way around this place and how easily things get distorted. I am Selim Pashazade. I don't make mistakes. By the time I heard what was being said, it was too late to correct it. I was indebted to my brother for what he did. I expressed my gratitude, but I suppose everyone's failure to recognize his deed embittered him, as did your rejection of him."

"I never rejected him," Yasamin protested.

"Didn't you?"

"He was not what I envisioned my future husband to be. I was expecting someone more like—" She stopped.

"More like me," Selim finished.

"Possibly."

"Ilker's death also came as a blow to him," Selim said. "He was the first to die of the janissary plague. They had been friends since they were children. But none of these things explain what he has done. It seems to me another is influencing his actions, although I don't know who that could be."

Yasamin thought of the puncture wounds on Murad's neck, but she didn't say anything. Selim held out his hand again. Yasamin was about to take it when two eunuchs, swords unsheathed, burst into the room.

"Selim Pashazade," one of them said, "submit to the will of Allah."

"I always do," he replied.

The eunuchs blocked the door and his only escape, but as they advanced on him, he ran and threw all his weight against the lattice on Yasamin's window. It shattered outward. He sailed through the air, down to the ground below. A flash of lightning allowed Yasamin to see him running into the garden. The two eunuchs ran out of her room without so much as acknowledging her.

Yasamin saw the eunuchs emerge in the garden to pursue Selim. Others joined them, but she lost them all in the trees. As the agonizing minutes dragged by, she sat at the window peering into the darkness, unable to see or hear anything but the downpour. The rain came in, soaking her, but she didn't care. She wanted Selim to escape. She wanted him to come back for her.

When lightning illuminated the world again, though, she saw the two eunuchs standing in the garden below her window, swords bloodied. One of them held Selim's severed head. Yasamin covered her mouth with her hand and backed away from the window. She felt her gorge begin to rise. As she fought to keep it down, someone behind her spoke.

"I warned them you would bring nothing but trouble," came the raspy voice, "but no one listens to an old woman."

Yasamin turned to face Nesrin. "I don't know what I've done to attract your ire, but for what it's worth, I wish I had never come here either. I should have stayed in Salonica and died in the same fire as my aunt and uncle."

Nesrin hobbled into the room, her cane hitting the floor with a rhythmic thud. She placed a bony hand on Yasamin's shoulder.

"You misunderstand me, dear," she said. "I know you've done nothing wrong."

"Then why do you dislike me so?"

"How much do you know about how your parents died?"

"I know they were murdered," Yasamin replied, "and I witnessed it. I didn't remember until … until last night."

"Do you know why they were murdered?"

"There was a fatwa—"

"No."

"But I saw it. I read it."

"A mere excuse. By Allah, child, do you know nothing about your own family?"

"Apparently I don't."

Nesrin snorted. "I suppose your aunt thought she was protecting you. Your father was an important man, Yasamin, more important than perhaps even he knew. He was charged by the Sultan himself with the keeping of a special artifact, just as his father had been, and his father before him going back more than a hundred years to a battle against the infidels, who were led by a man known as the *Kazıklı Bey*."

Yasamin stiffened at the mention of the *Kazıklı Bey*, the infidel prince from the letters of Kemal the army captain.

"Is something the matter?" Nesrin asked.

"No, I remember the name only from stories my mother and my aunt used to tell me to try to scare me. I didn't think that he was real."

"He was real," Nesrin said, "and he was a monster. His one goal was to destroy the Abode of Peace. By Allah's grace, the Sultan's army prevailed that day, and the *Kazıklı Bey* was killed. Your father's ancestor claimed to have been the one to kill him. As a reward, the Sultan created a special office for him and charged him with keeping the Impaler Prince's medallion in order to remind everyone of the inevitable triumph of the Abode of Peace. Your father was the last keeper of the medallion. After he was murdered, it disappeared."

"I still don't understand what this has to do with me."

Nesrin sighed. "It has to do with you, Yasamin, because it's the reason Hadice chose you as Murad's bride. They were convinced you knew where the medallion was. Murad has been overshadowed by his younger brother ever since Selim was born. He and Hadice both thought that if he could retrieve the medallion, he could finally gain his father's favor."

Yasamin shook her head. "I still don't believe my aunt would ever agree to anything like that."

"She didn't have much of a choice, Yasamin. You were unmarriable because of what happened to your parents. It's a miracle you weren't killed with them."

Yasamin remembered the man who had taken her and hidden her. "Yes, I suppose it is, but I don't know where this medallion is, and if Murad truly needed it to secure his place, what happened? What changed?"

"I believe he found it."

"What do you mean? How?"

"There are stories that say the Impaler Prince did not die that day on the battlefield, or if he did, he didn't remain dead. I believe the fatwa was engineered by him as a means of exacting revenge on your family and retrieving the medallion."

"That's impossible. You yourself said that the battle

was over a hundred years ago. How could he still be alive?"

Nesrin chuckled. "My dear, you are much too young to tell me what is possible and what is not. I have seen many things in my long life, and I can tell you this. There are dark powers in this world, and there are people who would think nothing of using those powers for their own purposes, no matter the consequences."

Yasamin wondered if she should tell Nesrin what she had seen.

"Now I fear he has come back," Nesrin continued. "For what reason, I don't know, but I suspect it has to do with you. I have tried to protect you. I wrote words of protection on your hands at your Henna Night. I had Murad give you the silver necklace. I've left charms outside your door on many a night. At least you are still safe, my dear. And I will do my best to keep you that way. As for Murad, his day of reckoning will come, sooner than he thinks."

She slipped something into Yasamin's hand, shaped like a teardrop, with a rough, bumpy surface—a head of garlic. Nesrin turned and hobbled out of the room, leaving her alone, the storm still raging outside her broken window.

Only a few moments later, though, Nesrin called out. "Ine! I need a light to see my way! Ine! Bring a candle!"

Yasamin rushed out into the corridor. Nesrin and Ine had their backs to her, silhouetted in the light of the candle Ine held. In her other hand, she held something else. The candlelight glinted off the blade of a knife.

"No!" Yasamin screamed.

Ine and Nesrin both turned to look at her, but Yasamin was too late. Ine buried the blade in Nesrin's side. A gurgling sound escaped Nesrin's lips before she collapsed to the ground like a sack of old clothes. Ine retracted the knife and threw it down, snuffed the candle, and ran.

Yasamin groped her way in the darkness to where Nesrin lay and knelt down beside her. A pool of blood already spread across the floor. The warm liquid soaked into Yasamin's trousers. The old woman still breathed, but each breath was more labored and shallower than the last. Yasamin felt for the place where the knife had gone into Nesrin's side. She tried to stop the flow of blood, but there was so much. Nesrin's breathing came in fits and starts, then stopped.

The next flash of lightning showed the knife lying in the congealing blood next to Nesrin. Yasamin picked it up. She recognized the jeweled hilt. It was the same knife Ayla had used to try to kill her in the abandoned washroom.

SIXTY-SIX

Berlin, Germany
12 August 1999

"WHERE IS HE?" ADAM ASKED.

"Who?"

"You know who I mean. Iskander. Alexandru. The *Kazıklı Bey*. Prince Vlad III Țepeș, the Impaler. The Son of the Dragon. Dracula."

The shadows churned and roiled, threatening to overwhelm Adam's tiny square of safety. He stood his ground.

"You risk invoking him by calling his names," Yasamin said.

"Let him come, then. Let him come and fight his own battles rather than have others do it for him. He did his own dirty work in Buda. Why can't he do it now? Where is he?"

"No one knows," she whispered.

"What do you mean?"

"He has disappeared."

"Disappeared? How long has he been missing?"

Her voice was quiet, her tone even. "For almost ten years."

Adam's eyes grew wide. "December 1989. The Romanian Revolution. The overthrow of Nicolae Ceaușescu."

She nodded.

"What happened?" asked Adam.

"If I knew that, I certainly would not be talking to you."

"That's why you want the medallion. You hope you can use it to find him."

"Possibly."

"What if he has purposefully gone into hiding? Or what if he has been destroyed?"

Yasamin's eyes narrowed. "He has not been destroyed."

"Do you have any clue where the medallion might be?"

"Dr. Mire, I don't have any reason to help you."

"Not yet."

She raised an eyebrow. "What do you mean?"

Adam didn't answer, posing instead more of his own questions. "Tell me about his dealings with Nicolae Ceaușescu. How long has he been manipulating history? What does he hope to accomplish?"

"Really, Dr. Mire, his desires are modest. He simply wishes to rule over his realm in peace. He has been trying to do so ever since the beginning."

"So at the turn of the seventeenth century, he was using Michael the Brave to build the empire he failed to build when he was alive. He used you to get close to your husband, so the Ottomans in Hungary wouldn't interfere."

"An astute assessment."

"Michael the Brave's letters ends before his execution, of course, and there is only a short note in Ioan Nicolescu's book about his death. I would have liked to know the real story."

Her mouth curled up into the twisted grin he knew would haunt him from that day forward, if there were, in fact, any more days. "Oh, but you can."

"Did *he* tell you what happened?"

"No. I found the priest who accompanied Michael the Brave that night." Her eyeteeth grew long and sharp. "Let's just say he gave me his confession."

SIXTY-SEVEN

The "confession" of Father Dumitru

Sâncrai, Transylvania
9 August 1601 Old Style

M Y HAND SHAKES AS I write this, my last letter.
Death lurks close by. She will find me soon, and
I fear I will not have enough time to tell this
story, one I have dared not share with another soul. There
are those who may brand me a lunatic, but I write only
the truth.

OUR PARTY THAT NIGHT CONSISTED of three—Prince
Michael, Alexandru, and me. The man we had come to
meet insisted upon it. When we reached the edge of the
churchyard, Alexandru stopped, refusing to venture any
farther toward the church, though the tiny building hardly
qualified as such. It was a pile of stones, devoid of decora-
tion save for a roughly hewn wooden cross on its roof.

"Go on, Your Grace," Alexandru said, "and you as well, Father. You mustn't keep the general waiting. I'll stand here, to keep watch."

A gust of wind threatened to blow out the lantern the prince held, but we kept walking even as the flame spit and sputtered, fighting for its life. I thought Alexandru's actions suspicious at the time. I made no secret about the fact that I never trusted the *boyar*, but that night I did not have time to work though his motives. No more than twenty paces into the churchyard, His Grace and I came face-to-face with the fat, grinning Albanian, General Georgio Basta.

"Your Grace," he said, "so glad you could make our appointment."

"Tell me what the purpose is behind dragging me out here in the middle of the night," His Grace demanded.

General Basta's smile widened, revealing his teeth. "My apologies, Michael, but it couldn't wait. We have much to discuss."

"What requires discussion in a graveyard?"

In the light of the lantern, the general's face took on a malevolent cast. "Your transgressions."

I watched His Grace in the dim light. Though he did not show it, I knew General Basta's comments incensed him. "My transgressions? You're one to talk, Georgio. You lost control of Transylvania and had to ask for my help. Now we're back to where we were two years ago. Why are we bickering in this graveyard when we should be working to push Jan Zamyoski and his Polish paymasters out of Moldavia?"

"I'm not talking about how you have ineptly squandered your victories, Your Grace. I'm talking about the company you keep. The emperor draws the line at making pacts with the devil."

The prince's eyes narrowed. "What do you mean?"

General Basta pointed at Alexandru. "I mean this monster you call your friend."

"Alexandru isn't a monster," the prince protested. "He's done more to stand against the threat of the Turks than anyone. He is a zealous defender of the Faith."

"Then ask yourself why he won't enter onto consecrated ground."

I thought I heard Alexandru chuckle.

"What are you saying?" His Grace asked.

"It's ironic. If it hadn't been for a goatherd doing decidedly un-Christian things in the woods one night, we wouldn't have known at all."

"Start explaining yourself, Basta," His Grace growled.

"A man named Lucian, who lived in the village of Şelimbăr, was tried and convicted of practicing witchcraft against his neighbors. By way of a confession, he told a story of something he witnessed in the forest almost two years ago on a chilly October night. He said he came upon two men arguing. One was tall and fair. The other was dark, with a black mustache. Andrei Cardinal Báthory and your friend Alexandru."

"That's impossible," His Grace protested. "How did this goatherd know who these men were?"

General Basta wagged his finger at the prince, much like someone would at a misbehaving child. "You forget, Your Grace, Cardinal Báthory's face was on all the coins. As for your friend Alexandru, a large medallion held his cloak in place. As it flashed in the moonlight, the goatherd could see it looked like some sort of serpent curled in a circle. Does that sound familiar to you?"

"What of it, Basta? Cardinal Báthory was already defeated, and everyone knows he escaped the battle only to be found dead—in the woods—a few weeks later. If Alexandru saw fit to hunt him down like the dog he was, then what is the harm?" His Grace glanced back over his shoulder and met Alexandru's eye. "I can't understand why he would neglect to tell me he did such a thing, but I'm certain he has a good reason."

"Oh, he does, a very good reason. They had an agreement. Cardinal Báthory let you win that day on the battlefield. In return, he quite irrationally believed Alexandru would grant him immortality."

Alexandru hissed. His hand went to the sword at his side, but he did not lift his foot to step onto the churchyard.

The prince laughed as he turned to face the general again. "Immortality? Now I know you're lying, Basta. Cardinal Báthory was many things, but he was not an idiot."

"I never said he was an idiot, Your Grace," General Basta replied. "You've heard the stories. Immortality is obtainable—for a price. The goatherd said that Alexandru was angry because you had nearly been killed in the battle, not to mention the fact that one of the Cardinal's men shot him. Tell me, Your Grace, did you ever ponder how a man could be shot at such close range and emerge unscathed?"

"Alexandru said it was merely a glancing blow."

General Basta raised an eyebrow. "Did you see him get shot?"

The prince shook his head. "Only at a distance."

"And did you see his armor afterwards? Did he show you where the pellets glanced off?"

"No," His Grace replied.

General Basta held up his hands. "Then how do you know he's telling you the truth?"

"Because unlike you, he is an honest man."

"He is not a man." General Basta spat out the words. "Cardinal Báthory's apologies and excuses fell on deaf ears. The goatherd said Alexandru pounced on the Cardinal like an animal. He ripped out the Cardinal's throat with nothing more than his hands and his teeth. And then he lapped up the blood gushing from the hole he made. If you don't believe me, why don't you ask Alexandru yourself?"

His Grace turned in time to see three soldiers emerge from hiding places in the wood surrounding the church. They charged at Alexandru. The *boyar* drew his sword and ran all three soldiers through before the unfortunate men had time to raise their own weapons, but in that instance I saw it, and so did the prince. Alexandru's dogteeth grew into fangs, and his eyes burned red like the fires of hell. Seconds later, his face reverted to normal, but it was too late. We had seen his true nature. The veracity of General Basta's story was no longer in doubt.

"Your Grace," Alexandru called.

The prince simply backed away, the pain of betrayal all too evident in his expression.

"Your Grace, you mustn't believe him," Alexandru said.

The prince shook his head. "I trusted you. I treated you like a brother."

"We are brothers," Alexandru replied, "bound by something even stronger than blood."

"Then prove it," His Grace said. "Step into the churchyard."

Alexandru bowed his head for a moment. When he raised it up, his eyes burned red with hellfire again. When he spoke, the voice was equally his own and not his own. "I could have made our nation great once more."

From everywhere soldiers emerged, swords drawn. Several of them seized His Grace, bound his hands, and forced him to his knees. From behind the gravestone nearest General Basta, a Roman Catholic priest appeared. He held a crucifix aloft and began to chant as he stalked toward Alexandru. The creature that masqueraded as a *boyar* shrieked, an altogether inhuman sound.

"Crux sacra sit mihi lux."

The Latin rite to repel the devil. I knew it well.

"Non draco sit mihi dux."

Draco. I never told His Grace I had eavesdropped on his conversation with the old Gypsy at the palace in Jassy. I hadn't been able to solve the Gypsy's riddle either. That night I cursed myself for being so blind. *Draco* is Latin for *snake.* "I do not want what the snake offers," the incantation says. *Draco* also means *dragon*, however. When the old Gypsy told His Grace he had to kill the man who bound himself with the snake, he meant Alexandru.

"Vade retro satana."

Alexandru screamed again and fell to his knees, but the pounding of my own heart nearly drowned out the sound.

"Numquam suade mihi vana."

"You've allied yourself with a child of Satan, Your Grace," General Basta said. Then he turned to me. "Please, Father, step out of the way. I am certain you had nothing to do with this."

I should have defended His Grace. I should have said something, anything, but one look at Alexandru's face— contorted in pain and rage, more animal than man—and the words left me. I stepped away.

"Sunt mala quae libas."

General Basta drew his sword and approached the prince. "Everything you have done, Your Grace, is tainted by your association with him."

"Ipse venena bibas."

With one last howl, Alexandru disappeared in a puff of greasy black smoke, just as General Basta's sword separated the prince's head from his shoulders.

SHE WILL SOON BE HERE. My only prayer, my only hope, is that someone will find this note I've scribbled and recognize the events of that inauspicious night for what they were. My faith in the Lord remai—

SIXTY-EIGHT

—✺—

Thessaloniki, Greece
9 August 1999

A DAM TRIED HIS HARDEST NOT to cry out as searing pain tore through his left hand. Sweat poured
down his forehead and stung his eyes. He had almost broken free, but the cuff still wouldn't fit over his
hand. He didn't know how long he had been in the closet.
The sun had set hours earlier, and in that entire time he
hadn't seen or heard anyone. For all he knew, they weren't
even coming back.

He didn't know if he could put himself through that
sort of pain again, but every time he felt like giving up, the
events of Nadiye's last night played over again in his head.

AT ABOUT EIGHT O'CLOCK IN the evening on the worst
day of Adam's life, the ringing phone jogged him out of a
doze. Nadiye's voice sounded frantic. She told him that
Serhan and his friend Tarik never showed up for dinner. A

quick trip to Serhan's dormitory room had proven futile. He wasn't there either.

Nadiye had always been protective of her brother. Everyone else in their family regarded him as the screw-up, but Nadiye saw something in him no one else could. Perhaps Serhan didn't see it himself. She made him enroll in university, even though he didn't want to, and she kept after him to keep his grades up, which he did most of the time. But some of the people he chose to spend time with concerned her.

"Are you at his dormitory now?" Adam asked.

"No," Nadiye answered. "His roommate said he and Tarik came in about an hour ago in a huge rush. They grabbed a bag from Serhan's closet and left. His roommate said they mentioned something about going to the lodge for a 'meeting.'"

"The dervish lodge in Eminönü he dabbled with last year? I thought that was over."

"So did I. Adam, the city elections are tomorrow."

He could hear the tremor of fear in her voice. "Nadiye, Serhan's a smart kid. He's not going to do anything stupid."

"I hope you're right."

The dervish lodge in question identified itself with the Bektaşi Order, the same religious order followed by the janissaries of the Ottoman Empire. This lodge, however, was also known for its outspoken conservative political views. They opposed the secular candidates running for office in the elections, candidates who were projected to win handily, barring something unforeseen.

"Where are you now, Nadiye?"

"At a pay phone across the street from the lodge."

"Stay there. I'm coming."

When Adam arrived, he didn't find Nadiye or Serhan. The lodge was dark. Adam, flashlight in hand, pushed open the main door of the medieval, dome-shaped building. It swung open with a creak that echoed through the black hall. Cold, damp air confronted him, and from somewhere in the darkness came the sound of running water. Adam crossed the hall's expanse. He could almost hear the droning dervish music the devotees used in their rituals. As he neared the back of the hall, the sound of running water grew louder until he reached a doorway. A sweep of his flashlight revealed a set of stone stairs leading downward.

As much of Istanbul was underground as above. Buried layers of civilization existed going back thousands of years to the time when Byzantion was a tiny Greek fishing village on the shores of the Bosporus. The stairs could have led anywhere—a forgotten temple, ancient waterworks, smuggling tunnels, catacombs. Adam knew only that he had to descend.

Before he could, though, he heard voices shouting and the sound of running footsteps. Seconds later Tarik and Serhan emerged from the blackness, as if ascending from hell. They collided with Adam, and the three stumbled to the stone floor in a heap. Serhan and Tarik scrambled back to their feet and kept running. Adam was a few seconds behind.

"Serhan," he called, shining the flashlight in their direction, "Serhan, it's Adam."

Serhan stopped and whipped around to face Adam. "What are you doing here?"

"Nadiye called me."

"Why would she do that?"

"Because she was afraid you were going to do something

stupid." The blood on Serhan's neck and hands glistened in the beam of Adam's flashlight. He grimaced. His breathing was labored. "Are you hurt?" Adam asked. "I think we need to get you to a doctor."

"It's nothing."

"It doesn't look like 'nothing.'"

"I'm fine," Serhan spat. "You wouldn't understand, professor."

"Where's Nadiye?"

Serhan shrugged. "How should I know?"

"We have to find her."

A noise echoed from down below, a low growl, like metal scraping on stone.

"Serhan," Tarik said.

"Don't worry. We're getting out of here now, something I would suggest you do as well, Mr. Mire."

Adam shook his head. "Not without Nadiye."

"Suit yourself, but remember I warned you."

He backhanded Adam across the face, and Adam tumbled backward to the floor. The flashlight clattered on the stone and went dark. Serhan's and Tarik's footfalls bounced off the shadowed ceiling as they ran for the door. Dazed, Adam lay for a few more moments in the darkness, gathering his wits before sitting up.

The same scraping noise welled up again, only louder. Whatever made it was coming up the stairs. As Adam scrambled backward on his hands and feet, his hand brushed against the flashlight, and he fumbled to get it working again.

The beam danced over the figure of a woman with long, dark hair standing in the doorway. She shielded her face from the light. At first, Adam thought it was Nadiye, but soon realized it was a different woman entirely. Her clothes were ripped and stained, and blood covered her hands. She reached a dripping hand toward Adam but jerked it back, as if suddenly burned. She shrieked and disappeared, seeming to dissipate into the darkness.

Everything inside Adam told him to run, but he knew he couldn't. He had to find Nadiye. Slowly, he stood and groped his way to the door. Probing for each step, he went downward. At the bottom, the dampness soaked through his shoes, and the low ceiling forced him to crouch.

"Nadiye!" he called.

He heard nothing in reply except for the ever-present water. With one hand on the slick wall, he took a few tentative steps. Only a few feet into the tunnel, he stepped on something. He stooped to pick it up, and his hand closed around a piece of wood. He drew his fingers along the length. It tapered to a sharp point. In the dampness, the piece of wood couldn't have been there long. He guessed Serhan must have dropped it.

Seconds later, a hand rested on his shoulder. Adam jumped and turned around to face Nadiye.

"Hello, Adam," she said.

Her eyes burned an unnatural red, and even as Adam stared at her, her canine teeth grew longer and sharper. He glanced down at the wooden stake in his hand.

THE MEMORY STEELED ADAM, AND he braced himself. While grasping his left thumb in his right hand, he slammed his right arm into the wall. The force turned his left thumb, and with a crack, the thumb dislocated, shifting inward. The pain shooting up his left arm nearly caused him to black out.

He sat for a few minutes, taking deep breaths, then

slipped the cuff off his left hand. He winced again as the cuff scraped against his injured thumb. With his hands free, he worked to pop the thumb back into place. While he could still move it, the pain doubled him over every time he tried.

The first step accomplished, he could do nothing but wait. As every minute ticked by, the angrier he became. It welled up inside him just as it had in Marina's office. Nadiye. Clara. He could have stopped it all if only he hadn't been so preoccupied with his own problems. Everyone in his life he had loved had been taken from him, but the truth he never wanted to confront overwhelmed him with undeniable clarity. It was his fault. Every time.

It would never be his fault again.

When the door finally opened an hour or so later, Adam was ready. The Chetnik made it halfway through before Adam threw himself against the door. His weight, combined with that of the heavy metal door, drove the Chetnik into the jamb. He came away with his nose mangled and gushing blood. Adam followed up with a right hook that sent him to the floor. He stepped over the unconscious Chetnik and into the hallway, which he found deserted. Adam wondered as he ran toward the exit if the unfortunate man lying on the floor had been sent to retrieve him or something worse.

He reached the door leading outside and threw it open only to be confronted with two more Chetniks on the other side, guns already drawn. Adam ducked between them and kept running. Bullets whizzed over his head. Adam recalled that afternoon when the Chetniks' aim had been suspiciously poor as well. They were deliberately missing. They wanted him alive.

With the Chetniks' footsteps thudding on the pavement behind him, Adam rounded the corner of the building and followed the alleyway back to the main street, where he discovered a movie had just let out of the theatre.

He ran toward the crowd and when he reached the edge, he joined in with the laughing, happy moviegoers. He ducked as he weaved in and around the clusters of people, glancing over his shoulder on occasion to see if the Chetniks were still following. The crowd began to disperse, people streaming into the coffee shops and restaurants lining the street. Adam chose a group of people close to his own age and followed them into a coffee shop. Fortunately, it was elbow-to-elbow inside. Adam pushed his way into a corner, away from the windows. He planned to stay there for a little while, until he thought it was safe to venture out again.

He didn't look at the man who sat down at the table with him until he spoke.

"Hello, Adam," Serhan said, grinning. "What are the odds of meeting up like this twice in one week? The universe seems full of coincidences sometimes, doesn't it?"

Adam had no words to respond.

Serhan glanced down at Adam's bruised and swollen thumb, his expression taking on mock concern. "Oh, look. You've hurt your hand."

He slammed his fist down on Adam's wounded thumb.

SIXTY-NINE

—∿∿—

Thessaloniki, Greece
10 August 1999

THEY LEFT THE CITY BEHIND, headed inland. Some-
time in the small hours of the morning, the car
pulled off the main road onto a long gravel driveway. The rocks crunched underneath the tires as the car
bounced over the rutted track. With every bump, the
muzzle of the gun dug into Adam's side. He sat in the
backseat, sandwiched between Tarik and Serhan, his
hands bound once again.

Tarik held the gun, a small .22 he had used to prod
Adam out of the café while keeping it hidden from the
other patrons. Adam had thought about running then, of
letting Tarik shoot him there, but he didn't want to put
anyone else in danger. His stupid decisions were his own.
He would bear the consequences.

Black shapes loomed on either side of the driveway,
gnarled limbs reaching out for the car and its occupants—
olive trees, misshapen from years of neglect. The car

crested a small rise, and a white house came into view directly ahead. The moonlight gave it a ghostly glow. Another car was already parked at the end of the driveway. The driver eased their car alongside it. Serhan opened the door and climbed out, and Tarik nudged Adam to follow. They began to push him around the house toward the back.

Adam studied the ramshackle structure in the middle of the olive orchard. One corner of the front porch sagged. The front door hung at an odd angle. The paint was cracked and chipped, and one of the chimneys had toppled. The house's darkened windows reminded Adam of the hollow eyes of a skull, yet they seemed to watch him, attentive, alert, as if in ghoulish anticipation. Adam held no delusions. He knew what he would see when their group rounded the final corner.

A hole had already been dug.

Two others waited for them, making five Blades total, including Tarik, Serhan, and their driver. Tarik marched Adam right to the grave and forced him to his knees at the edge of its dark, gaping mouth. Serhan knelt next to him.

"It didn't have to be this way," Serhan said. He held up the picture of Bahram Ashrafi and his future wife taken on their visit to Thessaloniki. "This woman. This Yasamin Ashrafi. It's her, isn't it?"

Adam choked down the words he wanted to say. "You found my satchel."

Serhan smiled. "Right where you left it. In the lady professor's office."

"The 'lady professor' had a name."

"I'm sure she did, but she's not the woman I want to talk about. You had pictures of this Yasamin—dozens. And stories, too. You've been thorough. You could say obsessed even."

"No more obsessed than you."

"I do what Allah commands, and I answer to Him alone."

"If there is any justice in the world, you will someday answer to Him."

Serhan glared. "You talk big, Adam, but that's all it is, talk. We never needed you, your unmatched knowledge Old Serbian, your fondness for obscure historical facts no one else knows or cares about, your brilliant deductive reasoning. We just needed your satchel." He stood. "Yasamin nearly robbed me of my sanity. We're going to rob her of her vile existence."

Adam snorted. "Or you'll die trying."

Serhan leaned down until his face was inches from Adam's. His lips were drawn back n a snarl. "You are the reason we're here now. You had your chance to cooperate in Banja Luka. Do you honestly think you could ever defeat her by yourself? All you had to do was let us help you."

"Like you helped Nadiye?"

Serhan let forth a string of curses and backhanded Adam across the face. The force of the blow almost toppled him into the hole. Serhan pulled an object from his pocket. Anya's gold hair clip, the one he had bought for her in Dubrovnik, flashed in the moonlight. Reddish-brown smears marred the etched pattern of roses.

"Anya," Adam whispered.

"Something to remember her by," Serhan said before he tossed the hair clip into the hole, where it disappeared in the shadows. He stood. "Good-bye, Adam. It's been a pleasure sparring with you."

As he walked away, Adam called after him. "You're not going to do it yourself? You're still a coward, Serhan."

Serhan stopped, but didn't turn around. "Not like you? Fearful of living his own life, trapped in the past, haunted by the ghosts of things that never were? We're all cowards, Adam. The difference is that I'm going to live to see the sunrise. Now if you'll excuse me, I have a plane to catch."

He nodded to the driver who had brought them there. The two of them disappeared around the corner of the house. Moments later, a car engine sputtered to life, and the gravel of the driveway crunched underneath the car's tires as it headed back toward the main road.

That left three.

Not great odds, especially with Adam's hands tied, but he was out of options. Without further ceremony, Tarik leveled his gun at Adam's head. Adam twisted to the side and rammed his shoulder into Tarik's knee. The gun fired, the bullet searing a path inches from Adam's face. Tarik toppled into the hole, and the gun fell from his hand.

Adam pushed himself to his feet in an effort to get to the dropped gun before Tarik clambered out of the grave. One of the other two Blades charged at Adam with his knife drawn. Adam ducked the man's swing and then planted an elbow in his midsection. The man's own momentum sent him tumbling into the grave as well, his surprised yelp cut off midway by a sharp crack when his head hit the opposite side. The Blade landed on top of Tarik, forcing them both to the dirt floor. Adam peered over the edge to see the man's neck bent at an unnatural angle.

Tarik heaved the Blade's body off and within seconds was already halfway out of the grave, again reaching for the gun. Adam stomped on his hand with the heel of his shoe and then tried to kick Tarik in the face, but Tarik caught his foot. Adam lost his balance and fell hard on his back.

The third Blade blocked his view of the sky. Adam

rolled out of the way just as the Blade's knife came down, sticking in the hard earth. Adam grabbed him by the leg with his bound hands, in an effort to make him fall. When that failed, Adam rolled again and bounded to his feet. He picked the knife up and squared off against the Blade, a barrel-chested man Adam guessed they brought along more for his skills with a shovel than his fighting prowess.

Adam charged, the knife held in front of him for an upward jab—about all he could do with his hands bound. The Blade sidestepped him with more agility than Adam expected and clutched his arm, trying to wrest the knife away. The two struggled back and forth over the knife until the Blade forced Adam off balance. Adam stumbled and fell, but the Blade couldn't arrest his own momentum, and he toppled on top of Adam.

Immediately, Adam felt something wet and warm oozing between his fingers. For a moment, Adam's eyes met the Blades, and in them Adam could see a mixture of confusion and pain. The Blade's breath came in short gasps. He reared up and rolled off Adam. Blood poured from the knife wound in his stomach. Moments later, the pain and the confusion—and the life—left the Blade's eyes. Adam climbed to his feet and turned around to find himself staring down the barrel of Tarik's gun.

"You're like the cat," Tarik said, a vicious grin on his face, "so many lives, but even the cat runs out eventually."

Adam waited for the gunshot.

It never came.

Tarik lurched forward. The grin vanished, his mouth thrown open in shock. He fell face-first to the ground, his arm hanging limply over the edge of the grave. A knife was buried in his back, almost to the hilt.

"Dr. Mire?"

Adam jumped at the voice. He peered into the darkness beyond Tarik's lifeless form. A man materialized from the shadows, approaching from the olive orchard. He had dark hair, save for a white streak that ran from his widow's peak to behind his left ear. He was dressed warmly for August—dress trousers, a long-sleeved shirt, and a vest. Something about the cut of his clothes struck Adam as anachronistic. His shirt was open at the collar, and he had rolled the sleeves to his elbows, as if he had come expecting a brawl. On his hands he wore black driving gloves. He carried a satchel over his shoulder.

Adam backed away. "Who are you?"

The man held up a hand. "I'm not here to hurt you. I did just save your life."

Adam grunted. "After what I've been through, you'll excuse me if I don't take that as evidence of your good intentions."

The man knelt next to Tarik's body and extracted the knife. It made a thick, wet smack that turned Adam's stomach as it exited the wound. "Let me untie your hands."

Adam glared.

The man sighed. He reached into his shirt and pulled out a crucifix on a chain around his neck. "I'm not one of them either."

Adam narrowed his eyes. "Then answer my question. Who are you?"

"Someone who wants to help, Dr. Mire. You do realize how out of your depth you are, right?"

"The thought has crossed my mind a number of times."

"You know where to find Yasamin." It was not a question.

Adam nodded.

"She has the answers you're looking for, but you'll have to get to her before Serhan and his band of fanatics." The man took the bag off his shoulder and tossed it on the ground at Adam's feet. "You'll probably want this."

It was Adam's satchel with all his books and papers.

"Why are you helping me?" Adam asked.

"Because I have to."

Adam glanced down at his bound wrists and the blade of the knife in the man's hand, gleaming in the moonlight with fresh blood. He held his hands out, and the man slashed the ropes.

"Hurry," he said. "Time is wasting."

Adam bent down to retrieve his satchel and noticed a thin, leather-bound book he had never seen before poking out of the top. The cover was worn and warped in places. The edges of the pages were mottled by water and mold. Adam opened it to discover a journal, handwritten in Romanian—the journal of Andras Iliescu, Mihai's father.

Adam wanted to ask how the man had stolen his satchel back from the Blades, how he had gotten the journal, any of a thousand other questions, but when he looked up again, the man was already gone.

SEVENTY

From the journal of Andras Iliescu

Bucharest, Romania
25 January 1941

MONSTERS ARE REAL, MY SON. Sometimes they look like the pictures in your fairy tale books. Sometimes they look like men. Sometimes they are men.

You are too young to understand war, Mihai, but you are not too young to understand hatred. Hatred is what turns men into monsters. For many years now, I have fought them. I thought I was, at least in some small way, making the world a better place. Now, I discover that my own hatred has made me into a monster as well. I write to you to save you from the same fate. Someday, when you are older, I will give you this journal. All I can hope is that when you have read it, you will forgive me.

Do you know why your mother and I named you Mihai? We named you after Mihai Viteazul, the Brave, the

343

great Romanian hero who first united the Romanians together into one nation. Maybe we were being foolish. We
hoped the name would make you brave, too. We knew you
would have to be brave in order to survive in our world.
It's not fair, not with this damned war about to come
down on all of us. The monsters thrive on death. There are
so many of them now. It's impossible for one man to turn
the tide. Perhaps that is why I've shunned my duty for so
long, but I can't turn my back any longer. Not only for
those who came before, but also for those, like you, who
will come after.

I cannot guarantee you a better life. I can, however,
stop participating in the acts of hatred that have fed the
monsters. That is my second apology. I expect you may
find it harder to forgive me in this case. What I am about
to tell you is offered by way of explanation, not excuse.

I was, before the war, a doctor, educated in the best
schools in Bucharest and Berlin. Upon completing my education, I could have taken a position in any hospital in
Europe. I could have opened my own practice in Vienna
or Prague and made a small fortune treating anemic old
ladies, but that is not the kind of life I wanted.

I learned of a tiny village named Belatori about two
hours southwest of Bucharest. The doctor there had recently died, and the village was in need of another. I was
more than happy to fill that role. So in the summer of
1937, your mother and I, having just married, moved
there. Not long after, we were thrilled to learn she was
pregnant with you.

The life of a country doctor suited me well. The people
of Belatori were mostly farmers, uneducated and superstitious, but they were hardworking, earnest people. In a very
short time, I grew to love them as family. Besides, even as

a man of science, I knew at least some of their superstitions were more than ridiculous nonsense.

But it all began to fall apart in the autumn of 1938. The daughter of one of our neighbors, a pretty girl with blue eyes, no more than fifteen years old, came to me complaining of stomach pains. It didn't take me long to diagnose the problem. She was pregnant. When I told her, she burst into tears. She said her father would turn her out of his house if he knew. She asked me if there was anything I could do to make it so she wasn't pregnant anymore. She begged. She pleaded.

At the time, the idea was appalling to me, so I refused, but I could not harden my heart to the desperation in her eyes. I offered to speak with her parents and intercede on her behalf. She calmed down a little, even though she still sobbed. I asked her who the father was. She wouldn't say.

The talk with her parents did not go well. As soon as I told them, her father began screaming at the poor girl, spewing every name imaginable. Then she accused a Gypsy of raping her. Her father stopped screaming. I looked at her in astonishment.

A group of Gypsies had set up camp near the village early in the summer. Their interactions with the village had been mostly peaceful. I had even treated a few of them for some minor ailments, but if you asked anyone what they thought of Gypsies, you'd get a curse and a spit in response.

The girl said one of the men had come to her while she was fetching water from the well. He'd grabbed her and forced himself onto her. She was lying. The well wasn't that far from the village. Someone would have heard her scream. And if she hadn't screamed, why not?

The girl's father was silent for a moment, and then he

stormed out of the house. He ran down the street, knocking on every door. The girl had set dry kindling ablaze. Within the space of two hours, the allegations against the Gypsies grew beyond control. The Gypsies had stolen chickens and eggs. They had cursed the cows and the goats to make them run dry. They had caused all manner of illnesses, from fevers to palsies, and more women—and even some men—spoke of waking up in the middle of the night to unwanted sexual encounters.

I didn't do anything to stop them from burning the Gypsy camp to the ground. I told myself it would not have mattered, that they would have done it anyway. I told myself I would have signed the girl's death warrant and put my own family in danger if I had exposed her lie. I told myself they were only Gypsies.

But on an evening a few weeks later, the gypsies came back. The sun had just set, and a cold moon hung barely above the treetops. I could see my breath as I climbed out of our old automobile. I had been in the city, buying medicines and supplies. The door to the house stood wide open. I could hear you crying.

Everything inside was torn apart. All the furniture was overturned. The contents of my desk were strewn across the floor. They were there. Three of them. Two men and a woman. They stood there as I walked in the door as if expecting me. The woman smiled. It was not a pleasant smile.

She had flawless olive skin and deep brown, almost black eyes, like still water reflecting a starless night sky. One of the men moved toward me. As he did, I saw who lay on the floor behind them—your mother. A deep red gash crossed her neck. I knew what they were then.

The monsters can't enter a person's home unless they

have first been invited, but they have ways of overcoming that limitation. They had used your poor mother to get into the house. They had charmed her. And then they had killed her.

I should have recognized the signs. I should have known from the rage stirred up in the village that they were already there. The monsters don't only feed when they come in the night. They whisper lies in the ears of the sleeping. They fan smoldering resentments into open quarrels. The discord they sow helps to conceal their activities, but I think they do it also because they enjoy it. Hatred nourishes them almost as much as blood.

"Wait," the woman said. "Maybe he knows where it is."

The medallion. They were after the medallion, like all the others.

"I don't know what you're talking about," I said.

She laughed. "Your wife told me the same lie. Of course you do."

"I swear I don't."

At that moment, you let out a fiendish wail from your crib upstairs.

"Do you swear on the life of your son?" the woman asked.

"You wouldn't."

"I've done worse."

She made a little motion with her head. Both of the men came toward me. Each of them had small, red marks on their necks, recently made.

"You destroyed our home," one of them said.

I backed away slowly, resisting the impulse to turn and run. If I had, they would have caught me without any effort at all.

"It wasn't me," I protested.

347

"You let it happen," the other one said.

Back and forth they went in an antiphonal chorus of spite.

"We're always to blame. For everything."

"We curse your crops and your livestock."

"We defile your women."

"We poison your wells."

"Everything bad that happens to you, we're the cause."

"Simply because you can't handle your own shortcomings."

I kept backing away, careful not to stumble over any upturned furniture. Inch by inch, I maneuvered myself around, leading them toward the kitchen. I had to keep them talking only a little while longer.

"Killing me won't give you what you want," I said.

"How do you know what we want?" the first one asked.

"You don't know anything about us," the second one added.

"I know that you have given yourself over to a monster when you didn't have to."

"What other option was there, besides bleeding to death on the hard ground?"

"Allowing your souls to go to their eternal rest, rather than damning yourselves to walk the earth forever."

They laughed.

"She seduced you both," I continued. "She hasn't given you anything. She's taken away all you had left."

"That's not true."

"We have our revenge."

"When we're done here, we're going to pay a visit to your neighbor."

"And his neighbor, and his neighbor, until there is nothing left of this village."

I fell over the upturned table. With a giant crack, one of the legs broke off. In one motion, I grabbed the splintered piece of wood and thrust the jagged end of it as hard as I could into the chest of the one nearest me. His scream left my ears ringing. In the split second that the other one was distracted, I picked up one of the kitchen chairs and heaved it at him. He deflected it without any effort, but it gave me just enough time to grab the ax hanging next to the door. Once I had it in my hands, it took me one blow to separate his head from his body. Still clutching the ax, I ran upstairs.

The crucifix on the wall above your crib saved you. She couldn't come near enough to do you any harm. When I entered the room, she stood a few feet away, staring darkly at you. By that time, you had cried yourself to sleep. She didn't turn around.

"Why do you keep it?" she asked. "It only brings pain. Pain and death."

"A promise was made," I replied. "My honor demands that I keep it, but you wouldn't know anything about that."

"You don't know anything about me."

"Your friends said the same thing, but you're all mistaken. I know what you crave, and I know the chaos you sow. I know enough to understand that you and everyone like you should be destroyed."

"And then what? The nations of the world will come together in peace and harmony? Don't fool yourself. You'll soon learn there are those breathing who are worse than I am."

Before I could even move, she threw herself through the window. The sound of shattering glass echoed for a moment and then gave way to utter silence. I checked to make sure you weren't hurt, and then I returned to the floor below.

When it came time, I couldn't bring myself to do what I knew had to be done. I lifted the ax above the prone body of the beautiful woman who had been your mother, but I could not bring it down to sever her head. I just stood over her body. That was the only time I cried. I knew some of the gypsies believed putting a silver coin in a dead person's mouth was sufficient to prevent them from returning. I did that, and I buried her in the forest.

As I put the last shovelful of dirt onto the grave, a rage filled me so intensely I felt I might explode, but I didn't direct my anger at the olive-skinned creature who invaded my home and destroyed my life. I directed it at the Gypsies. They had brought her there, of all places, where she would certainly have become aware of the medallion. They had probably sheltered her all summer, knowing exactly what she was.

After that horrible night, you went to live with your aunt in Timișoara, and I moved to Bucharest to find work. I rented an apartment across the street from the old synagogue. If I had known then what would happen, I might have found another place to live. As it was, I was able to find work in a clinic nearby.

I hope you never know true poverty. I saw it every day at that clinic. I saw illnesses that should have been wiped out centuries ago. I saw thirty-year-old men who looked like they were sixty, coughing up bits of their own lungs because they worked sixteen-hour days in filthy factories. I saw women of the same age with arthritis and stooped shoulders from making clothes in rooms barely lit enough for them to see. Those were the ones fortunate enough to have work. A few days a week I tended to the vagrants who frequented my streets. That winter, every last one of them froze to death.

I thought about you often. Whenever I could, I sent money to your aunt. Sometimes, I think if I had paid more attention to what was truly going on around me, I could have stopped the madness. It's probably wishful thinking on my own part. Each of us likes to think we have more of a say in our own individual destinies than we actually do.

At the end of the summer of 1939 the Germans and the Russians invaded Poland. Romania opened its doors to Polish refugees, thousands of them. To me, it meant only more sick, more poor. I worked from seven in the morning until eight or nine at night. I listened to their stories, but I found myself doing the one thing I was trained never to do. I discriminated among my patients. Any Gypsy or anyone who even looked like a Gypsy, I only halfheartedly treated. I never went out of my way for them, or even wanted to spend much time with them at all. Part of me didn't care if they died.

As if such a thing wasn't bad enough, the long days began to take their toll on me. My nerves began to go. In order to steady my hands so the patients wouldn't see them tremble, I stole small amounts of morphine from the clinic. One day, a fellow doctor, a Jew named Beniamin Gherwitz, caught me. I begged him not to tell the director of the clinic, but he did. I lost my job. I expected to lose my medical license as well, but then something of a miracle happened. At least, I thought it was a miracle at the time.

I was approached by another doctor from the clinic who said he had been watching me treat patients, and that he could help me. He told me about an organization that could use my skills. If I joined, he said, he could see to it I kept my medical license. That organization was the

Legion of the Archangel Michael, better known as the Iron Guard. I agreed.

I now fear I have made another mistake.

SEVENTY-ONE

Berlin, Germany
12 August 1999

"ANDRAS ILIESCU WAS THE SCION of Arnold
Pavle," Adam said. "Mihai scrawled his family
tree in the margins of his copy of *Dracula*. Alisa
Pavle left her village with her son and moved to Sibiu in
Transylvania. She called it by its German name, Hermannstadt, in her final conversation with Johann Flückinger, the army doctor. She learned not only how to protect her son from vampires, but to strike back at them.
The tradition was passed from mother to son, father to
daughter, until Mihai. He was the last of the vampire
hunters."

Yasamin cocked her head to one side. "Are you taking
up his mantle, Dr. Mire?"

Adam held up a hand. "I don't think I could, even if I
wanted to. When he died, something changed. Maybe
your theory about entropy is true after all."

"'Things fall apart; the centre cannot hold.'"

353

"William Butler Yeats."

"It has long been one of my favorite poems."

"Though I would think you might prefer the later lines: *The blood-dimmed tide is loosed, and everywhere The ceremony of innocence is drowned.*"

"Were you not paying attention when you read Andras Iliescu's journal? As I told him, you don't need us to destroy yourselves. You're already doing it without us. What good is worrying about the mote in another's eye when you haven't removed the plank from your own?"

"Even the devil can quote scripture."

"And does the mouth from which it comes change the point of the scripture? Why do you waste your energy on me? Are there dark things that lurk in the shadows after the sun sets? Yes. Do unfortunate humans sometimes come across those dark things? Yes. Are those dark things any more evil than your Caligula, your Adolf Hitler, your Joseph Stalin? No."

"I'm not concerned with their evil. That's the job of others. I'm only concerned with the evil that took Nadiye from me."

"And if it consumes you too?"

"Then I'll die knowing I did all I could."

"Probably the most astute thing you've said all day." She cocked her head to the side. "What now, Dr Mire?"

"We had a deal. I've told you my story. Now you finish telling me yours."

SEVENTY-TWO

Buda, Ottoman Hungary
29 Safar 1010
(19 August 1601 Old Style)

"THEY ARE AFRAID OF YOU, *hanım effendi.*"
Yasamin surveyed the breakfast of bread with butter and jam that Simon, the ebony eunuch, had brought her. She didn't want it, but she made a show of eating, so as not to offend him. Outside in the garden, she heard voices, happy, laughing, enjoying the warmth and the sun. She couldn't enjoy sunny days outside in the garden anymore. She couldn't endure the cold stares or the hushed whispers. She only ventured out at night, when she could sit among the shadows, alone.

She was not expecting the answer, though she knew Simon spoke the truth. "Why are they afraid?"

Simon sat cross-legged on a pillow across from her. She had insisted he stay for a few minutes. As one season passed into another—summer, to autumn, to winter, to spring, and back to summer—fewer and fewer of the *haremlık*'s denizens had anything to do with her. Simon was the only one who still talked to her. Not even Hadice could bring herself to look Yasamin in the eye.

"Because of your husband," Simon replied.

"But I am not him," she protested.

He raised a delicate finger. "It doesn't matter. Those who speak out against you ... have a habit of meeting unfortunate ends."

"But I had nothing to do with ... what happened. More than a year has passed. Nothing has happened since. Why can't they forget?"

"People remember when there is a reason to, *hanım effendi*."

"You are not doing a very good job cheering me up today, Simon."

He opened his eyes wide in mock alarm. "I didn't know cheering you was among my daily tasks. If you had only asked, I would have smiled and greeted you by telling you how radiant you look, even under these conditions."

A cannon fired, punctuating his remark. The war with the German emperor was not going well. Most days, Yasamin could see the smoke rising up from one battle or another.

"If we had to evacuate the palace, I wouldn't be very upset," she said. "I think I would miss the pomegranate trees in the garden the most. Maybe I would take a piece of fruit with me, and plant a seed wherever we stopped."

"But they are just blooming. There won't be fruit for several more months."

"Do you think Buda will fall before then?"

For a moment, a hint of panic entered his eyes.

Yasamin smiled. "It's not a trap. I'm not going to turn you in for treason. You can speak your mind to me."

"I think it is a distinct possibility we will have to leave very soon."

"Then perhaps I should gather some things together, just in case," she said.

"It might be prudent, *hanım effendi*." Simon stood and bowed. "I must take my leave now, but I will come around later, in case you need cheering up again."

"Thank you. I'll look forward to it."

He paused at the door. "*Hanım effendi?*"

"Yes?"

"This war. Those are not the conditions I meant."

Yasamin nodded. "I know."

Simon did not come back later. In the evening, after the echoes of the last of the calls to prayer faded away, Yasamin slipped out of her room. Moonlight or no moonlight, she could fly through the corridors like a ghost, her feet barely touching the ground until she reached the oak tree in the middle of the *haremlık* garden.

She was never afraid. Creatures lurked there in the dark that could kill her and leave her like Celibe—bloodless and terrified even in death—or carry her off without a trace, or make her like Rabiye. It didn't matter. They could come for her if they wished. But she knew they wouldn't.

Yasamin thought about Iskander as she sat with her back to the great tree and gazed over the black water of the pond. She wondered where he was, what he was doing, if he ever thought of her. A small part of her hoped he would yet return. Some days such thoughts were all that sustained her.

Still, hope had its limits.

More than once she had crawled to the edge of the inky pond and shattered its smooth surface with a probing finger. On nights when the moon shone, she watched as her reflection broke into a million pieces and as the ripples died, pulled itself together again. She thought about what it would be like to be the reflection, looking at herself from the other side, drowned underneath the water.

The moon was almost gone, so no other Yasamin looked back at her from the watery depths, nor did she receive any warning when the long fingers closed around her neck.

She flailed, trying to stand, trying to get away, but she couldn't break free. An odd sound found her ears. Someone chanted in a deep, guttural language she couldn't understand, but she recognized the voice. Simon. His hands pressed tighter around her throat, and she struggled to breathe. His chanting grew faster and more frenzied, and a new strain entered his voice, something low and gravelly, something less human.

Before she passed out, while she could still form a thought, she took the dagger from the sash around her waist, the same dagger Ayla had tried to kill her with and Ine had used to kill Nesrin. She thrust it backward into Simon's leg. The chanting stopped. The pressure vanished from Yasamin's throat. Simon cried out, his scream sounding like a crazed animal.

Yasamin jumped to her feet and pivoted to face him. He was stooped over, clutching his leg as blood spurted between his fingers. In his eyes, she couldn't see any hint of the Simon who had shared tea and gossip with her all through the long months since Murad had become Pasha. She saw only an unthinking beast. He bared his teeth and charged at her, despite the wound she had given him. A torrent of words, none of which Yasamin could understand, erupted from his mouth.

Yasamin turned to run, but he tackled her to the

ground again. She kicked to try to break free, but he clawed at her clothing, drawing himself on top of her. Yasamin held her dagger close. When he lunged for her neck again, she slipped the blade between his ribs. He lurched upward and Yasamin scrabbled away. He collapsed on the ground, clutching his chest. The sense returned to his eyes. He looked at her.

"*Hanım effendi*," he said, "I am so sorry."

"Who did this to you, Simon?"

"I did it ... to myself."

"To yourself? But why?"

"Where I come from ... there are those who create elixirs one can take if one is ill ... or for other reasons. My ... my father taught me, before I was taken away." He coughed until he spat blood. Several minutes passed before he could continue. "Tonight ... I took one that let me see ... the other world."

"The other world? The djinn—"

"Yes, those creatures you call djinn. And others."

With every breath a rattling sound emanated from his chest.

"Why did you want to do that?"

"If the Germans come here, *hanım effendi* ... you will flee to safety, while I ... will be left behind here ... to fight and die."

"That's not true. I wouldn't let that happen."

He tried to smile. "*Hanım effendi* ... there are some things beyond even your power. It would happen. And so tonight ... I wanted to see my future. What I saw ... I fear drove me mad."

"What did you see?"

His breathing had become shallow. His grip on her arm fell away. "I saw ... I saw the dark shadows gathering ...

gathering around you."

His last breath escaped him. Yasamin replaced her dagger and climbed to her feet. She struggled with the body, dragging it and rolling it in turn until she succeeded in pushing it into the pond, where it sank underneath the water to look up from below at those gazing in.

SEVENTY-THREE

Buda, Ottoman Hungary
1 Rabi' al-awwal 1010
(20 August 1601 Old Style)

THE KNIFE WAS A REMARKABLE instrument, the golden hilt encrusted with rubies and sapphires, the blade made of fine quality steel. Yasamin wondered how Ine had come to possess it. She passed her finger along the edge, with almost enough pressure to slice it open, but not quite. The knock interrupted her train of thought. She hid the knife in her sash before bidding whoever had knocked to enter. A eunuch opened the door, bearing what had become a familiar message.

"Your husband wishes to see you, *hanım effendi*."

Yasamin said nothing. She simply stood and put her veil across her face. She had tried refusing before. Defiance resulted only in two eunuchs dragging her to Murad's chambers and harsher treatment from him once she was there. When they reached the door, the eunuch remained outside. Yasamin did her best to hide her contempt as she entered. Since Murad became Pasha, he had abandoned his efforts to live an ascetic life of study and prayer. He had moved into his father's old rooms, decorated as one would expect for a Pasha—silk and satin pillows, gilded furniture, tapestries covering every wall. Yasamin found herself wishing for the quiet, awkward Murad she had rejected.

Murad stood waiting for her. He smiled and motioned for her to come closer. Gently, almost affectionately, he removed her veil. He wanted to talk to her first. Sometimes he never said a word, forcing himself on her and calling for a eunuch to escort her back to her own room when he was finished.

Murad's smile faded after he removed her veil. "Why do you glare at me so?"

"Why do you think? How long should I expect to be treated as a prisoner? I can't go anywhere without an escort, not even in the *haremlık*. One can only endure such conditions for so long."

"Yasamin, my dear, I've explained this. It's for your own protection. You are the wife of a Pasha, and I have enemies. At any moment, someone could try to bring harm to you in an effort to hurt me. I won't allow it. I don't know what I would do if anything happened to you."

"So you can hurt me, but others may not."

"Hurt you? How dare you say such nonsense. You have no right."

She pulled up the sleeve of her caftan to reveal the purple bruises on her arm. She could have shown him bruises in other places. "You stand here and claim not to have hurt me?"

The look Murad gave her was the same one he had given her the morning after their wedding—that of a sullen little boy. "I'm only acting the way you expect me to act, the way Selim acted toward women."

"Selim was not like that," Yasamin protested. "He may have been proud, even arrogant, but he wasn't cruel."

She realized her mistake too late.

Murad's eyes narrowed. His face hardened. He seized Yasamin by the wrist. "How do you know what Selim was like? Were you seeing him in secret?"

Yasamin shook her head. "No, Murad. I've already sworn to you I was not. The first time I ever spoke to him was that night he came into my room, the night he died. He tried to convince me to run away with him, but I refused. That is the truth."

"How do I know it's the truth?"

"You have my word," she said.

Murad regarded her coolly. "Swear it to me again. Swear on your life that you have always been faithful to me."

The words were about to lave Yasamin's lips when an image of Iskander leapt into her head. She hesitated but for a second, but it was a second too long. Murad struck her face with the back of his hand.

"Whore!" he shouted. "You can't say it, can you? You can't speak of your faithfulness because you know it's a lie." He cupped her jaw in his hand so she couldn't look away. "I will make certain you never again have thoughts of another man."

As Murad pulled her closer, Yasamin retrieved the knife from her caftan. When the gap between them ceased to exist and Murad's lips covered hers harshly, she plunged the blade into his stomach. It slid in easily after a small amount of resistance. Murad jerked and tried to pull away, but Yasamin gently, lovingly, placed her hand on the back of his neck and bent his head down.

"You're wrong," she whispered in his ear. "I was never unfaithful to you with Selim. I was unfaithful to you with Iskander, the janissary captain."

"No," Murad rasped tearing himself away, "not him. He wasn't supposed to touch you."

Yasamin glanced down at the bloody knife in her hand. Crimson drops fell from the tip and splashed on the floor. "What do you mean?"

A bright red stain blossomed across the front of Murad's shirt. As he clutched his stomach, the blood oozed between his fingers. He struggled for breath. "It was part of our bargain. He promised."

"What did he promise?" Yasamin shouted.

But Murad didn't answer. Instead he reached a blood-stained hand toward her, and in that moment all the pain left his face. He smiled. "Praise Allah for giving me a wife so beautiful."

His hand fell. He collapsed to the floor.

His very last breath carried her name.

Yasamin fought the urge to rush to his side, to try to rouse him and make him tell her what he meant by the things he had said. Instead she closed her eyes and struggled to calm her pounding heart.

"I have to admit I'm impressed. I didn't think you had it in you."

Yasamin knew the voice. She wasn't expecting it, but she wasn't surprised to hear it. She turned to see Iskander in the doorway to Murad's chambers. The eunuch was nowhere in sight.

"Where have you been?" she asked.

"You told me to go away, remember?"

"I didn't mean any of what I said and you know it." She

waved the bloody knife in front of her. "You could have stopped this."

Iskander shook his head. "No, it all would have happened exactly the same. Maybe not as soon, but eventually, Murad would have had to die. He was right. It was part of our bargain. I had to promise not to touch you. And I didn't, at least not in the way he meant."

"I don't understand, Iskander."

He stepped over the threshold. As he did he unpinned the medallion he wore on his caftan and held it out to her.

"Come now. You remember. You've seen this medallion before. You saw me wearing it the day I saved you from the men sent to execute your parents."

"That's impossible. That was ten years ago. You can't be the same person."

"But I can. I saw you, and I thought to myself what a beautiful woman you would be, if given the chance to grow up. I was right."

"Then why wait until now to tell me?"

"I couldn't. Not until you were ready to hear and understand."

"Understand what?"

"Your father had possession of this medallion," Iskander explained. "He kept it in a little mosque in the woods outside Banja Luka, a very pretty place."

"The same mosque in my tapestry, the one my mother gave me."

Iskander nodded. "Yes, that's the one."

"What did you do?" Yasamin asked through a clenched jaw.

"I made your father give the medallion to me. It's mine, you see."

"You're the *Kazıklı Bey*."

Iskander bowed. "That I am."

"How did you make my father give the medallion to you?"

He took another step forward, though Yasamin kept her knife between them. "I merely exerted my influence over him. I told him it wasn't right to keep something that didn't belong to him. He saw the error of his ways."

"Is that what you did here? 'Exert your influence'?"

"It is what I always do."

Yasamin felt the heat rise in her cheeks as the anger built. "You used everyone—the janissaries, Rabiye, Ine, Murad ... me."

Iskander grinned. "You forget those hapless German soldiers Selim and Murad stumbled across in the woods. And the one I attacked. Ilker, I believe was his name. I needed an invitation into the palace."

Hot tears fell down Yasamin's face. "I trusted you. Everything you said about me I believed. I thought you loved me. But it was all some sort of game to you."

Iskander took another step forward. "I would never play games with your heart. What I feel for you is real, Yasamin. It always has been."

Yasamin held the knife out in front of her. "Stay back! I won't let you do anything to me."

Iskander stepped forward again. "You know that won't hurt me, don't you? You were only able to kill Murad because I never completely turned him."

"The knife isn't for you," Yasamin replied. "It's for me."

Iskander's eyes grew wide as she turned the blade on herself. He lunged for her, but he was too late. The knife slid across her neck. It hurt less than she expected. She gasped and choked once on her own blood, and then she was falling. Iskander's face filled her vision, even as blackness crept in from the edges.

She tried to reach out a hand to him, but found herself too weak to move. She continued to fall, and Iskander faded away. She couldn't see anything anymore, and all she could hear was the beating of her heart, but even it slowed, and then stopped.

She didn't know how much time passed. She fell for a while it seemed, and then she realized she wasn't anymore. It seemed like she was floating. Everything was still black. Everything was still silent.

Then suddenly, inexplicably, images flooded her mind, enough for two lifetimes. The forest and the mountains she saw when dancing to the *kemençe* player's music. Battlefields strewn with bodies both Ottoman and Christian, ravens circling overhead in the red sky of twilight. Tortured souls, impaled on pikes, wailing in agony. A castle perched high on a precipice, overlooking a river coursing through the valley far below. Image after image, faster and faster, accompanied by the wild tune of the *kemençe* player. And with each image, a small piece of understanding. Yasmin's eyes fluttered open.

Iskander's medallion gleamed in the moonlight.

SEVENTY-FOUR

Berlin, Germany
12 August 1999

"HE SAVED ME FROM DYING," Yasamin said.

Adam shook his head. "You're lying. It couldn't have happened that way. You have to want it. You have to drink the blood."

"I tell you the truth and you call it lies. What would you have me say? Perhaps I truly did want it. Perhaps I still loved him, despite learning what he was and what he had done, despite knowing what I would become, despite my anger and my fear. I don't know what happened in those final moments. I told you everything I remember." Her eyes flashed red. "And now that you know the truth, I can't allow you the chance to tell anyone else. Pity. I like you. I haven't met anyone who could hold my interest for so long in quite a while."

"Then maybe I can hold it for just a little longer. I need your help, Yasamin."

If he could keep her talking for just a little longer …

"But I don't need your help, Dr. Mire. Tell me why I should spare you now, when you have nothing left to bargain."

"What makes you think I'm bargaining?"

She smiled. "Really, Dr. Mire. You've spent the last several hours telling me everything you know. You've been quite forthcoming, and I appreciate it, but I'm tired of this game and more than a little hungry." She glided across the floor, her hips swaying, her long black hair cascading past her shoulders. Her dark eyes drew him in, and when she parted her full lips to speak, her voice echoed inside his head. "Your arm must be tired from holding up that heavy rosary. Why don't you put it down and step away from the window?"

Adam's hand wavered. His every muscle ached to put down the rosary and step toward Yasamin, into the shadows that fluttered around her like a murder of crows.

Hail Mary, full of grace …

"I haven't told you everything," he said, shaking his head, fighting to resist.

… the Lord is with thee …

Her smile faded. "What do you mean?"

A clamor rose from downstairs as the front door to the townhouse burst open and heavy boots ascended the stairs.

"Süleyman's Blade is coming."

SEVENTY-FIVE

Berlin, Germany
12 August 1999

ADAM DOVE TO THE FLOOR as Serhan and five other Blades burst into the room. Yasamin hissed in fury, her alluring beauty melting like snow under the midday sun. Her exotic face replaced by that of a snarling animal, she became one with the shadows as her dark form flowed across the room toward the intruders.

Serhan raised his fist in the air. *"Allahu Akbar,"* he shouted. *God is Great.*

Two of the Blades met their ends immediately. Moving almost faster than Adam could see, Yasamin slashed open the throat of one, then the other. The two men fell to the floor, clutching at the gashes in their necks, futilely struggling to stanch the flow of blood.

Yasamin landed face-to-face with Serhan. She lunged at him with a clawed hand. Adam expected his life to end in the same way as the others, but at the last second Serhan threw up his arm. Yasamin's fingers curled around his wrist. A moment later she screamed as thick tendrils of black smoke rose from her red and blistered hand. Serhan had string of prayer beads wrapped around his forearm. He planted a boot in her chest and sent her staggering backwards, but she stayed on her feet.

One of the remaining Blades leveled a crossbow at Yasamin. She deflected the wooden bolt he fired with a simple swipe of her hand. Before the bowman could reload, she was on top of him. She knocked the crossbow out of his hands, sending him backwards into Adam, and they tumbled to the floor. Yasamin moved to finish the bowman, but another Blade diverted her attention with a thrown dagger. She barely dodged the knife, which stuck in the wall close to where Adam had been standing.

Adam and the former bowman both scrambled to their feet. The man regarded him with wide-eyed surprise for all of a second before his eyes narrowed and his mouth twisted in contempt. The bowman snatched the knife thrown by his comrade out of the wall. Adam evaded the steel edge, and when the bowman swung again Adam caught his arm. He tried to force the bowman to drop the knife, but the Blade wrenched himself free.

"Why are you attacking *me*?" Adam asked.

He lunged. Adam blocked him with a forearm and slammed him against the wall, but the Blade rebounded immediately and charged again. Adam sidestepped him, tripping him as he passed. The bowman tumbled to the floor, his knife skittering into a dark corner.

Adam stood over him. "I'm not one of her pets."

But the man had no intention of listening. He kicked Adam in the shin with his boot. As Adam staggered backwards, the bowman jumped to his feet. He punched Adam hard in the stomach. Dazed, Adam fell to his knees. A sharp blow landed at the base of his neck, and fireworks exploded behind his eyes. He struggled to stand up again, but found his legs wouldn't follow his brain's commands. When he looked up, the bowman loomed over him, recovered knife in hand, poised to slice him open.

"*La ilaha iallah*," the bowman said. *There is no god but Allah.*

But as he raised the knife to gut Adam, a bloody hand thrust through his chest. Yasamin, her arm dripping in gore, lifted him off the ground and threw him against the wall, his body leaving a crimson streak before joining the mangled form of the dagger thrower in a heap on the floor.

A flurry of movement to Adam's right caught his eye. Serhan, wielding a wooden stake, charged Yasamin. She pivoted and swatted him across the room. He smashed against a heavy table and fell to the floor where he remained, unmoving.

The vampire turned to face the sole remaining Blade. Panic filled the man's eyes. He tried to run, but before he could take even one step, Yasamin had traversed the space between them. She seized his neck with a taloned hand and lifted him off the floor. While his legs swung wildly, she tightened her grip until the Blade's neck snapped with a sickening crunch. His body went limp, and she tossed it to the side as one would a sack of trash.

Surrounded by the bodies of the fallen Blades, Yasamin's feral features faded, leaving her again the beguiling beauty Adam felt he had come close to understanding. She eyed him coolly, but any derision was gone from her expression. A hint of a smile, a genuine one, played across her face.

"Dr. Mire—"

Serhan rose up behind her and flung a string of prayer

beads around her neck before Adam could call out a warning. He pulled them tight, and her shrieks diminished to choked gurgles as she struggled to free herself, though her thrashing grew weaker by the second.

"This is for my brothers," he said. "*Bismillah al-Rahman al-Rahim.*" *In the name of God, Most Gracious, Most Merciful.*

"But how?" she croaked.

An exposed rib jutted from Serhan's side. His breathing was ragged.

"A Blade must know how to endure pain." Serhan spat. "You should have checked to make sure I was dead."

Adam's gaze met Yasamin's. With what must have been the last of her strength, she grabbed hold of Serhan's arms and twisted her body, forcing Serhan to pivot with her to keep hold of his garrote. Adam snatched the dagger out of the bowman's lifeless hands and hurled himself at Serhan and Yasamin. Clenching the hilt in both fists, he plunged the knife between Serhan's shoulder blades. Serhan lurched and let go of the prayer beads. Yasamin fell to the floor.

"This is for Nadiye, you son of a bitch," Adam whispered in his ear as he twisted the knife in Serhan's back.

Serhan toppled off Yasamin's still form. He struggled to his feet, but could manage only a few steps before collapsing again. He glared at Adam, blood erupting from his mouth and nose, and then the life left his eyes.

One moment Yasamin lay still as death, and the next she was tearing the prayer beads from her neck. Adam marveled as the raw skin began to heal.

She placed a delicate hand around the wound the beads had made. "Gratitude is not something I make a habit of expressing, Dr. Mire, but this once I am going to make an exception. Thank you. You might very well leave this room alive."

Adam forced a smile. "I suppose I should thank you as well, then."

She raised an eyebrow. "As I understand it, though, your life is in ruins. Wherever would you go?"

Adam's smile twisted into a smirk. "I'll miss the way you're always able to put things into perspective. I have some resources. I can find somewhere to hide for a while."

Yasamin bowed slightly. "I wish you luck. And I commend you on your well-executed plan for revenge."

Adam's blood froze. "What do you mean?"

She waved a hand around the blood-smeared room. "Come now, Dr. Mire. I have had four hundred years of experience with schemes and plots. Did you honestly think you could fool me? I heard what you said when you stabbed Serhan."

Adam clenched his jaw. "Whatever Nadiye encountered in that tunnel, it wasn't what killed her. Nadiye told me that Serhan lured her there. He killed her. And all because of me. Because it was unacceptable for her to associate with me, a Westerner, an American, and worst of all an unbeliever. He told her he had to do it before he would be deemed clean enough to join Süleyman's Blade. But something else was there in the dark. It attacked Serhan and drove him off, and as Nadiye lay bleeding in the dark, it came back for her. She was too weak to resist."

Her gaze bore into him. "And somehow Serhan got it into his head that I attacked him."

Adam held his expression steady. "So it seems."

"I was not there that night."

"I know that. Do you think I could ever forget the face of the woman I saw? I've tried, but I've never been able to find out who she is."

"A true mystery." Yasamin lifted an elegant finger to her lips and licked off the blood deliberately, as if proper manners existed for such an act. For all Adam knew, they did. "Why did it take you eight years to seek your revenge?" she asked, her voice carrying a hard edge of warning.

"Mihai's copy of *Dracula*. I always knew I would never be strong enough to take on Süleyman's Blade by myself, but a vampire could. All those clumsy inquiries about Dracula's medallion, I knew I'd attract attention."

"You didn't want Süleyman's Blade to find me."

"No. I wanted you to find them."

"Why would Mihai lead you to me?"

"You did destroy his family. Maybe it wasn't about the medallion for him either. Maybe he was seeking his own revenge but never had the chance to carry it out."

Her eyes narrowed. "Then you've failed him."

Adam's gaze fell on Serhan's body. "It wouldn't be the first time I've failed someone."

The last of the sun's purple-orange glow faded from the room.

"You should go now," Yasamin said. "I cannot guarantee your safety once you leave my home."

Adam nodded. "I will, but first a question. I made a mistake that nearly cost me my life more than once by underestimating the pull Dracula's medallion has, but now that I understand—"

She held up a finger. "For saving me from Süleyman's Blade, I will allow you to live, but that is all. If you want to know more about Dracula's medallion, you will have to find someone else to ask."

"But you said it would be dangerous if it ever fell into the wrong hands." Adam motioned around to the dead

Blades at their feet. "There are a lot of wrong hands. You may have neutered Süleyman's Blade, but the Chetniks are still out there, not to mention the Iron Guard and God knows who else."

"Heed my advice, professor. Go now and let others worry about Dracula's medallion. Only a handful of people in history can say they have faced a vampire and lived. You'd do best to accept my bargain while the offer still stands." She gracefully stepped over the bodies littering the floor and retired to her divan amidst the ever-darkening shadows. "Good day, Dr. Mire. I enjoyed our visit. Pray we never meet again."

SEVENTY-SIX

Berlin, Germany
13 August 1999

THE MAN IN BLACK GLOVES cleaned the blood off his knife and frowned. He hadn't enjoyed this one quite as much. The girl didn't struggle or plead for her life or recite prayers—none of what he had expected. She had simply glared at him, defiant.

"She did not abandon me," the girl said.

He held the knife to her throat. "If telling yourself such a lie makes you feel better, then go right ahead."

"She will find you."

He chuckled. "I'm counting on it."

After all, he wouldn't have revealed himself to Mire, that naïve American, if he hadn't wanted her to know. No, *naïve* was not the right word. Mire was cunning. He could never have survived an encounter with her if he weren't. Still, he had no idea what sort of game he was involved in, and as useful as Mire had proven himself to be, he would need to be dealt with soon.

He stood over the lifeless body of Yasamin's servant girl, watching the thick, red liquid pool on the floor underneath. A shame, but it wouldn't do any good having the police wonder where all the blood went, not when the mystery was supposed to be why her right hand was painted green.

He turned away, toward the window, and winced. Looking down, he pulled open his shirt to examine the burn mark made by the crucifix. There had been no other way to convince Mire of his good intentions. It would heal, eventually.

He climbed out the window and scaled the side of the building to the rooftop. He smelled the air, and his eye-teeth tore through his gums, growing into fangs. In such a big city, two murders in one night would not even raise an eyebrow.

It was time to hunt.

SEVENTY-SEVEN

Prague, Czech Republic
4 October 1999

ADAM BLINKED. HE CONTINUED TO struggle with the blue contact lenses he used to disguise his brown eyes. The waiter at the sidewalk café came over with his bill. As he signed his name, he scratched at his goatee, a recent addition as well, dyed to match his newly blond hair. Sometimes, he still startled himself when he looked in the mirror.

His fake government ID bore the name Edvard Novak. He told the people he met he grew up in Brno. He worked in the library archives at Charles University. He was quiet, preferring to keep mostly to himself, though he wasn't averse to having a few beers with his coworkers after his shift was over. He had a small, neat apartment near the university and even managed to keep his houseplants alive.

Sometimes, sitting on his balcony, watching the sun set over the medieval city, he could convince himself he was happy enough. He couldn't go back. Why shouldn't he make a life for himself there? He tried to put all the unanswered questions out of his head—Dracula, the medallion, Anya, the Chetniks, the Iron Guard, the mysterious man who helped him in Thessaloniki. He didn't want to think about any of it. But a dark, raspy voice never stopped whispering in his ear, telling him he didn't deserve to make a life for himself anywhere, telling him he should be dead. The voice wouldn't let the unanswered questions go. At night he sometimes dreamed of Clara or Anya, but mostly he dreamed of Nadiye.

And then there were the books. They were real, tangible reminders. He could feel their worn leather and cloth covers, pass their yellowing pages between his fingers. He had spent so many nights simply staring at them, willing them to give up their secrets. He still didn't know why someone had gone to the trouble to steal *The Life and Death of Michael the Brave* from the vault of a museum, or why Mihai dispersed his books as he had.

Finding Yasamin seemed part of Mihai's intent, but not all of it. Adam took Mihai's copy of *Dracula* out of his satchel and opened it to a page that had puzzled him ever since Thessaloniki. It contained another underlined passage, in which Dr. John Seward laments the death of his beloved Lucy Westenra:

There was a wilderness of beautiful white flowers, and death was made as little repulsive as might be. The end of the winding sheet was laid over the face. When the Professor bent over and turned it gently back, we both started at the beauty before us. The tall wax candles showing a sufficient light to note it well. All Lucy's loveliness had come back to her in death, and the hours that had passed, instead of leaving traces of 'decay's effacing fingers,' had but restored the beauty of life, till positively I could not be-

lieve my eyes that I was looking at a corpse.

The phrase "decay's effacing fingers" was an allusion to *The Giaour*, the epic poem by Lord Byron that introduced Western readers to the concept of the vampire. Adam had expected to find a copy of the poem waiting for him in Thessaloniki, not Andras Iliescu's journal. Of course, it hadn't mattered in the end, but the break in the pattern unnerved Adam.

Inside the copy of *Dracula*, Adam had also discovered several folded sheets of paper, which he clutched in his hand. They appeared old, older than the book even, and when Adam had opened them up, he discovered a letter written in 1892 by Bram Stoker. In the letter he transcribed a conversation with a man he met in a tavern in Venice while he was traveling through Italy with Henry Irving's acting troupe.

The man claimed to be from the city of Bistritz in Transylvania, but his travels had taken him to Ragusa where he found work as a sailor on merchant ships crossing the Adriatic to ports in Italy. Discovering Stoker was from England, he launched immediately into a lengthy story without affording Stoker the opportunity to decline. In Stoker's own words:

I WOULD LIKE TO ATTRIBUTE this man's wild narrative to his inebriated state, but the look in his eyes was not the unfocused gaze of a drunkard, but of a man deadly serious, imparting some grave and unwanted news.

"I met an Englishman once," the man told me. "Sad story. Very, very sad story."

"What makes it such a sad story?" I asked.

"When I was still a boy, the innkeeper gave me a few coins every once in a while to help travelers with their bags. I loved it for the money and because I got to meet new people. This Englishman came to town one day in the late spring. He said his name was Jonathan Harking, a lawyer from London."

Already I was having my doubts as to the veracity of this man's narrative.

"What could a lawyer from London possibly be doing there?"

The man took a swig from his drink. "That's what I asked him. He said his firm had a client nearby, that he was there on business because this client wasn't able to travel to England. I asked who the client was, if he was someone in town. He said he had to keep his client's identity confidential, but that he lived in a small village to the south of Klausenburg. When I stopped smiling, he asked why. I told him no one lived there."

"And why is that?" I asked.

The man shrugged. "It is a wild country, full of dangerous animals. The terrain is rough. I could not imagine someone would want to live there. The Englishman left the following day. Several of the others pled with him to wait a few days for the coming storms to blow over. He said his client expected him and he couldn't delay. We all thought it was the last we would ever hear of him."

"But it was not, apparently."

"A few weeks went by, and we all mostly forgot about the Englishman until someone came into town from Klausenburg. That night in the inn's restaurant, he told everyone who would listen his own story about the man some shepherds had found wandering in the woods. He was pale as snow and delirious, all but collapsing into their arms. They took him to a nearby abbey where the nuns tended to him."

"Your Englishman?"

The man failed to note the hint of derision in my voice. "In his state, he babbled day and night. It took them several days to figure out what language he was speaking. Finally, they found a priest who could understand him, but still none of what he said made sense. He spoke about strange and fantastical things."

"Such as?" I asked, despite myself.

"He spoke of a castle and a dark man and three beautiful women who seduced him and held him there, robbing him of even the strength to leave his bedchamber."

Here his story became too much. I did not bother to hide my incredulity anymore. "Three women?"

"Two raven-haired enchantresses, and one with golden locks," the man explained. "Some of the things he said apparently scandalized the nuns. He said their kisses were like fire and ice at the same time."

Having heard most of the story, I was determined to see it through to the end. "How did he escape these temptresses?"

"He did not say. He only explained that they were going to kill him, and so he had to escape. Despite wanting to stay and allowing them to have their way with him, he forced himself to leave the room and managed to find his way out of the old castle."

At this point, I could not help but challenge him. "But see here, what you say can easily be disproved. Even in such a remote area, someone would have to know the castle and its inhabitants."

The man shook his head. "There are ruins, but nothing habitable, nothing like what this man described."

"And what became of this Jonathan Harking?"

"He lingered on for a few days before he succumbed to his exposure, muttering until he breathed his last. Some of the nuns thought his last words were, 'Mina, Mina,' and took it to be the name of his beloved, whom he had left behind to make his fateful journey. Others heard a different name, one belonging to another woman entirely, if she could be called such. According to them, the name he repeated was, 'Jasmina, Jasmina.'"

THE WAITER CLEARED HIS THROAT, bringing Adam back to the present. "For you," he said, handing Adam an envelope.

"Who gave this to you?" Adam asked.

The waiter shook his head. "I ... I don't know."

Adam examined the envelope after the befuddled waiter walked away. He traced over his name—his new name—spelled out in elaborate calligraphy. The flourishes on the letters gave them an Arabic feel. As Adam stared, the letters twisted and coiled, like the branches of a bramble bush, until they resembled a different language entirely—something ancient and alien. The ink crept to the edge of the envelope and onto Adam's hand, encircling his fingers and crawling up his arm, branching and weaving, making patterns like a henna tattoo.

Adam threw the envelope onto the table. The spell broke. He looked around to see if anyone had noticed his outburst. Satisfied no one was paying attention to him, he picked up the envelope again and opened it.

Inside, Adam discovered an article clipped from *Liberation*, Sarajevo's daily newspaper. It was dated 16 March 1994, during the Yugoslav Civil War, when the Yugoslav army laid siege to the city. The article talked about several deaths that had occurred, deaths that could not be attributed to the shells falling daily. These bodies were found intact, but with their throats cut open and the blood drained from them. The police, the article said, were baffled.

Adam looked up in time to see a woman walking down the street, her back to him. Her skin was a shade of olive. She wore her long, black hair in a braid that swung from side to side with each step.

The shadows fluttered around her.

ACKNOWLEDGMENTS

This novel would never have been possible without the help of a number of people. To everyone, I'm grateful.

To those who saw the manuscript in all its stages of creation—Darin Kennedy, Rochelle Bryce, Jay Requard, Traci Loudin, John Hartness, Eden Royce, and the rest of my writers' group—thank you not only for your support and advice but also for your friendship.

Thanks to my parents, who never once told me I couldn't achieve anything I put my mind to.

Also, thank you to the many wonderful teachers I have had over the years, but especially Kristi Boroff Ferguson and Nancy White. Your passion for learning and teaching is a lesson I've never forgotten.

Thank you, Sharon Honeycutt for your thorough editorial services.

In addition, I would like to thank the host of authors who have contributed to my knowledge of the Balkans and the Ottoman Empire: Rebecca West, Robert Kaplan, Noel Malcolm, Misha Glenny, Jason Goodwin, Caroline Finkel, Orhan Pamuk, and many others. It is truly a fascinating part of the world.

Of course, Bram Stoker deserves credit for creating Dracula's Brides. More than a hundred years after his Gothic horror masterpiece was first published, *Dracula* continues to exert a hold on people, much like the vampire himself.

And finally, I want to especially thank my wife Lara for her patience, her encouragement, and her love.

ABOUT THE AUTHOR

J. Matthew Saunders, a native of Greenville, South Carolina, is the author of numerous published fantasy and horror short stories. He received a B.A. in history from Vanderbilt University and a master's degree from the School of Journalism at the University of South Carolina. He received his law degree in California and practiced there as an attorney for several years.

He is an unapologetic European history geek, enjoys the Celtic fiddle, and makes a mean sun-dried tomato-basil pesto. He currently lives near Charlotte, North Carolina with his wife and two children. To find out more, visit www.jmsaunders.com.